Morgen of Avalon

DREAMSPELL

☙

A NOVEL BY
CAROL J. WEAKLAND

ISBN: 1456347586
ISBN-13: 9781456347581

The House of Pendragon

Uther + Igrainne - Gorlois

Merlin - Morgen + Arthur - Morgause + Lot

Eliana - Rose ∽ Lohot - Mordred ∽ Gawain ∽ Gareth

The Sisterhood of Avalon

Morgen
Fairy Queen
Oryad
Tree

Tyronoe	Cliton and Cliton	Clitonea	Monronoe	Mazoe	Thetis and Thitis
Crone	Flower	Fire	Animal	Naiad	Slyphs
Earth	Flora	Salamander	Fauna	Water	Air

Dedicated to Peggy Williams,
Dennis Weakland and Jonathan, my guide

&

Special thanks to the women who have
proofread, edited, shaped, slaved over, and read
this novel time and again: Peggy Williams,
Laura Peterson, Michelle Gatts,
Michelle Savory, and Maureen Weetman.
Without you this novel would not
have been possible.

Prologue

"*Arthur, you must not die—not yet!*"

It was sunset: a thick, blazing epiphany that mirrored the tumultuous day. Morgen trembled despite herself, witnessing the death of her beloved country. Every breath, every fiber of her being championed Arthur's healing, a perilous task that ignored several truths essential to her own existence. She could not further divide herself by acknowledging the decline of their homeland—not if she intended to keep her own essence intact. What did it matter that they had spent twenty odd years securing peace throughout the land? Peace was an expensive luxury the masses had conveniently abandoned for gain.

A vein throbbed unsympathetically in Morgen's neck. She sent out a call to her sisters, those remaining and those dead and watching: ***Please, will you help me this one last time?*** There was no reply. Britannia, that grand old sovereign, sputtered her final breaths, far too weak to bolster further warfare. Her wounded and dying were desperate for solace, or anything that might help them avoid decay. No ultimate victor would emerge, not this time. Both sides suffered immeasurable casualties, souls that would never be reclaimed. How many lost entities approached the veil, whispering Morgen's name? How many dead Companions lingered, witnessing her efforts, aware that Arthur's life teetered painfully near the abyss? One slip and it would all be over. The endless stream of mind-numbing peace work that Morgen and the Sisterhood had conjured over the past twenty-eight years depended upon her ability to heal High King Arthur Pendragon, the man she had loved throughout time.

A sob involuntarily escaped Morgen's lips. Love proved far too insignificant a word to reflect the tiniest particle of what she felt for Arthur. They were bound as one entity, one heart that honored the same passions, the same goals, although each possessed a decidedly different means of expression. Perhaps that was why the healing energy surged within Morgen's hands only to retreat just as rapidly from whence it came.

Terror eclipsed Morgen's being, driving her heart at a violent rate. Healing was her essence, her birthright, the one gift that she, as Avalon's Fairy Queen, prized above all others. Why, then, did the divine energy lie dormant within her hands? Did her failing echo Arthur's decline? Was it possible that they were both so linked with Britannia that her symbolic death brought forth their own transitions?

I cannot, I will not accept that. I am Morgen of Avalon, and it is my destiny to heal Arthur Pendragon.

This is the only possible solution. The world must know peace once more.

Steely determination pulled Morgen upright as she placed both hands over Arthur's cleft temple. It was ragged, bloody; a huge, gaping chasm stained his golden hair crimson and dripped into his unseeing eyes. *You can do this,* she told herself over and over. If not for her past efforts, Arthur would long since have made his transition into the Otherworld. Somehow, someway, she must penetrate the barrier, the blockage that currently held her captive, withheld her gift from full expression. Britannia—*nay, the world*—demanded it.

Amber and gold light flared against Avalon's ancient standing stones, nearly blinding her with its brilliance. Only Arthur's jagged breathing, which grew so labored that Morgen thought his airway must be constricted, broke the silence. A swift inspection of his throat cavity, however, proved inconclusive except to further aggravate the head wound. Indeed, blood blossomed anew upon Arthur's brow, coating Morgen's fair arms, staining her deep violet gown. Why? Why must this particular circumstance evade her healing abilities? Morgen glanced up at the Eight Stone Sentinels, guardians from past times whose stalwart expressions remained determined, unmovable.

Come now, give me your blessings.

Lazily, a dark-eyed raven lounged upon the lone yew tree that commanded the center of the megalithic circle, but even he did not croak forth a reply. Taking a deep breath Morgen renewed her desperate bid to reclaim Arthur's life. All thought, all passion focused on the sacred words that connected her to ancient healing symbols, words that she almost knew better than she knew her own self.

Chante zey, chante zey, chante zey, eleaphrim Brigida and Dianecht. Ancient Ones, you gods and goddesses I have served from the beginnings of time! Help me save him!

Healing energy surged through Morgen's outstretched fingers with such fierce determination that she touched the wound firsthand. Although this act should have rewarded her tenfold, the energy rebounded, striking her squarely upon the chest. Light, sound, and memory mingled in one fantastic scream as her knees gave way, and she felt the soft, mossy ground kiss her cheek.

Drawing herself up on both knees, Morgen blinked back the tears that clouded her vision. Countless times she had successfully applied similar intervention. Why, then, did Arthur's wounds stubbornly refuse to close? Did the answer reside within Arthur himself? Was he actually thwarting her efforts? Surely he did not wish to die when so much remained unfinished!

The great camel-backed Tor on which she stood shook its green-tiered bulk ever so slightly, sending the raven high into the fiery sky. Something, some message, was about to impress itself upon her waking vision. Morgen instinctively looked up. A lone hawk, *a Merlin*, cried softly overhead. Fever thrilled through her veins. Yes, that was it— the answer! Merlin, her former love and Arthur's one-time rival for her affections, who remained imprisoned forevermore within the sacred hawthorn tree, often utilized animals, one of the few means of communication left to him. Circling low, the precious hunter gifted Morgen with a single tail feather before silently continuing its flight. The wind increased its passionate outburst. Tension swirled around her, accelerating the rapid beat of her heart. Merlin would never lead her astray. Who better understood Arthur than the very man responsible for his education, the man who raised him from infancy?

"Thank you, Merlin. Now I understand. The king is exerting authority over his subject. Well, two can play that game. I am Morgen of Avalon, and he will not deny me."

Although unconscious, Arthur appeared to have heard her, for his temple wept anew. Morgen breathed upon the crimson stream, noticeably slowing its flow. It was then she saw the breadth of his injuries. Terror eclipsed all thought, all emotion, laying bare her soul. Mordred's sword had cleft the brain as well.

Why? Why did they not come to terms? Why did they find it necessary to destroy each other?

A deep, muted hymn that originated from seemingly everywhere and nowhere at once answered, coloring the air a lifeless gray. Morgen had often heard the ancient ring stones sing in times of great joy or sorrow. Would they, the very guardians of Avalon, shift the balance in her favor? She had forgotten something, some bit of knowledge that lay waiting just beneath the surface, ready to break through. Why did she not see it?

How am I to bend fate so that it will kneel before me? Surely there must be some option I have not yet tried.

Dreams, Morgen…All answers reside in the world of dreams…

Yes, this was the answer! Why did she not think of it before?

Rubbing the precious tail feather between her fingers, Morgen blew on it three times, activating its essence. The wind rose to a fever pitch, tossing her deep, red curls until they danced as raging flame. Raptor energy, fierce, unblinking, true, swirled down upon her, filling her with a spirit stronger than her own fragile will. This was a spirit that could move mountains and alter the very course of existence. It was ancient, older than even Avalon itself, and capable of things Morgen had never dreamed possible. Dream proved the operative word. Indeed, anyone who viewed Morgen with earthly eyes at that moment would have seen a great winged being that hovered enticingly over the dying king, a harbinger of forgotten times. The spell took shape, altering the delicate balance of past, present, and future, rendering every detail available for inspection. There in the land of dreams, lay the truth. There the spell must convey the seeker, for all answers would be revealed within the span of three night's time.

"Listen carefully, dearest," Morgen whispered. "I will place you in the world of dreams. There you will linger until I reclaim my powers." Arthur's eyes flew open. A brief shudder animated his frame as she continued, "Hush now. Sleep, sleep."

Softly, gently, Morgen wove a lush cocoon of amethyst light around Arthur's wounded frame. "You are far removed from this mortal plane where death awaits." He tried to speak, but another pass of her hands diminished his form until he was mere shadow. "You exist in another dimension, another time. You will not age or weaken. Somewhere within the hidden mysteries of the past the answer will become plain. Then you—*we* will understand why *we* fail. Only then will healing become possible. Sleep, dearest, until I call you into my arms once more."

Morgen opened her eyes. Arthur—her love, her life—was gone. Gazing down upon the empty space where his broken body once lay, she felt hot tears spill against her cheeks. She had saved him—for a time.

The spell allotted her three nights to peruse the past—a past which obviously held some key as to why Arthur, Britannia, and even Morgen herself slipped ever closer to the veil.

Gathering Arthur's bloodied shroud against her heart, she began a rapid descent down the Tor, careless of its tiered labyrinth. This was not a time for following ceremony. Indeed, her work had just begun. Somehow she must solve the mystery of her own diminished powers. Only then would she comprehend how to wield them anew and thereby heal Arthur of his grievous wounds.

It is vital that I save Arthur. Whatever the cost!

The stones only increased their sad lament.

You cannot mean that I should allow death to claim him. Why, why can I not heal him this one last time?

This question consumed Morgen, propelled her forward, mindless of the fact that her feet found it impossible to navigate so steep a descent without stumbling time and again. Thankfully Morgen possessed enough fortitude to pull herself up and cease the downward tumble before she plunged to the bottom. She had to reach the Chalice Well, the oracle that would help her unlock hidden mysteries of the past. And so Morgen navigated the soft, rustling apple orchard, dodging in and out of familiar trees with the skill of one who had accomplished this impressive feat many times. She did not pause to caress the twisted bark or smell the delicate spring blossoms, so fervent was her pace. She had to stir the oracle's waters into action before Arthur became so engrained in his vision that she could not follow. It was essential that they view the same past simultaneously. Only then could they hope for success. The Chalice Well offered Morgen the best—perhaps the only—means she could conceive to follow Arthur's dreamspell, and so she approached the dimly lit threshold with a mixture of haste and reverence that even the orb-weaving arachnids, which silently witnessed her efforts, could feel.

Morgen fell upon her knees, oblivious to the ever-blossoming roses that cascaded over the well's intricate lid and shielded it from view. All around grew flora of such grace, such beauty: purple-hued violets, ivory snowdrops, and dainty-faced pansies, but even they escaped observation, so singular was her focus.

Ancient Ones, speak to me. Tell me, why has this punishment come to pass? I have a right to know, as does Arthur. Reveal to me everything you show him!

Casting aside the heavily thorned roses, Morgen pried open the well's lid, tearing her hand in the process. She muttered a faint reproach and then summoned liquid wealth from its origins deep within the Tor's center. Deftly, precisely, the Chalice Well, an oracle for the initiated or for those who easily bent time, began its charmed work. Vivid scarlet waters native to Avalon's red spring bubbled up from its mysterious depths, beckoning a closer look. Round and round they danced, a bright beacon that illuminated the clouded past. Morgen gazed beyond the water's heady depths, discerning her former haunt, a clear representation of St. Alban's monastery that allowed her to see, hear, and interact with images long spent. A familiar series of gritty stone walls claimed precedence. Sallow and utterly repelling were they, a feeling heightened perhaps by a multitude of unanswered prayers.

Amesbury Abbey…my home, my prison. Why show us this? How can this possibly affect Arthur? Why would he need to ponder the years I wasted within the harsh confines of that forgotten cell? Why blame the son for the sins of his father? It was Uther Pendragon's doing.

Yes, that's it! Uther is the key. Oh, how I remember your sharp tongue.

"Morgen is not my daughter. Do not tell me otherwise, Igrainne. I feel it in my bones."

CHAPTER 1:

Prisoner of the Past

The image of Uther Pendragon, Arthur's father and former High King of Britannia, took shape amid the watery canvas. He was still handsome then—tall, broad shouldered, and sporting a mass of golden hair that revealed only the faintest gray. Morgen shuddered despite herself. It was amazing just how much Arthur resembled his father. Uther's eyes possessed none of Arthur's warmth, however, only a studied glare that intensified whenever Morgen entered his presence.

"She is a witch, Igrainne. Surely you see that!"

This was the woman who had afforded Morgen the opportunity to live as a mortal, the being she once called Mother. It would be impossible to repay this debt throughout several lifetimes. Without Igrainne Morgen would never have known Arthur, never have helped orchestrate the reign of peace that set Camelot apart from the rest of civilization. Igrainne had risked everything when she adopted Morgen as a foundling child. The fact that she kept the secret hidden from Uther, at great risk to her own personal happiness, heightened her peril.

Uther was not a forgiving man. Igrainne knew this only too well. Perhaps that accounted for the sadness that infused her being. How beautiful she appeared: head downcast, a long veil of mahogany hair shielding her emerald eyes. Although well past forty years of age, Igrainne's long, slim form bespoke elegance. This was but a fair mask for the fiery heart that beat within her breast, the soul that instigated war between two of Britannia's elite commanders—all for the blessing of her favor.

"No! I swear she is innocent, not a witch at all!"

It was hauntingly clear that Uther had sensed the lie from its conception. Indeed, many of his friends readily confirmed Igrainne's mysterious disappearance while he was off battling Vortigern. Little did he dream this unaccounted time had secured Morgen's residency at court. Instead, he questioned whether Igrainne had betrayed him in that darkest hour. Surely the witch-child never originated from his seed!

If truth be told, Uther never possessed any tolerance for Morgen's "mystical oddities"—the little tricks she played on him, not to mention members of his court, an irritation that began when she was but six years old. Indeed, the first twelve years of her life she had turned the court upside down with her magical outbursts and trickery. This added further fuel to his growing distemper. The witch-child must be censored, sequestered far from court before she wreaked further havoc. Several important allies had already been lost thanks to her careless intervention.

"Every waking moment Morgen speaks of learning magic. No doubt she dreams of it at night. It is a pity Merlin resides so far away. He would know how to deal with her."

"Deal with her?" retorted Igrainne. "You act as if she has committed a crime."

"What would you call levitating King Urien of North Wales several feet off the floor while he was wooing her?"

A crimson flush colored Igrainne's pale throat. "I would call it very well bethought. Morgen is not yet thirteen years old. She is too young to think of marriage!"

"You were a year younger when pledged to Cornwall."

Cornwall… Uther always brought up Cornwall. Did he really believe Igrainne's betrayal of this man further endeared his own royal personage to her heart? The truth was a double-edged sword. Yes, Uther understood it only too well. That is why he played the card. If forced to choose between Uther and another, Igrainne always claimed Uther. There was no separating one from the other.

"Yes! Look where that union brought me!"

Uther brushed his lips against Igrainne's soft cheek, aware that she could not resist him. "I thought there was no complaint on that point. My caresses are but a small price to pay for the crown." When she did not respond, he added, "I am sending her away."

Although the attempt appeared futile, Igrainne made one last appeal.

"You already sent Arthur from me when he was a mere babe. I never knew him, never felt his touch. You cannot take Morgen as well. She is a fairy, Uther, I swear it—a foundling I adopted after our daughter died." A rosy flush brightened her features, but she did not stop there, "I never told you, for I knew how it would be. Morgen is not your enemy, Uther. She will offer assistance you cannot even begin to imagine!"

Stiffening at this intelligence, Uther inwardly raged. Suddenly everything made sense: his passion, his failing. This child was not mortal, but some otherworldly creature that possessed a motive he chose not to entertain. Did she intend to entice his approval as High King—or snare one who came after? Was it not probable that she sought to advise the future heir? Arthur! He must safeguard Arthur. Thank the gods Merlin schooled the lad far from court. He would make certain Morgen never met the prince, never exchanged so much as a simple glance with him!

"A fairy? You honestly believe that I would allow a fairy to offer me counsel?" The words spilled as venom from Uther's lips. "I have a difficult enough time swallowing Merlin's outlandish schemes. Let this be the end of it. I am sending her away to Amesbury Abbey. There she will be housed with nuns."

The reddish waters renewed their tumultuous dance, revealing Morgen's fourteen-year-old self housed in layers of protective white robes. Fragile to the point of delicacy, Morgen's ivory complexion, startling blue-green eyes, and tumbling mass of deep red hair gave her an otherworldly appearance that the nuns who surrounded her could not ignore. Indeed, far more often than not, it catapulted her into serious trouble. High on top of a weathered bench she stood, glaring, for the sisters had done the unthinkable and tried to cut her hair. This scene that had repeated itself over and over again throughout the two full years of Morgen's imprisonment within the abbey walls...

"Stay back!" Morgen cried. A subtle wave of her hand forced the offending cutlery to the ground where it remained unapproachable, blazing hot to the touch. Morgen had learned this trick to annoy Uther. In truth she simply wished to gain his love, his affection. When that failed she turned to other, far more devious ways of gaining his notice. This spell had served her well time and again, perhaps at no finer moment than when Uther toasted his newfound allies at the great Beltane celebration, took a great gulp of mead he did not realize was boiling hot, and then with a yelp of anguish released the goblet, splashing Igrainne and the nearby attendants with its contents. Morgen giggled despite herself, remembering the effect. If only she could duplicate the same results upon the dull, overly annoying sisters! What did they hope to gain by tormenting her day and night?

"I cannot comprehend how short hair brings one closer to the divine!" she cried, resuming the demeanor of one who has little patience for the unenlightened. "Long hair is a woman's right! It is her connection to all that is magical!"

"Magical?" sneered Sister Agatha, whose round face wore an expression of deepest loathing. "You dare mention magic here?"

Morgen stared back at her, grinning. *Do you really wish me to answer that question?*

Pausing in the midst of this reverie, Morgen reconsidered her situation. She was truly at the mercy of Agatha and the dull-witted sisters. Did she really wish to further fuel their anger? She was trapped inside a prison where fairies and nature spirits were considered unholy offspring of the devil. Where was she to turn if the nuns' simple punishments became more intricate, more brutal?

They were locked deep within the confines of Amesbury Abbey, a dark, somber structure where airy windows were replaced by harsh, unyielding stone walls. This proved fortuitous, for the nuns feared nothing so much as observation from the outside world. Amesbury was their kingdom, and its government fell under the dictates of Agatha, who answered directly to Uther Pendragon. How she managed to secure such an important position was a matter of much discussion among the younger novices. Surely she was not the High King's mistress. Nothing about Agatha's appearance suggested she had ever been beautiful; her figure was too thick, her eyes too peevish, her complexion a vivid puce that defied description. Perhaps that was why she attacked Morgen's glorious looks with such a vengeance.

Pausing once more to analyze the faces which gazed upon her with mistrust, Morgen softened her tactics. "I know that nuns are highly spiritual beings. I appreciate and respect your beliefs with all my heart. That does not mean I will bow to you. I am a fairy. Magic is my birthright. Despise me if you dare!"

This exclamation did little to further Morgen's cause, for the sisters pulled her from that lofty perch as if she were of no greater consequence than a feather. Down the narrow, gritty hall they conveyed her, grimacing at every word that spilled from her lips. Thankfully, they did not have to travel far, for the abbey was a small stone structure contained on minimal ground. Once they arrived at their destination, the sisters chucked Morgen inside a cramped, dark cell, and then set the iron lock in place. There, Morgen stood gazing out through the barred door, wondering what she might do to awaken their shallow sensibilities. Did not their own femininity, camouflaged as it was, plead the case better than mere words? No, the sisters wished nothing more than to sleep, eat, and utter prayers. Life's true wonders such as peace, beauty, and love were beyond their ken. Why did they ignore what they had been put upon this earth to accomplish? Why did they think that merely mouthing words would create change? How could she wake them, shock them into sensibility?

"Go on; lock me in my gloomy cell for days. The end result will be the same. I will learn the magical arts that you so fear. I will learn without book or aid of any kind. I am already stronger than most of you. The world will not be denied my gifts."

Several of the younger sisters hissed at her. Some even began to walk away. Morgen cringed, aware that her words were ill chosen. Her audience, small as it proved, was dwindling. There must be some way to turn them, some option she had not yet tried.

"Oh, poor sisters, do I unnerve you with my frank talk? You wish only to pray. I wish to be! Listen to me. Open your minds. Do we not all wish peace throughout the land? Let us work toward that goal as women. Let the men carry their swords. We wield a higher power that can stop the bloodshed."

"She's mad," Agatha grimaced, limping down the hall. Morgen's flailing fists had struck her kneecap, crippling her gait. "The High King said as much, and his word is law."

No one knew the agony Agatha had endured when Uther Pendragon had unceremoniously dumped Morgen upon her doorstep. Certainly she owed the High King much, but never in her twenty odd years' service to the veil did she dream of entertaining a devil incarnate. Pain screamed anew within her wounded kneecap, and she fell to contemplating revenge. Tomorrow she would see Morgen brought low no matter what the cost. Those stunning auburn locks would bring a pretty penny. Agatha felt justified in claiming every bit of gold for the abbey and its inhabitants, who had suffered under Morgen's wicked tongue. Down the gloomy hall she disappeared, finalizing her plans.

The battle lost, Morgen focused on her final witness, for all but the eldest nun had already made their departure. Her shoulders drooped, revealing a portion of the angst she carried inside.

Why did it seem she was destined to perish, locked away within this forgotten cell? Why did the sisters, who should be her friends, look on her as a demon possessed?

"Sister Portentia, why do your sisters hate me so?"

The elderly nun gave a whimsical smile. "We do not hate you, Morgen. It is not in our nature to hate. Holy sisters cannot equate magic with God, or even with religion. There is only one person I know who has ever spoken of such a union. He is currently focused on your brother's education. It is a pity you are not a boy, for I feel certain Lord Merlin would have accepted you as his pupil."

Hope flooded Morgen's breast. "Sister!" she cried, grabbing Portentia's knotted hand through the metal grating. "Do you know where I might find Lord Merlin?"

"No, I certainly do not," rang her firm reply. With that Portentia plucked Morgen's fingers from her hand and shuffled off down the darkened hall.

"Merlin!" the poor child cried, fluttering about the tiny cell like a caged falcon. "Merlin, where are you? Please help me find you!"

Everything happened so quickly that Morgen could not quite take it in. Somehow her large toe caught the edge of a tiny cot and down she fell upon the thrush-strewn floor, striking her forehead. It was at this moment of utter humiliation that a deep, weathered voice disrupted her tumultuous thoughts.

Do not struggle as a caged bird. Slow your breath-ing. Close your eyes and wait.

Morgen's heart leapt within her chest. "Merlin, is that you?"

CHAPTER 2:

The Arch Mage

Morgen did as she was told, keenly aware of the fresh bruise that throbbed incessantly upon her brow. Light danced beyond senses, beyond earthly vision, along the innermost corners of her third eye, illuminating a tall, thin shadow that stood scanning the horizon. Merlin cast back the hood of his raven-feathered cloak and gazed upon her with a quizzical expression. Energy ebbed and flowed between them, creating an impenetrable barrier that undulated with snakelike grace.

A brief tremor animated Morgen's youthful frame. This was a man who walked between worlds, a man who understood the living as intimately as he did the dead. He was never to be trifled with, never tricked. The only way to gain Merlin's attention was by earning it. Would he deem her, slight and insignificant, worthy of notice? True, she possessed physical charms that might interest him, but would a man of Merlin's stature allow himself to be swayed by beauty? The answer that welled within her mind was far from pleasing. Everything about Merlin's appearance was calculated to unsettle the

casual observer. Tall, dark, and arresting she could
call him, but that would be a disservice. Merlin was
not a handsome man, no—no one would ever call
him that. But his coal bright eyes, so penetrating
in their discernment, and the fountain of ebony
hair that fell about his shoulders in careless disarray, had an utterly beguiling quality about them.
A hawkish nose chiseled determinedly within his
long face added further character to his bemused
expression, as did the dusky beard and mustache
that appeared recently clipped. Every inch of
Merlin's long, thin frame fairly oozed power, but
that, as Morgen would soon unearth, was only
half his charm. It was time for her to speak. What
should she say? How should she address him? Pray
the goddess she did not make a fool of herself.
Perhaps a simple acknowledgement of his presence
would do the trick.

"Thank you for answering my call."

A sardonic expression colored Merlin's countenance. "Did I have any choice? Your hail fairly
pierced the heavens with its fervor. No doubt it
awoke half Britannia, not to mention my own
sleep-deficient soul. The next time you wish to
speak with me, try a silent summons. I assure you
that I will arrive in a far better mood."

Laughter spilled from Morgen's lips. She had
not expected Merlin to be amusing. "I did not realize that it was so late or that I was so loud. It pains
me to think I may have offended you."

Merlin struggled against the smile that threatened to expose his good humor.

"Why have you summoned me, little sprite?"

Rising, Morgen paced around her dusty, yellowing cell, watching little cobwebs drift to the floor. How much of her ill treatment should she reveal? Should she tell of the endless attempts to alter her physical appearance? The harsh confinement regularly inflicted upon her person? The disapproval that emanated from the other novices every time she walked among them? She did not wish to sound weak—not in front of Merlin, the arch mage.

Eventually the words, "I need your assistance," spilled from her delicate lips.

The wry expression instantly departed Merlin's face. "Why? Are you imprisoned?"

"Yes!" Morgen cried, matching his altered tones.

"Do not shriek in that manner. Do you wish your captors to hear? Use thought alone."

"I doubt that the sisters would care if…"

Merlin's lips twitched with mirth again. "Sisters? You are imprisoned by nuns? That is a fate most dreadful indeed."

"Do not laugh at me. I assure you this is serious."

Intrigued, Merlin asked the question that preyed upon his mind. "Who are you?" He drew near the undulating barrier, dark eyes scanning Morgen's fair person. Waves of pink and green energy leapt between them, assisting his appraisal. The lass possessed beauty beyond the mortal condition, a beauty rivaled by the elementals themselves. His heart beat a little faster as he registered her many attributes: the luminous sea-green eyes, the haunted smile, the glorious crimson mane that

flowed well past her tiny waist. Appearances suggested that she was still a child, yes, but a child of
such ethereal grace that she could only stem from
an otherworldly origin. How strange that this brief
sojourn upon earth had deprived her of most attributes she had possessed as a fairy. Indeed, as far
as he could discern, she claimed but two powers:
prophecy and healing. Each in itself was a magnificent treasure, but how could they ever satisfy her
when the whole of elemental magic was once at her
command? The transformation had also stripped
away her memories. Did she have any idea why she
had sought human form? What prompted her to
cast aside her post as Fairy Queen? Yes, it was true.
This slight child who stood so solemnly before him
was fairy royalty. For several hundred years she had
ruled a Sisterhood not unlike the women who currently held her captive. A bitter tonic, indeed.

The truth surrendered its secrets deftly, fuel-
ling Merlin's imagination. Oh yes, it all made sense.
Above all this, the fay longed for peace, for union
with the eternal other, things that one could only
achieve in mortal form.

"I should have known. Your look is far from that
of a novice. Indeed, you are a fairy in disguise—a
fairy who assumed human form for distinct pur-
poses. Do you remember them, Morgen?

"One involves your brother, Arthur. You will act
as an adviser—guide him toward adopting the ideology of the fairy once he assumes the title of High
King."

Merlin's form trembled and split at its core, altering beyond recognition. Up, up he rose, higher

than the greatest oak, a set of sharp antlers lancing his brow. Shining hooves appeared where his feet had once been, even as his body thickened, boasting a lush mass of rich brown fur. The ebony eyes alone remained unchanged, hauntingly intense, fixed as they were upon her person.

"Need I remind you that I am Arthur's adviser? He takes counsel from me and me alone," his voice boomed to the consistency of rolling thunder.

Nervous excitement flooded Morgen's being. What was happening? Merlin appeared far from amused. That much was clear. He wanted to diminish her power, to stem its flow at the source. She could not—would not—allow that to happen! Somehow, someway, she must reach him and make him understand the desperate longings of her heart. His altered appearance reminded her of Cernunnos, Celtic god of the Underworld: beautiful, awe-inspiring, one never to be crossed. This was the terrifying mage who had long since found his way into story and song. Was this the same person who actually schooled her brother?

Merlin bit back the laughter that threatened to escape his lips. The lass possessed spirit. She would not be intimidated by simple tricks or the weight of another soul that sought to overpower her. Indeed, Morgen stood her ground better than any other youth he had ever met, save one. Pleased with her response, he softened his tactics and returned to his true features.

"There is no need to remain silent, Morgen. I felt it imperative that you understand my position. You ask my assistance in gaining magical powers.

Yes, I know that is why you have summoned me. I also know that it would be disastrous if I helped you achieve this goal."

Confusion flooded Morgen's being. Surely she did not hear him aright! Surely he did not mean to reject her! Why, why would he do this? Was it possible that such an advanced soul looked upon women as insignificant, inferior life forms, never to be trusted, never to be taught? Could he be so heartless?

With a flurry of white robes, Morgen burst through the energy vale that had enforced their separation. Suddenly she was standing within a forest, lush, dark, and foreboding.

A thick canopy of hemlocks rustled overhead. It was midnight or sometime thereafter, judging by the relative darkness. Behind Merlin flickered the remnants of an aging fire that sharpened his features, highlighting every wrinkle and line of his face until he appeared almost haunted. This did not affect Morgen in the slightest, for she resumed her pleas as if nothing of import had occurred. "Please, Lord Merlin, do not turn me away. I swear that I will not interfere with your counsel of Arthur. I know you never accept female students— but please, listen! I will succeed in every test you set before me. I will achieve all that you expect of a boy—even my own brother!"

Morgen paused, her eyes irresistibly drawn to a cloaked form that lay unmoving upon blankets of fragrant pine needles, his fair hair illuminated by the waning firelight.

"Is that him?" she asked, taking a step forward. "Is that Arthur?"

Before Merlin parted his lips to speak, she knew the answer. Yes, this was the brother, the heir incarnate Uther had safeguarded against all enemies the day he surrendered him to Merlin's care a full sixteen years ago. They had never met, thanks to the High King's interference, an act that further affirmed his gross dislike of her.

Merlin countered her move, placing himself between Morgen and his sleeping charge.

"Yes."

"May I see him?"

"No."

Puzzled by Merlin's actions, Morgen tried to brush past him, but it was not to be. One move of his weaponless hand cast her back several paces. Morgen marveled at this. He had not even touched her! "How…?" she stopped short, remembering her true intent. "Why may I not speak with Arthur? He is my brother."

A slight tremor animated Merlin's frame. She did not remember the truth, not yet. Just how much he should reveal proved problematic. Certainly Uther would never approve. Perhaps concealment was the best, the only option for the present—until both Morgen and Arthur were mature enough to understand their bond.

"Sit down, Morgen," he soothed, gesturing her toward a decaying, moss-covered log that appeared conceived for that very purpose. All around them messengers of the forest hooted and cooed, witnessing this exchange. A lone barn owl swooped low, grasping hold of a steady branch overhead. Thus lodged, he fixed his gleaming eyes upon them.

Merlin did not speak again until Morgen had complied with his request. "I know this will be difficult for you to understand. Believe me, I wish it could be otherwise. It is imperative that you do not meet Arthur just yet."

"Why?" she asked, defiance coloring her sea-green eyes.

"You will meet Arthur when the time is right, and not before."

"I do not understand."

"I do not mean that you should."

Morgen stared at the arch mage, perplexed. What new impediment was this? Surely he did not believe that she wished to harm Arthur. That would be the height of foolishness. She wished only to converse with Arthur, to let him know that she too walked the same earth, breathed the same air, and that she was quite, quite alone. There could be only one reason Merlin denied her this meeting.

"Uther has put you up to this. He despises me— keeps Igrainne distant and fettered. Can you even begin to imagine the nightmare that was my life at court? The nuns are little better. They think I am a demon possessed. Arthur is all I have in this world. He is my only brother. Without him I am alone. Completely alone."

Every hoot, every coo, every snuffle ceased its expression. The barn owl flapped its pale wings, intent, listening. Silence lingered between mage and fay, a silence laden with emotion and another feeling the latter chose to ignore. As Merlin became increasingly aware of its presence, however, the sardonic smile returned to his lips. He had met her, this fairy lass, years ago when just a lad—an outcast lad to be precise—who spent his days and nights sequestered in a lonely cave, always striving toward perfection of his magical craft, far from the cruel townspeople who sought his life. Indeed, Merlin's childhood had been fraught with death threats, stoning, and all manner of physical abuse from the locals, who saw only his difference and feared its affects. And so he fixated his life, his attentions, on his true love, his obsession: magic. Every waking moment was spent alone in this unrelenting study until a beautiful fairy clothed in moss and roses took pity on his plight. She was there for him when no one else cared, always supportive, forever exasperating in her endless chatter, so lovely, so thoroughly irritating that he banished her with a careless spell, an act he regretted to this day. Suddenly the fairy stood before him reborn, seeking his assistance, and he could only remember how she had touched his heart so very long ago when his own unworthiness had made love impossible.

"Are you really alone, Morgen, or is that just an excuse you use to feel sorry for yourself?"

Morgen met Merlin's dark gaze and trembled. Perhaps he hit the mark with undue ease. Although smiling he looked altogether different, unsettlingly so. His ebony eyes latched onto her with a fierce tenacity that bespoke passion, though age and inexperience kept her thoroughly oblivious to its expression.

"You will not always be with me."

A chuckle spilled from Merlin's lips. "I am not as old as that."

Morgen laughed outright at his discernment. "Is there nothing I can keep from you?"

No response came forth, no sound beyond that of Arthur's enchanted breathing. Merlin watched her intently, moonlight playing upon his smooth brow. Here was the rub, the very fly in the ointment that could either sever their brief relationship or send it soaring past the highest peaks. She wanted knowledge, not love. Indeed, the two rarely combined with any uniformity; but in this case, he saw the possibility swell as some delicate rose blossoming upon the vine. It was up to him. He would either foster the love, the affection, or sever it forevermore. In any case he could not be her teacher—not when she affected him in this manner. No matter what she said, the answer would be the same.

"You are passionate," he offered at last when the silence no longer served them. "Use that passion to convince me of your worthiness to study magic." Having said this, he leaned back against an aging hawthorn tree, breathless and agitated. How would she respond?

Excitement flooded Morgen's being, drawing her forward until she stood but a hair's breadth from the mage. This was it! She would plead her case and either succeed gloriously or slink back to Amesbury Abbey with tail tucked between her legs. Morgen little cared for that analogy. It made her think of a male dog. A faint pricking at the back of her skull forced her to reassess the image, for she could sense something of import, something she could use to her advantage. All at once she understood. She was to appeal to his masculinity, force him to view her as a woman of worth. The words flowed from Morgen's lips as honey through a sieve.

"I am a woman—or will be soon. The feminine is in all ways magical—a dark knowing amid the present masculine light. You are the sun, Merlin. I am the moon. We are meant to unite and bond as one. Only then will I become the greatest enchantress Britannia has ever known. I will tell the world that I owe everything to you! I will glorify you, Merlin, with every mote of my being."

Merlin sought her hand with one swift movement, aware that his heart was beating faster than it had in quite some time. What man in his right mind could refuse such an offer? She was strong, gloriously beautiful, and fervent in her beliefs, everything he had ever dreamed of in a woman. "Dreamed" proved the operative word. Indeed, women did not figure prominently in any portion of his life. Suddenly, in the midst of Merlin's thirty-eighth year, all that was about to change. It was as if the fairy of moss and roses had reached into his imagination, pulled out the woman of his dreams, and adopted her wit, her knowledge, her physicality all for his pleasure. "You misjudge me, Morgen. It is not that I blatantly refuse to teach female students. I have yet to find the lass worthy of such a gift. Are you that lass, Morgen?"

"*I am.*"

She was so passionate, so determined that absolute denial failed him. Every whisper, every breath of the forest spurred him forward. Firelight played against her glorious locks, lending them an intense crimson hue—the color of love, of passion. What would it be like to hold her in his arms, feel the press of her lips against his? Aware that his thoughts were running wild, Merlin reined them in, drawing himself back to purpose. Why not spend time with her, grow accustomed to her? Morgen possessed magical gifts of her own that needed little bolstering. Perhaps she would absorb additional powers simply by being in his presence. Surely this was the best, the only way. Was it not better to make her work for the gift than to offer it freely, openly?

"Perhaps," rang Merlin's enigmatic reply. Releasing her hand, he strode off several paces, losing himself in a clustering vine that proved to be none other than mistletoe. The significance startled him. What was he to do? Arthur was already casting off the heavy bands of sleep. It was vital that Morgen depart long before his eyes opened. Perhaps if Merlin told her but a portion of the truth, it would set all the players in motion. Slowly he turned and faced her.

"There is another reason you adopted human form, Morgen. You also seek a romance with your other self—the one you have loved throughout time. This will complicate matters tenfold, for magic and love do not mix."

Morgen stared unblinkingly at Merlin. *Love?* What made him bring up such a deplorable term in the midst of her argument? *Love with my other self? What other self?* So many questions begged for answers that she had no option but to thrust them back into the deepest corners of her mind. Love would not help her win Merlin as a teacher. Love was an inconvenience unworthy of attention. She had witnessed Igrainne and Uther share their passionate displays more times than she could stomach. Why would Merlin mention such an unappealing prospect? Was it possible he had twisted her words so that they appeared to desire love? Perhaps this was a test—the means Merlin chose to determine how serious she was about magical study.

"What do I care for love or romance? It is magic that consumes my being. Please, Lord Merlin, accept me as your pupil!"

Narrowing the distance between them, Morgen clasped the mage's bony hands, unprepared for what would follow. Energy surged as their fingers entwined, spilling along their wrists and down the length of their arms. The barn owl gave a low hoot before soaring off, free and unfettered. How still, how solemn mage and fay stood, gazing into each other's eyes. The ebbing firelight leapt forth, bursting with expression, as if it were the light to reveal all souls that belonged to each other. Merlin widened his eyes, aware of its significance.

Suddenly Morgen understood why. Time shivered and split, revealing a moonlit lake and the hauntingly familiar lovers who sought its misty shores. A lone wolf howled as Merlin's lips blazed against Morgen's throat. All was passion and stardust. This was not the first time they had spent thus entwined, nor by the look of it, would it be the last. The vision slowly dissipated, transporting Morgen back to Arthur, Merlin, and the dark-clad forest that housed their beings. One question alone burned within her brain.

"Merlin, are you my other self?"

CHAPTER 3

The Feather

Morgen awoke with a start, her cramped body aching feverishly from head to toe. She was lying face down against the rush carpet exactly where she had landed the previous evening, legs twisted uncomfortably beneath her. Slowly, methodically, she unraveled her aching frame, desperate to remember what had transpired. Surely she had slipped beyond the cell's boundaries; surely much time had elapsed since then. Unfortunately the lack of proper windows made it impossible to tell whether it was day or evening. Shadow and yellowing stones peppered her surroundings, rendering the cell haunting in its simplicity and offering but a single, moldy hunk of bread for food, a cracked water jug, and a small chamber pot tucked away in the darkened corner.

Casting her head back to relieve the dull ache in her neck, Morgen sat up, struggling against the heavy bands of sleep that still weighted her mind. Images of a golden-haired youth struggled forth only to be suppressed by a tall, dark man whose face remained obscured within the hood of his raven-feathered cloak. Morgen trembled although she did not know why. Something familiar about both figures played upon her sensibilities. These were allies, friends that would help her escape the white-robed women who currently held her captive. Their names were *Arthur and Merlin*. Yes, of course! She had seen her brother and his magical protector last night!

Morgen rose to her knees, pulling the snowy robes back up over her shoulders, conscious that far too much of her ivory flesh was on display. This action dislodged something soft from her garment that drifted lazily to the floor. For a moment Morgen thought it was a spare bit of cloth, but then she realized that it was a feather. Clasping the bluish-gray bit of fluff between her fingers, Morgen noticed that a coal-black marking wove through its middle. How intricate, how glorious it shone amid her humble surroundings. All along its delicate edges ran a thin strip of white, lending a dash of purity to its already magnificent composition. How had something so foreign, so delicate found its way into her locked cell? Was it possible that the feather had attached itself to her boots during their outing? Or were its origins supernatural? If those midnight wanderings had really introduced her to Merlin and the sleeping Arthur, was it not possible that this feather solidified the meeting?

"Well, at long last the lazy child is stirring," sneered a haunting, unwelcome voice.

Morgen looked up. She had not time to gather her thoughts before a dark shadow loomed over her, blotting everything else from view.

"Where did you get that?" Sister Agatha fairly spat. No doubt she had been watching Morgen for some time before making her presence known. Her plump, round face appeared swollen, misshapen. Perhaps it was the shadows that pervaded Morgen's cell that affected this change. In any case Morgen thought Agatha looked even more ghastly than usual.

Little did Morgen dream that throughout the night, Agatha had been stung by several miscreant bees that had mysteriously found their way into her locked cell. This explained much of Agatha's ill humor. Something in the back of the disgruntled nun's mind suggested that Morgen was behind this assault, although how this could be when the child was locked up proved problematic. Tolerance for deliberate misconduct was not a luxury she would permit. The feather demonstrated that Morgen had been somewhere off limits to her station.

"She's awake!" cried a weathered voice that reminded Morgen of crackling embers. Another face swam before her, one that personified beatific grace. Sister Portentia smiled down upon Morgen, offering wordless blessings. "We were worried, child. You lay as one dead."

The light reflected in Portentia's gaze forced Morgen to look twice. Something familiar, something comforting resided within their fathomless depths. Portentia's concern was palpable. Against all odds she truly cared whether or not Morgen still lived. Unlike the other sisters steadily streaming into her cell, she exuded good will and compassion. Morgen smiled back and kissed her wrinkled cheek.

Portentia flinched at the sensation. Intimacy of this sort was not something she was accustomed to at Amesbury—or anywhere else for that matter. Indeed, her limited experience with the flesh was not of the sort that fostered such displays. Somehow with this child it was different. Portentia made allowances, for she saw so much love within Morgen, such a need to be recognized and appreciated. This child, strange as she appeared, held the key to their future. If only she could convince Agatha and the other sisters of this simple truth. Portentia's eyes widened, fixating on the feather clasped between Morgen's trembling fingers. Perhaps it was time for the child to reveal her true colors.

"That is not a simple feather from one of our fowl," she cautiously began, just loud enough so that everyone could hear. "It belongs to a hunter, a bird of the air, a Merlin if I am not mistaken."

It was impossible for Morgen to camouflage the look of awe that lit her expression. "Then it was not a dream. I really did it. I really met Merlin last night," she whispered, clasping Portentia's hand.

Unfortunately Portentia was not the only sister who overheard this exclamation. A low muttering overcame the other novices, gaining in force and sensation until Agatha took measures to still its passion. This portion of the abbey, meager as it appeared, fell under her absolute authority. Thus it had been since she had arrived at Amesbury. Morgen, no matter who she was, would not undermine the discipline Agatha had wrought through twenty odd years of service to the veil.

"Give me that!" she cried, wresting the precious feather free from Morgen's faltering grip. "The king will hear of this. He has given me leave to punish the child freely. This feather shows that she has either been consorting with a demon or has somehow used the black arts to walk through locked doors."

Grasping Morgen's long, thick tresses, Agatha pulled her up to standing, and then struck her full across the face. "Are you a witch? Are you?"

Pain flooded Morgen's cheeks, leaving them flushed and tingling. A witch? What ever gave Agatha that idea? Hadn't she told the dull fool time and again that she was a fairy? Even if she were a witch, what did it matter? Were not some witches good? Did they not serve humankind in positive ways? Why must Agatha repeatedly turn something beautiful into sin? Gazing at the combined Sisterhood, Morgen saw that their faces echoed Agatha's revulsion. Did they actually believe Agatha's ludicrous claims? Surely they did not think she wielded black magic?

Morgen offered no verbal reply, but made a valiant effort to reclaim her lost treasure, twisting and flailing against her captor. Another slap followed then another. Exhausted by lack of sleep and enforced starvation, Morgen slumped forward, stunned. What should she do? Must she endure this unjust punishment, or strike back? Her head reeling, her senses askew, Morgen felt the blows increase their expression until she could feel no more.

"Answer me! Are you a witch, one of Satan's own minions? The church burns witches who are beyond redemption!" Clasping Morgen's delicate chin within her terse fingers, she cried, "Look at me, child. Why is this feather so important to you? Is it a gift from your master? A means by which you will communicate with him?"

"The only witch I see here is you!" Morgen cried as Agatha buffeted her cheeks until they felt raw. Sensing that Agatha's foot lay dangerously near her own, Morgen slammed her heel upon it. The fact that she was currently bootless little aided her efforts.

A low growl burst from Agatha's lips as she reasserted her grasp on Morgen's locks, drawing her up so high that the poor beauty was forced to stand on tip toe. "You are Satan's minion!"

Balling her fist, she struck Morgen in the stomach, an act that thoroughly terrified the sisters. This punishment far exceeded anything they had experienced to date. What if Agatha's claims were unjust? What if Morgen was innocent? How would they answer the High King when he learned that his very own daughter had been abused in this manner? All eyes watched with increasing horror, tense and uncertain. Should they intervene? Perhaps Agatha was exceeding her authority. No one moved. Few even dared breathe, so precarious was the situation.

Finally Portentia could bear it no longer. She had to speak—no matter what the cost.

"Stop this madness! Morgen is a fairy—not a witch! She has told us this time and time again. The feather you hold *is* a gift from her master. He is not a demon, but the arch mage himself!" She paused, witnessing Agatha's stunned expression. "I speak of Merlin—the king's own adviser. This feather indicates that he has accepted Morgen as his pupil."

Near delirium, Morgen felt her knees give way, and she found herself exclusively supported by Agatha's fingers entwined within her flowing tresses. The pain was immense, but she did not cry out—not this time. Something was happening, something she did not understand. A low, dull throbbing centered within her heart, growing in breadth and intensity. If only she could use it to gain release! Another innocent was suffering because of her indiscretions. Indeed, Agatha was refocusing her assault upon the elderly Sister Portentia.

"How do you know so much, Sister?" Agatha glared through narrowed eyes, twisting Morgen's glorious mane into a long, narrow column perfect for cutting.

"I know," came Portentia's simple response. Stepping forward, she released Agatha's fingers, an act that allowed Morgen's hair to spill free until it streamed over her shoulders and down the small of her back. "Are you willing to risk Merlin's wrath simply because you despise his pupil?"

"The 'arch mage,' as you call him, holds no power here," Agatha cried, reclaiming a fistful of locks that had shielded Morgen's eyes. "If Merlin disapproves of my actions—the very actions his king desires—then let him come and save her!"

Morgen struck Agatha's foot again with the base of her heel, this time grinding down upon the tendons until Agatha gasped with pain. "You mistake yourself! I need no man to save me!"

This act little aided Morgen's cause, for Agatha cast her back against the stone wall with such force that it knocked the wind from her lungs. Agatha looked surprised by her own strength, but this did not stop her from fumbling within her robes for a knife. A few decisive steps brought her back to Morgen's side.

Portentia tried to stay the effort, but it was no good. "Please do not go through with this," she exclaimed. She knelt by Morgen, placing the water jug against her lips. "The child is ill. She needs food and rest."

Morgen responded by directing a wide stream of water at Agatha's peevish eyes. This proved most satisfying, for Agatha never anticipated such a response. The excess water burst against her bloated face, splattering her formerly pristine robes with spittle and blood.

Finding herself drenched, Agatha reasserted her grip while she rid her face of excess moisture with her free hand. "If I did not know better, I would say the witch has cast a spell on you, Sister. Morgen needs to be saved from the mage and all forces of darkness!" Singling out two exceptionally wide-girthed sisters, she spat, "Hold her!"

At that moment Agatha finally secured the much-desired knife from the folds of her newly mired robes. The conspiring nuns launched forward, each grabbing Morgen by an arm, a task not for the faint hearted. Indeed, Morgen struggled against them as if she *were* possessed of a super human strength. In the ensuing confusion, Portentia was flung backward and lost her footing altogether.

Agatha did not pause to aid the elderly nun or even ascertain if she was hurt. Instead, a wide smile spread across her face as she deliberately ran the knife's blade back and forth against the wall, sharpening it while she fingered Morgen's curls with derision. "It is time you live by our edicts, minion! You will be humbled in every aspect of your person. You will be simple, plain—a lass of no visible attractions. I have waited long for this moment. Off come those red locks!"

Morgen's heart beat wildly within her chest. She knew not what to do. They must not cut her hair. Long hair was a woman's right. It was her connection to everything magical...yet how was Morgen to wield this inherent magic without use of her hands?

"The mage will no longer desire you when you are shorn like the rest of us!"

Portentia regained her footing, this time with even greater passion. "Sister, please!" she intervened, staying the dagger with a touch of her hand. "Morgen is a princess. She is not meant to be plain as the rest of us."

"She is a foul witch. The king has already sanctioned this act!" With this utterance, Agatha broke free and made good her threat.

Several novices, Morgen chief among them, gasped as a thick cluster of curls fell to the floor. The act accomplished, Agatha made ready for a second pass, a look of supreme pleasure coloring her blotchy countenance.

Energy boiled within Morgen's core, demanding release. Relaxing to purpose, she felt it flood her hands. This was it! This was the key! She must mold the magic to do her bidding. Slowly, methodically, she framed a picture of release in her mind's eye, then saw it fulfilled. At that moment everything clicked into place. Morgen felt it. The nuns felt it. Somehow, miraculously, she lifted her arms. Away flew the dagger, embedding itself in the chamber's sallow walls. Agatha and the younger nuns leapt back, setting her free. Instantly the stray feather found its place back into Morgen's trembling hand.

"You are evil," she cried, "far more evil than I ever conceived. I will not tell Lord Merlin of your transgressions—for I do not wish to see you harmed. I will, however, remember everything you ever did to me."

Casting a softer glance at Portentia, she continued, "I will also repay every kindness shown me here. I will repay it tenfold."

This said, she turned on heel and marched defiantly through the unfettered door.

"Wait, child, where are you going?"

Portentia's kindness stilled the rapid pulse of Morgen's temper. Suddenly, she was drawn back to the previous evening's encounter with Lord Merlin. They were in the midst of a conversation that had all but evaded her memory, a conversation that answered this very question. Merlin gently held her hand within his own.

"There is a place that calls you day and night—the place of your origins, the place of your being. It will haunt you forever. Go home, Morgen. Remember your destiny. I will find you there."

Morgen gazed into Portentia's eyes and whispered, "I am going home."

CHAPTER 4:

home

Day bled into night, and night sped day as Morgen wandered alone amid rolling hills, fragrant grasslands, and forests green, uncertain of her ultimate destination. Thankfully her pale nun's robes were easily replaced with a green gown of woven stuff that some fortunate mistress had cast aside when her figure grew too ample to fit its slender casing—at least Morgen's faultless intuition told her as much. She plucked the discarded garment from a ditch where it lay forgotten. After a reasonably good airing, she donned the well-worn material and marveled at the admirable camouflage it provided. This was especially useful as she traversed bramble thickets, clustering ivy vines, and an endless array of lacy weeds. How wonderful it felt to be free—free of the oppression she had suffered within Amesbury Abbey's decaying walls! This new life, however, did offer up challenges she had never previously contemplated, the most noticeable of which was securing food.

A far from subtle rumbling within Morgen's stomach routinely reminded her that she was hungry, so hungry that the humblest repast proved but a distant memory. The nuns had weakened her resolve with harsh treatment, starvation, and physical abuse. Those memories, however, paled when compared to her current situation. She was, after all, mortal. If she did not find food soon, death would ultimately follow.

Dipping her ivory fingers into a bubbling stream, Morgen knelt down and sipped its life-giving water. Her stomach lurched painfully at the strange sensation, but soon accepted the gift without further reproach.

All will be well according to your belief, prompted her inner voice.

Morgen cautiously observed her watery reflection, marveling at its unexpected brilliance. Mirrors were banned at Amesbury Abbey, so she had not glimpsed herself for a very long time. Surely this young woman whose bright smile flashed back at her was some other waif, some foundling robed in forest green. She was beautiful; perhaps ethereal would offer a more apt description, her long, wavy locks layered at the forehead and temples where Agatha's blade bit home. It was a surprisingly even cut—one that would not mar her delicate looks. A new mass of curls unexpectedly adorned her heart shaped face, accentuating it as never before. Would Merlin approve of this alteration? Would he visit her before time and distance irrevocably drew them apart?

Perhaps one day. One day, but not too soon.

This unspoken promise prompted Morgen to draw Merlin's talisman, the blue-gray feather, from a leathered pouch that hung about her waist. The difficult journey had not altered its delicate constitution, a fact well illustrated as it stood without further prompting in the palm of her hand. A familiar voice, originating from everywhere and nowhere at once, urged her to blow on this treasure three times.

Puzzled, Morgen scratched her head and then did just that. The wind moaned low against several clustering hawthorn trees, drawing her focus. Back and forth their nimble limbs dipped, lulling all thought, all emotion. Peace, contentment, and bliss whispered their promise bright and true. Morgen found herself slipping deep under this unexpected spell. There she lingered until a subtle pricking at the base of the neck indicated that she was no longer alone. Whirling around, she found a gentle flop–eared rabbit admiring her efforts. The mottled darling raised itself up until supported exclusively on its hind legs and then pawed the air, literally begging attention. Morgen could not dismiss such a broad sign.

"You are a messenger from the gods—the Ancient Ones. What is it you would tell me?"

The rabbit circled around three times and dipped its forelegs in the cool, clear water. Morgen mimicked its actions, awaiting further instruction.

Fair daughter, follow your heart's longings to the place of all beginnings.

"Yes, I want to explore. I want to know who I am. Can you tell me that?"

You must find the answer yourself. Journey within.

Further articulating this point, the hare stared directly at the water's mirror surface.

Morgen followed suit, slowing her breathing, for it seemed appropriate.

You are a part of this world, but not of this world. Indeed, you walk between space and time. Come home, Morgen. Fulfill your destiny. There is a reason you claimed mortal form—not to terrorize nuns, but to help.

Realization burst through Morgen's meditations.

"Arthur! I must help Arthur! He needs me now more than ever! Yes, I know that it's true. I feel it with all my being—even if Merlin and Uther keep us apart. Wait for me, Arthur. I will find you."

Everything happened so quickly that Morgen could hardly follow it. Cool, blue light poured from the hare's orbs, nostrils, and mouth, deftly altering every aspect of its delicate composition. Its legs, torso, and tail lengthened. Its fur grew richer and denser. Suddenly an amber-eyed fox stood before her. It spoke not a word, but winked meaningfully, then gave a brief wave of its rusty tail before plunging headfirst into the bubbling creek. Morgen took a deep breath and, without hesitation, followed in its wake. Down, down through the moss-green brew she swam, delighting in each new sensation that caressed her being. The creek was widening, lengthening into an endless sea, or so it appeared to Morgen's untrained eyes.

She had no need to draw further breath, or exhale, for a force higher than herself offered assistance. Morgen never contemplated where this guiding presence originated, perhaps due to the fact that strange spirits that sported both scales and fins observed her progress. Darting back and forth, they eyed her with a discerning gaze, ultimately seeking shelter behind plant, root, and water vine. Morgen wondered who they were and why she found them "odd."

One being appeared to read her thoughts, offering up a wayward smile that showed kindness, rather than irritation. Morgen's heart beat faster, for his physique proved immense, larger than any deity she had ever imagined. Long white hair fairly danced around his sea-green face, adding merriment to a normally stalwart expression. Cloaked in billowing robes of reed, moss, and algae, he towered over her, a magnificent monarch of the deep.

At his side swam a glorious, fair-haired nymph also robed with various sea treasures. Fish scales and shells adorned a silvery turquoise gown that swirled round her lithe frame. The light in her eyes proved disarming. Who could not love her? Who could help but follow her lead? Beauty and strength fairly emanated from her being—a fact made all the more tangible by a jewel-encrusted sword clutched purposefully in her hand. Morgen took note of this magnificent weapon, aware that it held some future significance.

The fair nymph smiled, offering wordless encouragement.

"I am in the presence of Lir MacMannon and the Lady of the Lake, guardians of all waters?"

The maiden nodded reassuringly, brandishing the sword three times.

"Thank you for guiding me through this first test. I am honored beyond all imagining."

It is we who are honored, Morgen. Indeed, our future hopes begin and end with you. Step forward. Claim your inheritance. If all goes well, one day I will stand at your side, beamed the fair lady. Gracefully, she circled around Morgen, an act that slowly propelled the pale beauty up toward the mirror surface. Lir further aided this endeavor, repeatedly brandishing his whalebone staff until the lake fairly sang its exuberance. Bubbles burst with pleasure, and glassy waves parted to provide an unexpected glimpse of blue sky.

Freed of the water's embrace, Morgen felt cleansed, born anew. She cast one glance back at Lir and his lady before the glittering waters closed, shielding them from view. Morgen found herself lying facedown amid a blanket of reeds. A loaf of brown bread adorned with fresh berries and fragrant cheese awaited her inspection.

"Thank you. I am ever so grateful for this food."

Slowly, carefully, Morgen tore off a small chunk of bread and brought it to her lips. The taste was exquisitely nutty and sweet, almost as if it had been drenched with honey. Another chunk found its way down her throat, then another. Morgen fairly choked under its influence. She was not generally a glutton, but the food was so delicious, so satisfying that she couldn't help it. The berries proved more heavenly still, far better than ambrosia. Even the cheese, which normally would have made her stomach curdle, tasted most satisfying.

Morgen wrapped the remains of her feast in the reedy blanket and then gingerly gained her footing. Where was she? What place had offered her this lifesaving repast? Amethyst mist swirled low, drawing focus away from the clustering apple trees that nodded their welcome. A lone heron plucked an undersized pike from the drink and with one swift motion threw it skyward so that it landed headfirst in its gaping maw. Swallows softly cried overhead, a low breeze carrying them to and fro as they pirouetted, sky-bound. A brief sigh escaped Morgen's lips. Never before had she felt so peaceful, so complete. There upon the shores of a moon-shaped lake she stood, admiring its brilliant landscape. Soft, glistening waters lapped at her feet, reflecting a canvas of color and light.

The mirror image proved hypnotic, capable of drawing her inward toward points unknown. Turning around she saw the countryside dappled with iridescent magnificence. Here and there gateways into other realms burst forth gleaming, only to withdraw just as rapidly from whence they came. Morgen paused, spellbound. Should she enter, or remain lodged within this magnificent haven? Everything around her appeared so different from Amesbury, or even the early years she spent at court. Green, rolling hills dotted with hawthorn and yew trees, ancient beyond imagining, stretched far as the eye could see. Morgen wanted to explore this virgin territory firsthand, but her gaze was drawn by a brilliant, camel-backed Tor that held its head high among the clouds. Earth, water, and blue sky perfectly intermingled in this sacred haven—a fact

that was not overlooked by its previous inhabitants.
A tiered labyrinth, a dirt footpath, long since over-
grown with grass and weed, hand-carved into the
rising ground, spiraled endlessly up the vast climb
toward a circle of megalithic stones situated upon
its smooth crest. Birds of every shape and size war-
bled peacefully together amid tumbling roses that
blanketed the lower levels in pink, crimson, and
deepest purple that shone black, and even sunshine gold. Suddenly, Morgen remembered her
truth.

*Avalon! It is Avalon that welcomes me into her
blessed arms! Oh, you beautiful island of mist, reed, and
apple blossom, how I have missed you. How I have longed
for you day and night. Now I remember! How strange
that my brief time as a human stripped me of this truth.
You are my essence, my soul. Avalon, you are real, far
more real than any place I have ever known! You are forever the bridge between fairy and humanity. Britannia's
health and wholeness originate within your breadth and
being. You are my home, my birthplace. Guide me; show
me what it is I must do.*

A low hum that seemingly emanated from everywhere and nowhere at once drew Morgen up a
winding path that encircled the Tor. How soft the
emerald grass felt beneath her feet as she traveled
higher and higher. Somewhere along the second
or third pass she encountered two rabbits pressed
nose to nose. She had to smile at so precious a
sight. A promise of romance lingered in that quiet
exchange. Morgen felt this intuitively, but gave it no
further consideration, for the rabbits broke apart
at her approach and fled. The wind increased its

passion, birthing little dust storms that danced to and fro before dissipating. Morgen recognized this at once as evidence of fairy activity, and she smiled. She was close—so close to realizing her life's purpose! This knowledge quickened her step, and soon she achieved the lofty summit. Louder and louder the wordless song grew—so vibrant at this point that there could be no further doubt of its origin. Why, the very stones were singing, welcoming her home. Morgen bowed before these cool divas, awaiting instruction. When it was not forthcoming, she threw caution to the wind and danced around the circle, caressing each megalith with a soft, affectionate touch. They were tall, curvaceous beauties of midnight gray that sparkled amid the late, afternoon light.

Morgen paused upon viewing a hollow tree that originally must have commanded the circle's prestigious center point. Hopelessly uprooted, she lay resting her leafless head against one rocky companion, as if dozing, dreaming. Morgen tried to right her, but the tree, though hollow, proved heavy, and she was weak from near starvation. The trunk did not budge an inch. Morgen tried again and again, aware that she was waging a hopeless battle. Finally she plopped down beside the trunk and brought her fair head to rest against its hollow, unprepared for what would follow. Energy surged through the dried bark, spilling out amid the empty branches, dead twigs, and dull trunk until it encompassed Morgen's fragile being. Light, sound, memory all came alive in that moment, rendering everything past, present, and even pieces of the future, clear for her inspection. Indeed, the whole of Morgen's life purpose revealed itself with such unabashed brilliance that a cry of joy escaped her lips.

Even Merlin had not understood the full scope of her mission.

"Now I understand! This is why I became human," she rejoiced as the stones increased their low chanting. "I am your queen, the one who will evoke peace throughout the land!"

Fairy Queen of Avalon...The supreme honor of this lofty title enveloped Morgen with its tantalizing embrace. Had she not told the sisters at Amesbury that she was destined to accomplish great works? As Avalon's queen she would represent the fairy on earth. All those quirks that had set her apart from other mortals and made her an outcast among the sisters and everyone at court were suddenly rendered sublime. She was a mistress of healing, prophecy, and wisdom, and she would share those qualities with everyone who crossed her path. Indeed, that path was destined to one day carry her back to court where she would stand beside the High King. His spiritual guide, his counselor she would be. A low tremor raced through Morgen's frame—an unsought harbinger of some knowledge desperately trying to break through that she was not yet ready to entertain. She had so much to take in, so much to consider. Each of the aforementioned gifts, precious as they appeared to be, was but a portion of her calling. It was equally her destiny to walk between the narrow thresholds of life and death and guide dying souls through the veil when their time came. Such were the gifts The

Ancient Ones had bestowed upon her—the gifts she would share with the world.

"I am your *peaceweaver*—she who channels light to all who wage war. Let me begin the sacred task now!"

The misty landscape beckoned her forward until she stood at the very edge of the Tor and cried, "Peace now and forever! Peace blanket Britannia! Peace be upon all beings and peoples of the earth!"

A low rumbling deep within the Tor drew Morgen from this passionate reverie. Avalon was speaking to her, offering counsel through the very stones at her feet. Yes, she was the peace weaver, but men were hopelessly accustomed to war. As she would see this very night, it was the only thing that many understood.

The eight grand megaliths fell silent, offering warning. A siege, an insurrection—one that intimately affected every last soul Morgen held dear—was about to be unleashed upon St. Alban's monastery. Instantly Morgen's feet were in motion. How she understood this communication proved a mystery, but there was no time for explanations. She entered the stone circle once more, aware that the megaliths were conversing with her. Their words, soft as quicksilver, spilled through her anxious brain.

Make haste, Sister! St. Alban's is under attack. Igrainne, Uther, Arthur, Merlin, and a handful of the king's guard are trapped. You must act now before it is too late.

Relying on an instinct that felt painfully familiar, Morgen approached the wounded tree and stepped inside its hollow, awaiting further instruction. When it ultimately came, she wished she had already made good her exit.

Yes, Uther is dying. Remember your life's purpose.

CHAPTER 5:

Insurrection

Remember my life's purpose?

Orgen followed an intricate series of steps down the tree's hollow innards, oblivious to everything but a profusion of sound. Swords clashed and men shouted amid a chorus of feminine screams. She saw nothing at first beyond the downward spiral of knotted roots, but then a full-fledged vision consumed her, revealing the royal family—*her family*—trapped within a large dining hall. Morgen recognized Urien of North Wales, whose tactless marriage proposal had earned him a levitation, and another petty king, Lot of Lothian, husband to her half-sister, Morgause, as leaders of the would-be usurpers. No doubt they intended to seize Arthur's crown before it was irrevocably placed upon his head.

Remembering the fair-haired youth she had viewed asleep upon the forest floor, Morgen pondered his current whereabouts. Where was Arthur in all this madness? Slowly, distinctly, she scanned the bloodied warriors with her inner eye, pausing at a tall, golden-haired lad who kept watch over

the fallen Uther. *This* was her brother, the future
king—but only if he survived. She wanted so desperately to warn Arthur of Lot's duplicity, but there
was no need. Indeed, Arthur's agile sword stalled
the advance, leaving the would-be usurper visibly
stunned by his youthful skill. Suddenly Lot was
sprawled upon the ground, legs splayed beneath
him. Arthur moved in for the kill, but five other
miscreants swelled forward, allowing Lot time to
reclaim his stance. This did not bode well. Morgen
breathed a prayer for assistance, but it was unnec-
essary, for Arthur's foster brother, Kay, and best
friend, Bedivere, raced to his side. Together they
acted as one entity, beating back the five with coor-
dinated defense. Another group surged forward,
past Kay, past Bedivere, straight for the dying
Uther, but Arthur's blade proved too lethal a deterrent. He moved with such speed, such surety, such
grace, it was impossible to overcome him.

A sudden stirring drew Morgen's attention.
She could just discern Igrainne struggling to
escape through a servant's door, albeit with little
success. The movement also caught Urien's eye.
He motioned a burly man forward, little imagining that a mass of swirling silks would impede his
progress. The queen's lady-in-waiting, Guenevere
of Carmalide, stood blocking his path, sword
drawn. Tall, golden haired, and surprisingly steady,
she appeared well versed with the blade.

"You will not pass," she said, blue eyes narrowing with a fierce determination that defied her
opponent's edge.

A huge grin animated the man's heavily bearded face as he lunged forward, hardly anticipating the agile sword that bit his side. Instantly the grin was replaced by a look of utter incredulity. Down he fell, clutching his side, blood blossoming upon the thrush-strewn floor.

Morgen did not wait to see any more. It was perfectly obvious what she must do. The servant's door needed clearing to provide an escape route for her mother. And so she stepped free of the dark protective root structure and found herself situated within a small prayer chapel that boasted white-washed timbers and pale dressings that appeared hauntingly ghostlike in their familiarity. How many times had she visited this humble place? How many times had she left its hopelessly pure alters, ashamed of her own name?

The only person that can truly make me feel ashamed is me—and only if I allow myself that power.

A series of screams claimed Morgen's focus. Out into the shadowy monastery, she stole, careful to remain unseen—a task which proved easy enough, for the hall was completely deserted. Morgen pressed forward, pausing only once she reached the great hall's shattered door. What was it she intended to do? How was she to offer assistance? Aware that her heart was pounding at an alarming rate, Morgen answered the question herself. Many a lazy summer day she had spent at St. Alban's, days in which she had shirked all other duty in favor of exploring its various haunts. This knowledge informed her that the servants' quarters lay directly ahead.

Stealthily pressing forward, Morgen pondered the whereabouts of the inhabitants of St. Alban. Where were the monks, the prior, and the bishop, who never strayed far from these hallowed walls? Surely Lot and Urien would never harm men of the cloth. Morgen shook her head, remembering that both Lot and Urien followed the Old Religion. Monks and their prior, even a bishop, could not stop an insurrection. Either they lay hiding somewhere or they were already dead.

Tying her heavy skirts at knee length, Morgen cast all such morbid thoughts aside. Off she raced, ignorant of what lay ahead. Igrainne's escape must be her focus. If that went smoothly, she might slip inside the hall itself and heal some of the guard.

Morgen skidded to a halt just outside the servants' chambers, breathing hard. Casting caution aside, she threw open the door. A huge platter of what appeared to be duck lay upon the pitted serving board, awaiting consumption. Heavy wooden goblets, plates, and wine vats stood perfectly ordered along with a profusion of bright fruits and vegetables: apples, pears, carrots, and plump, ripened peas. Indeed, everything appeared as it should be—with one unfortunate exception. Corgan, the merry-faced cook who once told her fairy tales as a child, lay unmoving in a broadening puddle of scarlet. It was his body that currently blocked Igrainne's intended escape route.

Morgen entered the room, swallowing hard against the terror that tested every fiber of her being. *Why do I fear the inevitable? Death will claim us all at the proper moment, heedless of impediment. Death does not discriminate when claiming its due.* Morgen knew within her heart of hearts that she was to act as advocate of the dead and dying, and so she mentally reaffirmed her purpose.

This is my life's work. I must help the dead find their way home.

Gazing down upon the cook's cruelly lacerated throat, Morgen shivered ever so slightly.

Corgan, it is I, Morgen. I am here to guide you home. Take my hand.

A pale, bluish energy slowly spilled forth from the very pores of Corgan's skin and fixed itself around Morgen's slender wrist, an act so gentle, so easy that it almost felt normal.

Dear child, I always knew you would come for me. Tend to the others first. I will watch over you in this time of peril.

Thank you, Corgan. We will save Igrainne first; then tend to Uther.

Once a fairy princess found her way to earth...

Morgen paused, remembering how many times Corgan had told her this romantic tale filled with knights, dragons, and a dashing, golden-haired prince.

Did you know?

I might have guessed, rang his bemused reply.

Softly Morgen kissed the pulsating blue light, then grabbed hold of Corgan's stiff ankles and pulled. Since Corgan was a small man, she dragged him easily. The door swung wide, freed of its burden. Igrainne instantly took advantage of the situation, motioning the bloodied Guenevere toward their haven. The man who had been foolish enough to take on this fair sentinel lay forever silenced, his sightless eyes bent toward some imagined haven.

"Come, Mother," Morgen whispered, clasping hold of the queen's arm, "we will see you to safety."

Igrainne's breath faltered slightly as she recognized her foundling daughter reborn, no longer a child but a maiden of such delicate beauty that she could only be a fay. "I don't believe it," she cried, wrapping her trembling arms around Morgen's shoulders. "Is it really you, Morgen, lost for so long, yet now found?"

Morgen reeled at the sensation. How wonderful it felt to be embraced by someone who loved her, someone who cared that she also inhabited this earth.

"Yes!" she cried, conscious that mere words would not express her true feelings. Oh, why did they have to meet this way, when their lives were threatened? Why did fate play such thoughtless tricks with their emotions? Morgen wished only to thank Igrainne for the gift of mortal life, but the sensation of touch, warmth, and trembling spurred her back into movement and action. Any further delay could prove fatal. "Come, Mother, we must be off!"

Racing out of the servants' quarters as fast as her cumbersome gown would allow, Morgen led both women down the mouth of a shadowy tunnel that came to an abrupt halt deep beneath the monastery wine cellar. Darkness eclipsed their vision, throwing all other senses into heightened awareness. It was oppressively dank and musty in this forgotten place. Morgen pressed a lone torch against the moldering stone walls and watched as it burst into flame without further prompting. Both Igrainne and Guenevere gasped at the sight, yet it was not enough to stay the disgust from their features when they realized the scent of decay came from moldy straw at their feet. Apparently one of the wine vats had burst open and spilled its contents on the dirt-laden floor. Morgen ignored their looks of repulsion and continued securing the torch in its iron holding. This accomplished, she inwardly pondered her next move.

Igrainne, impressed by Morgen's fortitude, drew her softly against her breast. "My darling, how is it you are here? I was told that you lodge with the sisters at Amesbury Abbey—that you have lodged there these past two years."

Morgen smiled as she stroked Igrainne's lush, dark tresses. "You forget, Mother, that I am a fairy in disguise. I will always know when my family is in danger."

Igrainne looked up at this. "Yes, of course. I should have known." Clasping Morgen's hand, she trembled anew, "How could this have happened? How, when we are so well guarded? St. Alban's has always been Uther's haven. He came here to heal, but now…"

Words failed Igrainne momentarily as she searched her daughter's eyes. When she did speak, it was with rapid determination, as if to outrun the very miscreants that threatened their existence. "How powerful is your magic? Can you stop this madness? Arthur desperately needs your assistance. He is all alone trying to defend his father."

One question plagued Morgen's mind. Indeed, it had been assaulting her consciousness since she first entered St. Alban's shadowy halls. "Where is Merlin? Why is he not here?"

"Merlin left shortly before the attack," Igrainne cried, pacing to and fro amid the sticky floor covering. A soft squishing sound accompanied each footstep, lending a further hopelessness to their situation.

Morgen looked beyond this discomfort and continued her questioning. "He left? That makes no sense, Mother. Surely Merlin would foresee an attack on the royal family. He would never abandon us."

Something snapped within Igrainne's deportment, for her vulnerability disappeared, and she looked every inch a queen. "I neither know nor care where that creature has gone! I think only of Uther. Did you see him, Morgen? Did you see Uther?"

Morgen flinched inwardly. Even now Igrainne thought only of her precious husband. "Arthur will safeguard his father," she said flatly.

Igrainne underwent another mood shift, this one so rapid that Morgen feared for her mother's sanity. She appeared a mad woman, tearing her glorious hair even as her eyes flashed with wild, inwardly raging fire.

"But he is so ill! This could kill him, Morgen. I must go back!"

Before Igrainne could make her escape, Morgen took hold of her shoulders and thrust her back against the slimy walls. "Do you wish to die as well? Stay here, Mother," she cautioned, motioning Guenevere to the queen's side. "I will see to Uther."

The warmth of Morgen's person slowly worked its magic upon Igrainne until she knew reason once more. "Oh, my darling, it is too dangerous for you. Lot boasted that he and Urien had already slain two women."

"I think one of them was Gwyneth," Guenevere offered as she wiped the bloodied sword against a bit of molding straw. "Urien wore her sleeve."

Morgen looked up. Guenevere was a tall, slim beauty with long golden hair that fell well past her waist and eyes that rivaled the summer sky. Her demeanor, though respectful, was solid, unwavering, determined. She would not allow Igrainne to throw her life away for a hopeless cause. This knowledge helped Morgen breath a little easier. Guenevere would continue to safeguard the queen. Oh, and she was destined for Arthur. How that bit of information had fallen upon her unbidden, she dared not conceive.

A low, dull ache assaulted Morgen's brow. *I don't have time for this*, she inwardly groaned, methodically rubbing the spot until the pressure ceased its expression between her brows.

"Poor Gwyneth," whispered the queen. "She was your age, Morgen, scarcely a woman."

Morgen held Igrainne tightly, as if the world must fall away. So much remained unspoken between them, so much emotion that neither dared broach. Should she use the moment to dissolve this lingering silence? If truth be told, it seemed a waste of valuable time. Somehow the words, "I will help Uther if I can," filtered through her lips of their own volition, and her fate was irrevocably set in stone.

Igrainne stared at Morgen unblinking. "You would do that for him?" Her surprise caught all three women off guard.

"I do it for you," she said, pausing only to kiss her mother's cheek. "You will be safe here."

Igrainne knew better than to impede her daughter's decision, so she simply let her go. Little could she imagine that they would soon be forever parted; little could she dream of Morgen's true future. Instead Igrainne only saw a tiny, flame-haired beauty racing fearlessly into the vast unknown before Guenevere claimed her queenly hand and led her deep into the vast labyrinth that was St. Alban's cellar.

The tunnel seemed long this time, filled with unexpected twists and turns. Morgen fell more than once, so frantic was her pace, tearing her green gown at the waist and bodice. Quickly she regained her footing. This was no time for false modesty, and so she raced on. Her pace was so frantic that a stitch assaulted her side. Still she moved forward, somehow regaining the hall outside the servants' quarters with remarkable speed. Doubling over at the waist to better catch her breath, Morgen heard the door fly open. Out staggered a wounded Urien of North Wales. Lean and tightly muscled, he sported light brown hair and smoldering green eyes that could steal a woman's soul at a single glance. A nasty thigh wound preoccupied his attention—one that had drawn him from the fray. Urien had just tied Gwyneth's pearly sleeve above the gash when his eyes fell upon Morgen. A low whistle issued from his lips.

"Morgen, my sweet," he sputtered in a thick, husky voice that readily bespoke pain. "Is this a new fashion, or are you playing the role of harlot tonight?" he grinned, indicating her torn bodice. "Come closer. I merely wish to admire you. A piece of that lovely garment will help save me. In any case it no longer shields you from view. Come now, I do not ask much. You can hardly deny me this one request."

This said he made a lunge for her gown.

"I will always take great delight in denying you everything, Urien," she taunted, easily evading his grasp.

Urien drew the sleeve tighter, but could not conceal the groan that escaped his lips. "Always is a very long time, Morgen. One day you will come to love me."

Morgen offered up such a fierce glare that Urien gave way to laughter. Using an agility that clearly surprised them both, he pinned her hard against the wall with the unmarred side of his body. His left hand softly played against her breasts, just concealed within their torn casing, as his right ripped a long sheet of fabric from her skirts. Luckily this set the ill-tended knot free so the balance spilled back over her legs, shielding them from view.

The assault reminded Morgen why she had so vehemently objected to Urien when he made his initial proposal: he nurtured a fierce hunger that could never be abated, never be fulfilled, a hunger that extended beyond his holdings in North Wales to everything that captured his greedy eyes. He must possess a thing wholeheartedly or die. As simplistic as this man's makeup appeared, it did not fully cover the scope of his existence. He desperately wanted Arthur's crown, of that she was certain. The fact that Uther lay near death made the endeavor extraordinarily easy for Urien. Or did it? Arthur was winning, by the look of things. Was it not Urien that left the fray wounded and failing? If truth be told, she did not fully understand Urien, nor did she have any desire to understand him. He was lewd and crass, his ill-conceived behavior never to be borne.

Morgen fiercely lashed out with her hands and feet, making it impossible for Urien to secure the additional material above his wound.

"This would be so much easier if you chose to cooperate."

"Why, so you can murder me as you did Gwyneth?" she spat.

A frown graced Urien's brow. "What—you mean the little raven-haired lass? Well, she did put up a fight when I took her maidenhead, but rest assured I left her alive and smiling. In fact she sent me off with her sleeve. No woman ever leaves my arms unsatisfied. Now, beauty, allow me to offer *you* ample thanks."

It was with a kind of controlled horror that Morgen watched Urien fasten his mouth against hers. Never before had she been kissed by a man— something about the act seemed almost barbaric, as if he wished to swallow her whole. He tried to pull her closer, but thankfully the wound interceded.

"You will forgive me, beauty, but..."

With a swift motion, Morgen slipped her right elbow free and slammed it against her oppressor's neck.

Urien reeled with the impact. His grip faltered, and Morgen found herself captive no more. Tearing the dagger from Urien's belt, she made ready to drive it through his heart.

Would you so easily commit murder, little sprite?

Morgen froze, her hand poised within striking range. It was Merlin's voice! So he was alive! In fact he was somewhere nearby!

Merlin? Where...?

It is not Urien I think of, but you. Make haste, little sprite! Attend the king!

All thought of supreme vengeance was abandoned in that moment. Offering Urien one final kick to the shin, Morgen plunged recklessly through the servants' door, dagger clutched tightly in her hand. Sound, sight, and metal swirled around her in one great dance of death that rendered movement difficult at first, for Morgen not only had to navigate past the blade-wielding living, but also the dead who littered the floor. Swords thrust and clamored around her, hapless of rank or title. Somehow she slipped past the copper-headed Kay, past the sure-footed Bedivere, and even past Arthur himself, who was yet again steeped in combat with the traitorous Lot.

There behind this wall of Arthur's brethren, Uther lay forgotten, gasping for breath. His skin was a dull gray, almost devoid of life. Morgen knelt beside the poor soul, aware that he would soon slip away. Softly she stroked his fair beard, unprepared for the jolt of life that blazed through her veins. What strange curiosity was this? Uther was dying—of that there could be no doubt—but his body felt alive with vitality. Something was wrong, out of sorts. This was not Uther but...

Yes, Morgen, it is I, Merlin, in the guise of the king. Merlin!

A wave of relief filtered through Morgen's veins as she stooped to kiss Merlin's moist forehead. How could she not have seen? It was so obviously Merlin in the king's habit. No doubt Lot and Urien were far too concerned with the insurrection to unravel this clever illusion.

"Merlin, I knew you would never abandon us! Where is Uther?"

"There is no time for explanation," Merlin barked with irritation. "This is war!" Pulling Morgen down by the hair so that her ear fell just above his lips, he continued in softer, albeit no less biting tones. "Go to Uther and attend him as best you can while I create this diversion. It is the only way he may survive this madness. Lot and Urien will hardly seek elsewhere if they think him dying before their eyes. Quickly now. You will find him in my chambers at the west end of the monastery!"

"You do not wish me to help you here?"

"What help can you be in battle?" he snapped. "You are a healer. Go, see to Uther!"

Morgen quickly released Merlin's arm and then, through clever maneuvering, slipped away unnoticed. She tried not to think of Merlin's cold reception or of the fact that Corgan still clung to her wrist. Arthur and Merlin would see the insurrection fail—of that she was certain. At present she had only to concern herself with Uther, a true challenge considering his contempt of her person.

Onward she ran, pausing merely to catch her breath before entering the bishop's chambers. Perhaps the gods would be kind...

CHAPTER 6

Secrets Revealed

Deep within the bishop's chambers lay a tiny room that safe-guarded the religious icon during times of unrest. It was here that Merlin sent the dying king when Lot and Urien made bold their attack. Merlin felt confidant that its occupant would remain undetected, as it was inaccessible to all save those who knew where the hidden trigger panel lay. Indeed, this is precisely why the enchanter had taken great pains to secure the adjoining chambers for the prince and himself.

A wise move, Morgen mused as she reached the chamber. She paused, fingertips brushing the doorframe. Could she do it? Could she forgive Uther his past transgressions and offer him the healing his ailing body so desperately craved? It was time to press forward, time to conquer those deep seeded fears that haunted her existence. As Avalon's Fairy Queen, she could do no less. Royalty must acknowledge equals and comprehend the other's needs and goals no matter how dissimilar they may appear at first blush. Even a dying monarch understood that.

Take heart. Uther will be glad of your assistance, Corgan graciously reassured her.

Morgen was not so certain of that statement's validity. Pausing just outside the secret door, she caressed it with her sensitive fingertips. Suddenly, all of Uther's nastiness, all his vindictive pleasure came back to haunt her. This was Uther Pendragon, the oppressor divine, the man who had exiled her to Amesbury Abbey and Sister Agatha's "tender" care.

Morgen gripped the door to better thrust her rising temper back into submission. Instantly, the hidden trigger snapped open of its own volition, and she saw Uther flailing about like some great fish cast hapless upon the pitted shoreline. He was trapped, paralyzed, and unable to save himself. The picture was at once so pitiful, so hopeless that Morgen trembled.

Nothing, not even the previous vision, had prepared her for that sight. Uther, formerly so handsome and vibrant, appeared shrunken, as if what little of his flesh remained was tightly stretched against bare bones. His hair, dulled by premature graying, straggled upon his brow, partially camouflaging the purple shadows that diminished both eyes. She watched his feeble attempts at escape, aware the door had already swung back into place. No doubt he anticipated a swift dagger to the chest. When at last he registered that it was Morgen and not some usurper bent on his destruction, the age old mask of disgruntled monarch slid across his countenance. Morgen carried but two items, a torch and a simple washbasin, which forced a sneer to his lips.

"I come at Merlin's request," she said, securing the fitful torch upon a cobweb-infested wall hanger not dissimilar from the one she found several floors below.

"*You?* What do you want with that?" Uther spat as a bit of water splashed his chest. "Is it your intention to drown me then? I make a very easy target. You could finish the task and no one would be the wiser."

Morgen laughed at his mock anger, aware that it helped him feel stronger, more thoroughly in control. Why had she never taken time to comprehend the man behind the crown? Surely there was more to Uther Pendragon then met the eye. How else could he have won Igrainne's heart? Was it possible that underneath this veneer of gruff, stern behavior lay a kinder, misunderstood soul? The proposition gave Morgen some pause, so she voiced the question that plagued her mind, "You believe I am your murderer? Life would have been far more pleasant had I settled upon that course of action. Unfortunately, someone beat me to it. No, Uther, I am not your executioner, nor do I have any intention of finishing you off now. Be at ease. Let me aid you as I can."

Slowly, deliberately, she waved her hands above his wounded frame, willing the healing energies into expression. The task was easy enough, one that required little thought but true intent. Instantly, she felt warmth flood her hands, brilliant and strong, spilling through her palms as it encompassed Uther. Healing was one of two abilities she had brought with her from the Otherworld. The other, prophecy, told her that Uther knew nothing of this gift. Indeed, he knew little of her at all.

Uther blinked but kept silent, his eyes ever mindful of the deep, violet light that permeated his body. How comforting it felt to be bathed in this unexpected celestial radiance. Indeed, it would have been beneficial if he had known Morgen possessed this "oddity" long before his decline. Observing the changeling child with a discerning eye, he noted how wholly she championed his recovery. Why she even bothered, he could not conceive. His past conduct toward her hardly fostered such devotion.

Using her middle finger, the fire finger as it were, Morgen offered a pronounced tap upon his chest, an act which propelled the healing current straight into his weakened heart. The sensation spiraled up through his throat and forehead before it ultimately came to rest at the crest of his skull. Understanding broke through Uther's senses with such brilliance that it slowly began to extinguish his fear. There in that forgotten cell, Uther gazed into the eyes of his healer, forgetting anger or reproach. She was assisting him, helping him make the transition, for it appeared futile to expect recovery.

"By the gods, girl, what are you doing to me?" he jested in simulated panic.

Perfectly aware of his tactics, Morgen fixed her eyes upon him and smiled. "I am offering you healing of heart, mind, and spirit," she said simply. "Your poor body, I fear, is beyond my humble talents."

A chuckle escaped Uther's cracked lips, "Igrainne has often told me as much."

Morgen's cheeks flushed crimson. "I did not mean to suggest..."

"I know you did not," he said, capturing her warm hands within his own.

"You need not worry for Igrainne," Morgen offered, unsettled by this close contact. "She is hiding beneath the wine cellar. I made sure of that."

A sigh of relief escaped Uther's lips. The little imp had done it! Somehow, beyond all hope, she had relieved the cold, dry fear that consumed him. Never had he dreamed that Morgen could serve him so well. Igrainne, his other self, would survive the insurrection, even if he did not. "The gods be praised," he breathed, somewhat labouredly. "She is well."

"She is well, indeed, and missing you terribly. It took every ounce of my strength to keep her hidden. Igrainne seemed to think that finding you was more important than safeguarding her own life."

A fine mist colored Uther's eyes. "That is so like her."

He loves her more than anything else on earth. This truth fostered the forgiveness that had long evaded Morgen's heart. All the suffering, all the anguish, all the red-hot anger Uther had forced her to endure was extinguished by his great reverence for Igrainne. A man that felt so deeply was not beyond hope or redemption.

I will try again. Perhaps some form of healing, no matter how miniscule, may be possible.

Morgen had just replaced her palms against Uther's narrow chest when he cried, "Enough of that! Give over the healing. It is time we spoke candidly."

Drawing near the shallow washbasin, Morgen cleansed her hands, a necessary precaution to remove any negative residue that often accompanied the healing exchange. Indeed, each healing was as unique as the individual patient, and sometimes, as in Uther's case, the patient's decline was so advanced that not even a healer gifted as Morgen possessed the ability to call him back from death's embrace. This normally would not have halted her attentions, but once the patient had rejected the healing, several unspoken laws came into play. Healing was only offered to those willing to accept the gift. Once the magical treatment had been rejected, the healer had no choice but to wash her hands of it and find another worthy of her service. And so Morgen did just that. Slowly counting the steady pulse of her breathing, she pressed each palm methodically against the tattered green gown to relieve the excess water, and then faced the king. She had waited her entire life for this conversation. Pray the goddess she did not waver under Uther's stern gaze. How would he react to the truth? Would he welcome her honesty, or cast her back into the darkened halls?

With characteristic discernment, Uther spoke straight to the point. "Why have you adopted the guise of my daughter? What is your purpose here, lady fay?"

Morgen was indeed surprised, not so much by the question, but that Uther had bothered to ask it at all. "I am here to help your son. You had no wish to heed my counsel. Arthur, however, is a different man."

Uther shifted his weight uncomfortably, a difficult task considering his weakened state. The low, dull fear that had plagued him since he learned of Morgen's true identity reasserted its grip. Arthur would bend to her will as no other. He sensed it intuitively. If only he possessed the strength to banish Morgen, consign her to some foreign outpost where Arthur would never see her, never even dream of her existence.

"Forgive me, I did not mean to offer insult," Morgen sighed, aware of his discomfort.

Uther swallowed back his venom. "I know that, girl. You are perfectly right in suggesting that I would never have accepted your counsel. Merlin has a hard enough time convincing me of his outlandish schemes. Why, then, would I listen to a child, even if she be fairy born? Arthur may be open to otherworldly counsel, but I would caution you against it. A man must make his own destiny. Do not seek to alter that which is his birthright."

How little Uther understood his son's true purpose. How little he dreamed that Arthur's existence was part and parcel of Morgen's being! Somehow she must make him understand that Arthur shared with her the same bonds that tied him to Igrainne.

The truth of this realization hit Morgen squarely between the eyes, and she spoke without thinking.

"I do not move against destiny, Uther. If I did, you would not be dying now."

Bile rose in Uther's throat, forcing him to stay his reply. The air, the life-giving breath itself seemed to exit his lungs as he slumped back against his pillow. It was over—his life, his existence, all gone forever. Morgen had given him the gift of peace. He would not cast it away for a moment's anger.

"You have heard my counsel, Morgen. See that you heed its wisdom in the years to come."

Morgen offered a brief nod of her silken head. It was useless to further plead her case, for death sat poised to claim its due. Healing was no longer possible for Uther Pendragon, no matter how much effort she put forth. It was over. Never again would he torment her. Never would he consign her to an earthly prison. It was time to place past sorrow aside and guide him through the veil.

Redoubling her efforts, Morgen cast a white light around her charge and watched breathless as it lifted him several inches off the bed. Uther appeared unaware of this new development. Indeed, his attention was bent on several muffled voices that drew ever near.

"We are discovered, lady fay. Fly—steal away while you can."

"I will not leave you, Uther. I have come to take you home."

"Let us be gone then."

With that Uther trembled and breathed his last, his body collapsing against the shallow bed, still shrouded with light. The secret door swung open as Uther's essence latched itself about Morgen's right wrist. She heard a sharp intake of breath.

Morgen looked up. There before her stood the most dazzling youth she had ever seen. It was Arthur that met her gaze, tall, golden-haired, and breathtakingly handsome. All of Merlin's plans had come to naught. They were spellbound, each held by the light in the other's eyes.

"Who are *you*?" Arthur asked, his voice barely concealing disbelief. "Are you real?"

CHAPTER 7:

The Cauldron of
Rebirth

Morgen, make haste! You have lingered too long!

It was Merlin's thoughts that shattered all focus, demanding attention.

"Forgive me," she breathed, finding it nearly impossible to tear herself free from Arthur's gaze. "We will meet again."

Arthur stared at her reeling, heart pounding wildly within his chest. "Meet again"? *Yes, we have met before somewhere long ago, high upon a lonely wind-swept hill. I can almost see you and hear the timber of your voice. You are dearer to me than my own existence, my own sweet love who forgives all except the one thing that drives us apart—war.*

A rapid series of events followed that defied discernment. White, icy light, blinding in its brilliance, eclipsed the narrow chamber, forcing Arthur to shield his eyes. A low cry escaped his lips as something four legged and excessively

agile whirled around the space where the beautiful maiden stood, utilizing such speed, such grace
that the very air wrinkled in its wake. He reached
for his weapon, but it no longer occupied his scab-
bard. Had he not placed it there but a moment earlier? Suddenly, Arthur knew with a thrill of agony
that the maiden too was gone, the knowledge of
which forced another cry from the very depths of
his being.

Morgen trembled at the sound. It was that of
a twin soul being torn from its other self without
hope of restoration. She tried to reassure him,
but the light, so pure in its composition, eclipsed
all meaning. Arthur, Uther's body, the very room
itself melted away into nothingness, and a sensation of falling embraced her. Morgen flung her
arms around the beast's neck and held on tightly
as they plunged into bitter darkness.

"Wait, please!" Arthur cried. "At least tell me
your name!"

The voice repeated itself and then grew fainter
and fainter until it could be heard no more.

Morgen struggled against the sorrow that
welled within her being. All focus must be placed
on the task before her. The spirits of Uther and
Corgan were her priority—not the golden-haired
prince, but oh, how his voice inspired the innermost cords of her being.

He was still searching for her, unaware that
Uther had expired. When that shock came, he
would soon forget her. On she traveled through
the dim, chilled light, arm draped around her
mysterious guide's smoothly muscled shoulders.

Morgen could just discern the pale outlines of a stag, noble in its deportment, that led her forward, eyes bent on the frozen levels below. His expression was kind. Though his fur appeared snowy white, it was warm and soft to the touch, and his eyes, when they flashed upon her, were an unearthly blue. Never before had Morgen seen so beautiful a creature.

I come on behalf of my Lord Cernunnos.

The stag's words sounded clouded at first, as if it were difficult for him to arrange his thoughts into a language Morgen could decipher. He need not have worried, however, for she understood him perfectly. Indeed, she thoroughly comprehended that this was the beginning of her life's purpose as an Underworld guide. Cernunnos was, after all, the Celtic god of the Underworld.

And of all animals, the stag aptly supplied.

Morgen offered a caress to his graceful back. Down an exceptionally slender, snow-covered path they trod—one that spiraled and coiled its way deep into the bowels of the earth. Morgen clung tightly to the stag's neck—so precarious was her position. Indeed, every step she took threatened to cast her off that narrow trail and into the seemingly bottomless abyss.

You may ride upon my back if that would be helpful, he suggested, pausing to better register her reaction.

Then we both would learn what it means to fly.

A low chuckle bubbled from the stag's ivory muzzle. Before Morgen could voice another concern, he had settled her into the perfect crook of

his back and set forth down the snow-laden path
once more.

How did you...?

Some secrets are better left unspoken.

Morgen smiled at the stag's coy demeanor.
No doubt he was a magical creature whose gifts
extended beyond her own shallow comprehension. The very lilt of his gait suggested as much.
His grace exceeded anything Morgen had ever witnessed. Indeed, one movement flowed into the next
as if he were dancing. Morgen admired the bright
stag to distraction. As a result the journey sped
by without making any further impression until
Morgen started from her musings. How much had
she missed while admiring her guide's prowess? It
was then she took note of her stark surroundings
with heightened interest. Her eyes, slowly growing
more accustomed to the absence of daylight, registered that everything appeared shrouded in white,
black, or silver. No sound rang out beyond that of
the stag's hooves as they crunched the icy snow.
The air was sharp with chill and faintly musty.

One day, she too would assist others along this
route.

Thank you for coming to my aid, she offered, pat-
ting the stag's lean, smooth flank.

*Think nothing of it. We are almost there. Oh, my
name is Myrddin.*

Morgen froze. *Myrddin? Is that not an ancient
variation of Merlin?*

Time shifted and blurred, as if they covered a
vast distance with one great bound. Morgen found
herself standing outside a huge gate of sharp white

pikes that stretched far beyond her limited vision. She frowned at first, for the pikes appeared to be unevenly matched, bound as they were together by thick bands of various colored hair. Morgen shivered as she ran her delicate fingers against the macabre structure. The hair was obviously human and the pikes well-honed bone. No doubt they had belonged to a bevy of mortal hosts. That clearly explained why the gate and wall were so oddly composed.

You now stand at the Underworld gates, Myrddin supplied, answering her unspoken question. The deep blue of his eyes sparkled meaningfully, and a smile graced his fair countenance. Nuzzling her hand, his form shimmered then was no more. In his wake appeared an ebony sow lolling beside a low cauldron that lazily bubbled and sputtered its welcome. Morgen's eyes grew wide. This was the cauldron of rebirth. The sow appeared to read her expression, for she spread her broad mouth into a half smile. Waddling forward, she placed her moist snout against Morgen's fingers.

Feeling rather foolish, Morgen addressed the sow's endearingly chubby form. ***I am in the presence of Cerridwen, dark mother to us all?***

The sow nodded her thick, smooth head. ***Welcome, Morgen of Avalon. You are correct in your assumption.*** This is ***the cauldron of rebirth. Place the souls of the king and cook inside and they will be born anew.***

Corgan, who needed no further prompting, rapidly began uncoiling himself from Morgen's fair arm. Every appearance indicated that he was eager to begin life anew. Softly, his essence hovered before Morgen, a bluish light that fairly glittered with pleasure.

Thank you, child. I always knew you were destined to achieve great things, but I never imagined you would guide me back into the womb. I will always remember you. I will always bless you.

Morgen bent forward and kissed the pulsating light. *Be well, be happy, be whole.*

The light that was once Corgan slowly spilled into the cauldron and became one with its soupy composition. Although the bubbling broth appeared a rich brown, here and there bright colors burst forth, reflecting individual traits. No doubt it took longer for some individuals to release their personalities than for others. Morgen watched the magnificent spectacle, spellbound. Had she ever surrendered her will to the cauldron? Did fairies combine with mortals in the collective? Was that how she became human?

A fine question, indeed, Morgen. The ebony sow continued, analyzing her with the weight of its sloe-black eyes. *What of your other charge? Is he so cowardly as to hide behind your skirts? One would hardly believe that he was once Britannia's High King.*

Uther's essence showed no sign of movement except, perhaps, that it clung with even greater tenacity to Morgen's wrist. After a lifetime of exacting judgment on others, no doubt he felt uncertain about his own reckoning.

Morgen smiled despite herself. *What is it, Uther? What is wrong?*

I have no desire to be boiled with a cook. I am a king!

He further emphasized the point by tightening his grip to such an extent that Morgen felt her hand tingle.

*You **were** a king,* Cerridwen aptly supplied. Slowly, she waddled over to Morgen, gazing up at Uther's light, which deepened into a dull, red brown.

You are now simply one of my children.

The sow further emphasized this point, guiding Morgen until her wrist dangled low over the bubbling brew. Round and round the heated broth swirled, gaining momentum as if it needed impetus to leap up and claim the unwilling Uther.

My work is not yet finished. I have to help my son. War is…

War is and was and unfortunately always will be until man adopts another path. That will be your task, Morgen, the dark sow grunted, gazing up at her through twinkling eyes. *Help man see another way. Then Arthur, your son,* she continued, glancing back at Uther, *will truly become a king among kings*.

Uther's light still remained uncertain, growing a deeper, richer red. No further movement occurred until the sow butted Morgen's leg with her rounded head. The time for reckoning was at hand. Her next thoughts did not wax gentle.

What is it you fear most, Uther—the loss of your identity? Unless, of course, you are an arrogant sot who will not mingle with the collective.

Once again came the determined head butt— this time with such force that it loosened Uther's hold, and he dangled free before securing another grip around Morgen's fingertips. How much longer could this impasse endure? Surely, the dark goddess had a trick or two she had not yet revealed.

I fear stupidity! It is the height of folly to be boiled when so much remains to be done.

Impatience flooded Morgen's being. It was her job to bring Uther home, and she was failing miserably. Perhaps if she spoke to him as a daughter, some understanding would spur him into action and so she put her thoughts into words. "Uther, I know there is no love between us…"

That is your interpretation of my feelings!

"I am here to help you, Uther. Please let me guide you forward. If you remain, if you linger forever on the outside looking in, you will be lost. Your spirit will become earthbound, a ghost, an echo of the past that can neither help nor hinder a cause. Please Uther, this is the best, the only way you may aid Arthur. Come back as someone dear to him, someone who can make a difference. That is what I did."

You have known him before? Uther questioned, analyzing the lilt of her voice, the rise and fall of her breast, those very things that had exasperated him in life. Suddenly, he understood. Everything— the masquerade as a human, the portrayal of a princess—made sense. She did it all for Arthur. *You have loved him before. You love him still.*

A brief nod of the head served as Morgen's reply.

Well, that settles it. If a fairy lays prior claim on my son's affections, I have no choice but to come back immediately and warn him of the fact. Arthur has no idea what disaster awaits him. Complete your duty and do not pause, lady fay.

Morgen knew not whether to laugh or cry. Slowly, she lowered her hand until it dangled but an inch or two over the boiling liquid. The pressure that Uther exerted relaxed momentarily, but then renewed its vigor, stiffening once more. He was waging a violent battle with himself, unwilling to release everything he "knew" to be true.

Finally, I can say it. I need your help, daughter. I cannot do this alone.

That is why I am here, Uther. I know you never cared for me, but now I may assist you in this one small way.

Morgen carefully unwrapped the glowing light from her arm and then touched it with her lips. There was no response, except that it brightened to an emerald green.

Be happy, Uther. Come back as a joyful person next time.

Is that possible for such a one as me?

Anything is possible if you will it, supplied Cerridwen, shifting into her true form—that of a lovely old woman with dark, wrinkled skin and hair whiter than the purest snow.

You are wrong about one thing, Morgen, Uther mused, slowly loosening his grip.

What is that, Uther?

I do care—more than you will ever know. Why else would I place you in a nunnery?

With that, Uther Pendragon released his fragile hold, finally content to mingle among the collective unconscious. His green light sputtered fitfully as it hit the brown broth and then dissipated. Morgen paused, considering Uther's departure. This man had affected every moment of her mortal existence. Suddenly he was gone forever—no, not forever. Uther Pendragon was part and particle of her being. That bond would never be severed until she too mingled with the collective—perhaps, not even then. A low humming called Morgen from her private reverie. It was Cerridwen, smiling her approval.

Well done, Morgen. Your first venture as an Underworld guide has been a success, she said with warmth, slowly stirring the cauldron's contents with a spoon that appeared to be made out of huge incisors. The act appeared barbaric, inhuman, but this hardly dampened the goddess's appeal. *Now another soul begs your attention.*

Morgen blinked, remembering the golden-haired prince who still awaited her at St. Alban's monastery. "Arthur?" she whispered, drawing his glorious form and face into mind.

A sharp clucking colored the air. *How easy it is to cast aside wisdom for beauty. Is Merlin so soon forgotten?*

Cerridwen's humming recommenced as if nothing of import had occurred. Round and round she stirred the cauldron's contents, careful not to spill the slightest drop against the ice-encrusted ground. Morgen swallowed before answering, aware that she had gone against the mage's wishes when she spoke to Arthur. Perhaps a reckoning of another sort awaited her return.

Merlin seeks me? Why would he?

A subtle shaking of Cerridwen's head proved her answer. Morgen marveled at how lush the goddess's white locks appeared even in the Underworld, where absence of color or abundance was the norm. Her dark skin glimmered with power, the kind that lay just beneath the surface, waiting. Her eyes, though fixed upon the cauldron, read Morgen clearly as a scribe analyzing his masterwork. Indeed, she knew all, understood every nuance, every question from its conception.

Do not forget the feather, Cerridwen said at last, so carelessly that Morgen was not quite certain she had spoken. *It is a token—not, as you suspect, of Merlin's willingness to become your teacher, but of his undying devotion.* Down came the mask of confidant and Cerridwen revealed, perhaps, greater detail than she intended. *He needs you now more than ever.* The cauldron teetered precariously as she shifted her grasp. Morgen, fearing the worst, rushed forward to aid her. *Do not be foolish, child,* she said, brushing off the well-meaning gesture, her eyes sparkling approval. Placing an ebony hand against Morgen's shoulder, she cautioned, *Listen carefully. Something has happened—a rift between mage and pupil. Arthur blames Merlin for his father's death. Perhaps I should not have told you this, but there it is.*

Blames him? How is that possible? Merlin did not poison Uther!

Cerridwen watched Morgen intently before answering. The child loved both men; with whom would she side?

No, but he also neglected to tell Arthur that Uther was dying. Now the future king feels betrayed by his teacher. He has cast aside his one true ally—his counselor. You must help bridge the gap between them or all will be lost.

Once again a bemused expression puckered Cerridwen's lips. Dire as this turn of events appeared, she was enjoying Morgen's reactions. It was anyone's guess whom she would choose. Merlin stood on even ground with Arthur.

But how will I…?

How indeed, Cerridwen chuckled. *A beautiful maiden loved by both prince and counselor. How will she ever guide them toward reconciliation? The answer lies in Avalon.*

Cerridwen cast her toothy spoon aside, then picked up the once-smoking cauldron without flinching and, demonstrating a strength that belied her seemingly fragile being, carried it through the ivory gates. A low creaking emanated from the ivory hinges, one that clearly revealed disuse; it was not often Cerridwen walked out among her people. Morgen marveled at this and watched as the bony gate swung shut, zealously guarding its treasure. Uther, Corgan, and the goddess divine disappeared within, leaving Morgen alone to ponder her own return route home.

CHAPTER 8:

Fallen from Grace

Long before Morgen exited the tree's hollow innards, she sensed that Merlin was present in Avalon, anxiously awaiting her return. Her suspicions proved well founded, for once she climbed out of the toppled trunk, the enchanter drew all her attention. There he sat within the ancient stone circle, looking like some lost urchin, cross-legged and introspective, drawing energy from the eight gray sentinels that sparkled their pleasure amid the late afternoon light. His dark eyes sprang open at Morgen's approach, displaying a certain vulnerability, but he did not move to greet her. "Forgive me, Merlin," she apologized, aware that her cheeks were burning. "It was not my intention to meet Arthur."

"What is done is done," he said in a cool manner that displayed his displeasure more readily than a passionate outburst. "Come, sit beside me."

Morgen did so, conscious that her heart was beating rapidly. What if Cerridwen was right about the feather token? Did that mean Merlin *had* pledged himself to her? If that were true, why did he remain so distant? Surely he did not think she had chosen Arthur over himself. Surely...

"What may I do to ease your pain?" Morgen finally whispered when the silence between them became too broad to bear. "I know of your quarrel with Arthur."

Merlin looked up at this but said nothing. His eyes met hers with a fierce intensity that mirrored his suffering. Slowly, he clasped her hand then brought it to his lips. "Help me through this agony. I cannot find my way. Indeed, I am lost to all sensations beyond those found within your presence."

Drawing his chilled fingertips against her lips, Morgen returned the gesture.

At long last she understood the feather's true meaning. Clasping the deerskin pouch that hung between her breasts, she knew that it lingered inside, waiting. Would she accept the gift or cast it back in the mage's face? She had, after all, asked to become his pupil. Instead, he thought only of binding himself to her. Merlin viewed her as a love, not a scholar. Was her worth not greater than this? Did she not deserve to be educated? How would she play out this game? Cerridwen spoke of his great need. Should she not help him through this difficult time and decide later? Surely a healer could ease his torment as nothing else.

"Merlin, I am flattered that you have chosen me among all women who grace the earth—flattered, yes, but altogether conscious that love is not what brings you hither. You are here because of Arthur, because of the quarrel."

Suddenly, Merlin was on his feet, pacing. "He sent me away—wishes to be rid of me, all because I failed to warn him of Uther's demise. How was I to tell him that his father had been poisoned? How, when I was sworn to secrecy on the subject of his birth? Uther demanded that I treat Arthur as an orphan until a fortnight ago. That is when our plans began to unravel. You must understand; Arthur has been fanatical about unearthing the truth. He has dreamed his entire life of meeting his father. I hoped I had filled that void, but..." Merlin's voice trailed off, even as the stones' soft, hypnotic melody echoed his sad lament. Somehow their song gave Merlin strength for further confession. Round and round the circle he paced, hardly daring to catch Morgen's eye. "It was cowardly of me. That is the truth plain and simple. I was a coward, afraid to tell my one charge information that intimately affected his life. I feared I might lose him to Uther. Now I have lost him altogether."

Altering course, Merlin caught Morgen in a wild embrace that swept her off both feet. "Forgive my foolish bleating. I know not where else to turn. If not for your own sweet person, I will run mad."

Morgen saw that Merlin desperately wanted to kiss her, caress her until all the pain drained away. Deep inside she understood that it was not so much love that Merlin inwardly bled for, but healing. She would heal him and leave the question of romance for another time. "I think you are neither a coward nor mad, merely an adviser who cares too deeply for his charge. It is time you accepted help from another. Lie down among the stones, and I will heal you."

Merlin gazed at her intently, a soft smile playing upon his lips. "I have never received so tempting an offer," he sighed, allowing her to guide him down against the heavily winded grass. "If my circumstances were less dire, I might think this a romantic proposition."

Warm laughter spilled from Morgen's lips. "Yes, men always think such things."

"What does a mere slip of a lass who has spent so much time in a nunnery know of men?" Merlin asked, arresting her hands when she attempted to place them against his brow.

Delighted that Merlin could still find humor amid heartache, she replied, "I have observed Uther, the guards at court, and Urien of North Wales long enough to read a man's thoughts, especially when they turn toward wooing."

Merlin gazed up at Morgen, his expression unreadable. "What am I thinking now?"

A bright flush animated Morgen's expression. She drew her long locks over the torn green bodice of her gown and took a deep breath before making a reply.

"I choose not to say. Rest assured, Merlin, that my offer of healing is genuine—not a ruse to seduce you. There will be time enough later to explore such inclinations, should our thoughts tend in that direction."

Merlin opened his lips to reply, but thought better of it. Resigned to the foreign role of receiver, he relaxed his tense muscles and shut both eyes.

This was the signal Morgen had been awaiting. Claiming a dark mantle from Merlin's shoulders, she knelt upon it, shielding her already ruined dress from further soiling. The ground was still moist from frequent rainfall, and she marveled that Merlin did not object to the fact. Positioning her hands above his brow, she silently asked the divine healers, Bridget and Dianecht, for assistance, a request they honored with all due haste. Lush healing energy spilled through Morgen's palms and straight into her wounded charge. Merlin started at the sensation, perhaps because of its intensity or perhaps he did not deem her capable of such gifts. Regardless, she smiled. With this act she would prove her true worth. A sharp pricking at the back of Morgen's skull forced her to recant that thought. Healing was not meant to be used to further her cause. She must focus exclusively on Merlin and forget his past disregard. At least the great mage was making an attempt to be open, but oh, how he flinched as the divine energy targeted his reeling mind. An intense chill consumed Morgen's being—one that stemmed from the negativity being sucked free of Merlin's body. He was releasing some of the angst, albeit slowly.

If truth be told, Merlin was not a model patient. He possessed far too much pride to release his healing exclusively unto Morgen's care. Still, she did not waver, redoubling her efforts even when his legs began to spasm. So much anger and pain lodged within his soul that this was the only way he could release it. The tremors continued until Merlin sat up and forced his body into submission.

The look with which he fixed Morgen was haughty, as if he were beneath such indignity. Merlin refused to appear feeble, and soon a wall of resistance rose between them. Aware that she was but a hair's breadth from losing him, Morgen folded Merlin in a soft embrace and guided him back against the soggy ground. There he lay, gazing up at her, uncertain. It was altogether clear that he did not wish to experience any further humiliation. If Morgen could continue without evoking a similar reaction, then she had his blessing, if not...

Placing her hands directly against the crown of his head, Morgen breathed a prayer for assistance. It was vital that she not shame him. The energy began its charmed work again, this time focusing exclusively on Merlin's troubled thoughts. A low sigh escaped Morgen's lips. Had she trespassed on some forbidden ground? What secret was it that Merlin sheltered with such tenacity? What agony did he not wish her to see?

Healing often unveils those thoughts that haunt a person's sensibilities, drawing the healer deep within their charge's psyche until they stand as one and the same. In this case Morgen felt herself meld with Merlin to such an extent that she lingered inside his very skin, viewing the Great Hall at St. Alban's as it was but a few hours earlier. Uther's body lay within a hollowed-out log, awaiting burial. Merlin looked up from his devotions, aware that Arthur stood nearby watching. Slowly he rose and bowed his head.

When Arthur spoke, his voice was steady. "You have betrayed my trust."

"Betrayed?"

The look of utter perplexity that unhinged Merlin's expression must have communicated itself to Arthur, for Arthur rounded on the mage with mounting anger.

"You, who know so much of healing and magic—you could have saved him!"

Healing? Surely Arthur understood that healing was as unique in its expression and abilities as the person for whom it was enacted. In Uther's case too much internal damage had been suffered, leaving no means to pull him back, reclaim him, no matter how gifted the healer. Merlin was clawing, scratching to regain his delicate footing. What brought on this shift of consciousness? Surely Arthur understood that he was enacting the king's will in keeping his identity, not to mention Uther's illness, secret. Surely Arthur comprehended that every task he had undertaken over the past sixteen years had been executed for his welfare.

"I have told you before that magic does not work that way!"

"No, it only works when and where you wish it!" came Arthur's firm rebuff.

The sad truth filtered through Merlin's veins. It was cowardice that brought them to this impasse. No matter how much he mouthed otherwise, Merlin should have told the lad everything. Fear governed his tongue, holding it in check, the fear that he would lose Arthur. This realization far from softened Merlin's response, "Arthur, I cannot force destiny to fit your private whims."

Something clicked within Arthur's brain: the fact that he was just a heartbeat away from assuming the role of High King. No one, not even his counselor, had the power to deny him anything. Why, then, did the sorrow reflected on Merlin's face, not to mention the fact that he was responsible for it being there, make him feel guilty? He had just lost his father. Surely this gave him the right to make demands. Arthur watched Merlin intently before voicing his decision. Aware that dismissing Merlin when he was so broken would wound him as nothing else, Arthur did just that. "I wish to be alone with my father," he said. "Do not return until daybreak."

Oh, goddess, Morgen breathed into the misting air. *Help me ease this breach between prince and counselor. Britannia needs their combined brilliance, not dissolution based upon a misunderstanding.*

Determination flooded Morgen's being as she searched the catalogue of her mind for every healing technique that might magnify her efforts. Surely some symbol she had once used in the fairy realm could pierce the barriers Merlin had erected around his mind. Shifting one hand against Merlin's heart while the other reasserted its presence upon his crown, Morgen whispered the word, "*Seleaphrim.*" Merlin's breathing slowed noticeably even as a low moan escaped his lips. The steely nerves, muscles, joints, and tendons that he held so tightly relaxed, and then regrouped before she could do anything further. "Do not fight me, Merlin. I am trying to help you."

"My needs are not as they appear, Morgen."

Morgen felt an invisible presence push her away from Merlin's frame. Aware that it went against every unspoken rule of healing, Morgen repositioned her hands, this time directly against his skin. It was wrong to force healing upon a person if he was not ready to accept it. Yes, she knew this intuitively, but that did not stop her efforts—no, not this time. *Seleaphrim.* The word shone as quicksilver in her mind. Again flowed a rush of energy, vital and discerning, drawing her deeply into Merlin's essence. Oh, how she felt his pain—so brutal in his condemnation of himself! That was part of her gift brought forth from the fairy realm, the gift of empathy. Indeed, Merlin's inner torment was so immense that Morgen trembled. Poor Merlin, certain he had lost Arthur and...

It was then she glimpsed the image Merlin kept buried deep within his cavernous thoughts, camouflaged from all detection save that unearthed by this one irrefutable spell.

"Who are you? Are you real?"

A single tear spilled down the length of Morgen's cheek. *I am responsible for his anguish every bit as much as Arthur is. Our connection torments him.* Clearly the mage saw what Morgen chose to ignore: the unspoken past connection shared between the golden-haired prince and herself, of such intense recognition that it seemed the very air must melt for expression of it.

Merlin's thoughts twisted inward. *I have lost her forever.* The vision wavered and was seen no more.

"You have lost nothing," Morgen said, bending low to kiss Merlin's forehead. Merlin arrested the effort and brought his lips squarely against her own. The sensation was at once irresistible, spellbinding. Healer that she was, Morgen did not break the exchange. Indeed, she kept fast to her purpose, channeling the tonic, even though Merlin's lips claimed focus. Energy swirled between them, born of this odd pairing. Waves of pink, green, and indigo commenced a heady dance, mirroring their passion. Morgen caught only glimpses of this magnificent spectacle. Although the healing was still active, she no longer felt capable—or worthy—of its conception. Perhaps it was a spell Merlin had placed upon her or the fact that their individual gifts blended in this exchange; but Morgen no longer felt conscious of her actions. It was instinct alone that charted her course. Merlin's lips broached no other option. Oh, how warm he was, how strong, how vital, the very muscles in his lean, smooth arms growing more possessive, more demanding. The tide turned as Merlin grabbed hold of her hips and coaxed them flat against his groin.

Morgen tried to pull away, but he held her, wrapping his right leg around her thighs, holding her fast against escape. This was not a totalitarian restriction. Indeed, Merlin would release her, should she demand flight. Morgen felt that instinctively. Oh, but each time he kissed her, all such thought sped away. Magic flowed between them, revealing glimpses into dimensions previously unknown. Voices, soft and enticing, whispered confessions never imagined, never dreamed. They were not alone. Indeed, the wealth of the universe held them fast within its fiery cradle, uniting every fiber, every sinew as one. Morgen's senses lengthened to such exquisite perfection that they felt as keenly sharpened as a dagger's blade. The mage was masterful at manipulation; his lips and hands, velvety smooth, slid up and down her torso, drawing her ever nearer to ecstasy. His scent—that of earth, leaves, and musk—proved heady and utterly inviting. They were still fully clothed, but that made little difference as their forms softly entwined.

"No woman has ever touched my heart so deftly as you, little sprite," the mage whispered, burying his face within her silken locks. "Indeed, no woman has ever suffered my caress."

Morgen's thoughts turned inward. Was Merlin a novice when it came to love? Was it possible he was every bit as virginal as herself? His actions suggested otherwise, but then he could be drawing on the universal consciousness that guided their union. It pleased her to think that Merlin had waited his entire lifetime for her, but then most of his life had been devoted to preparing for and educating Arthur. What time had he for love? What time had he for her? This would most likely prove a one-time union. Even if the visions indicated otherwise, she was hardly a match for Merlin.

Think not on it. You are exceptionally well versed in love's mysteries, Morgen. How can it be otherwise? You are our Fairy Queen.

Ignoring the sinking feeling that she was being watched, Morgen thrust these concerns aside. The stones were speaking, offering shrewd reminders of that ultimate purpose that fired her imagination.

Why did they have to be so present, so watchful? Could she not have a moment's freedom, especially when it came to love?

Laughter welled within Morgen's mind. Whoever or whatever was observing her thoughts hardly amused her. Merlin was staring at her, gently caressing her cheekbones with the tips of his fingers. The light in his eyes was spellbinding, reflecting something so tender, so emotional within their hypnotic depths that she voiced the question earlier than she intended.

"Do you love me, Merlin? Why pledge yourself to a maiden you have met only a few times?"

Even in the waning twilight, Morgen saw that Merlin colored, uncertain how to respond.

"Do you not see?" he whispered, folding her within his arms. "You are my heart, Morgen—the very blood that flows within my veins."

Slowly she undid the ties that bound his ebony robes at the throat. His skin was dusky, a soft sheen of mist clinging to the dark hairs that lined his chest. Wiping the fine residue free, Morgen became aware that the healing energy still bled from her fingers. Merlin sensed it as well, closing his eyes, as if praying.

"You are both love and teacher to me," she confessed, easing the robes further off his shoulders, "although you swore that it could never be so."

"For us, little sprite, magic and love are one and the same."

Passion drew them back against the dewy grass, this time with such fierce compulsion that neither could escape the other's lips. Merlin claimed the dominant position, pressing Morgen fast against the moist earth. He eased the torn gown from her body with such slow, delicious strokes that she felt herself a pearl being urged from its shell. Night fell fast around them. All was stardust and moonbeam. A distinct humming broke forth as the stones added their private symphony, soft, fated, desperately sensuous. Morgen experienced it all with an exquisite agony. Yes, she loved Merlin, adored him to distraction; but there beyond the magic, the moonshine, another man claimed her attention. Arthur's voice haunted her perceptions, called her through previously unvisited dimensions, until her spirit breached St. Alban's monastery, where he waited with open arms. There, beyond the brilliantly colored veil that undulated between them, she could just detect his well-muscled outline, strong, clean—in a word, brilliant to the eye. The veiled lights plummeted as falling stars, revealing a sight that set her heart pounding.

Gone was Avalon Tor, gone Merlin the mage, gone everything Morgen knew to be real. It was not the soft, mossy earth upon which she lay, but a thrush-strewn floor. It was no longer Merlin that caressed her, but Arthur the prince incarnate! They were entwined as mistletoe around the sheltering oak, glistening, naked and warm.

When Arthur spoke, Morgen felt she must expire else the dream fade and she find herself forgotten once more.

"Surely now, you will tell me your name."

She laughed at this, but said nothing, shifting her body so that it fit him perfectly, an act which practically spurred Arthur into confession.

"We have known each other before. The first moment I saw you I knew—I recognized you from somewhere long ago. Please believe me. I would do anything for you, even give my life to see you safe. Truly, I will be your husband if you will have me."

Once again laughter chilled the air, cold, hard, biting, an inappropriate response to so heartfelt a declaration. The words that issued from her lips were altogether brutal, unfeeling. How could she be so thoughtless? He loved her! How could she threaten his very existence?

"I do not ask your life—not yet at least," her response oozed as venom from a desperate adder. "It would not serve my purpose if you were to die before you became king."

Die? The words fell as a dagger plunged straight through Morgen's heart. Why would she want Arthur to die? Darkness eclipsed all thought, all sensibility. How could she have strayed so far from Avalon and Merlin's embrace? Was it possible that she had happened upon some alternate reality where words and deeds fell contrary to their intended mark? Had she happened upon some fairy land where she was no longer in control, but a mere observer? Soft petals of golden energy fell fast upon Morgen's pale skin, offering explanation as to why she felt off kilter. Every inch of her once lithe body waxed swollen. Indeed, she was gathering flesh at such a rapid rate that her arms, belly, and thighs appeared plump, if not decidedly voluptuous. Had she not been near starvation but a scant hour earlier? Surely, this was no dream, but some waking nightmare!

The look of terror that eclipsed Arthur's expression echoed her sentiments. He had just become one with her sweet body when the transformation began its ungodly work. "I do not understand," he whispered, controlling his voice to keep it from quaking. "What is happening to you?"

Pain flooded Morgen's femininity to such an extent that a cry broke forth from her lips. She was a maiden no more. Again, she gazed upon her consort and trembled. Merlin was before her, dark, slim, utterly beguiling; but even as she kissed his lips, Arthur's golden hair, bronzed skin, and brilliant blue eyes usurped his place. A scream lodged in Morgen's throat. She could see them both, mage and prince, making love to her as one, each present, yet separate in their unique aspect. The horror of this fantastic encounter left Morgen increasingly faint, reeling. She must somehow break free without wounding her loves. The stones once again exerted their authority, fairly shrieking their warning. The fate of Avalon, indeed Britannia, depended upon her compliance.

Morgen closed her eyes and prayed as she had never prayed before. Voices whispered their intelligence; but she could not discern their meaning so caught was she in this passionate dreamspell. All sensation told her that she had left the Tor behind and lay locked in Arthur's bronzed arms. Indeed, she felt the crush of strong, youthful torso against her rounded belly, the press of his battle hardened fingers against her full thighs. *Arthur, something is terribly wrong. I don't understand it, but we have to break free of this. Do you hear me? Save yourself while you still can!*

Silence proved her only reply. Arthur stared right through her, claiming precedence over his dark tutor. His look, one of perplexed horror, terrified her as nothing before. What was it he saw? Not Morgen, but some lascivious seducer bent on his destruction, drawing him ever near release. It would be over in a heartbeat. Morgen sensed that at once. She had to act quickly. She had to comprehend the true nature of this disastrous encounter. *Who am I? Not Morgen of Avalon, but...*

A subtle dialogue played within the forgotten corners of her mind, offering a hint to the answer. She was a queen, a wife, a mother. She had birthed many children—all of them boys, gifts to her liege lord, a cunning Angle based in Lothian, but now all that was forgotten; now she would conceive a king.

Conceive a king? Understanding broke through Morgen's consciousness as daylight streamed upon the steely blue standing stones, casting their glittering faces into bold, brilliant hues. Their words, equally unclouded, realized her worst fears. This was a vision, not some magical feat that combined the two men she loved most into one delicious whole! Yes, Merlin kissed her, embraced her; but Arthur made love to another woman somewhere deep within St. Alban's monastery, unable to break free. Indeed, a witch—or something like one— held him fast within her person, claiming his precious seed, which she would use as a weapon, the future means of his destruction. Suddenly Arthur reclaimed control over his voice.

"Who are you?" he cried, trembling with revulsion. "You are not *her*."

The words stiffened as ice about Morgen's heart. She had tricked him—her face, her form had forced him into a union he had no desire to entertain. Their past love, so pure in its conception, had been his undoing because of one woman's mad desire for revenge.

"No, of course not," the red witch sneered through finely polished teeth. "You would hardly wish to mate with your own sister." Her dark hair cascaded into two bands across Arthur's arms, forcing them into submission, iron strong as they were, preventing escape.

"I do not understand," he said, utilizing the full force of his considerable strength to break free. "She—that maiden is my sister?"

Cold, cruel laughter flooded the great hall. Uther's body lay within the hollowed-out log but a few paces away. Once sunshine filled the sky, countless followers would pay their respects to the fallen king. The witch fixed her gilt green eyes on Arthur and smiled. "It comes as a surprise that you could desire one of your own family, does it not, my prince? You thought that you made love to Morgen, when in reality you became one with me. I am only your half-sister, so the crime is not altogether dire."

Arthur renewed his bid for freedom, but it did no good. He was trapped as a fly in a spider's webbing, clawing against invisible waves of energy that held him in place. "What game are you playing? Release me!"

"Poor, poor Arthur lost his father, even as he has lost his soul. I will keep you inside me until I know our son has been conceived."

"Who *are you?*" he asked, pale as death.

Merlin leapt to his feet, his eyes full of fire. *"Morgause!"* he cried.

The wind rose to a fever pitch, and Morgen knew no more.

CHAPTER 9:

The Red Witch

Betrayal. The word repeatedly assaulted Morgen's being until she sat upright, head reeling. Pressing her trembling fingers against each temple, she coaxed her frantic thoughts into submission. How much time had passed since Morgause's gross transgression? How many horrors had superseded the last since her enforced slumber? A scream still lodged unexpressed within the back of Morgen's tender throat. It had been *her* usurped face and form that brought this agony upon Arthur. If they had never met, never gazed upon one another... Merlin's warning suddenly appeared quite prophetic. He had done everything within his power to prevent their meeting— to delay the inevitable upheaval of their emotions. And why? Had he known that this betrayal would follow?

Darkness had come, darkness at daybreak. The gathering storm clouds swirled low as if stalking some enticing prey. Wind pelted Morgen's fair countenance to such an extent that it became difficult to draw breath. Thankfully the stone circle offered a reasonable amount of shelter or she might have found herself flung off the Tor. This was no storm of its own making, not when the sky cried its fury. Lightning flashed its wicked smile, revealing the mage as he conjured what appeared to be a portal that mysteriously swirled inward, oblivious of space or time.

"Do not follow me!" he cried, stepping into the crackling vortex. "Wait for my call!"

With a burst of golden light, Merlin was gone. Silence followed, a piercing silence that thoroughly tormented all sensibility even as it brought Avalon back into balance. Everything appeared normal, untouched. The sun had recommenced its upward trek across the sky. No hint of wind, no promise of rain darkened its aspect. Avalon presented a placid, tranquil countenance, belying the truth that haunted perception. Morgen rose to her feet, drawing the increasingly shabby gown about her person. She had been used by her own half sister, Morgause, as a means to seduce Arthur. How? *Why?*

Racing down the Tor at breakneck speed, Morgen gasped as her toes connected with a variety of stones, brambles, and weeds. She *was* barefoot after all. Perhaps that was the reason tears spilled down her pale cheeks. Perhaps it was something else entirely. In any case it was vital that she reach the water quickly—be it the lake itself or better still, the well! Yes, the well was closer! Down, down the Tor's camel back she plunged, unmindful of the carefully tiered path, clutching a stitch in her side. It was the lush apple orchard that beckoned

Morgen forward, a bevy of heavily laden boughs that welcomed her approach.

Here and there exposed roots caught her delicate footing and she toppled, cursing her own existence. Why could she not be more agile? Merlin was trying to save Arthur while she lay immobilized in the mud! Drawing herself upright she recommenced her flight, conscious that the arch mage might be enduring a life or death battle with Morgause. Why did Merlin forbid her assistance? Why did he deny her right to aid him?

Bursting through a layer of curvaceous yew trees, Morgen slid to a halt just short of the Chalice Well's rusty seal, her feet torn and bleeding. Violently, she tore at the cover, ignoring the creaks and groans that came from its hinges, ignoring the pain that strained her fingernails to the breaking point. The lid was heavy and uncooperative from disuse, but Morgen's efforts were soon rewarded, and she found herself peering into the water's smooth surface. Poised for spell work, it placidly reflected the sun's radiance overhead. Morgen paused only to splash a few droplets on her forehead; then she knelt so she could look directly into the unbroken surface.

Show me Arthur and Merlin. Are they together?

The rusty water swirled round, revealing earth, sea, mist, and sky in one great melding, a brilliant painting that muted the senses and lulled the mind. Image after image whisked through the reflective lens until it came to rest full stop upon the Great Hall of St. Alban's monastery. Dark as a forgotten sepulcher the hall festered, graying stones barely brightened by the waning torchlight. The first rays of daylight struggled through an unfettered window, illuminating subtle patches of thrush-strewn floor. Once again, Morgen noted how empty the large chamber cavity appeared, devoid of monk, prior, or bishop. This was the hall where all great people were received, all pilgrims waited—the few furnishings decidedly humble, even for a proper monastery. Near the far wall lay a single trestle table, upon which Uther rest deep inside his burial log. A handful of benches and a couple of well-made cross chairs also peppered the room. Everything else had been removed—no doubt to accommodate the masses that would soon arrive to pay their final respects to the High King... *Everything but the siren who wrought his destruction.*

Morgause lounged upon Uther's coffin, crimson bodice half laced and legs spread wide. She did not appear fat but full through the breasts, hips, and thighs, an altogether stunning beauty with pale skin, dark, streaming hair, high cheekbones, and emerald eyes. It was easy to see that this was Igrainne's daughter, so similar was their coloring, but the malice that defined Morgause's expression quickly forced one to question any such ties.

The red witch laughed aloud, her thoughts coloring the rusty waters as easily as if they had been spoken.

A life for a life...One child born of lust grows to manhood, and another is conceived to destroy him. And so the circle revolves round. There is such poetry, such beauty in the conception. Can you not see it, Uther? Long ago you struck my father down so you could lie with Mother.

Arthur was born of that mating. Now with his *seduction I repay you tenfold. What a shame that you are not here to see your precious son brought so low. Ah, but I must not mourn too much. This is, after all, a cause for celebration!*

Unholy laughter filled the cavernous hall, shook its very foundations as Morgause placed her clenched fists against Uther's chest and pummeled him over and over.

Finally you're dead—dead! Uther, bastard usurper, great Pendragon, husband to my bitch mother, and oppressor divine, you are no more! Never again will you torment, abuse, and oppress me. Never again will you marry me off to a loveless petty king and think yourself well justified. Today I am justified—*all thanks to a clever disguise and an even more potent poison. My one regret is that you cannot see my complete triumph over your person! Now poor, dear Arthur will pay for your crimes!*

A half smile twisted Morgause's lips. Arthur had proven himself a generous lover, thoroughly attentive to her needs. There he lay so still beneath her feet, fully capable of inspiring desire. Half brother or not, the lad was incredibly handsome. And then there was the real purpose behind his seduction. Morgause patted her belly and smiled.

"Well, Uther," she sneered, casting his body from the hollowed log so that it toppled to the floor, "your son acquitted himself quite well."

Morgause paused as if expecting some retort; then when it did not come, she laced up the bodice of her crimson gown. Uther was dead. His harsh tongue would torment her no more.

Yes, Uther, the High King was gone, but one who served him whisked through the silent monastery as if he had no more substance than wind or light. The huge chamber doors guarding the Great Hall were flung open, and a voluminous shadow spilled inside, expanding in length and breadth until it resembled the one form Morgause feared most. Tall, dark, demonic, no one would ever doubt that Merlin was the son of an incubus as was so often rumored in fireside tales.

Morgen gasped, still locked within the well's reflection. *Merlin!* The image that assaulted her vision proved terrifying. Surely this was not the man who had kissed her so passionately. No. This was a demon brought forth from the lower realms bent on one task: Morgause's annihilation. Several heads taller than any mortal he stood, eyes glittering black fire and bristling hair that stood on end. So lethal was Merlin's aspect that he appeared wolf-like, once gentle hands twisted into clawed appendages, and teeth into razor sharp fangs that bespoke vengeance. The red witch was doomed, utterly, hopelessly doomed, for it appeared impossible to escape so ferocious an enemy.

Indeed, Morgause sensed this, for when she saw that fateful shadow take shape, a tremor animated her frame. The king's counselor stood before her, eyes narrowed into two black coals, barely concealing their fury. All thought of escape fled in that moment. No, she must stand and face whatever followed and pray that she was cunning enough to protect herself and the newly conceived child that harbored in her womb. Slowly, deliberately,

Morgause stretched her shapely legs around Arthur. This was her first victory over the Pendragon clan. It was vital that she not allow their enchanter to dilute its potency. Perhaps that is why she set all her assets into play and blew Merlin a soft kiss.

Merlin hardly blinked, so set was his purpose. One glance around the seemingly dormant hall told him more than he needed to know. The fact that Arthur lay as one dead suggested the witch controlled his spirit. It was Merlin's task to restore Arthur's essence within its frame, then deal with Morgause and her bastard offspring.

"What you have done you will undo and quickly," he hissed, making good his approach. A subtle flick of his wrist cut off the airflow that fortified Morgause's lungs. He took some solace as the magnificent beauty choked and sputtered, clawing wildly at her throat, but did not stop there. Merlin redoubled his efforts, tightening the invisible pressure upon Morgause's airway until her face took on the ruddy hue of her gown and both eyes bulged wide. Only at the final moment when it seemed she must expire did he offer release. The command given, Merlin watched, unmoving, while she desperately lapped up much needed air.

Realization burned Morgause's aching lungs. It was impossible to defeat Merlin with courtly tricks. No, he must be taunted, tested before she uncovered a weakness that rendered him vulnerable. "I assure you Arthur initiated the liaison all by himself," she breathed, aware that her voice was rebelling. "You would have done the same, had you been in his place." Slowly, seductively, she ran her fingers along the crimson bodice that only half concealed her ripe breasts. If this did not move him, then he was a statue, indeed.

A sharp flick of Merlin's hand cast Morgause back against the hapless trestle table that housed Uther's coffin. She grabbed the log for support but found herself unceremoniously thrust into the hollow where Uther once laid. Before she could draw breath to utter a counter curse, the lid flew into place, securing her fate.

"I will leave you there a little while, Morgause, so you may reflect on this night's transgressions. Think how many souls have suffered by your hand. It would be well within my rights to conveniently forget you even exist."

A fierce cry pierced the air. Morgause clawed and pummeled the heavy oak lid with the desperation of a wild animal trapped in a hunter's snare. Freedom was her prime directive—once that was procured, she would strike the wound where it bled most freely. Merlin was not without vulnerabilities. Oh yes, she understood the subtle working of his sheltered heart. It was always the heart that proved a man's undoing, that and his loins; she sneered, slowing her frantic action.

Let him think I have surrendered, and then we will see how it falls.

Finally, after Morgause's efforts grew increasingly feeble, her low voice penetrated the confines of that wooden prison. "I have something you want, Merlin. Release me and we will begin negotiations for your precious Arthur."

Off flew the lid. Morgause instantly emerged, gasping for breath. Slowly she pulled herself free of the log but lost balance and soon joined the deceased Uther and his living, albeit enchanted son down upon the thrush-covered flooring. Merlin's face wore a distinctly smug expression, something she could not, *would not* abide.

Thrusting her clawed fingers into Arthur's golden hair, she crooned, "Do not look so pleased, Merlin. The prince is mine."

Thankfully Merlin had anticipated this. Indeed, it was the very reason he had cast her back against the monk's table. He wanted Morgause to touch Arthur again—to think that she had won. Only then could he force her to set him free. There he stood watching Morgause manipulate Arthur's essence within her nimble fingers, playing with it carelessly as if it were some child's toy. By the gods she was revolting! Instantly, the coffin flew at him, followed closely by the table and cross chairs. Utilizing the same energy flow he had managed when affecting the witch's windpipe, Merlin easily brushed each missile aside so that they landed several feet away, splintering into fragments.

"Poor Merlin," Morgause crooned, kissing Arthur's forehead and temples, "so ashamed to admit that the Sight has already failed you once this night, so ashamed that Morgen's charms kept you from your charge—that and the fear of a perpetually empty bed."

A bright flush colored Merlin's throat. He had anticipated this too. Oh, yes, that is why he took such pains to keep Morgen away. This was a woman's magic, always and forever centered on seduction—something he could not stomach, not when it often rendered a man weak as a newborn babe. "Let us shift matters back to where they belong. You will free Arthur."

"Careful, Merlin," she hissed, placing Arthur's essence between her teeth, swirling it back and forth as if it were some rare delicacy that she would consume only after thoroughly relishing its taste.

"I know everything about you—every strength and your hidden weakness. Can you honestly say the same about me?"

The torch flame leapt high, gaining momentum as it streaked toward Merlin, who mentally rerouted its course so that it landed at his feet. Morgause burst into wild laughter as she watched Merlin stamp out the blaze but was unprepared when he flew forward, caught hold of her jawbone, and forced Arthur's essence free. Securing both hands behind her back with mere thought, he watched the pearly energy mass drift slowly down into its rightful place, namely Arthur's golden head.

The effect was immediate: Arthur gasped, as if waking from a nightmare. His startling blue eyes flashed open, taking in the cavernous surroundings, but his voice and limbs remained frozen, unable to break Morgause's spell.

"Cut the cords that bind him," Merlin whispered, "and do not tarry."

An unexpected movement forced Merlin's attention to the nethermost corner of the hall. There lay a pale, slender figure robed in a white shift, hands and feet bound by red velvet cording—a figure that surprisingly resembled Morgen!

No! I told you; I warned you to remain in Avalon!

The stricken beauty turned her sea-green eyes upon him and sobbed fresh tears.

"Merlin, forgive me. I should have listened."

"So young, so innocent," Morgause whispered, producing a sharpened sickle blade from the folds of her crimson gown, "so unblemished by the touch of man. Is she not the perfect virgin sacrifice? Oh, yes, I forgot. My little sister is no longer a virgin—thanks to you. Perhaps her sacrifice will be even more effective now that you have known her."

The effect was immediate. Merlin reasserted his hold, but it was no good. Morgause had already gained her freedom. It was impossible to fathom how she had cleared his range of vision without so much as stirring a single hair on his head, but somehow she stood over Morgen, holding the blade against the delicate skin of her throat. The sight, the very image left Merlin incredulous. Morgause did not possess that kind of magic. It was undoubtedly a ruse to confuse him, leave him divided from the truth. Merlin willfully gathered his thoughts and replied. "That *thing* is a mere apparition. Morgen remains safe in Avalon. I know this to be true."

"Are you so certain? The Morgen *I know* would do anything to aid the man she loves."

"Merlin, no! That isn't me!" Morgen cried from her forgotten post. The well's ruddy waters swirled higher and higher, slapping against their stone casing. "Merlin, hear me! See me! Merlin, I am still in Avalon—at the well!"

Energy was building, boiling inside Merlin's veins. He had neither to move nor act but direct it with his mind. Instantly the blade was cast from Morgause's hand by an irresistible force that left her digits swollen and shaking. She grasped for the weapon but could not manipulate her throbbing fingers to the task. Every inch of her body felt bruised, beaten. Perhaps that is why her feet offered no resistance as they forcibly carried her back to Arthur.

"Release him," Merlin nearly choked, so great was his fury. The witch had something planned, something he did not yet see. It was vital he free Arthur before this monstrosity came to pass. No other option was acceptable. His fingers tingled as they snapped once, forcing her down low upon both knees so that her head brushed the floor. The action was unnecessarily harsh but exacting.

"You cannot save them both," she grimaced, raising her face high enough so she could meet his gaze. "Whom will you choose?"

"Release Arthur now. I will not ask again."

Morgause had no choice but to follow Merlin's bidding, certainly not when his eyes burned a crimson hue. So intense, so hypnotic was this transformation that Morgause found she could not look away. It was with an almost mechanical precision that she forcibly moved her swollen hands over Arthur's heart, forehead, and groin, severing the ties that bound them. Arthur gave another sharp intake of breath then closed his eyes once more, the spell no longer commanding his action. It was sleep he needed, pure, undisturbed, dreamless sleep that healed the soul.

Morgause sat cross-legged, seething. The prince was hers no more.

Go on, Merlin, think of me as defeated, and we will see who wins the prize.

It was almost pleasant to watch Merlin cradle Arthur like some huge, sleepy child, thoroughly dependent upon his father, or whatever post the mage held. That gesture expressed a sweetness and a gentleness that she could prey upon. How strange that the arch mage who had never allowed anyone to touch his heart was rendered vulnerable by his attachment to both Arthur and Morgen— how strange and indescribably wonderful! Slowly, diligently, Merlin blew a cleansing draft along the lad's shell, thoroughly erasing any last remnants of magic that clung to him, completely unaware of Morgause's true intent.

In a trice she slipped away unseen, skirting the long hall until she easily secured the forgotten blade within the folds of her gown. Footfall after footfall brought her closer to Morgen's writhing form, and still the weary enchanter did not move. Bending over her half sister, Morgause kissed her pale cheek then swung the blade high.

"No, Sister! Please, I have done nothing to you."

Merlin looked up. His charge was at long last stirring, muttering questions that could not be answered with simple replies.

Blood flew wide, painting the air a grotesque hue, the result of the red witch's knife slicing open

Morgen's heart cavity. Surely this was a dream! Screams flooded the chamber with such abject horror that Merlin was no longer certain if they originated within Morgen or himself. Somehow the mage gained his feet, reeling, even as he released the still woozy Arthur back against the floor.

"Why do you stand there gaping?" Morgause crooned. "Heal her. Only you can make her whole."

Was it possible that Morgen had ignored his warning? Was it possible she had left the safety of Avalon? He had no time to ascertain the truth, for if this were the real Morgen, delay would prove fatal. Merlin staggered forward, past Uther's decaying corpse, past the gloating Morgause herself, until he reached Morgen's side. Blood blossomed upon her chest and hands even as it coated the floor. Kneeling beside her, he swiftly placed both hands against the gaping wound. His eyes closed, rendering him oblivious to all other sensations than those found within her person. This act demanded total concentration—so grievous was the injury. He knew that Morgause danced nearby, laughing wickedly at his progress but ignored her all the same. Healing was not his forte. That gift belonged to Morgen. Why then, did she remain so still? The truth struck him at that moment, but it was too late; for even as he sensed Morgause's blade swinging high, he felt the power surge within his hands. He could not waver—not if Morgen was to survive. Time slowed as the blade began its downward arch. A moment more would see her restored.

Wild in her despair, the real Morgen cried one last warning. "Merlin, this is a trap! Save yourself!

Oh Goddess Cerridwen, aid him, help him block her blow!"

Deftly the sickle struck its intended mark, and a chunk of Merlin's ebony hair flew into Morgause's hand. Merlin's eyes flashed open. Gazing down upon his beloved fay, he watched her form quiver then meld with the swirling air. He had wasted his time, his energies on a false vision. Suddenly it was imperative that he save his own soul.

"Are you trembling yet, Merlin?" Morgause gloated, twisting his coarse, dark hair between her fingers. Round and round she spun, conscious that the enchanter could do nothing to stop her. Each move, each twirl of her malevolent dance brought Morgause closer to the door, closer to escape.

Merlin drew himself up to full height and faced her with a steely expression. "I have nothing to fear. Yours is a feeble power bred of potions, hexes, and deception."

"I could accuse you of wielding no less than the same," Morgause simpered as she held the cluster of Merlin's hair aloft so that it tickled the ebbing torch flame. "Was it not by your deception that Uther gained access to my mother's chambers the night Arthur was conceived? Was it not by your hand that my father died? You are no better than I, Merlin, for all your supposedly good intentions."

A chill lanced Merlin's spine as he trod forward mechanically, devoid of his normal grace. She was right on that point, but not altogether correct in essentials. "I do not call on black magic to serve my desires."

Perhaps not, but it will be those very desires that bring about your undoing. Now that I have a part of you, there will be no escape!"

Merlin lunged forward, hands raised even as the ebony lock flew high, eluding his grasp. The torch flame sputtered then consumed the token whole, glowing brighter for the sustenance it provided.

"Great Sulis, my goddess, my guide, hear your daughter's cry! May you, Merlin, never know true love in a woman's arms. May you always question whether she really loves you or means to destroy you instead. For on that day when you feel most blessed, she will have no choice but to betray you—cast you into bitter darkness. Great Sulis, hear me now!"

The mage stared unblinking, only half aware of Morgause's abrupt departure. Numbness crept through his veins, consumed his being. It was useless to offer pursuit. One day Morgause's vile deeds would prove her undoing. The same was true of her unborn son. Until then Merlin need only fulfill destiny's bidding. His place was with Arthur, always Arthur. Yes, Arthur was his priority now and forever.

"And so it comes," he whispered almost dispassionately. A woman *had been* his undoing. The still small voice within had always known it would be thus.

Arthur rushed to his side. "Merlin, what is it? What has she done to you?"

Gazing off into a vast sea of nothingness, the wearied counselor replied, "A man cannot avoid his destiny."

A soul-wrenching cry escaped Morgen's lips. "Merlin, no! You must not allow her this victory! You are the greatest enchanter this world has ever known. Do not accept this madness."

Silence proved the only answer Morgen would receive. Hope evaporated, dwindling with the low hum that colored the breeze. Slowly Morgen turned her tear-stained face toward the misty Tor. The stones were calling her into their sheltering embrace. Back up the increasingly familiar path she trod, keenly aware that any romantic ideals she held for the future were forever crushed. Merlin was all but dead to her. And Arthur, *Arthur,* would never dare think of her again except when it came to deception. She was dead, dead to them both.

"That is not true. Their love will not be dissolved by this curse," soothed a familiar voice that reminded Morgen of finely ground sand, a voice that carried her back to Amesbury Abbey.

Morgen paused upon reaching the crest. There before her stood a beautiful old woman with long, ivory-colored hair that fell in graceful waves about her shoulders. Her periwinkle blue eyes fairly twinkled with warmth and perception.

"Sister Portentia?" Morgen gasped in recognition.

"Come, greet me by my true name. I am Tyronoe. It is time I reintroduce you to the Sisterhood."

Soft hands encompassed Morgen's shoulders, drew her into the stone circle. A rosy flush burned her cheeks as she watched the sentinels quiver then yield up their fair treasure; for out of the depths of every last one of them appeared a sprite.

"It is time you learned the truth, Morgen," they chimed in earthly unison. "We are your sisters—the wise women of Avalon."

CHAPTER 10:

The Sisterhood

"Sisters?" Morgen whispered, her mind reeling amid this startling revelation of sound, vision, and light. "What truth? Surely there are many truths that remain hidden to my mortal eyes."

Smoky clouds swirled overhead, obscuring all but the purest beams of cool, white light that penetrated their pervasive shrouding. It was the perfect mixture of fair and dark, innocent splendor piercing the deep excess of passionate display. The sight was not lost on Morgen. This elemental showcase mirrored her own soul in its currently divided state—a state which she shared with Arthur, who stood ready to claim his crown. Arthur would soon be hailed High King of Britannia, and she...

Tyronoe smiled, reading her thoughts. "You are queen, the leader of our Sisterhood, if such a title may still exist. Each and every last one of us desired this mission, but you were ultimately chosen."

"Me? Why me?"

"Why?" the flower spirits, Cliton and Gliton, giggled as they darted about on iridescent wings that mirrored the finest petal hues, pausing only to catch stray rain drops on their delicate tongues. Neither childlike nor maiden, they skirted between the two extremes, small, lithe, and flexible with a soft fringe of buttercup yellow hair that framed their oval faces, faces that exuded joy. "She wants to know why!" Thrilled to be free of rock, earth, and all restrictive casing, their happy banter proved contagious...contagious for everyone save Morgen, whose face wore an agitated grimace.

Is it really their intent to taunt me? Am I that pathetic? Haven't I already suffered enough, losing Arthur and Merlin this day? Why must I bear their insipid banter? Insipid...perhaps I am being unjust. Their word play is carefree, but not without merit. I, too, wish to be free— free to understand what I am and what I have lost.

Casting her eyes upon the fairy contingency, Morgen marveled at their composition, so varied, so extreme in its appearance that she could not believe the term "sisters" applied to any but a hand- ful of them. Every nuance, every aspect of ethe- real femininity found expression there. Childlike bloom so alluring in its youthful attraction was not to be overshadowed by maiden appeal, sensuous in its purity, or matronly devotion, steadfast and true, and the age-wise crone that saw far more than eyes ever confessed. Wings that reflected the fair- est rainbow colors graced nearly every back, but even those lacking in this gift appeared capable of flight. Yes, the sisters were striking and beauti- ful beyond expression, but that was not what drew the eye. They were committed to a goal that defied boundaries, a goal that fostered the freedom to choose anew.

Tyronoe slipped her slim arm around Morgen's waist, an act that lent strength and conviction. She was rock hard, solid as the earth from which she sprang, fully prepared for Morgen's irritation and in no way diminished by it.

"You, Morgen," she gently supplied, "possess certain gifts that will be called forth to benefit our cause. It is your task to win both heart and soul of the king. This is how you will ultimately manifest our goals."

A starling danced among the northern gales, her throaty song overshadowing the storm before wind and rain carried it past discernment. Morgen watched unblinkingly the lovely bird's progress. Truth slowly penetrated her sensibilities, tearing the veil that perpetually blinded sight and clouded mind. Arthur was her other self, her lord, her life, the very reason for her being. They were two entities bound as one through a common love for Britannia and her people, a love fed by mutual affection for the Otherself. Why then, did she not rejoice at such knowledge? Why did the very mention of Arthur make her shy from love? They were not meant for each other—not in this life. Did not everyone look on them as brother and sister? This was madness! Another man claimed her thoughts, her passions. Merlin was more a beloved to her than Arthur could ever be. A dull note sounded within Morgen's chest, left it hollow without hope of restoration. Merlin had effectively divorced her, stripped his life clean of her influence. His mind spoke this action clearly and without any doubt on this point; yet that was not why Tyronoe watched so intently. She, the ancient, ever-patient wise woman, was awaiting Morgen's reply.

"Arthur? You speak of Arthur?"

The act of voicing these words further quickened Morgen's raw humor. Had they not just witnessed the terrible violation unfold? Did they not comprehend that Arthur was dead to her? All the love, all the passion they might have experienced was gone—gone forever—not to mention the point that presented an insurmountable barrier. Morgen wrested her hand free from Tyronoe's gentle grasp. "One vital fact that you seemed to have forgotten: he is my brother!" she said with a sharp finality.

"In name only, Morgen," Tyronoe soothed. Her gentle expression was that of a forbearing grandmother. "Your connection with Arthur has never encompassed that particular association."

"Never has, never will," the Sisterhood chimed, giggling amid Morgen's frustration.

Never will… Destiny wrapped its luxurious fingers around Morgen, drawing her back through several lifetimes. There she stood, fingers entwined within those of a tall, golden-haired man whose startling blue eyes mirrored the summer sky, a man who instinctively spoke the language of her heart and mind, understood her thoughts and desires sometimes better than her own self, reverberated to her inner song as no other being ever could; but one inconsistency, one failing continuously tore them apart. Remembering this sorrow, the man's expression waxed melancholy, a mood echoed by the deepening clouds. The stone circle rose high around them, offering shelter from the impending storm. Wind buffeted Morgen's tender skin, made it feverish, desperate; but that was not what left her so unsettled.

"I must go. Britannia—our child—needs me," he whispered, aware that this declaration would do little to aid his cause.

"Do not speak to me of the country or the land. I have seen this all before. Each time it draws you from me, keeps you fettered until we wither away. We are meant to share this lifetime together—not apart."

The golden-haired man pressed his lips against hers with such abandon that she was rendered temporarily mute. They were free, elemental, never burdened by a higher authority than their own consciousness, which displayed impeccable purity. "We can never be apart, dearest. Remember our eternal bond. We are one in heart, mind, body, and spirit. Nothing can ever change that—not even the impending battle. War is and was and always will be."

"Unless we find another way, my love. Unless we find another way."

Another way. A vast tunnel yawned wide, coaxing Morgen toward its hypnotic depths. The golden man clasped hold of her wrist, but it was no good. Suddenly, she was gone, catapulted through the tunnel's dark recesses until she stood once more among her fairy clan. All eyes fixed upon her, watching, waiting. If the vision proved true,

Arthur was anything but her brother. Yes, this was a fundamental knowledge she had always known yet never fully understood. She was not daughter of the High King and Queen, but a foundling never accepted or trusted. Why should they? What madness would possess a Pendragon to accept an elemental child born of wind, earth, fire, and rain?

A vigorous stirring at Morgen's feet called her attention earthward. Delicate, white flowers flooded the emerald Tor so rapidly that Cliton and Gliton were propelled several inches off the ground without use of their wings. Indeed, the glorious cascade found its origins within their own gentle beings, a truth that lent grace and movement to its upward progression. High they stood atop this magnificent bower, dispelling warmth and light. Everything about their aspect, their being, appeared lit from within. Such joy, such bliss was displayed upon their flowery faces that a smile soon colored Morgen's lips. She wanted to love them and understand them, but she felt unequal to the task.

"Dearest sister," Cliton beamed, "Arthur is the most wondrous of mortals."

The Sisterhood fell into musical laughter that threatened to paint the heavens a brighter hue. .

*I cannot love him. I cannot...*Morgen inwardly chanted, although she was not quite certain why. What was it about Arthur that evoked within her such a vehement response? She did not even know him—well, certainly not in this life.

"What woman in her right mind would not wish to live and breathe in his arms?" Gliton continued, catching hold of Morgen's fair arm so she must meet her gaze. This information was far too important to be dismissed so lightly. "You alone have been given that gift. Arthur loves you more than life itself, though he may not realize it. What is it you fear: that he will reject you or that his passion will consume you whole?"

Morgen grasped hold of Gliton's shoulders and shook her soundly. "You wish me to bind with Arthur, to become his love—his wife?"

"Here in Avalon, you are already husband and wife."

Everyone fell silent, staring, waiting for this truth to fully penetrate Morgen's consciousness. Gliton gained her release but did not travel far, concerned that she may have revealed too much too soon. Thankfully the sky periodically wept salt tears, aiding her cause. Water was the medium that best reflected emotion, transformed it if the individual allowed such healing, or in the worst case, further magnified their folly.

And so the rain did its work, falling upon Morgen's upswept face, soft and deep, altering anger and distaste into a more palatable dish. So much vital information lay waiting for her to accept. Could Arthur truly be her husband? The intensity of their first meeting indicated as much. The vision had shown them united at this very place, speaking vows that transcended time. If they were man and wife, why had *she* made such a spectacular mess of things? Why had she taken mortal form as Arthur's sister? Their marriage could never be acknowledged because of this choice.

What bizarre, forgotten motivation forced this seemingly irrational decision?

Morgen gasped back the sob that threatened new understanding. The air felt thick and full, ready to dispel a great quantity of rain. Distant thunder rumbled a warning note, a low prelude that welcomed the unearthly darkness that slowly, deliciously encompassed the Tor. This was an elemental storm conceived by the Sisterhood itself, one that would affect Arthur's current failure or success. She was feeling woozy; a state no doubt inspired by the play of lightning that fired her tearful gaze.

"You wish me to reclaim Arthur's heart?"

A chestnut-haired beauty walked forward, every pore of her translucent skin oozing command. She was tall, proud, regal, one that knew power and welcomed its presence. Fire colored her knowing smile, added brilliance to her smoky eyes. A painted quality about the fay made Morgen look twice. No one else among the gathering possessed highlighted lips or rouged cheeks. This fairy wished to stand apart, to be acknowledged as an individual, not a member of the fairy clan, a trait that could prove dangerous if she moved against the pact. Some distant memory stirred Morgen's consciousness, heightened her thoughts. A rival stood before her—someone who wanted and had once challenged Morgen for what she already possessed. Was it Arthur that stood between them or the gift of mortality that this brash elemental desired? The fay boasted no wings and needed none, so sensuous, so strong was her psyche, a trait echoed by her low, rich voice.

"It is already done, Sister. That is how Morgause was able to seduce him. She understands the hold you claim over Arthur—better than you do, my dear."

Morgen did not appreciate this suggestion yet bit back her harsh reply. This fairy was quick with her sharpened barbs. She wished to wound and did so without hesitation. It was vital that Morgen not respond in kind, especially if she *was* Fairy Queen. Instead, she focused on something concrete, something that had yet to be acknowledged. "What of Merlin? What of the love we share?"

A smile graced the fay's ruby lips. "We have no objection to Merlin, Sister. He too will play an important part in manifesting our goals."

Morgen bristled, despite her best intentions to remain calm. Something behind the fairy's words made her wary. What further part was Merlin destined to play in this grand tragedy? Morgen inwardly reproached herself for labeling the pact "tragic." She had no idea what future awaited them. In any case this fairy with the smoldering eyes instantly rubbed her the wrong way. She was too proud, too arrogant. Every nerve, every particle of Morgen's being wished to wipe that self-satisfied smirk off her face. What right had she to command Morgen's future? Who was she? And why did everything about her make Morgen cringe?

"This is Glitonea, matriarch of flame," Tyronoe carefully supplied, her periwinkle eyes offered silent warning. *Do not press too far, not yet. Your answers can await another day.*

Morgen inwardly scoffed. Matriarch… If Glitonea stood so high in the Sisterhood as to command the title of great mother, why was she not the Fairy Queen? Surely this fay born of fire and passion would revel in Arthur's love. Why then was she not entrusted with this task?

Melodic laughter issued from each and every member of the Sisterhood, including Glitonea. So lovely, so magical were these bell-like tones that they gathered strength and vitality, rebounding off megalith, creeping bowers, and even the hollowed tree. Surely the whole of Britannia could hear it! "This love, your love has been arranged, Morgen, arranged from the beginnings of time," they fairly sang.

Certain that any more such levity would make her scream, Morgen paced round and round the stone circle, further analyzing the Sisterhood. What were their gifts, their passions? Did they too possess an agenda, a plan for the greater good, a plan that demanded every particle of their commitment? Were they free or fettered by past choices? Each and every one of them stared back at her, some with marked discernment. Most were elementals, like the fiery Glitonea, or the earth-wise Tyronoe. A few, however, such as Gliton and Cliton, appeared more attuned to flowers, plants, and trees. What was the common link that bound them—beyond that of being fairy bred? Why were their lives, their existence, linked with Arthur, herself, and Britannia? Further questioning appeared a necessary discomfort she must endure.

"Surely securing Arthur's heart is not my only reason for existence."

Twin spirits, linked by their common medium of the air, drew her focus, each utilizing pearly wings to convey them several feet above the rain-sodden ground. Fair Thitis was the most maidenlike of the fay, with silvery blonde locks and a willowy frame, fluid, athletic, and true. Her voice, breathy at first, strengthened with speech, softening Morgen's heart, priming it for what would follow. "No, but it is a very integral part of your mortality, the part that links all others together. Without Arthur you would never have agreed to become mortal."

"You are a peace weaver, Morgen," Thetis interjected, tossing her rose golden mane so that it did not camouflage both eyes. She was less grounded than her sister, wilder and carefree, her voice rich and warm as the summer breeze. "Peace," she explained, "now and forever is your, *our* goal. Arthur has become an agent of war: the Red Dragon, he who will unite Britannia's children with the sword. It is you who must help him remember that peace is the ultimate achievement. The unity he seeks may only be maintained through peace, eternal peace."

A distant memory stirred Morgen's consciousness. *Peace now and forever. Peace blanket Britannia. Peace be upon all beings and peoples of the earth.*

Understanding blossomed, gaining in strength and conviction until it split open her grieving soul. Yes, this was her truth, the essence of her being. It had been apparent the first moment she rediscovered Avalon. The insurrection, Uther's death and Morgause's betrayal had temporarily distracted her; but that upheaval transformed her, made her ultimately more receptive to its meaning. Over and over the chant echoed through the innermost cords of her mind, guiding her steps, offering new hope and inspiration.

Yes, how could I have forgotten? This is the reason that I was born. This is the reason I sought mortality.

At last Morgen understood why life's injustices appeared so pronounced beyond Avalon's hidden veil. For fifteen mortal years she had struggled against the current, thoroughly forgetting her life's purpose. All that was about to change. How light she felt, free of the darkness that clouded her past, free to assist Arthur, Merlin, and Britannia and thereby to enrich the world. Peace was the worthiest of all goals.

"Peace and healing," beamed a small, dark figure that appeared no larger than an eight-year-old child. She boasted neither wings nor the inherent beauty the other sisters possessed, yet her spirit held a dazzling quality that beckoned one to take a closer look. "You are a healer, Morgen. Never forget that."

"Thank you, Sister," Morgen cried, throwing her arms around the tiny fairy, conscious how rare it was to find someone smaller than herself. The fay's movements, her very essence waxed lyrical, echoing bird, bee, and bear cub. She could run faster, leap farther than any other sister present, yet to acknowledge such natural accomplishments was beyond her ken.

"My name is Moronoe," the fay supplied, calling the low-flying starling so that it roosted on her sun-bronzed arm. Softly she stroked the mottled feathers that graced the bird's head and was rewarded by a warm cooing sound. "I embrace the animal realm—watch over them in times of trouble, offer guidance when it is prudent. Just as you are guardian of the forest, so I am guardian of her children."

This knowledge set Morgen's cheeks aglow, for she loved both flora and fauna as if they were her own being. Suddenly she understood why. Her eyes fell upon the toppled tree that once stood so proudly amid its sister stones. This tree—now devoid of life—was her all but forgotten charge. Aware that everyone awaited her next move with bated breath, Morgen approached the downed beauty and laid her head against its withered trunk. "For fifteen years you have dwindled without your spirit—a mere shadow of your former self. Forgive me, dear one. You have allowed me life, even as yours was taken away."

The floodgates opened, evoking tears in a blessed ritual whose origins spanned well beyond memory or time. Each droplet, each tear that caressed the mossy trunk forced an inner trembling that stirred the phloem, cambium, and heartwood back to life. From everywhere and nowhere at once came a whisper that rode the breeze, as if the tree itself were speaking. ***You are a healer, Morgen. Fulfill our destiny.***

Focusing all thought, all determination to infinitesimal precision, Morgen placed her hands against the vast hollow and willed the healing energy to begin its work. With no hesitation or pause, the white light instantly spilled through her palms into the open wound, carefully knitting the lifeless wood together. A low rumbling deep within the heartwood served as her reply. Branches swayed, roots snapped, and a plethora of leaves burst forth, not to be outdone by the long-congealed sap that flowed anew within the tree's throbbing veins. Using an almost superhuman strength, Morgen pulled the rotted trunk into a standing position and then willed its roots to draw nutrients and water.

Mazoe, a twilight-eyed fairy whose almost boyish form stubbornly refused discernment, remained half hidden behind her foster stone. She had an endearingly elfin appearance with short, dark locks and long limbs, barely concealed by a blue ankle-length tunic and a quaint upturned nose. A mere nod of her bobbed head supplied an increase of rain. Although she ducked once more behind her megalith, the gesture could not be mistaken. Here was a naiad, thoroughly attuned to her element divine. The shyness, the seeming defiance was puzzling, but Morgen did not trouble herself further on Mazoe's account. One day her story would unfold.

The tree shuddered, noticeably this time. Buds burst open along its tangled branches, a steady progression that signaled life renewed. Bright, newly fleshed green blanketed upper and lower canopies accompanied by swaying boughs and roots that stretched their pleasure. A collective sigh escaped the Sisterhood's lips. This is what it meant to be alive—a treasure unparalleled! Each and every one of them felt it, including the long-absent Fairy Queen. Indeed, this unmitigated joy, this quintessential bliss communicated itself to Morgen, and she at last understood the wealth of its importance. She was a dryad, the fairy who blessed this tree with her presence; the tree lived inside her, helped her to thrive and prosper in days past. This single yew that formed the pinnacle of the stone circle's magical powers was a threshold, a gateway into Britannia's heart, a threshold into all times past and present, known and unknown.

I will never forget you again. No matter how far I travel, I will always return here and offer you sustenance and hope. This is my pledge to you, dear one.

Without faltering, Morgen fixed her eyes upon the Sisterhood and continued, "This is a pledge I make to each and every one of you. From this moment forward, life begins anew for all of us."

The Sisterhood responded in kind, bowing their heads in a show of reverence. Even proud Glitonea and shy Mazoe did homage to their Fairy Queen as heavenly fire flashed overhead, increasing the feverish play of light against dark. All participants stood ready, each poised to evoke her magic. Placing her hand palm down against the yew tree, Morgen grew preternaturally still. "It is time for Arthur to claim his power," she cried, eyes mirroring the fire that played overhead. "Let us go to him. Let us be there to witness his triumph, aid him if necessary, for he is our agent of peace."

And so Morgen lead the Sisterhood through the sacred yew tree's twisting innards, down the root-bound staircase until they came upon a clearing, and the sound of untold footsteps and human vocalizations drew focus. They were in a shallow forest thronging with people, eyes bent forward, seeking salvation from a prince who had yet to be tried. Morgen gave the signal and the Sisterhood drew up their hoods so they would remain unrecognized. There Arthur kneeled beside the sword so carefully lodged within an aged altar stone. Countless boot prints around the sacred relic offered some indication of the sheer numbers that had likewise tempted fate. Each, without exception, had failed. The only difference was that Arthur knew himself destined to succeed. Merlin had primed him for this, day after day, year after year, and now he stood ready to meet fate head on. A subtle stirring behind the prince made him turn, revealing the form, the essence of his dead father: translucent, majestic, thoroughly commanding. Little did he dream that this was Merlin's gift to him, a rendering of his father's essence, the thing he desired most now that he stood poised to claim victory.

"Thank you," Arthur whispered, deeply moved by his father's appearance. "This moment would not be complete without you."

The shade bowed its head and replied, "Heed well Merlin's teachings, my son. Do not allow Lot and Urien to distract you from your purpose. Now, as your knees kiss the earth, feel its power. Claim it as your own!"

Arthur did not need further prompting. "Guardians of the earth, wind, water, and fire, heed my cry! I am Arthur Pendragon, Britannia's heir come to claim what is rightfully mine. Assist me, guide me, if you will. I am your vessel. Use me to heal Britannia, to right all wrongs that bleed her dry. Let me be her soul forever more!"

An audible gasp raced through the Sisterhood as one by one they rose, independent of wings, high above the rain-sodden ground. Here was their signal—the chosen sign agreed upon long before Arthur drew breath but uttered with a selfless devotion of which they had never dreamed. Here, truly, was a king for all time! The request was already granted, and in such a manner that Britannia would never forget.

All the lessons, all the understanding that were part and particle of Merlin's teachings came to play in that moment. Silent and still, Arthur mentally drew divine energy through the earth, to the balls of his feet, until it fairly coursed up legs, torso, and head, firing his veins. It was then he reached for the sky. "As above, so below."

The wind rose to a fever pitch, whipping Arthur's fair locks into a perfect halo around his head. As he touched the gleaming hilt, Uther's image fractured into a thousand points of light. Each wove a merry path up and down the blade, much like fairies at play on Midsummer Eve. Cries broke forth at the unearthly sight. People were teeming everywhere. It was a miracle they had come to witness, a miracle that transpired before their eyes. Few noticed that Arthur's orbs blazed at that moment. He was hailing the elements of water and fire. Thunder echoed above. Taking this as his cue, Arthur freed the sword from its sacred tomb. Silence fell as a silvery lightning bolt lanced the sky. Arthur pointed the sword high overhead and allowed sacred fire to christen the blade. Somehow, miraculously, he remained untouched throughout the entire exchange.

"Thank you, Ancient Ones," he whispered above the rising wind. "Now I am truly one with all things."

Morgen and her sisters clasped hands, forming a circle unnoticed by the masses. Rain fell upon their upstretched faces, bathed them with purpose. A new king was born, a champion for peace. Cries burst forth from each and every one of them, cries born of passion intensified by years and years of bloodshed when fairies and all beauty, all innocence that they represented, had been virtually forgotten. Here and now was the time to cast aside the restrictive chrysalis that had kept them imprisoned for so long and re-emerge as glorious agents of peace. Yes, war was still part and parcel of Britannia's existence. The blackened clouds indicated as much. One day, however, Arthur's great light would pierce these funereal shrouds. It was a new Britannia he promised, a Britannia born of love, peace, hope, and the Sisterhood would use their individual gifts to aid the cause.

"Come, Sisters!" Morgen cried. "Great work awaits us. Work of the most sacred kind."

CHAPTER 11:

The Missive

"Why did you not tell me the truth?" Morgen sighed as she sat mulling over a spare bit of parchment clutched tightly within her hands. It was a brisk, midwinter day, and although Avalon's lakeshore and grounds were clear of any snow, a decided chill flavored the air. Staring out across the moody lake, Morgen remembered the first time she had witnessed the sacred isle in full bloom. Gone was the vibrant spring color, replaced by a cooler, steely-blue mist, foam, and cloud. The apple trees had long since given up their fruit and the blanketing roses cast forth their buds. Even the cattails bowed their heavily laden heads, ready for winter's embrace. Morgen glanced up, remembering that Tyronoe stood patiently beside her. "Why did you pretend to be the helpless Sister Portentia? Why did you not come to my aid when…?"

"I did, if you recall, aid you on numerous occasions," came Tyronoe's overly patient answer. She smiled, and then offered Morgen a thick, chalky rock that easily fit into the palm of her hand. "You are avoiding the task, Morgen. What is it you fear? Arthur is already in love with you."

"Well, then it is an image, an idea he loves. He does not know me."

"Arthur does not fly against destiny. He remembers—at least some part of him remembers—the divine vows you made to each other."

Morgen stared mutely at the rock, which had smudged her hand. It was meant to be used as a writing utensil. Why must she do this...*thing*? Why must she force this communication? Arthur was thoroughly consumed with war. What time had he for sisters, lovers, or women in general? Would she not better serve Arthur—serve Britannia—by continuing peace work within Avalon's blessed grounds?

"Write the missive, Morgen. It is the simplest way to initiate contact."

With a slight groan, Tyronoe stretched, favoring her back. The mortal shell she had chosen for habitation with long, ivory hair, well-wrinkled countenance and tall, but increasingly stooped deportment, did not always serve her well, as it possessed numerous maladies associated with old age. Yet Tyronoe seldom complained or allowed her periwinkle blue eyes to register frustration.

Instantly Morgen was on her feet. "Allow me to heal your back, Sister."

A wry smile crinkled the edge of Tyronoe's slim lips. Although ancient she was a beautiful woman that would make any man look twice. That, no doubt, was what it meant to be a fay. "Write now. Heal me later," she smiled with wry amusement.

No further words were spoken. Indeed, none were needed, for Tyronoe set her heels in motion and soon disappeared among the tall well-frosted reeds.

Cool gray waters slapped incessantly against the shoreline, heightening Morgen's feelings of disconnect. She was alone, deserted by the sisters who lost patience with her inability to accept Arthur as her Otherself. Indeed, she could detect no movement, no hint of life beyond the great blue heron that patrolled the icy waters. Morgen plopped down upon a bright almond-shaped rock that overlooked the lake's testy countenance. Rubbing her palm against the stone's glittery surface, she marveled at its smooth texture. No doubt the water level was once high enough to soften its harsh edges. Why then could the lake not repeat its work and soften her unyielding heart? Why all the fear, the self doubt? She was an attractive mortal, capable of inspiring admiration. That in itself felt gratifying beyond measure. It also proved an equally unpleasant curse. Yes, men desired her, longed for her company, but they also wished to keep her fettered. Urien of North Wales proved an excellent example. He would hide her away amid his mountain fortress and keep her distant, inaccessible, if she wed him. Would Arthur's dominant nature follow suit? Would he even care that she was destined to help him evoke peace throughout the land?

Feeling that any more such supposition would drive her mad, Morgen peered into the lake's watery mirror. A thin layer of mist hung low, brushing the cool surface, lending an otherworldly flavor to its aspect. Morgen leaned forward until her delicate nose touched the liquid chill. The result was instantaneous. Bone-numbing cold raced through her veins, forcing her back upon the rocky perch. Certainly this was her just reward. She was foolhardy, blind if the sisters were right. She had shunned Arthur, the man with whom she had shared so many lives.

Why did she shun a soul mate that had once been part and particle of her being? What was it that made her vehemently resolve not to love the High King? She had seen him, if only momentarily: tall, blonde, and gorgeous, and by all accounts well gifted when it came to wooing women. Yes, every eligible maiden of Britannia wished to win the High King's heart. That is why untold numbers shadowed his campaign across Britannia, a new lass filling his bed every night. Why did Morgen not follow suit? She could not help but shiver at the thought. Just beneath the watery surface an answer festered, waiting for expression. The Fairy Queen inherently knew why she had chosen to become Arthur's sister, a deliberate decision that necessarily kept them apart. She had to accomplish some task, some goal independent of the High King, something she could not fulfill if they were married—something destined to keep them at odds. That forgotten task did not reside within fifteen-year-old Morgen's consciousness. It did, however, explain why her protests appeared so pronounced. This time their union was forbidden. This time it possessed the power to destroy them. The

Sisterhood understood everything—of course. But they said nothing, offered no further illumination. Indeed, they acted as if the impediment did not exist. Did that also imply that they were ignorant of the Fairy Queen's true goal, a goal that might very well transmute her love into hate, force her hand so that she was no longer Arthur's soul mate, but an enemy of the most intimate kind?

A determined smile colored Morgen's lips as she stretched the parchment wide against its rocky canvas. She must step forward and meet fate head on if she ever hoped to answer that question. In other words she must convince the new High King that he could not live without her—a simple task if the sisters were right about their connection. Bending low Morgen mulled over how to begin the missive. How might she engage Arthur's interest amid so much war? Aware that Merlin had reaffirmed his belief that she still housed with the nuns at Amesbury, she set chalk to parchment and began.

Amesbury Abbey
Midwinter
Dearest Arthur, Red Dragon, and High King of
Britannia,

> *Greetings, Brother, I hope you are well—or as well as anyone who suddenly finds himself king of a war-torn country can be. Are the insurgents still giving you trouble? Have you found a way to annihilate the usurping dread? Oh, this is madness! I must simply write my heart and be done with it. Dearest, cannot you bring all this fighting and bloodshed to an end? Why not befriend*

the Saxons instead of slaughtering them day and night? We will all sleep better.

Morgen absentmindedly rubbed the chalk between her fingers, questioning whether or not this approach was too harsh. Arthur really did not know her. Would he welcome her council, dissonant as it was from his own reasoning? A moment's further reflection indicated that she should press on. It was vital that Arthur become acquainted with her views. Clutching a reed blanket against her shoulders to better ward off the morning chill, she continued.

> *I wish to see you, but the nuns keep sharp watch over me—punish me for the slightest indiscretions. Yes, this must sound trivial to a man of your station, but I assure you it is more than mere unpleasantness. Arthur, they have tried on numerous occasions to cut my hair. How would you like to have a bald sister? Come now, tell the truth. Help me, dearest. I beg you. Cease the war and set me free. It is as simple as that. Britannia will thank you.*
>
> *Love,*
> *Morgen*

Morgen read the missive over and over again until she knew it by heart; she then placed the neatly rolled parchment inside a tiny basket that boasted leather tethers stitched into its woven composition. No sooner had she done so than a lovely hawk lighted upon her arm. Soft blue-gray plumage accentuated with fine brushstrokes of black covered his crown, wings, back, and tail feathers. He blinked at her expectantly, awaiting instruction. Those fierce golden eyes instantly belied the generous heart which beat within his mottled breast. Morgen knew this—else she would not have asked his assistance. The devoted raptor graciously allowed Morgen to stroke his fair chin and brow as she fastened the tethers to his anxious talons. Delivery proved his joy, his rapture, especially when it was on Morgen's behalf.

"Cerifus," she whispered, pressing her lips against the soft, dark feathers that adorned his crown, "please take this to Arthur Pendragon, High King of Britannia; bend time if you must, but deliver it without delay. Convince him to respond if you can."

Cerifus blinked his wide golden eyes once more, exuding confidence that he would do just that. He rubbed his feathered head against Morgen's cheek and then became one with the misting air.

A sigh broke forth from the depth of Morgen's being. It was done. She had only to await the response, which would certainly come. Time ticked away at its ever-steady pace, but Morgen had no stomach for it. There she sat shivering upon that lonely rock, while the High King and his counselor raced about Britannia, beating back those vultures who threatened her safety. Feeling altogether forgotten, she pondered destiny's demands. They dictated that she remain secluded, unable to assist except in the most inconsequential manner. Inconsequential? Perhaps that was not correct—not in its essentials. She and the Sisterhood did aid Britannia on a daily basis. The fact that people did not suspect or dream of their intervention proved an increasing source of frustration. She wanted to be acknowledged, recognized for the great work that consumed her being. Impatience was slowly consuming Morgen's thoughts and actions, silently demanding its due. Why must she wait? Why was it impossible for her to see Arthur and Merlin right now?

Casting her shivering body against the frost-covered rock, Morgen gazed full into the lake's surface. "Ancient Ones, you who have given me mortal life, reveal Arthur Pendragon, the great king! Show me his current whereabouts and dealings," she cried, little imagining what would follow.

Indeed, everything happened so quickly that Morgen had not time to brace herself. Invisible hands encircled her torso, forcing her facedown into the freezing waters. Flailing and pummeling against fate, she struggled to break free, but soon arrested the attempt as a full-scale battle shattered the underwater world with its volatile brilliance. Suddenly, irrevocably, her own disaster was rendered inconsequential by this torrential siege. Death filled her nostrils, coated her aching lungs. This was not a simple scrimmage; it was an all out blood bath. Everywhere she looked, men were dying. Was this a vision of Arthur's current struggles?

"Yes, I'm here, Morgen!" a hauntingly familiar voice answered, using a frequency that no one else could decipher, a voice that belonged to none other than the High King himself.

Somewhere lost within this cataclysmic frenzy, Arthur fought alongside his men, alongside *Merlin*—though it was impossible to decipher either king or mage among the mass of warring bodies that whirled with a dancer's precision, belying their horrific legacy of death. The tide had shifted against Britannia's new ruler at Guinnon Hill Fort. There he fought not only the Saxons but also a dissonant group of petty kings including Urien and Lot, those individuals who believed he was a bastard, unworthy of the crown, the kings that Uther had so feared when he placed Arthur in hiding all those years ago, the kings that had ultimately arranged the High King's death. Yes, Morgause was the ultimate assailant, but every one of these petty kings, native Britons all, had signed the death warrant and now they sought to kill the son, even if he was their best hope for salvation. And so brother fought brother, an act of sacrilege so severe that it could never be forgiven. Morgen tried to scream, to force them to cease, but a cloud of bubbles erupted anew in thick, angry protest, hailing the appearance of Lir MacMannon and the Lady of the Lake. The two water deities nodded their greetings, their eyes set, unblinking. It was not Morgen they came to accuse but the people of Britannia! Lir halted the frenzied warriors, dissolved their impressions, and with a flourish of his whalebone staff, restored the lake to its tranquil, albeit freezing splendor.

You have now seen Arthur's current predicament. The question remains: will you aid him or continue your peaceful life of noninterference? We, those of us you call "Ancient Ones" will no longer stand aside and witness such evil where brother kills brother. All who inhabit Britannia are our children. Take heed, Morgen. Act now or we will take matters into our own hands.

Terror consumed Morgen's being. Did that mean the Ancient Ones would destroy all who inhabited Britannia? Before Morgen's lips fully formed the question, Lir and his lady disappeared, leaving behind a frothy trail that lingered amid this poignant warning. Morgen had not time to question their desertion, for she found herself lying face down upon Avalon's Tor, the thick earth heaving beneath her. No hint of moisture clung to her person, no indication of watery trauma. She was inexplicably bone dry. How or why little seemed to matter. Morgen's course was clear. Arthur, Merlin, and the people of Britannia desperately needed intervention. Oh, yes, she and the sisters had sent previous assistance, but this time was different; this time they could not fail. The earth underfoot, trembling its fury, indicated that Britannia teetered near destruction. The battle must cease, or the very island itself would be lost.

Deep within the stone circle, every last member of the Sisterhood waited, eyes bent on their queen.

Staggering to her feet, Morgen cried, "Arthur has been attacked by Saxon and Briton alike. Brother destroys brother. The Ancient Ones stand ready to crush one and all. We must change their minds."

Each fay turned to her respective stone, the receptacles of their various gifts, while Morgen drew near her tree and commenced once more the work that had originally conveyed them to the mortal plane. Pure white energy flowed from their outstretched hands into the gray sentinels, which shivered slightly as they prepared the precious treasure for release. Wave after wave of light enveloped the stones, fairly lifting them from the earth's embrace. Up, up the life force climbed, higher and higher as the sisters' chants filled the air.

"Peace now and forever. Peace blanket Britannia. Peace be upon all beings and peoples of the earth."

Every thought, every intention came together in that moment. Indeed, anyone who gazed upon the Tor would certainly gasp at the vivid peace work manifesting in physical splendor. Brilliant hues of blue, green, and purple energy danced above the circle, gaining power and intensity until they burst forth in one immense sending.

"Hear us, Arthur. Hear us, Britons. Hear us, Saxons. Yes, you hear us each time you bring about the death of another. All life is sacred. You know this instinctively in your bones. Stop the fighting. Be a catalyst for change. Bring an end to the bloodshed. Peace. Peace."

Morgen watched the healing energies exit her delicate fingers in a downward spiral that fed the tree's humble roots before it burst newborn into the earth's welcoming embrace. A low rumbling met her efforts. Perhaps the Ancient Ones would forgive man's folly. Thitis and Thetis focused sending the life force into their medium of sky, the very air itself, while others channeled blessings through the stones, through cool, liquid puddles, and even a crackling fire. If Britannia was failing, every inch of her beloved frame needed attention. Affirmations of peace poured across the landscape far and wide. How many Britons would act on these vibrations? How many would follow the one, true path of peace?

Morgen's cheeks grew deathly pale. *Is all of Britannia deaf to our pleas? Is it all for naught?* her inner voice cried.

Never give up, Morgen, Merlin's deep, weathered voice seeped through her mind. *We all wish the same conclusion. Keep sending your gifts of peace. This battle is all but concluded. Casualties are heavy, but Arthur remains king. He must remain king until the end of his days. That is the only way Britannia may survive as we know it. Hold fast to your efforts. He will call for you within a fortnight. Your missive was well bethought. The thought of a bald sister really put the fear of God into him.*

A burst of laughter escaped Morgen's lips. *Only you, Merlin, can find humor amid so much pathos.*

Suddenly mage and fay were easily conversing through the medium of thought as if there had been no estrangement between them.

You came up with the horror tactics, Morgen.

The nuns did that all by themselves. Pray, do not let Arthur wound them too grievously. Oh, and tell the good king that I will await him at the fortress of Caerleon.

You overstep your boundaries, Morgen. Arthur will send a guard for you. It is paramount that you await their arrival.

You seem to forget, Merlin, that I am not in Amesbury.

No, but it is easy enough for you to find your way there.

Do not be absurd, Merlin. I absolutely refuse to return to Amesbury.

I will see to it that the guard awaits you at the gates. That way you need never see the sisters.

Merlin!

You have a fortnight, Morgen. No more. Make ready for departure from Amesbury a fortnight from this very day.

CHAPTER 12

Caerleon

Swish, crunch, swish. Morgen counted the tread of her dainty palfrey as it propelled her ever so slowly forward. She and her four-man escort, consisting of Bedivere, Lucan, Dagonet, and Bors, had been traveling at a snail's pace so long that date and time had long since ceased their meaning. Each rolling hill, each virgin, rock-lined stream all tucked within a green cacophony of turf, moss, and woody shrubbery melded into a familiar whole that defied individual discernment. Yes, the West Country was beautiful and fertile, but Morgen and her heavily muscled companions no longer registered its attributes. The men, member of Arthur's elite knights, were, in any case, far too preoccupied with safeguarding their precious charge. Certainly she did not blame them for that. Travel, especially slow travel hampered by palfrey and the ideology that a princess must be pampered, was proving excessively tedious.

Morgen glanced once more at her entourage, analyzing their various attributes. This course of action had delighted her for the first day; but it soon grew stale, perhaps from overindulgence. Yes, she found Bedivere, a small but darkly handsome knight who also happened to be Arthur's earliest friend, charmingly flirtatious, always ready with a barb, quick, eager to please, and thoroughly smitten with her. The same did not hold true for Lucan, whose manner appeared far too haughtily internalized for her taste. Introspective, slim, boasting hair of golden brown and moss-green eyes that read her a little too deeply, it was clear that Lucan did not like her, which in truth did not matter all that much. Dagonet and Bors easily made up for Lucan's indifference with their boisterous gestures and overzealous expression. The black-haired Bors, whose heavily bearded face wore a perpetual grin, overshadowed his less massive comrade both in bulk, which was vast indeed, and volume. He could not laugh loud enough or sing with greater fervor, all in the effort to please Morgen. More than once the blondish, winningly conniving Dagonet, whose robust figure made Merlin appear of no more consequence than a slender reed, fell back on his favorite pastime, tormenting Bors, by arranging strategically placed thorns on his saddle or filling his boots with pesky ants. The end result left Morgen breathless with laughter. Men certainly were a bizarre species unto themselves. Yet, now as they drew ever near Arthur's military fortress, the mood shifted to quiet subservience. Morgen followed suit, altogether conscious that anxiety swelled within her breast. Why did she feel that every step of the dapple-gray palfrey's hooves conveyed her closer to destruction? Why did doom color the thick, heady midsummer air?

It was well past midday when Morgen and her escort finally reined their horses into the sprawling military fortress that Arthur called home. She could not see the inner sanctum at first. She saw a long, winding barrier that consisted of elevated guard towers situated at each of the four corners and a dilapidated wall that boasted powdery beige stones, piled with seeming haste, so that they stuck out at odd angles here and there. Irritated by this ill-favored blockade, Morgen wondered when, if ever, they would gain entrance. Lodged deep within the rolling hills that boasted the glistening river Usk on one side and a lush green fairytale forest on the other, Caerleon camouflaged itself from discerning eyes. As a result the legionary structure saw little warfare. No doubt that was why its previous Roman owners had packed up, leaving behind much, if not all of their belongings: beds, tables, benches, and even an old Roman bath, which delighted Arthur's forces to no end. Thus Arthur claimed this forgotten fortress as his home, a home no one else apparently wanted.

Home, indeed! A burst of wry laughter escaped Morgen's lips. This caused her guards to shift uneasily upon their mounts. Oh, yes, they knew what she was thinking. It appeared that sheer luck alone held the powdery beige stones captive within their decaying mortar. One swing of a proud battle-axe, if not an overly zealous wind storm, would bring it down. How would such an inferior barricade protect Arthur and his men from determined

Saxons? Bedivere, who winked at her forbearance, readily concurred.

"Perhaps Caerleon needs a lady's touch," he chuckled, eyes twinkling with amusement. "No doubt Arthur will enlist your aid."

Morgen smiled despite herself. Bedivere, for all his cleverness, possessed a thoughtful, arresting demeanor that readily bespoke intelligence. She noted again his slight build and dark coloring native to those northern dwellers known as Picts. Although Bedivere vehemently denied any familial connection to such a marauding race, his companions secretly delighted in the belief that a stray Pict may have at one time shared a bed with some unsuspecting ancestor.

"I think a miracle is in order here," Morgen mused, mulling over this supposition.

"Believe me, it is high on Merlin's priorities. Unfortunately he is often consumed with advising Arthur."

"You refer to the battle of Guinnon Hill Fort."

An unexpected groan served as Bedivere's reply. Suddenly the merriment was gone. "And the treaty with Lot and Urien." Leaning quite near so that they all but touched, he added, "That really has them at odds."

Morgen fell silent. A treaty with Lot and Urien? Was it possible that Arthur condoned such folly? Certainly Merlin would not approve. Perhaps it *would* take a *woman* to guide the High King toward reason. Why then should she not grasp the reigns? They had, after all, grown close through the constant exchange of missives. Arthur believed that his responses went to Amesbury, when in reality Cerifus always ensured they reached Avalon. Morgen smiled and colored at the thought. A wealth of youthful charm bubbled throughout those memorable parchments. How had such a seemingly gentle youth become the legendary warlord already remembered in myth and song?

A sigh escaped Morgen's lips as she remembered Arthur's response to her hints that he should end the war. Indeed, she still saw his determined writing clearly etched into the parchment's soft facing.

Caerleon
Winter

Dearest Morgen:

Universal peace... If only life were that simple. Even if the Saxons left Britannia, I still have Lot, Urien, and countless petty kings to appease. None of them believe that I deserve to be king. Apparently, there is some dispute over my conception. Urien of North Wales swears that I am illegitimate!

Arthur

Morgen's response had been sly.

Amesbury Abbey
Early Spring

Dearest Arthur:

That is ridiculous. I am the one whose origins should be questioned. I am not your sister, but a fairy in disguise.

Love,
Morgen

Caerleon
Spring

Dearest Morgen:

   Do not make me laugh. I am in the midst of war right now. You a fairy? How did you come to be placed as a princess?

Love,
Arthur

Amesbury
Spring

Dearest Arthur:

   Call me to court, Brother, and I will explain all.

Love,
Morgen

It was Midsummer. Six moons had waxed and waned since Arthur had promised to send for Morgen. Why had her arrival been so delayed? Was it possible that the High King and his adviser had been creating some foolhardy agreement with Urien and Lot all that time? Did she have anything to do with that treaty? Bedivere's searching eyes intimated as much. He was on his guard, unwilling to divulge too much information. Following Arthur's orders no doubt. Oh, they could not reach court soon enough! Once she saw Arthur and looked into his eyes, she would know the truth. He could hide nothing from her.

   After skirting along the frail wall for a seeming eternity, Morgen was surprised to find the bronzed entranceway standing wide open—as if in welcome. A snarling wolf, not a red dragon, unexpectedly adorned the metal facing, and Morgen was reminded once more that this was not truly Arthur's fortress but a former Roman haunt. Bedivere gracefully lead her through the threshold, the bulk of her escort following behind. Although she craned her neck, it was impossible to see the central structure through a thick network of sheltering oaks that hid all but snatches of brick and timbered roof from view. Caerleon was but two simple, utilitarian levels, built of the same beige stones that guarded its decidedly humble facing. This was all Morgen could glean, for a lush garden courtyard fairly teeming with men lost in the execution of military exercises arrested her attention. Sweat glistened against their exposed limbs through the woven fabric of their tunics, revealing musculature that she had never dreamed possible. Yes, her guard proved likewise endowed, but they were covered in layers of leathern armor, leaving much to the imagination. There before her stood strong, vital, keenly bred fighting men, who knew their craft better than their own name. Few were older than twenty years of age, yet that only heightened their appeal. Morgen had never seen so many attractive men. How athletic they appeared, each capable of inspiring admiration! She gazed but a moment longer before a series of calls echoed among the ranks. Heat flooded Morgen's cheeks as every last warrior turned his gaze upon her then shifted into a regal salute. It was at that moment she saw *him*. Arthur stood at the center of this impressive gathering, tall, golden haired, and imposing, the guards flanking him on either side. Across Britannia these men were known as the Companions, the loyal followers that did Arthur's bidding in all matters great and small. Each held his sword in bold salute. Bedivere and the members of Morgen's train did likewise. It would have been an understatement to suggest that she, the wayward princess, felt honored.

Sliding off her befuddled palfrey, Morgen raced toward Arthur, barely considering rules or decorum. She had waited an entire lifetime to be reunited with this man. It made little difference what the others thought of her. This was to be the first true meeting—the one that would determine their fate. Morgen knew it was imperative that she not disappoint Arthur.

She had little to fear, for Arthur broke rank and met Morgen halfway. Catching her in a wild embrace that lifted both feet off the emerald grass, he spun round and round until it seemed the very earth must dissolve. His eyes were a sparkle just then, fueled by an inner fire Morgen did not see. Brother and sister they were to those who watched so intently, a fact all but forgotten by the enamored king.

Suddenly the touch of Morgen's flesh, the close proximity of her person stirred memories he had not experienced since their first meeting at Uther's deathbed. He had shared many lives with her, this woman who knew Arthur Pendragon better than himself, the woman whose heart beat in time with his, who had loved him unconditionally, understood his quirks, his idiosyncrasies, indeed, praised them, and even accepted his failings until it came to the one point that drove them apart. What was it? Why did he sense that she would shun his love if they were so connected? She was so close, so bound to him; they were melting into each other as they had once done when Britannia was fresh born, mother and father of the land and her people. Was this past reality or merely a deep seeded dream? All this bliss, this angst assaulted Arthur's sensibilities as they spun round and round, leaving him increasingly vulnerable, a fact which had not yet communicated itself to Morgen.

A whirl of faces, sun bronzed and dreamy, met Morgen's gaze. She threw her head back and watched the heavily laden oak boughs sway, the delphinium blue sky swirl among fluffy cloud formations, and the distant hills—broad, green, and expansive—spin around. They were secluded far from civilization, lodged within nature's bosom, the perfect place for forging new alliances. The sound of a nearby fountain, trickling its merry greeting, drew Morgen's focus. She saw the bronzed basin, elevated several feet above ground level by a fluted stand that boasted the same coppery hues; indeed, she noted that the fawn's mouth remained perpetually *O* shaped so it might spew a thin, watery stream but did not give it full credence. Everywhere she looked she saw cultivated beauty. Foxgloves poked their majestic crowns through thick, blanketing ivy, and crimson-hued rose bushes sprang up here and there, utterly glorious and unexpected.

Unexpected proved the word to describe the moment. One glance at Arthur's bewitched expression set Morgen's heart pounding at an alarming rate. The sisters had warned her of this. Arthur was in love with her—an honor to say the least. Was she prepared for such adoration? Should she reciprocate before these men? Slipping from his arms, she could not help but admire how *handsome* he was, utterly breathtaking in beauty: tall, sun bronzed, golden, and surprisingly starry eyed, and the rugged planes of his face, nose, and chin finely chiseled as if by some master carver.

"Arthur, dearest, at last we meet," she recovered, kissing his cheek. "Is it possible that you are Red Dragon, Britannia's Warrior King who has freed our land of Saxon rule? Peace reigns supreme now and forevermore thanks to your good work."

Morgen smiled serenely up at Arthur, waiting. The idea had been planted. How would Britannia's High King respond to such prompting?

"Peace now and forever," Arthur sighed, claiming her hand. "What a dream you weave, Morgen. If only it were true. The battles with Lot and Urien *are* but a memory. Our Saxon foes, however, are not so easily placated."

He paused, once more contemplating the delicate planes of her face. *Look at her, so dazzlingly perfect: the manifestation of my deepest desires. It is as if I dreamed her into existence. Surely I have seen her before—known her before. One might almost believe that she* is *a fairy. Perhaps that is why she outshines the brightest star.*

Remembering himself Arthur regrouped with surprising ease. Indeed, it was essential he do so, for Morgen was staring at him with a discerning eye. "Dearest, welcome to Caerleon," he said, swiftly kissing her brow.

Little remained to do but embrace and hope the bulk of their conversation progressed with greater ease.

Morgen faltered as she felt herself crushed within Arthur's well-muscled arms. He was so strong, so vital, truly a king among men. Instinctively, she placed her head against his chest and marveled at the breadth of it. Uther in all his impressive glory had never attained such physical perfection. Perhaps Igrainne would disagree, but Morgen knew she was right. Arthur was hot and sweaty from activity, but she hardly noticed, for some familiar note sounded in her brain.

I remember his touch, his scent, the incredible warmth of his person. The sisters spoke true. We are bound to each other. Still, I must overcome it. There is a reason I am thought of as his sister. I am not here to admire Arthur but to help him achieve peace.

"Why not end the war here and now?" she said, drawing back so she might meet his gaze. "Call the Saxon king, Cedric, to Caerleon. Make compromises. Share Britannia with our Saxon brethren and all will be well."

Arthur bit his lip but failed to hold back a chuckle that cost him dearly. Indeed, the bemused look on his handsome face spoke volumes. He found Morgen's "interference" highly entertaining. What did this "sweeting" know of warriors and fighting? Did she imagine that they would sit down at table and enjoy a little party while discussing terms of peace? Cedric was ferocious, a man of metal, blade, and steely sinew, the least vocal opponent Arthur had ever entertained. The likelihood of this veritable lion entertaining peaceful discussions was not much greater than the possibility that Arthur would one day surrender his throne.

"Forgive me, dearest, but you make it sound so simplistic," he said, holding that image in mind. "Do you really think that we could come to terms of peace simply by talking?"

Morgen drew a deep breath before answering, "Yes, I do."

The reaction was instantaneous, swelling through the ranks and even attaching itself to Dagonet and Bors, who had just returned from seeing the horses safely sheltered. Everyone, even these devoted members of her guard, were chuckling, a sound that could not be diminished no matter how much they shuffled booted feet. Arthur struggled to remain composed, but Bedivere's barely concealed snort broke his resolve. It was a valiant but futile attempt at suppressed mirth. He laughed outright then bit his lip.

Morgen felt her cheeks blaze crimson. What did she expect? They were men, after all! Gazing around she met Bedivere's sparkling eye and watched as he sheepishly toyed his boot back and forth against the thick, silky grass, fingertips pressed to his trembling lips. He did not want to hurt her; nor did Bors and Dagonet, who began rapidly stripping off their heavy armor so they appeared otherwise occupied and in no way connected to her distress. Lucan had already disappeared into the ranks. How typical. Men were utterly and completely impossible when it came to reason! Swallowing her pride, Morgen forced all focus back on the High King.

"Arthur, do not laugh at me. This is serious."

"I know that, Morgen," he gently soothed, pressing the palm of her hand against his lips. Up came the mask of diplomacy, instantly masking his true feelings. The act was so seamless, so inherently natural it became apparent that Arthur was already quite gifted at playing king. "Forgive me, but I have seen a bit more in the way of battle than your own sweet person."

Beyond the increasingly loud chortling, the outright levity that consumed his Companions, Arthur also knew another feeling inspired their reactions; they admired Morgen to distraction. This of course was pleasant ogling, but decorum dictated that it go no farther, and so he added, "Keep your wits about you, friends. Remember, she is mine."

This was not to be borne, not to be tolerated. The High King of Britannia was certainly full of himself. What right had he to treat Morgen as a piece of property? The words, "I belong to no man, Brother, not even you," spilled out of her mouth before she could check them.

That did it. Each and every last one of Arthur's men burst into an explosion of laughter. Quite a few edged closer, Bedivere, Bors and Dagonet included, observing the exchange with rapt

attention. This was the first time they had witnessed Arthur verbally jousting with a woman.
They did not want to miss even the tiniest thrust of
the opposing javelins.

Arthur was not at all bothered by this. How
often had Merlin drilled him on the principles of
diplomacy? Here it was: that very lesson brought
to life, but in such a manner that he and the arch
mage had never conceived. Morgen was hardly a
petty king or an insurgent. She was a gloriously
beautiful, intelligent woman who spoke her mind.
It took every last bit of his training to keep from
unintentionally insulting her. Not that he wished
to belittle her, but her commentary was so amusing. The Companions would have much to say
regarding this exchange when they later recon-
vened. Imagining that conversation, Arthur's smile
grew even broader.

"See what you have done, Morgen? You have
made me look foolish before the Companions."

"It would not be the first time," Bedivere volunteered, barely camouflaging a wink at Morgen
from his new elevated vantage point, draped across
a low hanging oak bough.

"Nor the last, I assure you," came Arthur's most
amiable reply.

Laughter erupted anew, so great was their
camaraderie. Morgen witnessed the exchange with
mixed emotions. The ranks had long since lost
their congruity, Companions having claimed whatever seating was available, be that stump, wall, or
grassy turf. This was a tightly woven group, every
bit as close as the relationship she shared with the

Sisterhood. What place had a female amid so much masculinity? How would a woman, even a princess, convince the High King to exchange his battle lust for thoughts of universal peace? It was her task to evoke such a change, but how—*where*—was she to begin?

A light breeze stirred Morgen's tresses, tossing them back and forth as many tongues of flame. The sight was not lost upon Arthur. He was spellbound, bewitched by this woman, his sister. Suddenly the task before him appeared altogether uninviting. He no longer wished to imagine treaties or former foes who desired alliances. Indeed, he wanted only to spend time with Morgen, to understand the heart, the soul that dwelt within such stunning packaging. Her beauty dazzled him, yes, but that was not the whole of his attraction. They were compatible in a way he had never imagined possible: each bent on similar goals, yet bolstering discordant means of attainment. Placing her fair arm against the bronzed length of his own, he escorted her through the foxgloves, winding ivy, and crimson rosebushes, away from prying eyes.

"Arthur, do not mock me," Morgen warned, wishing she had never left Avalon. This breach, increasingly more pronounced each moment, proved that men were beyond all comprehension. Did they always inflict their viewpoint on others? Did they ever consider the great responsibility women bore as savior of their race? Was it not through women that all dreams manifest? Surely Arthur, *the great king*, understood that. If not, he was ignorant indeed.

Arthur glanced at Morgen as if reading the thought. His countenance wavered, revealing a sight that made her increasingly wary. He was *concealing* something, something that concerned her, something that caused him heartache. Was it Morgause's seduction come back to haunt him, or another matter that currently consumed his attention? "What is wrong?" she questioned, feeling his fingers tighten about her arm. "What is it that you are not telling me?"

They paused beside the tarnished fountain, cautious, wary, and barely conscious of the thin stream of water that trickled from the fawn's frozen mouth, a flow that suppressed all mirth. Still seething, Morgen struggled to compose herself when Arthur's thoughts unexpectedly filtered through her mind.

Urien…How can I give her to Urien?

"No!" she cried, slapping her hand against the discolored basin so hard that angry water droplets littered the air. "Arthur, I have known nothing beyond convent walls for three years! Now you would marry me to Urien of North Wales for the solvency of your ridiculous treaty? Urien does not love me. He desires only to place himself in contention for your throne!"

Arthur's blue eyes widened as he clasped her trembling hands. "Did you just read my mind? Merlin must hear of this!"

Stifling a groan Morgen sought out a drooping oak bough several paces away and wound her fingers into its leafy greenery, keenly aware that the Companions still struggled to discern their conversation. They had not resumed their military exercises but fairly gaped at her, conscious that she might very well defy the king. Bedivere was fielding questions from his lofty post, supposedly about herself or the journey or something of that sort. Men were all around him, listening with rapt attention. Suddenly Morgen felt Arthur's strong arms encircle her waist.

"Dearest, the treaty is still delicate," Arthur whispered so close to her ear that his lips accidentally brushed her hair. "Caution must be exercised at every turn. I wish you only to entertain Urien's proposals..." He paused, turning her so they must converse eye to eye, "...not accept him. Will you do that for me? Will you trust me as you do no other?"

"Trust you? Why should I do that?"

The subject of trust proved a bitter tonic. Morgen found it more than a little disconcerting that Arthur asked for her trust, especially when he had already promised her to an ogre. Had there been discrepancy of trust in their former lives together? Had their love tested this issue firsthand? She gazed anywhere and everywhere but in his eyes, mentally taking note that the fortress appeared large enough to house several legions. Arthur and his men could certainly not fill this vast enclosure. Numerous balconies dotted the pockmarked façade with uniform regularity, offering Morgen the belief that most rooms boasted this feature. She wished to go inside to affirm this possibility for herself, but Arthur's next question claimed precedence.

"Do you love me, Morgen?"

Oh, goddess, there it was—the uncanny ability Arthur already possessed of reading *her* mind. Well, she had better get used to it, for it was not possible to hide affection from one with whom you had shared several lifetimes. Where was Merlin? Why did he remain so hauntingly absent?

"Yes, I love you! But I am not ready to give my life for you, not yet! Marry me to Urien and I will die."

Arthur stared at her unblinking. This woman, his sister, was so different than anyone he had ever encountered. How was he to mold her ideals so that they mirrored his own? You might as well speak commands to the ever-changing wind, he thought. She was watching him through a pair of seething blue-green eyes that questioned his kingship. Well, it was certainly not the first time someone had done that.

"Are you always so passionate?" he asked, drawing her even further into the canopy of green. Here they could converse freely, away from those overly astute eyes. Silence grew heavy between them. Indeed, they didn't speak another word until they reached a pitted wooden bench plopped directly beneath a prodigious oak tree. Arthur motioned Morgen to sit, then took up residence beside her. This done, his words tumbled forth in one great stream.

"Forgive me. My experience with women is limited and not altogether pleasant. I am not certain of the proper way to broach such subjects with you."

He glanced at her hopefully, certain this kinder, gentler method would evoke her trust but soon saw his mistake. He too wished for Merlin but knew the mage had no intention of making an appearance at this first meeting. And so Morgen's reply proved quick and altogether biting.

"On the contrary I hear you are quite the ladies man, that a new maiden fills your arms each night."

Arthur flushed scarlet but did not deny it. "They follow me on campaign from battle to battle, always appearing when I bed down. Believe me I do not seek them out. They are just there...always there. I assure you they never inhabit Caerleon. In any case I have no lasting experience with any of them. In truth women give me some pause..."

"Why, what happened? Did someone break your heart?" Morgen fairly blurted, before realizing her mistake. What insanity had prompted her to broach Morgause's deadly manipulation, an act of treason that could never be forgotten?

Unable to stay the hiss that escaped his lips, Arthur stared at her, horrified she might guess the truth. His mind grew desperate, reeling, no longer conscious of diplomacy. It was vital that Morgen never comprehend his folly, yet how was he to ensure this when she was so adept at unearthing his thoughts?

"You had no idea of her true identity. You could not help it."

Suddenly, Arthur was on his feet, staring as if he had been slapped full across the face. *She knows!* he thought. *How is this possible? Not another word must be spoken or I will die. Surely she understands that! Why then does she keep speaking? Why does she stare at me as if she comprehends all?*

Morgen responded also using her thoughts. ***It was not me, Arthur. I would never treat you so abominably!***

Arthur's features twisted so that he appeared increasingly vulnerable—a child with authority that surpassed his years, his station. Thank the gods he had taken her far from the Companions so they need not overhear his shame. Few men beyond Merlin, Bedivere, and his foster brother, Kay, knew the truth. Fewer still understood the full magnitude of Morgause's seduction. If that tidbit ever got out to the people, he would meet challenges against his authority that would make the Saxons pale by comparison. Taking a deep breath, he steadied himself. *I must remember myself. I am High King. Nothing Morgen can say or do will ever change that. Now show her who commands Britannia.*

"That is enough," he said, clasping hold of her arm. "I forbid you to say another word!"

This brief stab at reasserting authority did little to stop Morgen's reasoning. The longer they spent on this subject, the less time Arthur would devote to Urien's request, so she persisted. "Morgause is a witch. What could she hope to gain by seducing you?"

The fact that Morgen spoke of the seduction, that she, the woman he thought he had taken in his arms, intimately understood the betrayal but remained ignorant that his heart was irrevocably broken, that he would never love another, hurt worse than almost anything else he could conceive.

How was it possible for her to peer into his deepest darkest secret and not even weep? *Oh God, I must escape her eyes. They follow me everywhere—even in my dreams! Does she not see? Does she not understand?*

One option remained. Arthur set off at a brisk pace, his long legs narrowing the distance that existed between him and the Companions. It was essential that he reclaim his authority. In any case Morgen would think twice about broaching his agony there. Oh yes, he knew that she followed at his heel but only increased his pace, praying distance would render her mute.

Morgen increased her pace, struggling to match Arthur's long strides. Everything was going horribly wrong. Arthur surely hated her now. Why had she done it? Why had she broached the forbidden topic? Somehow, someway she had to win Arthur back or he *would* give her to Urien! "Brother, please!" she cried, grasping hold of his ivory tunic with trembling fingers.

Anguish spiraled Arthur around with such unexpected speed that he caught hold of Morgen, pressing tense fingers against her shoulders. Did she not understand his rank? No one, not even a sister, spoke such horrors to a High King! "Yes, Morgen, I am your brother. More importantly, I am your king. My thoughts are not to be shared with anyone. You will never read my mind again. Is that clear?"

"Yes, Arthur," she whispered, awestruck by the light, the shade, the very torment that colored his beautiful eyes. How tragic that his youthful exuberance was clouded by a witch's spell. Black magic, however, always struck back at its servants tenfold. One day Morgause would endure agony beyond her wildest imaginings. This was cold comfort, indeed. How many years would pass before evil claimed its due? It was impossible to fathom how many other individuals would suffer at her hands. Morgen faltered, lost in the dazzling blue of Arthur's tormented eyes. The look, the emotion pierced Morgen's soul, drawing her back to another place, another time. Arthur lay entwined with her—*no, entwined with Morgause*—once more in the shadowy depths of St. Alban's Great Hall. The red witch mechanically suffered his caress, all the while hatching her plot, a plot that included a golden-haired boy who stood beside her, innocently gobbling cherries. He pressed his blood red lips against her cheek then watched as she resumed her own distinct face and form. Suddenly Morgen understood, yet the truth proved so unnerving that it nearly made her retch.

"Yes, Arthur, I will bow to your decree, but there is one last thing I must tell you—one last thing you must know. Morgause bore you a son."

Moonlight Escape

Sleep did not come easily for Morgen. All thought, all contemplation continuously centered on Arthur's trials, Merlin's absence, and the proposed treaty. Hour after hour she watched liquid shadows play against her gloomy walls, brightened only by waning candlelight. Her chamber was large, roomy, boasting an oversized raised bed of Roman design, side tables, similarly hewn, and a walk-through window that opened up into a highly prized balcony. She had noted this much before night fell. Indeed, Arthur kept her figuratively guarded so long that it was impossible to bathe, let alone take a good look at the fortress. That would have to wait until morning. The fitful lighting was so dim, so muted that she could detect only shapes and forms, larger furnishings that appeared to be draped with a network of cobwebs or some such masking. In any case it did not matter. She was alone in another dismal cell without hope of rescue, for this time the High King and his mage were her jailers.

A shallow basin filled with water prompted
Morgen to splash her tear-strewn face over and
over until she regained some semblance of calm.
This was her life, the life she had chosen for herself, devoid of hope, inspiration, or love. Urien was
a man incapable of understanding her, a man who
did not comprehend the fine workings of her spirit.
This she knew intuitively. How then could she ever
contemplate such a marriage? Surely there must
be some way of appeasing Urien without sacrific-
ing herself. Why then could she not see it? Why
did everything—even the filmy draperies, woven
sheets, and fine deerskin trappings that adorned
her bedding—appear calculated to inspire acceptance? Groaning, Morgen stretched out upon the
untried bed, so large in its composition that it
nearly swallowed her whole. Surely such a fine bed
was meant for a king and his queen, not some tiny
princess who knew only rock, moss, and Avalon's
mystical apple trees. A soul-wrenched sigh escaped
her dry lips. Avalon...her hope, her dream...how
had the accursed treaty ever come to pass? Even
if Merlin had been instrumental in its conception,
he certainly never intended this horror. No, Urien
must have caught both counselor and king unprepared. That left them no alternative other than to
offer her as bait. If so, she had only one option
left—flight.

Slipping out of the oversized bed, Morgen pad-
ded barefoot to the gauzy coverings that adorned
her balcony window. One glance outside revealed
an altered courtyard bathed in an otherworldly
glow. Morgen stepped fully into the moonlit

brilliance and sighed. The air was alive with information. There she stood motionless, clad only in a creamy shift that left little to the imagination, desperate to glean those answers that evaded her reasoning. She must escape Urien's proposal—no matter what the cost.

A sharp falcon's call arrested her thoughts, rattled her senses. Oh, how she missed Cerifus. Indeed, the joyful reminder of her raptor friend brought momentary solace before Morgen continued her agonized musing. She had only one way to feed Urien's desires and still remain free. She would become his lover, not his wife. Again came the mournful cry, closer this time. A shudder of realization animated Morgen's spine, for it was not a falcon that hailed her, but a Merlin. Indeed, Merlin stood witnessing her efforts from his own moon-drenched balcony, a scant four rooms away, his piercing eyes aglow. Morgen's heart leapt at the sight and then just as suddenly hardened against it. Why had he remained absent? Why had he not even bothered to make an appearance upon her arrival at Caerleon? She saw but one way to unearth the answer.

I wondered when you would deign to appear.

They were so near each other, but a few doors or balconies away. Morgen never dreamed that Arthur would offer her a chamber in such close proximity to his adviser. The thought, while vaguely unnerving, offered possibilities. Perhaps this unorthodox choice could be used to her advantage.

Moving with a shadowy grace, Merlin shifted so that they faced each other before offering his thoughts. *That sounds more like a reprimand than a greeting.*

When she did not respond, he continued. *It appears our thoughts are locked upon the same point. I believe we should combine our talents. Together we will find a solution that is agreeable to all. Now draw a cloak about you and meet me by the courtyard gate.*

Morgen nodded her acceptance, aware that Merlin had unearthed her plan. Wordlessly she slipped inside the dim chamber, calculating her response. No doubt he intended to question her. How do you hide such plans from a man who knows all? Throwing a lightweight riding cloak over her creamy shift, Morgen breathed a prayer for assistance, took a right turn outside her door, and began a trek through the torch-lit labyrinth of halls that should have led to the garden but never offered the necessary outlet. Round and round the narrow halls spiraled, snakelike, offering Morgen little hope she would find the gate. Earlier that evening Bedivere had led her to her chambers after a series of stops that took him here and there and left Morgen so confused that she almost did not know which why was up or down. Yes, she was a prisoner, a prisoner of Caerleon's maniacal, incomprehensible configuration. Had the Romans made Caerleon's interiors so difficult to discern because they wished to thwart enemy invasion? If so, they had succeeded quite admirably! Flight appeared an increasingly futile option. Indeed, escape was impossible, if she could not even find the exit door.

On and on she trod, feeling utterly hopeless until Merlin's long, slim shadow loomed into view.

He too was similarly clad in night robes and cloak. Indicating that Morgen should follow, he pressed forward, effortlessly navigating each unorthodox curve until he took an abrupt turn to the right and sallied through the courtyard gate, which stood open as if awaiting their presence. Relieved, Morgen stepped across the bronzed threshold, noting that it also boasted a snarling wolf design. Merlin bent his steps toward an ancient oak whose exquisitely twisted trunk invited confidence. Devoid of Companions and Warrior King, the courtyard revealed its secrets, boasting abundant flora that spanned the full front of the fortress. Some of this was well tended, especially near the entrance doors where she met Arthur and his men that day; but just beyond the rose, ivy, and foxglove, Morgen detected vines and shrubbery so exuberant that they probably had not seen maintenance since its Roman guard made good its departure. As a fairy this pleased Morgen, who fostered the belief that nature should always remain untouched, never forced into submission. As a princess Morgen knew that Arthur had to impress those allies and potential enemies that sought his grace—so she appreciated the well-groomed entranceway.

I think we will do well, Merlin began in voiceless speech, *to communicate through thoughts alone. Otherwise I will be placed on trial for leading the princess in a midnight tryst.*

This thought tore Morgen from her midnight musings. Fairly snorting she pulled her soft, green cloak close and plopped down upon a tangled mound of roots. *It is certainly not the first time you could be so charged.*

The mage said nothing but fixed his eyes upon her, unblinking.

Very well, Merlin. I will try to be civil, she began, only half meeting his gaze. *It is quite a dilemma. I had almost decided to offer myself as Urien's...*

Lover. The air trembled with import. *Yes, I know.*

A frown graced Morgen's fair brow. Arthur had forbidden her to read another's thoughts. Did that same restriction not also apply to Merlin?

Merlin sighed. He had been caught red handed. *It was not necessary for me to trespass as you think. Perhaps I already know you a little too well.*

The breeze thoughtlessly intervened once more, tossing Morgen's flame-colored forelocks until they camouflaged both eyes.

Drawing close, Merlin gently brushed the stray ringlets behind her ears. *Forgive me. It was not my intention to intrude upon your musings,* he continued, sitting opposite her lovely countenance. *But once you entered the balcony, I did not resist being drawn in.*

The hour was late, and the entire courtyard possessed a fairytale quality about it that had been lacking earlier that day where men brandished cold, harsh steel, dispelling all but the most potent magic. Low hanging mist gently blanketed turf, tree trunk, flora, and fountain, bathing them in a pearlescent glow that sparkled its dewy welcome.

Morgen offered up a mischievous smile, her heart slowly warming to Merlin. *Well, I suppose you are forgiven. I would have done the same.*

There was no help for it. Merlin chuckled outright. It was so refreshing to see Morgen, to converse with her alone, even if it be on such a distasteful topic. A part of him was almost thankful for Urien's demands. At least they had conveyed Morgen to Caerleon. In any case her bizarre counteroffer left much to be desired. Arthur might very well shatter a sword if he heard it. Although Merlin pondered equally dire measures, he chose not to divulge them just yet. Instead he mentioned the obvious.

Dreams evade you this night. How fortunate for me.

Fortunate? Surely the arch mage saw that she was far from pleased. Perhaps at one time she would have relished a moonlight tryst, as he called it; but currently she was struggling to keep afloat amid a sea of deception! Arthur, for all his supposed goodness, had withheld vital information as to the real reason for her visit, and so had Merlin.

I am in no mood for riddles, Merlin, she intimated, perhaps a little too harshly.

Merlin was not about to be baited. "I have often thought that the world is but a dream," he whispered, drawing even closer, conscious that the mist and the romantic setting played to his advantage, "and that life itself is nothing more than illusion."

Silence served as Morgen's response. She was not about to make this easy for him. How many months had bled away since their last meeting?

How many days lost, remembering all the tenderness that had been shattered by a witch's curse? Why even now, in the thick darkness, he was far more guarded than their last meeting. No hint of romance or passion was present. He was only the king's advisor bent on solving a dilemma. After all, that is what he did best.

Merlin reconfirmed this estimation with a flash of his coal-black eyes. *Look to the stars, little sprite. Perhaps we will find the answers there.*

Casting her eyes upward, Morgen marveled at the clear, bright sky. True, much of the celestial vista was concealed by leafy canopies, but she could detect several heavenly constellations and one piercingly bright star that begged attention. It was all too easy to lose herself in such excess, which was, undoubtedly, Merlin's goal.

I once was of the same opinion, yet six moons waxed and waned without any word from you. Now I find myself nearly drowning in their depths.

Merlin bit back the retort that threatened to escape his lips. By the Ancient Ones, Morgen was overly dramatic! One might almost imagine that she was an actor presenting a well-rehearsed play. As with all performers, Morgen needed applause, appreciation. It was his task to exult her, sing her praises to the very heavens.

Drowning? That cannot be. You are all stardust and moonbeam, little sprite. Indeed, you share their essence. That is why you must stay the course.

What does it matter to you, Merlin? You no longer love me. Morgen stood for additional emphasis, setting Merlin's hand free. The courtyard grounds

grew preternaturally quiet, observing their inter-
actions with rapt attention. Indeed, the oak trees
craned their leafy crowns, the foxgloves swayed,
and even an interested nightingale stayed its flight,
roosting silently overhead. *If I become Urien's lover, I
can keep close watch on him.*

A shift of energy occurred, a flash of light.
Every attempt at humoring the princess disinte-
grated, leaving the air raw, bare, and seething.
Merlin no longer cared to participate in her petty
theatrics. She was totally forgetting her rank, thoroughly ignoring the importance of her purity. He
paused, remembering just how close he came to
altering her virgin state. Yes, the vision, the sending had *felt so real* that Morgen believed she was no
longer a maiden, a falsity he was not yet ready to
dispel. In truth he had ceased his amorous attentions just short of epiphany, denying them both
the ultimate prize. It was Arthur she had felt inside
her, the thought of which made Merlin's stomach
churn. That was something the High King must
never know. In any case if both he and Arthur had
been denied Morgen's gift, certainly Urien had
even less right to claim it. Merlin paused, remembering his position as king's counselor. No one, not
even Arthur, questioned his rulings. This princess
must be humbled, if that was, indeed, the only way
to help her see reason. Merlin also gained his footing, towering over her petite frame. "Morgen," he
said, speaking aloud, "you will not do this."

The nightingale shrieked, leaving its green
roost far behind; yet neither mage nor fay gave it
full credence. Morgen's face flushed crimson. She

had been waiting for just such a power play. The
arch mage knew how to bait her. Oh, yes, he understood that very well! "Are you ordering me? I do
not respond well to orders."

"I thought not, little sprite."

"Why do you keep calling me that? Yes, I am
little. What of it?"

Merlin's smile was disarming. Morgen had no
need to feel defensive. Her small stature was a great
advantage that she did not yet comprehend. In any
case it had already attracted more than a few men
of note. Did she not see that? Did she not glean the
power she wielded within that tiny frame?

Aware that he was not going to answer, Morgen
felt her patience fray a little further. Casting herself
back down upon the ground where their discrepancy in height lacked verification, she remembered
how he had once promised to teach her the magical arts. She had yet to see any such teachings. Had
there brief relationship merely been a ruse to gain
her favor? She saw no easy answer. She watched
him stalk toward the tall foxgloves, either lost in
thought or desperate to escape her company. The
moon shone full upon his long black hair, which
extended down the length of his narrow back,
melding perfectly with the raven-feathered cloak
so voluminous that it concealed all but a hint of
white night robes. Merlin truly was an unearthly
sight, something born of demon, mist, and shadow.
Most women would flee his company, but Morgen
found him utterly arresting. In any case it did not
matter. The treaty, if not Morgause's curse, kept
them apart.

When the silence had extended so long that even the shy tree frogs had recommenced their song, Morgen continued, "If you wish to be rid of me, Merlin, then why not agree to my plan? It will cost you nothing."

"Ah," Merlin stopped at this, and faced her, "but it will cost *you* dearly, more dearly than you can imagine. Give me a moment and I will present a new solution."

Merlin commenced pacing back and forth across the shadowy courtyard, startling several magpies that rooted the grounds for juicy grubs. Morgen noted a tenseness about him she had never witnessed before. Indeed, he appeared thoroughly flummoxed. All round him nature stirred. Squirrels chattered, prodigiously interested in his progress, even as a snowy barn owl offered a series of low hoots, and a sweet, stubbly hedgehog waddled by, watching, waiting, lending energy to his endeavors. Time ebbed and flowed until one renegade magpie lighted upon Merlin's dark head, fairly knocking the sense into him. Suddenly he came to a halt, locked in a tangle of ivy. Freeing himself from both magpie and the unwanted restraints, he quickly regained her side.

"Morgen," he said, softly placing both hands against her shoulders, "it is surprisingly simple. Give me leave to explain. Your beauty and wisdom will garner suits from Britannia and beyond. Do you see where my thoughts tend? I cannot believe I never conceived it before. Urien must woo you along with the other suitors. Arthur really has no choice in this matter. That is the only way we may ensure peace among one and all. Urien will have no hope of becoming your husband—unless he wins your heart. How strong are his prospects on that point, Morgen?"

Morgen's frame quivered ever so slightly. "The answer rests entirely with you, Merlin."

"Does it, indeed? Then I pronounce you irrevocably safe."

Morgen threw both arms around Merlin and began plucking stray bits of vine from his ebony locks. He looked every inch a green man, wild and virile to the core. Suddenly it made no difference that he had not visited her for six moons. Suddenly she did not care that he had been instrumental in constructing the treaty that might ultimately send her into Urien's bed. Morgen wanted only to love Merlin, to kiss him, caress him, to show him the depth of her feelings. It was impossible for her to be Arthur's love in this life. Why then should she deny herself Merlin? Pressing him back against the oak tree's knobbly, weathered trunk, she gave into desire wholeheartedly. Indeed, Morgen drank from Merlin's mouth as if it were some forbidden delicacy.

"Why have you avoided me for so long, Merlin?" she whispered, conscious that the tree aided her efforts, reconfiguring its bark so that it welcomed rather than stabbed the mage. "Is it possible that you no longer care for me? If so, why kiss me now?"

"It was *you* who first kissed *me*, Morgen. Take care not to forget it," he said, softly rubbing the tip of his hawkish nose against her delicate counterpart.

"Oh, yes, the blame must always be placed upon me. I am the renegade fairy, the little sprite who cannot be trusted—unless it be one of those rare moments when romance suits your fancy."

Merlin shifted position so that Morgen rested against the tree's ever-changing embrace. "Tread carefully, little sprite. You are on dangerous ground. Remember, I am a man like any other. My heart is just as easily broken."

"Is it just as easily won?"

CHAPTER 14:

Old Wounds

Morgen slept long and deep, unaware that the first half of the day had already spent its wings. Indeed, only a royal summons could successfully wrest her from that dreamy slumber. When the crisp knock sounded at her chamber door, she felt confused by the unexpectedly trussed amber and green surroundings that met her eyes. Bed, tables, and tapestries all boasted the same rich dressings, which admirably camouflaged the Roman, if not utilitarian design. Yes, this was unquestionably a man's room, but whoever took time enough to see it feminized made certain that each strategically placed drapery or frill softened the stark edges and lent warmth to its brisk feel. Even the elfin tapestries indelicately thrust upon her crumbling walls were intended to inspire, uplift all darkening thoughts. How could they not when the subtle breeze from her open balcony window made them wave to and fro, offering the illusion that they winked at her, sharing her pleasure. Beautiful gowns hung liberally, draped here and there, further masking the well-dressed furnishings. This was but a mask for a true state of disrepair. Fresh watermarks broadened just over-head, wearing away the powdery stone façade and rotting timbers that composed the roof. Slowly memory stirred. She was housed within the for-tress of Caerleon. These gowns were, no doubt, Arthur's peace offerings.

A second series of knocks shattered her focus.

"What is it?" she cried in obvious frustration. "Cannot a body wake of its own accord?"

"Forgive me, princess," chimed Bedivere's apologetic voice through the thick confines of her oak door frame, "but Arthur has requested your presence."

Deerskin coverlets flew wide as Morgen leapt from bed. Merlin was waiting for her. He had prom-ised to approach Arthur with the new proposal at daybreak. By the look of the sun it was already very near midday!

"He apologizes that there is no one here to attend you," Bedivere continued, thoroughly non-plused by Morgen's previous outburst. "I certainly would be willing, but somehow I do not think that was entirely what he had in mind."

Such a mischievous quality informed the sug-gestion that Morgen could not help but laugh. "Thank you, Bedivere. Tell Arthur I will attend him directly."

"I will do just that," rang his amused reply.

Morgen heard Bedivere hesitate as if awaiting some final response. When it did not come, he started off down the hall at a brisk clip.

Left to her own devices, Morgen set about choosing the gown that would serve her best. Arthur had hired numerous dressmakers weeks in advance so that she might truly look a princess. Glancing over the various styles and colors which adorned her ample furnishings, she thought that he had indeed chosen well. Each piece was exquisitely made of the finest and, no doubt, most costly materials. The question was which gown would best aid her cause: the flowing angel-sleeved beauty that boasted layer after layer of shimmering color from lapis to amethyst, the brilliant white gold made of some exceptionally clinging material that would, perhaps, fit her a little too well, or the dazzling azure—long, formal and beautifully cut. Morgen paused, considering. What did she know of Arthur? Yesterday he had been but simply dressed. Did that mean he cared little for color or fabric? If so, why had he gone to such lengths to see her beautifully adorned?

A sigh escaped Morgen's lips. She should dress for herself, not Arthur. The multi-layered amethyst concoction was instantly her favorite, ethereal, dreamy, and ultimately feminine. Morgen lifted the voluminous skirts and allowed the soft layers to slip through her fingers. Yes, this appealed to her, but what of the man who controlled her destiny? Would it make Arthur take such note of her that he could not stomach any thought of separation? What color would he wear? Irresistibly her eyes were drawn to deep, lush forest green edged in gold. The material was substantial, yet silken to the touch. Without further consideration, Morgen slid the gown over her creamy shift, taking note of the way it draped against her figure. Yes, this piece would do very well. The fact that the bodice was exceptionally low cut would further aid her cause.

After lacing up the gown in record time, Morgen dragged a much-abused comb through her unruly mane, washed both face and hands in the basin, and then sprinkled a handful of Avalon's crushed rose petals down her bosom. This was the best possible preparation she could make on so short a notice.

Out the door she flew, uncertain where king and mage currently met. The task of unearthing their whereabouts was daunting to say the least, especially after her midnight confusion. The halls appeared deserted again, with no hint of Companion or servant anywhere. This time Morgen chose a different path, bending her steps to the left, conscious only that her inner voice acted as guide. She passed a large dining area, also deserted, keenly aware that hunger gnawed at her vitals. No doubt the men had long since finished their breakfast. That meant she would have to wait until the midday meal, which she hoped would begin soon. Finally, after wandering another few minutes without seeing anything other than what must be individual bedchambers, Morgen turned into a large oval hall that boasted one bronzed door guarded by a chestnut-haired knight who appeared to be awaiting her presence. He was of average height and build, the traditional Red Dragon tunic he wore barely concealing his musculature, which was appealing, but not so overly pronounced as to make him appear weighted down. A flash of his blue-gray eyes indicated that he recognized her at once. Indeed, he bowed so low that Morgen feared he might have trouble straightening, an awed expression painting his finely hewn features. It was then she took closer note of his person, for something about his aspect and form appeared almost too beautiful for this world. The eyes were large and luminous, the cheek bones high, well defined, and the nose, chin, and oval composition of his face appeared almost feminine in aspect. *Almost but not quite.* Morgen recognized this at once. She too possessed that ethereal energy. Did that mean the knight was fairy born? This was a question Morgen dare not ask on so brief an acquaintance, yet she must begin somewhere.

"Good day. May I have the pleasure of knowing your name?"

"Accolon, my lady," proved the knight's fairly breathless reply. A soft sigh escaped his slim lips as he gently pressed her hand within his own. His palm was well calloused, as were his fingertips, a natural result of wielding a sword.

"I am happy to meet you, Accolon. Perhaps someday soon we will come to know each other better. At present, however, I must find Arthur and Lord Merlin. Can you tell me where...?"

Accolon fairly flung open the door behind him, a soft flush coloring his cheeks. "They await you inside, princess."

"Thank you, Accolon." Morgen paused as if she wished to say more, then thought better of it and entered the room without a backward glance. The

door snapped shut behind her, Accolon fulfilling
his duty.

The chamber Morgen entered was large, dank,
and dusty, devoid of any direct sunlight but that
found struggling through a gauzy drapery unceremoniously tied back at its nape by a length of rope.
Circular in composition, the room was bare and
unadorned, boasting few furnishings on which to
rest or recline but a couple of cross chairs, a ragged
bench, and a dragon-backed throne Morgen knew
had once belonged to Uther. This however was
far from the most curious sight that met her eyes.
Both king and counselor were huddled over hun-
dreds of carefully written vellums. These objects,
which she could only presume to be petitions, were
cast in wild disarray upon a strangely undersized
table that seemed ill equipped to house such abundance. The picture itself appeared so comically
ludicrous that she could not help but giggle.

"Good morning, Brother, Lord Merlin. I hope
this day finds you well."

Arthur, who was clad in a simple tunic and
pants, which also happened to be forest green,
rapidly straightened, then groaned at the shock it
provided his much-abused back.

"I do not mean to offer reproof, Morgen, but
'good day' is far more in order."

When Morgen merely laughed at this assessment, his smile broke forth anew. His eyes skimmed
her figure, perhaps a little too zealously, and then
shot back to her face, brimming with admiration.
"What a vision you are in that green gown."

Merlin shifted uncomfortably on his cross chair, wishing that he were leagues away. The room, so expansive in its relative emptiness, no longer seemed large enough to contain all three of them. Fixing his eyes on the petition still clutched in his talon-clenched fingers, he made note of Morgen's silence, then fell again to perusing the contents.

"In fact," Arthur continued, indicating his own garb, "we make quite the pair." He beamed again and then recommenced rubbing the troublesome spot along his spine. "Strange...that I am already old at nineteen."

Instinct drove Morgen forward until she tentatively clasped his hand. "Hardly that," she supplied, conscious once more of his warmth, his scent, which reminded her of spice and windstorm. "You have seen more battles than most men thrice your age. If there are no objections, I will ease your pain."

Clearly perplexed, Arthur paused, trying to decipher her words. Surely she meant something other than the thoughts that plagued his mind. One look, one glance from her sea-green eyes possessed the power to heal him, but what did she truly suggest? They were already dressed as a couple. Why then was it so impossible to contemplate them joined as one?

"Never hesitate to use one's gifts," Merlin suggested with a wry lift of his brow.

Morgen glanced openly at her love, unprepared for what she would find. Gone was the arch mage who had kissed her so passionately in the moonlight, leaving behind a steely adviser coiled in his chair—cold, calculating, and detached. Why did he not return the look? Surely he knew her eyes were upon him. What was wrong with Merlin? Did he think Arthur would not approve their love? Perhaps it was much worse than that. Perhaps Merlin *did believe* that love was nothing more than a momentary distraction.

Aware that Arthur was watching her intently, Morgen quickly thrust all such feeling aside. Negativity of this sort did not suit her. Indeed, it did not serve anyone. Only one task possessed the ability to convey her beyond petty speculation. Healing was forever her focus, her very essence. Why should she not share it with Arthur?

"Please sit down, dearest," she said, looking up at his impressive height, which made her feel no more than a fledgling child. Why, her head barely reached his heart! "It amazes me how anyone can be so monstrously tall."

Warm, rich laughter issued from Arthur's lips. Yes, he had noticed the discrepancy between them, but it only increased his delight. Amused, he sat upon a low, pitted wooden bench, an act that produced further strain, peppered by an additional groan.

"That is much better," Morgen pronounced well satisfied. "Now I can reach you." Placing her hands so that they just hovered over Arthur's tender back, she silently asked assistance of the divine healers, Brigit and Dianecht, conscious how the requested warmth animated her palms, the very onset of healing. The way the energies flowed through her person spoke of something eternal. Softly she blew against Arthur's spine. This would further relax the afflicted area, for it was clenched tight as a fist. Arthur gripped the table, uncertain.

"Relax, Arthur," Morgen mused at his overly cautious antics. "I will not hurt you. Surely you know that, dearest. I want only to help."

"Yes, of course, I..." he paused, searching for words. "I will try to be more cooperative."

Morgen marveled at this, remembering how Merlin had previously blocked her healing efforts. This man before her—Arthur, High King of Britannia, was very different, indeed. Taking courage, she placed both hands against Arthur's spine and watched him tremble as he received the gift. Clearly fascinated he reached across his chest so he might clasp her slim wrist. Oh yes, he appreciated her efforts! Without further prompting the energy increased its power tenfold. Heat blazed through her palms into the afflicted areas. Indeed, the rush of energy was so impressive there could be no doubt Arthur really had damaged the muscles along his spine.

"Your hands are so hot; they almost burn me," Arthur exclaimed in good-natured surprise, releasing hold of her person. "What are you trying to do, Sister, render me incapable of finding you a husband?"

Morgen forced a smile. "The life force is healing your much-abused back. Please allow it to work without further comment or reproof." Arthur bit back the next comment that hung upon his lips. Directing the healing energies with her mind, Morgen shifted both hands several inches over the offending spasm. This act treated not only Arthur's body, but all energy fields surrounding his person. "You may proceed with your kingly duties," she said, certain he would no longer taunt her.

Arthur glanced at her with some amusement. "As you are the current topic of discussion, I hardly think…"

"Am I?" Morgen interjected almost mischievously. Turning Arthur's head so that it faced forward, she refocused the energy deep into his complaining muscles.

"…you will accept any of our suggestions with grace."

"Am I really such an ogre?" she questioned, seizing Arthur's shoulders.

"Certainly not. You are…" Arthur paused while he caressed his back with tentative fingers. "That is amazing, Morgen. The pain is gone. How did you ever learn such a thing?"

"It is as I have told you, Arthur. I am a fairy in human form. Healing is one of the gifts that I brought into this world."

Arthur's expression changed as he seized upon the new possibility before him. "If you are a fairy, then I can hardly claim to be your brother. Perhaps I should add my name to the list of suitors who seek your affections." He indicated the mass of vellums stretched indelicately upon the table.

Swallowing hard Morgen stared wide-eyed at the throng of proposals. "Those petitions cannot all be for me."

"Better than half seek to woo you—perhaps more. We have barely addressed this lot," Merlin supplied, lifting a handful of missives that awaited their perusal.

"No..." she whispered, conscious that Arthur had a country to maintain. Her own feelings were inconsequential at best. She was but a choice prize available to the highest bidder. No doubt every High King's sister bore this heavy burden. Why even Arthur himself was pursued by masses of eligible females. Suddenly it became clear why he never denied them. This was a sanctioned ritual in which they displayed their "attributes" before the king.

Arthur watched Morgen's countenance wax pale as marble, then just as quickly blaze crimson. Potential wooers of this sort obviously made her uncomfortable. And why not? She was only four-teen, or was it fifteen? Many of those recent years had been spent in the company of nuns. Men were a commodity with which she was not altogether familiar. It was his task to put her at ease. "Thank you for healing my back," he sighed, purring his pleasure like a contented lion. "I cannot convey how many times we might have utilized your tal-ents during a siege. Merlin is also a healer, but I must so often use his gifts to other ends that mere mortals attend my men."

Alive with purpose Morgen did not hide her enthusiasm. This was how she could serve the country and guide it back toward a peaceful exist-ence—as a healer! Arthur had inadvertently stum-bled upon the very topic that plagued her mind. "You need only ask, Arthur, and I will gladly accom-pany you on campaign."

Sadly Arthur's pronounced reaction was not what Morgen expected. Darkness clouded his normally sunny features, wrinkling his smooth brow until it appeared furrowed and immoveable. He rose quickly claiming his authority and then spoke without hesitation, "Absolutely not. Have you any idea what Saxons do to our women?"

"This is all very interesting," Merlin carefully intervened, aware that Arthur was but a heartbeat away from losing his temper. "We seem to be avoiding the point of discussion. Countless marriage proposals have been made on your behalf, Morgen. One in particular must be immediately addressed. Will you hear our counsel?"

An unmistakable groan escaped Morgen's lips as she plopped into a large cross chair that felt deliberately carved for discomfort. The action was smooth and seamless, and she thought herself quite the accomplished thespian. Arthur would never know that she had already plotted this suggestion with his adviser by moonlight. "Proceed, Lord Merlin," she sighed. "I am all alight to hear what you would say."

Merlin hardly missed a beat, so steady was his answer. "I have already told Arthur of our discussion last evening."

Surprise pierced Morgen's well-planned theatricality, pulling her up so quickly that the chair nearly tottered to the thrush-lined floor. What kind of game was Merlin playing? Had he actually told Arthur of their midnight rendezvous?

"He agrees that your proposal to seduce Urien is entirely out of the question."

"How dare you?" Morgen's cry lodged within her throat, the sheer magnitude of betrayal nearly choking her. "It was my place to broach that topic with Arthur—not yours!"

Arthur intervened with great skill, analyzing her reactions from every angle. This was a complicated woman, one that readily defied classification. It was vital that she understood him, comprehended how he would never allow such sordid tactics! "Morgen, it is better this news came from Merlin. I probably would have started breaking things had you thrust such a preposterous idea upon me unawares."

Morgen's expression wavered slightly. The chamber, the mood was darkening by the minute, not because of any elemental storm but due to the tempestuous nature of its three inhabitants. "It is not preposterous! I only entertain the idea because it will help you. Why can you not see that? As Urien's lover, I could unearth his plots before…"

"Enough. There will be no more said on this point." Arthur fixed his gaze upon her, communicating the finality of his decision. This was the king speaking, head held high and not to be questioned or defied. After a necessary pause, sunshine returned to his expression and he appeared almost mischievously happy. "Urien will simply take his chances with everyone else. If he wins your heart, which seems altogether unlikely, then he will claim you as a bride. If not I will find someone else to his liking."

Morgen relaxed ever so slightly. "Are you suggesting that I am easily replaced?"

Another delightful quirk registered itself in Arthur's brain. Morgen was not altogether as self-confident as she appeared. "You seem to be missing the point," he explained, placing both hands firmly upon her shoulders. "We have just offered you a way out of this accursed marriage proposal while leaving room for the treaty to remain intact."

Wasn't that the very point? Urien was capable of dissolving all their plans if she was not a component of his reward. "The treaty will only remain intact if Urien accepts."

Arthur's confidence was disarming. "Oh, Urien will accept. He has no choice."

"Very well, Brother," Morgen sighed, standing on tiptoe so she might lace both arms around his neck. Why she had done this was impossible to say, but the end result made her shiver. Indeed, Arthur stared at Morgen, unblinking, as if nothing else could be more important than the length of each ginger lash that framed her sea green eyes. Morgen gazed back at him intently, trying hard not to bait him.

"Arthur, I believe you have a smudge of chalk on your nose," she finally said, reaching up to rub the offending mark away.

The effect was immediate, kindling Arthur's eyes so that they clearly spoke his passion. "May you always be near to catch me when I fall from grace," came his low reply. Thankfully he caught himself and quickly recovered, his face beaming sunshine once more. "Yes, I think I will keep you with me always. Those fellows," he indicating the overly abundant petitions, "can shift for themselves."

"Oh, yes, Arthur! Keep me with you always," Morgen cried, covering his face with kisses. Arthur returned the gesture, perhaps a little too zealously, lifting her up so that their lips met. Both king and fay froze locked in the exchange. Neither knew how to resolve the intimacy. The kiss had been far too pronounced for a display of sibling affection.

Sisters, what have I done?

Morgen saw at once the future implications of her mistake and tried to break free, but Arthur would have none of it. Slowly, gracefully, he began to propel her around the chamber in a delightfully unscripted dance, lifting her up so that both feet skimmed the floor.

"You are light as a feather. Why, one might almost believe you could fly. Tell me, sweet Morgen, are you still a shapeshifter?"

Confused by the assumed intimacy of their actions, Morgen quickly said the first thing that crossed her mind. "Set me down, Brother."

The finality of Morgen's tone brought Arthur to an abrupt halt. His fair brows drew together questioningly as he relinquished hold of her. "I meant no disrespect, dearest. Forgive me." The words sounded strangely hollow as they escaped his lips.

Everything was going terribly wrong. Morgen had been so close—so close to securing his approval, but in that strange twist of fate, she had pressed her advantage. Suddenly Arthur, High King of Britannia, stared at her as if he had been slapped full across the face. She had wounded him without intending it.

Bending her head low, she whispered, "Forgive me, Arthur. It is I who has been disrespectful."

Arthur instantly helped her up, his face a mask of concern. "You must trust me, Morgen. I swear that all will be well."

Once again they embraced. This time Morgen trembled at the sensation. It was vital that she tread carefully, never to lure Arthur into such dangerous territory again. What was she thinking, kissing his forehead, his cheeks, his eyelids? Of course he had misinterpreted the gesture! Her one thought, her intent was to heal the fresh wounds she had just inflicted upon his person. "You asked me a question. Shapeshifting is one area of study in which I do not dabble."

Pleased that they had moved beyond the awkwardness, Arthur followed her line of thinking. "But that night when you were at father's death-bed, I saw you change into a stag—a white stag."

"A stag, Arthur?" Morgen attempted an ill-fated laugh. "If I were determined to shapeshift, I would hardly choose a stag—a hind, perhaps, but not a stag."

How much should she tell him? Was Arthur ready to hear the length and breadth of her abilities? Did he really want to know why she had traveled to Caerleon and risked everything, including her sanity, to stand by his side? A quick glance at Merlin answered her queries. This was not the time for such confessions.

Say something convincing, Morgen, then allow me to change the subject.

Drawing a deep breath, Morgen did just that. "Arthur, I assure you that was illusion—nothing more. Merlin did not wish us to meet just then, so he made it appear as if I became a stag."

"The princess speaks true," Merlin offered, skillfully drawing focus. "I have no doubt that Morgen would be quite excellent at shapeshifting if she put her mind to it. I will be happy to oversee her studies as time permits."

This was it—a tantalizing opportunity that shimmered its promise. It felt wrong to meet Merlin's eyes so Morgen looked to Arthur, who nodded his approval. Here was a victory won! They could see each other without escort, match wit for wit in magical study and whatever other opportunities came their way.

"Thank you, my lord." Morgen smiled, drawing near Merlin so she might clasp his hand. "You will find me an apt pupil."

"I have no doubt of that," Merlin said a little too casually. He felt it was dangerous to seek her eyes, but it would seem far more noticeable if he did not. The fact that she held his hand made it imperative he do so at once. Caution sounded its warning note. Merlin knew that everything would be revealed in that moment—that Arthur would discern their love, but there was no help for it. Indeed, he met Morgen's gaze, and his worst fears were realized.

Arthur drew breath to speak, then froze, reading the depth of their intimacy. Color drained from his bronzed face. His own adviser, who never looked at women, appeared to be inexplicably in love with his sister—*No, a fairy who pretends to be my sister. A fairy with whom I have spent several lifetimes.* It was all so complicated; Arthur felt his brain was about to implode.

By the gods, how could this have escaped me? How— when did they ever meet? Merlin has been with me all the time, every day, every night. How is this possible? Did he visit her at Amesbury? Did they meet at St. Alban's? Yes, Morgen just said they had communication at St. Alban's, so that must be it. But how could Merlin have labored on that treaty without saying a word? Am I to bind her to my counselor when petty kings are willing to lay down their arms to secure her as wife? How is this to be answered? How am I ever to bear losing her to another?

Arthur blinked rapidly as if trying to center his thoughts and then spoke, perhaps rather too abruptly, "Well, the next month should be fairly uneventful until Mother arrives. Did you know that she currently lodges at your old haunt—Amesbury Abbey? She arrived there just after your departure."

Morgen tore her eyes from Merlin, reeling at this intelligence. "Igrainne is at Amesbury? Oh Arthur," she cried, unable to regain his side fast enough. If only she had communicated the tiniest bit of information about the treatment she suffered at Agatha's hands. "You must get her out of there at once. There is a woman, Sister Agatha, who beat and tormented me!"

Thunder animated Arthur's expression. "She would not dare," he fairly hissed through gritted teeth. "Did you know this?" he continued, fixing Merlin with fierce, discerning eyes. Anger simmered beneath the surface, ready to burst forth in one great explosion, which the king barely held in check. His eyes blazed fire, narrowed into two points of blue flame. It was suddenly clear why Arthur was so feared on the battlefield.

"Yes," Merlin acquiesced with bowed head, "I knew, but I did not comprehend the full depth of abuse until I spoke with Morgen firsthand."

It happened so fast that Morgen had not time to react. Arthur seized the goblet from which he had been drinking and hurled it against the stone wall with such force that wine sprayed in every direction, along with pieces of stone, pewter, and powdery residue. Merlin never flinched, undoubtedly accustomed to such abrupt mood swings, but Morgen stared thunderstruck as if seeing the High King for the first time.

Arthur closed his eyes, forcing his anger into submission. "You must believe me, Morgen. I had no idea that you were being abused. If I had the slightest idea, I would have marched in to Amesbury with the Companions and turned the tables on this *Agatha*. Take comfort," he continued, pausing to stroke her hair. "No one, not even a sister of the cloth, would dare abuse a former high queen. The fact that she hurt you will go hard on her."

Claiming his hand so she could bring it to her lips, Morgen could not stay the next question. "What will you do to her?"

"Leave that to me," he added lightly, his eyes seeking Merlin with an unspoken command that escaped Morgen's comprehension. He then sat down with ease upon the dragon-backed throne and seamlessly continued where he had left off.

"Urien and Lot will follow after Mother's arrival. You should have ample time to hone the craft by then. Go. Break your fast, dearest. Leave us to sort out this mess."

"But I wish to stay and help!"

Arthur would not be put off. Indeed, his demeanor was yet again that of a monarch fully consumed by his duties. "Once I release Merlin, the two of you may pursue whatever magical arts suit your fancy. I must drill the men, and as you have been so gracious to restore my back, I will face no hindrances. Bedivere will show you where the food is housed. Oh, and you will also meet my foster brother, Kay. He was wounded in battle and has since been overseeing the court as my seneschal."

"Perhaps I may heal his wounds," Morgen suggested, pleased with this new opportunity to prove her worth.

Again came Arthur's cool reply. "I have no doubt you may—if Kay allows you to touch him. I would not count on that. He is a little out of sorts these days."

"Well, I will see to that," Morgen proclaimed with assumed relish. She would win Arthur's confidence back with this act of healing his foster brother. Surely then he would see the important role she was to play in shaping Britannia's future.

After receiving doubtful looks from each corner, Morgen gracefully pivoted on heel and made good her exit, leaving the shadowy chamber complete with mage and king far behind.

Bedivere, who stood in Accolon's place, nodded his greeting. "So it is adventure you seek.

The question is, are you brave enough to follow?"
Without another word they took a left turn and set
off toward the west quadrant of the fortress, otherwise known as Kay's domain.

CHAPTER 15

Companions

Dark, musty, and almost entirely devoid of natural light, Caerleon's mead hall was oppressive, almost smothering in its stagnancy. Why, the very air was so thick of sweat and fumes that Morgen necessarily placed a cloth over her nostrils to keep from retching. The honey-stoned hall shone sallow, but this did not camouflage its expansiveness nor hide the fact that the vast chamber was built to serve more than one Roman cohort with ease. Indeed, men of all stations, from the lowliest foot soldiers to the elite Companions, were squarely planted at long, wooden tables that bore pits and gouges that hinted at excessive usage. Bent over a luncheon consisting of bread, stew, and watered mead, few men bothered to look up until Kay's grainy baritone burst through their midday libations.

"You may willingly play nursemaid, but I have no time for it! Tell Arthur I said so."

The cry was low and guttural, like a wounded animal making one final attempt to defend its turf. Morgen winced despite herself and watched the soldiers nudge each other good-naturedly. Apparently they had heard this mottled tirade before.

Bedivere appeared with a roomy basket stocked full of fruits and breads amid the clamor and clang of heavy cooking utensils. One whirling specimen nearly succeeded in bashing his shoulder, but the agile Companion deftly stepped aside, well acquainted with Kay's eccentricities.

"Feast well, you smitten fool!"

"I assure you we will!" rang Bedivere's merry reply as he dodged yet another cooking projectile.

A grunt of displeasure was followed by another inordinate crash. Kitchen servants were running this way and that, seeking shelter from Kay's seemingly violent outburst. The event was comical even as it waxed poetic. Kay, for all his bravura, was not a happy man.

"It appears, sweet princess, that you will be spared this day," Bedivere chimed, as he plopped down upon a battered three-legged stool that teetered precariously before accepting his weight.

"Spared?" Morgen repeated, her eyebrows lifted in faint bemusement.

Nodding toward the ominous, smoke-stained kitchen door, which stood deceptively open as if in welcome, he continued, "Kay has been…detained."

"Haven't I enough to do around here without trading gossip?" Kay sneered, poking his large coppery head out the door, revealing just a hint of his broken visage. Shadows played against his brow, forcing it into almost lumpy relief. "I leave that to you, Bedivere."

Casting his hazel eyes on Morgen, he gave a brief snort, and then added, "Enjoy feasting with the Pict, my lady."

Morgen burst out laughing as Bedivere turned a brilliant shade of crimson. Another crash burst forth from the kitchen, and Kay withdrew his scowling countenance, much to the chagrin of both princess and knight, not to mention numerous other observers who banged their goblets with rowdy appreciation.

Apparently laughter was the only medicine that Arthur's foster brother found palatable. Life had dealt him a cruel blow, one that left his face, his form hauntingly distorted, twisted, and battered beyond that which was physically pleasing to the eye. Morgen shuddered despite herself. Kay's appearance was not one to inspire admiration. An angry red scar ran unceremoniously from his right eyelid to his left lower lip, visibly marring his strong features, blurring them into an eternal grimace. Not that Kay would ever have been handsome; he was too large, almost gigantic in height and breadth, fully capable of dwarfing even Arthur. The coppery hair that framed his seemingly misshapen head jutted out here and there as if incapable of lying flat. Cropped short, these untamed locks accentuated rather than hid his wounds. His eyes were large, fiery hazel, bloodshot—no doubt from too many choleric outbursts. The nose, broken at some time, had healed at a curious angle that made him look like he was perpetually twisting his head, but this was not the most curious thing about Kay's appearance: something seemed almost inhuman, bestial, the way the scar pulled his flesh, indeed, distorted it from eyelid to lip. Morgen was about to question Bedivere on its origins when he sprang up, basket in hand.

"Why not break your fast outdoors? What say you, princess?"

It did not take long for Morgen to voice her approval. Bedivere leapt up and with an overly gallant bow offered his arm. Together they picked their way through the mead hall, careful not to disturb the feasting troops who had returned to consuming their stew with zeal. Drops of airborne gravy and mead spattered Bedivere's uniform, the red and gold dragon tunic that all members of the Companions wore religiously. Thankfully Morgen dodged these edible projectiles and kept her gown mercifully unsoiled.

Upon entering the courtyard, Morgen immediately broke from her escort, intent on dining beneath the canopy of a giant oak tree that boasted the pitted bench she had shared with Arthur when that unmentionable secret surfaced a scant day earlier. Bedivere followed, pausing only to spread wide a well-used deerskin upon the lanky grass so he might better display the delicate fare of fruits and breads for her inspection. This done, he situated himself on a low-hanging bough of the ancient sentinel, obviously pleased with the opportunity it gave him to better admire her person.

"The sun must be envious of you, princess," he said, dangling his booted toes so they just fell short of skimming her locks. "Hair of flame, skin of snow."

"You should see me by moonlight."

"Name the night and I will be there."

Bedivere was only half jesting. That made Morgen pause. Did she really wish to foster such admiration—especially when it would lead nowhere? Surely Bedivere knew that. She was destined for Urien, *goddess help me*, or some petty king—if not the High King himself. Had not Arthur suggested that he add his name to the applicants that vied for her affections? That was before he became cognizant of her feelings for Merlin. A hot blush colored Morgen's cheeks as she remembered Arthur's reaction. He was hurt, puzzled, to say the least. How was she to interact with him, knowing that he understood her feelings for his adviser?

Aware that Bedivere was staring at her a little too intently anticipating her answer, Morgen voiced the first thing that came to mind. "Tell me everything about court. Arthur speaks only of training for battle. Is it possible that you enjoy no liberties beyond those provided by the sword?"

Bedivere easily saw through this device and reclined back against the trunk in assumed rejection. This did not last long, for a renegade piece of bark stabbed his tender back, and he shot up like a bolt, swinging his legs over the bough so that he faced her blooming countenance. "We are all bound to live and die by the sword, princess. It is our sole purpose for being. We are here to defend the people of Britannia—you included. A difficult task to say the least, but someone has to do it." He winked at Morgen, then fell back to admiring her person, propping his hands against branch and trunk so that he might easily swung back and forth by simply adjusting his weight.

Bedivere's small, compact build gave him the look of a dark elf, especially when he was in a mischievous mood. He had a certain arch of the eyebrow, an impish twist to his smile that only heightened this effect. Yes, he was dashing, magnetic, thoroughly appealing, and…entirely wrong for her. Why could he not see that?

"Tell me of your time in Amesbury," Bedivere continued, "Arthur said that the nuns tried to cut your hair. Is that true? If so, the Companions would have rallied to your defense, be they ladies of the cloth or not."

Bedivere fairly vaulted off the tree limb and landed gracefully at her side, an action so seamless that it appeared natural he would kneel, claim her hand, and bring it to his lips again and again, each time moving in a little closer until they were separated by little more than a prayer.

Fairly affronted, Morgen slipped free. Bedivere's attentions had become too marked for her taste, which meant diversionary tactics were necessary. Glancing around the courtyard, she saw nothing to aid her cause—nothing but the high Roman wall that blotted the surrounding countryside from view, something she very much wished to see. Scampering to her feet, Morgen embraced the far west corner of this crumbling encumbrance and attempted to scale it, an act which achieved its desired effect when Bedivere ceased his romantic maneuvers and raced to her side.

"Wait!" he cried, offering instant restraint as he placed his arms about her tiny waist. "Arthur will skin me alive if you fall!"

Morgen saw at once that his concern was real. Not that Arthur would truly punish Bedivere for her folly, but he might make his life excessively uncomfortable. Well, Arthur need never know about this little diversion. In any case he would never hear about it from her lips. Everything was so guarded, cautious in this new world of Caerleon. Morgen desired only to see, explore its hidden secrets, understand its Roman composition, but this was denied her at every turn. What was Arthur hiding? What was it he did not wish her to see? Scanning the surrounding landscape from this lofty vantage point, Morgen found a vast expanse of open field that led almost absent-mindedly to an ominous forest, ancient and seemingly untouched by the hand of man. Morgen's heart beat a little faster. Oh, how she wished to lose herself within this virgin woodlands, cast aside all thought of treaties and men until she was no longer Britannia's princess, but a dryad, born of leaf, acorn, and barky embrace. Bedivere would not understand this, however, so she said, "Where is this amphitheater I hear talk of day and night? Do the Companions really train there for battle? Is it really so vast as to encompass such exercises?"

Slowly Bedivere pulled Morgen down from the unstable perch and offered her shelter in his strong, steady arms until they reached the sun-baked deerskin hide, where he gently deposited her. "You cannot see the amphitheater from the courtyard. If, after breaking your fast, you still wish to view it, I will happily escort you there."

Morgen nodded her assent and then took a bite of crisp apple. Relishing the sweet taste that reminded her of wildflower infused with honey, she mused that the diversion had proved exceptionally short-lived, a fact blatantly confirmed when Bedivere recommended his barrage of questions. Fixing her gaze on twisted vine, tree trunks so ancient they defied time, and flower petals whose delicacy kept even the most nimble wasp from gaining foothold, she did her best to remain detached. These were questions that could only stem from the male psyche, and naturally they made the velvet hairs on the nape of her neck bristle.

"What is it like to live only with women? Are they catty? Do they slash with their talons if you let your guard down?"

Morgen gave up all pretense of interest in Bedivere's one-sided discourse. The day was hot and muggy, forcing beads of sweat down the delicate planes of her nose. Unfortunately the green gown she wore was far too substantial for this weather, a fact she would have discerned if she had taken time to step out her balcony window before choosing attire. A fine washing was in order this night—if not sooner. Bedivere appeared thoroughly unaffected, his Red Dragon tunic boasting no marked evidence of sweat. He was still waiting, so she answered, "Would you have me give away all secrets at once, Bedivere? Please let me eat this apple in peace."

Bedivere laughed—perhaps a little too vigorously—then took up another line of amusement. As Morgen was not altogether forthcoming with information, he provided the entertainment by offering many interesting—and sometimes sordid—facts of court life. Kay had not missed the mark in calling him a gossip.

"It is such a pity," said the impetuous escort as he settled down beside her, insinuating himself so close that Morgen shivered despite the warmness of the day. "Kay's temper has grown most foul since his wounding at Celidon Woods."

Yes, this was it! This was precisely the information she needed to know. It was vital she not appear too interested, however, or Bedivere might withhold truths necessary to her success. Listening intently Morgen carelessly plucked a lush strawberry from the basket and toyed with it until her pale fingers dripped with the excess. Bedivere countered by staying her hand so he might better press the fragrant berry to her lips. The act was sensuous, if not overly forward, considering Bedivere's rank. Did his amorous nature always get the better or him or was it just his best friend's sister that solicited such flirtatious attentions?

"Go ahead," he whispered, releasing the berry once she had claimed it between her teeth. "It is sweet, like you."

Swallowing the fruit whole, Morgen pulled away, wondering what Arthur would think of this behavior. No doubt he was accustomed to Bedivere's romantic maneuvers. Were all the Companions equally adept at wooing? Did Merlin ever take heed of their expertise? Every move, every word came so naturally to Bedivere. He felt no angst, no uncertainty as to whether this interlude would cost his soul. Here she paused. *Do not be unjust. Merlin already possesses your heart—no need for him to resort to such tactics.*

"Tell me more of Kay," she said, positioning herself on the bench in such a way that Bedivere could not easily take up residence beside her. The ancient pine which supported Morgen's perch lulled her into a sense of calm with its enormous trunk, flaky bark, and low-hanging needles that tickled the crown of her head. It was safe here and comfortable.

"You will make me jealous with so much talk of him," Bedivere sighed, collapsing fully against the tawny grass in assumed rejection. The deterrent had been duly noted. When no reply came, he continued in a nonplused manner, "Lot nearly broke his back; that is why he cannot walk straight. And the scar—that is a gift left behind by your intended."

"Urien?" Morgen interjected, aware that a full account of the vision she had experienced in Avalon's frigid waters was about to be laid bare before her. Sitting forward she felt the bench anchor her against its woody restraint. "I thought you battled the Saxons at Celidon Woods," she prompted, setting the bait in place.

Bedivere sat up, aware that he at last held her attention. "We did, but not before Lot and Urien had their say."

"It's a wonder you were not destroyed—with foes attacking from every side."

"If not for Arthur's military skill and Merlin's magical intervention, it might have been a massacre. The two of them are a wonder to behold on the battlefield. Thankfully the casualties were minimal. Kay was one of the exceptions. When all was said and done, he nearly gave his life for Arthur that day."

Bedivere stood, drawing quite near so he might whisper, "It will be difficult to find him a wife, with that scar. What a sad plight for a man."

This said, he wiggled in beside Morgen, conscious that the brief span of a hilt separated him from her soft, ripe lips. Bedivere narrowed the distance intent on stealing a kiss, but it was not to be. Indeed, a far from subtle clearing of the throat made both individuals start, then quickly part as they sought its well-timed source.

"Bedivere, the king awaits you at the amphitheater," declared a melodious-voiced Companion, who advanced rapidly through the bronzed gate. Thick layers of shade camouflaged his aspect, making recognition impossible until his stride brought him full into the sunlight, revealing a medium build, curling, chestnut mane, and luminous eyes that instantly identified him as the warrior bard, Accolon. Arthur had spoken much of Accolon's musical gifts and, suddenly, Morgen longed to hear them.

"Your announcement is ill timed, Accolon," Bedivere exclaimed, leaping to his feet so he might dust off any last hint of grass that clung to his crimson and gold tunic. Eyes cast down, it was clear that he also fought against embarrassment that colored his dark expression. Perhaps the forward behavior that he exhibited was not typical after all.

Accolon, on the other hand, appeared delighted with his timely interference. The grin that stole across his face was lively, animated, far more so than he had demonstrated that morning. "I think only of the princess," he beamed, offering Morgen a slight bow. "Anything to spare her undue discomfort."

Bedivere whirled around, seething. "You will answer for that," he spat, tapping his sword. Two steps brought him a simple blade length from Accolon, who echoed the gesture. Suddenly they were circling each other, eyes narrowed, a lethal dance that dismissed the fact their matching red and gold uniforms clearly proclaimed them brothers bound in service to Arthur.

Everything happened so fast that Morgen momentarily thought she was dreaming. Reality pressed its clarifying fingers against her brow, however, and she leapt up, determined to stop the folly before it drew first blood. "It was meant in jest, Bedivere," she soothed, stepping between the two Companions, an action which brought both individuals to an abrupt halt. "In any case I am hardly worth such a price."

Both Accolon and Bedivere fixed Morgen with a look that refuted any such claim, then fell back to contemplating each other, fingers caressing their sheathed swords.

"I thought all the Companions were supposed to be friends," she intervened, placing her soft fingers against Bedivere's flexed arm.

The effect was immediate. Bedivere turned from his opponent, smiled appreciatively at Morgen, then bowed, relaxing his guard. "You must understand, princess, that it is rare to have a beauty among us. I imagine you will see most of us acting the fool in your presence. I do hope you will forgive our folly."

Morgen offered her hand, relaxing ever so slightly when Bedivere responded by pressing it to his lips. "It is already forgotten."

Bowing again Bedivere quickly pivoted on heal, already bent on gaining Arthur's side. He did not glance back or bother to contemplate what would happen during his absence, for it was already beyond his control.

Aware that the departing Bedivere had just disappeared beyond the bronzed gate, Morgen smiled once more. It was clear that Accolon had no intention of leaving just yet. Indeed, he had planted himself square upon the thick turf like some fledgling tree, not altogether comfortable with its position. "I hear that you are a bard," she gently began, noting his uncertainty. "One day I will ask you to sing for me."

A jagged sigh escaped Accolon's lips. His handsome countenance blazed red, but he quickly mastered it. The princess had found the one topic that always rendered him eloquent. "It would be an honor," he replied, pausing as if ready to say more. *Perhaps we may share a song together.* The words fairly swirled around his brain. Unfortunately, as fate would have it, Accolon found he could not give them full voice, so he smiled nervously, bowed low, then set off after Bedivere.

A peal of laughter unexpectedly escaped Morgen's lips. Men were beyond all comprehension. Would Accolon and Bedivere really have come to blows over her affections? By the gods, what good could ever come of that? They were fighters that thought of little else. That was all. Thankfully women used softer, more enchanting methods when it came to dealing with matters of the heart.

Assuming that the wayward enchanter was still otherwise occupied, Morgen's thoughts revisited Kay. Strolling around the courtyard, she noticed a great variety of late spring flowers in full bloom: honeysuckle, snap dragons, and some curling vine that reminded her of sweet pea, yet without its heady fragrance. These spoke to her soul, prompting it toward apt contemplation of the ill-fated, rust-haired giant. His look, his manner was that of an unkempt ogre, or so Morgen imagined, for she had never seen a rendering of this mystical beast before. No doubt the assessment was faulty, if not unjust. Kay had not wished this calamity upon himself. What must it be like to exist in a constant state of anger, raging at the unjust hand fate dealt his humbled soul? Could one live well in the shadow of a foster-brother turned king? What of the knowledge that you nearly gave your life to save this man? How could you interact with him on a daily basis, viewing his strength, his physical perfection, while you lingered in the darkness like a festering wound?

Suddenly Merlin stood before her, an expression of great warmth coloring his features.

"It is good of you to consider helping Kay," he said, drawing her hand within his own. "Unfortunately you will find it somewhat difficult to gain his trust. Believe me, I have tried. Kay's physical wounds are nothing to those which still bleed inside."

"I will do what I can."

"Good."

Mage and fay fell silent. Eyes met and lips parted, though each maintained a safe distance. The air grew heavy with the scent of jasmine and wisteria, lover's magic as it were, for no such plants inhabited Caerleon's courtyard. The scent was heady and enticing, capable of leading them down paths previously unexplored. Perhaps that is why Merlin deftly broke the spell.

"Are you ready?"

A giggle escaped Morgen's lips. "That depends on what you have in mind."

Merlin colored and then involuntarily took two steps backward. "I think it best if we put last night behind us," he said, almost dismissively.

The fountain claimed his attention, for his hand sought the bubbling water that cooled its steaming basin. Well past its zenith, the afternoon sun only increased its splendiferous heat. Plunging his hand down into the shallow excess, Merlin fixed his gaze on some object seemingly lost in its glittering embrace. Or was it that the mage simply wished to avoid the conversation altogether?

Morgen knew the latter was true, although she did not understand why. Locked in contemplation of her lover's words, she haphazardly brushed away stray water droplets that adorned his ebony-feathered robes. The fountain had perhaps too zealously done its work. Soft winds whispered their approval even as the tree limbs overhead shivered and moaned. A cool, blue light slowly encompassed Merlin's form, altering it with an almost iridescent splendor. Where this light originated Morgen had not time to contemplate, for a shadow of antlers sprung full upon his crown, godhead of Cernunnos himself. Morgen was transported back to her first meeting with Merlin—when he had similarly altered into the Underworld god. Who was this man who stood so silent before her? Surely this was not Merlin but some deity of old. Was this the reason he did not wish to bind himself to her? Gods rarely chose mortal women to be their loves, but then Morgen was not a true mortal…

Merlin gently took Morgen's hand and placed it against his chest so she might feel the rapid beating of his heart. Light danced around his tall, slim form, nearly blinding Morgen with its fiery brilliance until all traces of the sacred horns were burned away.

"I am but a man, Morgen. Never forget that. I possess the same feelings that every man carries inside. Believe me when I say that there is reason to pause."

Here it was again! The same hesitation, the same denial of Merlin's feelings, brought forth to sever any love between them. The arch mage simply did not trust her.

"It is not as you believe," he whispered, forcing himself to remain calm. "We must know each other's souls before any intimate relationship should be contemplated. We do not yet comprehend certain things about each other that might..."

"Why not speak the truth, Merlin? You do not trust me!"

"If only it were that simple. The truth is much darker I fear. *I am not free,* Morgen."

CHAPTER 16:

Curses and Enchantments

"Not free?"

A cricket steadily chirruped its welcome, oblivious to the sorrow that filled Morgen's breast. Stirring from its midday stupor, the courtyard yawned, offering up a heated symphony of bird, rodent, and insect song. This intrusion of sound appeared no less irritating than the buzz of a striped bee that methodically moved from sweet pea to honeysuckle, forever bent on its work. Morgen observed all this as she contemplated Merlin's words. Not free? What precisely did he mean by that?

"Your heart belongs to another?" she whispered, not quite meeting his gaze.

Merlin closed his eyes to blot out her pained expression. "No. My heart is yours. The difficulty lies in the fact that I am not free to give it."

"I do not understand," she said, simply taking Merlin's hand, so calm, so steady that it belied the midsummer heat.

"Think, Morgen, think. You know the answer."

The bee, tired of such shallow expression, landed on Morgen's fair arm and stung her with firm intent. "Wake up!" it fairly cried, then without so much as another breath, curled up and fell to the ground.

"A sting that claims one's life," she whispered, stooping to secure the tiny guide between her fingers. Softly she drew forward and tucked its furry shell into a fragile nook of the twisted oak, a final resting place. She paused to help the dear soul cross the threshold, then turned her eyes once more on Merlin. "The curse—you speak of Morgause's curse. Surely an enchanter of your talents and the fairy who loves you can thwart any curse of Morgause's creation."

With one swift motion, Merlin fairly swooped to her side, his black robes curling around them as smoke, claiming its intimacy with flame. Clasping her hands tightly within his own, he continued, "Do you really wish to take that risk? I think not of myself but of you, Morgen. Do you realize that if we fail you will become the means of my destruction? The curse states that the woman I love most will have no choice but to…"

"Lock you within a cave and leave you for dead. Yes, I know. I must one day ask Morgause how she dreamed up such a hauntingly romantic curse." Here Morgen pressed Merlin's dusky face between her hands and pulled it low so she could kiss each eyelid separately, an act so soft, so seductive that Merlin did not bother to hide the shiver that traveled the length of his spine. "Now, Merlin, I must ask you a question," she continued, maintaining the embrace. "Do you really think anything lodged within this world or the next could tempt me to destroy you? I would kill myself first. Surely you know that."

Merlin straightened, setting her hands free. "That is precisely my point, Morgen. I know *it would kill you* to be involved in my undoing. Why should we sacrifice ourselves for Morgause's gain?"

"The true sacrifice would be for us not to love each other. I believe that is what she intended. United we are formidable, indeed."

Merlin's hand carefully sought Morgen's enflamed forearm and cooled the bee's work with a gentle touch. This done, he softly drew her into his arms, resting his lips against her ivory forehead. The courtyard grew preternaturally quiet, bereft of twitter, croak, or hum, apparently enthralled by their plight.

"We will see," he whispered into her silken hair. "Time will tell."

They remained blissfully entwined, listening to the hypnotic rhythms of each other's heart before the mage gathered strength and spoke again.

"I have promised to teach you shapeshifting. Come, we must make haste," he exclaimed, casting a wary glance at the late afternoon sky. "Arthur will expect us back before dark-fall."

Without further ado Merlin quickly set out through the gate, staff in hand, ebony robes billowing behind him. He did not wait for Morgen or even pause to see if she followed, but kept both eyes fixed on the afternoon horizon.

Hoisting her heavy skirts, Morgen was fast upon his heels. The pace Merlin set was strenuous; he was seemingly unconcerned with the fact that she wore a restrictive gown. Still, she trod up and down the hill-laden fields, navigating sun-baked weeds that poked and prodded her shallow slippers and shadowing Merlin's every move—agile, spirited and utterly fay. This was, after all, the West Country, renowned for its rolling terrain. If nothing else the fast-paced jaunt gave her an opportunity to explore her surroundings—away from Arthur and his endless array of well-meaning guards. Waves of deep green sleeves and skirts swirled around her nimble form, whispering melodies of forgotten lore. They were drawing near the forest—lush, ancient, and most inviting.

Soon, Morgen thought, *soon I will be home.*

Merlin turned and offered her an appreciative nod.

Unable to stay her enthusiasm, Morgen raced past him. How many years had passed since she last enjoyed the forgotten wonders of forest splendor? Seemingly a lifetime. Not once during her royal upbringing had she been allowed this extravagance, and certainly not in Sister Agatha's anal keep. Avalon possessed an apple orchard, ancient and utterly magical in its conception, but Morgen never had the opportunity to explore beyond the lake's subtle boundaries. Longing pierced her breastbone, calling her forward until she passed

Merlin, so swift in his progress, and sped head-first into woodland bliss. Bursting through the deliciously leafy threshold, she allowed its majesty to swallow her. Sylvan green colored her senses, heightening them to a fine point that made her one with the thick, noble trunks, boasting masses of heavily laden boughs that swayed high overhead. She had been correct in her earlier assessment: Caerleon's forest possessed a virginal quality, as if it were entirely untouched by man. Scores of knowing ash, oak, and thorn opened before her, offering welcome. Softly they whispered of daylight and passion as a forgotten melody poured from her lips. She was home at last!

Understanding softened Merlin's expression, as he too entered the leafy abode. Morgen was, after all, a dryad—he had known that all along—a dryad once clothed in moss and roses who offered a poor, witless enchanter love. Unlike the sylphs of the air or the undines of the sea, Morgen was most connected to tree, leaf, and acorn—those very aspects of nature which enthralled his own senses. This too was Merlin's private world, a world that strengthened him in times of trouble. Here he would determine whether they should move forward as one or forever sever the ties which bound them, the very thought of which left him bewildered. Indeed, Morgen's song was hauntingly beautiful, stirring memories of days gone by, so beautiful that Merlin necessarily sat down upon a decaying log to center himself. The melody was familiar, one that had haunted his thoughts on the eve of their first meeting, one that the moss-clad fairy had sung to his youthfully careless, disheveled self night after night. Here she was, newborn and ready to love him even after he had banished her from his presence so long ago. Oh, what an exquisite picture she painted, dancing enchantingly from tree to tree!

A sweet, fragile hare peered out of a jagged opening in the log's shell and fixed its moss-brown eyes upon Merlin. Wriggling her pink nose, she gathered his scent. A decision was made in that moment, and so she joined him, approaching with measured gait, softly, carefully. The mage smiled. His lips whispered her sacred name so quietly that none save herself could hear. Without further ado she nestled against his arm, offering a measure of trust even before he earned it.

"I have much to learn from you, little one," he sighed, stroking her mottled brown fur.

The hare cooed and snuggled closer, perfectly content to be the object of his affection. Together they watched the lovely maiden awaken trees from their deep slumber, a graceful dance that carried them beyond thought or discernment but was one with all things great and small.

Leaves rustled and shimmered as Morgen wove her way in and out of their lowered boughs, stirring tender leaves with a quiet touch. How cathartic it was to embrace each beauty that met her eye. Softly she blew warm air against trunk, branch, and root system, awakening the ancient guardians who shivered and swayed their great bulk so they might bow before their goddess divine. The act was ethereal, otherworldly, filling Morgen's heart with such love that she could have expired at that moment and wished for no more. Reality, however, has an ever practical way of interrupting such notions and thereby found the perfect means to call Morgen from her dreamspell.

Merlin's haunted gaze was the agent, a gaze that spoke everything he kept hidden behind layers of self-imposed restraint. The fact that he was embracing a hare made little difference. Indeed, his eyes blazed with such intense passion that a shudder animated Morgen's spine. Yet this was not the most astounding sight that claimed her attention. Just behind Merlin stood a tall, breathtakingly beautiful maiden with long, golden hair that fell well past her knees. She was dressed in a soft white gown that billowed behind her, accentuating every curve of her sensuous frame. Merlin remained oblivious to the maiden's presence until she wrapped her fair arms around his neck. He appeared surprised but accepted the kiss she bestowed upon him, and another, followed by an endless string of endearments strung together in one great play of seduction. The action reminded Morgen of a spider capturing its beloved prey within a silken web. She tried to call out a warning, but no sound issued from her lips. A cave loomed wide before them—one that threatened to swallow Merlin whole. Surely he saw it! Why did he not move to save himself? Why did he cling to the enchantress as if she were his life's breath and being? Passion bound them lip to lip, draining Merlin's sanity, if not his powers, leaving him ancient, bent, and frail, his hair white as newly fallen snow. A scream lodged in Morgen's throat as she raced forward. Only she possessed the power to save him. Only she claimed the ability to call him back from his living tomb. It made little difference that the dark-haired Merlin, still untouched by spell or enchantment, captured her in his arms, arms that were free of any enchantress save herself. It made no impression whatsoever that he, the arch mage, whispered time and again that all would be well.

Morgen saw nothing beyond the cave's stiff darkness, felt nothing beyond Merlin's lips as they caressed her aching temple. Something was wrong, something that lay just beneath the surface of expression. They were in the forest. Twilight had already come and gone, ushering up a pregnant moon. What was it? What could she not yet see?

A sharp cry pierced the night with its prophetic warning, "Nimue!"

"Merlin, you must never return to the cave! Not unless I am with you!"

The arch mage froze rooted to the ground, fully cognizant that Morgen had seen his future demise. He tried to speak, but her desperation blotted everything from mind.

"A woman with long golden hair will lure you there under the pretense of love, and then when you have all but achieved your passion, she will cast you into oblivion where I cannot save you. We will be separated throughout the course of time."

Startled by this insight, Merlin questioned how Morgen had seen his assassin, a feat he had never achieved of his own volition no matter how hard he tried. Renewed purpose drove him forward,

and he placed his fingers squarely upon her trembling shoulders as if he could shake the particulars
out of her, but she fell limp in his arms and knew
no more.

CHAPTER 17

Forgotten

Merlin, the cave! Do not enter the cave!
Morgen awoke with a start, heart pounding, beads of sweat pouring down her fair cheeks. A perfect sea of deerskin coverlets flew in every direction as she leapt from bed. Where was she? Why did Merlin not answer? Surely he would not leave her side at such a critical moment, unless…unless it was already too late.

Glancing down at the newly hewn rush clippings that tickled her anxious toes, Morgen gained some sense of her surroundings. Amber tapestries of elves and woodcocks camouflaged the otherwise threadbare walls before her—honey-colored stone walls that boasted cracks that even this fine veneer did not hide. The huge bed and the watermarked ceiling all spoke volumes. This was not the forest—no, not even Amesbury Abbey, but Caerleon, home of the High King and his Companions. How was it she had come to be housed within this aging prison once more? Where was Merlin? Why had he left her side? Surely he knew, surely he *understood* some part of the vision and sensed the urgency behind it. Surely he wished to question her about its content. Surely...

Merlin, where are you? Why would you abandon me at such a critical time? Is it possible that you are advising Arthur while I linger in despair?

The promise of love so potent in its twilight exchange slowly dissipated with the dull morning light. Yes, Merlin was advising Arthur. Morgen felt it intuitively in her bones. How characteristic of him to place courtly matters above love—how characteristic and utterly self-serving. When the country and its people superseded his own passions, he need not think of love or even acknowledge its existence.

Morgen paused, remembering her own part in the country's salvation. Love and its acquisition had eradicated all thought of peace from her mind with surprisingly remarkable ease. Here lay the difference between herself and Merlin. Was she negligent in placing her own needs before that of Britannia? Did she not deserve to be happy, fulfilled? Was that asking too much? *Yes!* her inner voice prompted time and again. Her divine purpose, her very reason for being, began and ended with the High King—a king destined to unite Britannia under one flag, one rule. Certainly Merlin was a part of this great work, but Morgen's relationship with the famed enchanter ended there. The love they shared was allowed but not encouraged. The sisters had kindly accepted Merlin as an end to some unfathomable means of which she knew nothing.

Stepping briefly out onto an all but sodden balcony, Morgen allowed the steady flow of rain to wash away her unspent tears. Muted grays enveloped the once green landscape, her sylvan woodlands, her shimmering river all bedecked in somber hues that blended as the many colors in a charcoal relief, rendering each distinction mute. A moderate tempest had descended upon Caerleon, which meant Arthur and his troops would remain inside throughout the course of the day—a fact that little soothed Morgen's darkening humor.

Aware that she must take some sustenance, the bewildered princess slipped back inside, dried off the excess raindrops with a roll of deerskin, showering liberal attention on her overly exuberant hair. Water is often the enemy to wavy locks, and Morgen's unruly mane proved no exception. When the fine bone comb Arthur had newly bestowed upon her displayed several broken teeth, Morgen cast it aside and began training the waves around her fingers. This enterprise took some time, and Morgen found herself growing calmer with every twist of her auburn locks. Finally by midday she felt centered enough to leave her sallow chambers behind.

The whole of Caerleon proved alive with activity, jammed beyond proprietary limits with Companions, knights, and foot soldiers thoroughly lost in games they seldom had time to appreciate or the simple exchange of tales. They lounged about, draping their battle-honed bodies across bench, chair, and table. Everywhere Morgen went it was the same. Seldom, if ever, did these men get the chance to simply relax. Britannia was far too combustible a commodity to allow such excess. They praised the rain, embraced it, did everything they could to celebrate its timely appearance.

Drawing near the kitchens, Morgen found herself face to face with her former escorts Dagonet and Bors, who had just emerged dripping wet from the chambers that housed the old Roman baths, fully robed with large towels that offered some modesty but not enough for Morgen's peace of mind. Although pleased to see them, she could not help but blush, which set their renowned horseplay into action. They winked at Morgen with such enthusiasm that she knew a jest would soon follow, so she swiftly turned the corner, blotting out their amused expressions. On and on she trod diligently, greeting each man who crossed her path.

Finally, upon reaching the kitchens, she found the smoky entrance door closed, shut tight against intrusion. This did not stall Morgen's advance, for her hunger was great, and soon she was in possession of apples, marbled cheese, and dark bread. She marveled at how efficiently the kitchen staff ran, even without Kay's overbearing influence, fully absorbed in preparations for the evening meal, though that was hours away. Every metal pot, every wooden plate shone clean, neatly stacked, fully prepped for the next feeding. The scent that wafted from the stone pit proved intoxicating, though Morgen little cared for meat. She breathed in its heady aroma and remembered those youthful days spent at Uther's court, a black fortress upon which fortune smiled for a time. Here the stone walls possessed a red hue that reminded her of some masonry concoction that she witnessed in the Amesbury kitchens. A shudder raced up her spine. Did the red stem from sacrificed animals that shed their blood for human consumption? Nausea animated her stomach, drove her out of that bloody pyre until she stood once more ensconced in the smoky mead hall. Aware that one too many eyes watched her hand still the incessant churning of her stomach, she began to fear what conclusions they might draw, so she made off with her simple gains and quickly sought refuge within her chambers once more.

Time marched forward, painting heavy shadows against her amber tapestries so that the elves slowly stretched their limbs as if waking from a long sleep. Nightfall was rapidly approaching. It hardly seemed possible that an entire day has passed without any word from Merlin. If he was trying to avoid her, then he was succeeding most admirably! When the enforced solitude became intolerable, Morgen set out yet again, this time with a steady heart. It came as no surprise that Merlin was locked inside the advisement chamber with Arthur. The fact that the irritatingly charming Bedivere denied her entrance, however, proved more than a little disconcerting. Naturally Morgen sent in a verbal protest. The only response she received was an invitation to dine later that evening in the king's chambers. Was Arthur displeased that she and Merlin had failed to return before nightfall? Suddenly Morgen felt certain that it was Arthur himself behind these separation tactics. If this were indeed true, then the uncooperative weather had made it very convenient for him.

When dusk departed without summons of any kind, Morgen sent a request for instructions. A message came back via Accolon that Arthur was still debating some particularly sticky points on the proposed treaty and that she should not wait. Thankfully Accolon's presence meant that Morgen need not dine alone. He was sensitive, compassionate, and pleasant to admire in an otherworldly way that made her feel so at home. If nothing else, he offered pleasant, articulate conversation. Why, his enamored sighs alone bolstered her tender ego. And then there was his glorious voice.

Remembering Arthur's boast that Accolon's singing ability rivaled that of the gods, Morgen requested a song. Little did she dream that the inspired bard possessed a gift that would lift her out of the dark mead hall and carry her far beyond consciousness, thought, or active dreaming to a higher plane that few ever attained; or that he was, indeed, more than he appeared: a handsome, but singularly humble knight.

Well pleased and proud that Morgen longed to hear him, Accolon pulled a dusty lap harp from its anchored spot high upon the darkened stone wall and drew close, so close that they almost touched. What followed next sent a hush throughout the packed hall. Knights, foot soldiers, kitchen staff all turned from their occupations and fixed their attention on Accolon, breathless, certain of what would follow. They knew his prowess, applauded his fortitude in performing for the princess, and took a collective sigh as the bardic knight set fingertips to harp strings and allowed his voice to flood the smoky, cavernous chamber with the purest, most heavenly sound.

At first Morgen could not quite hear the words, so glorious was the vehicle through which they flowed. A golden voice it was, one that sent thrills up and down her spine. Casting a quick glance around the hall, she saw that everyone else was equally spellbound. Not a breath, not a hush altered the perfect symphony or overwhelmed its hypnotic power. Tears filled Morgen's eyes, although she could not be sure why. Never before had she been so affected by a human voice. Accolon's exquisite tenor spilled through the dusty hall, crystalline like the midwinter breeze, utterly pure in its passion. This *was* a gift of the gods, one that few mortals could ever attain. Why, then, did Accolon waste his time carrying a sword? Surely there was more to this gifted Companion than met the eye.

"I regret I have but little time to spend with you this evening," Accolon apologized after finishing his solo to a thunderous pounding and thumping of goblets against wooden tables, dusty floor, and rocky walls. "They are expecting me on watch."

A length of shadow pooled at Accolon's feet, spilling fast up the stone wall, gathering shape and substance, a shadow that bore his height, bone structure, and physicality, and for a single moment, it appeared that a form stood directly behind him, willing speech. Morgen started at the words that flooded her consciousness, words not of Accolon's making, words that originated from the mysterious shade.

"We have known each other from the very beginnings of time. Trust me, call me forward, and you will remember why."

Morgen was on her feet. The dreamy-eyed knight had an element of prophecy about him. And now it appeared a shadow self, perhaps a past life entity, stood waiting to be heard.

"Who are you, Accolon? Tell me what you know."

A myriad of eyes were upon them, watching the exchange between bard and princess with rapt attention. The heartless knights were wagering for or against their trembling companion, little aware of his discomfort.

Accolon took a deep breath and spoke the first words that came to mind, aware that they made little sense. "You are my destiny. Nothing more. Nothing less." His lips softly caressed her hand, glad for the distraction when she did not offer a response.

At this rather delicate moment, Kay appeared, spouting orders. Several of his men were haphazardly ridding the much-abused dining hall of its abundant refuse even as they witnessed the drama unfolding. Aware of their distraction, Kay quickly unearthed its source. A good tongue-lashing followed, punctuated with snorts of disgust. This accomplished, Kay dragged his wounded carcass through the cluttered hall, out the far doorway until he disappeared down a set of stairs that evidently led to the dungeons below.

Aware that any magic the moment held was now broken and that all eyes were still fixed upon him, Accolon laughed uneasily. "I see our good seneschal finds *you* as despicable as the rest of us."

A chorus of laughter filled the smoky air, reaffirming the fact that they were not alone and that every move, every word exchanged was open to inspection.

Morgen colored and then cleared her throat in an attempt to regain some dignity. "Forgive me, Accolon. We both have work to do."

Without another word Morgen broke from Accolon and set off in pursuit of Kay. She heard Accolon call after her but did not acknowledge his plea. It was vital she take some measure to still the violent beating of her heart, an act best accomplished in service to another. Thus she followed Arthur's seneschal into the very bowels of Caerleon, a haunted, web-filled pit that boasted minimal illumination.

Kay was somewhat shocked to find Morgen standing among the aging mead barrels, cobwebs clinging to her azure gown. "What are you doing here?" he bellowed. "Arthur will hardly approve of your fine gown being mussed in such a place as this."

The cellars were indeed filthy, infested with a thick network of spider webs, mold, and chilled dampness that perfectly accentuated the dirt floor long since turned to muck.

"The gown is unimportant," she said, carelessly allowing the bright blue hemline a thorough mud bath. "I have longed to speak with you."

"What could you possibly have to discuss with me?" he spat through cleft teeth.

Morgen raised her hands so that they were parallel with his shattered frame. "Life has dealt you a harsh blow, Kay. I will set that aright."

Muttering a heartfelt prayer for assistance, Morgen instantly felt the flow of energy spill through her outturned palms. Distant healings were not much different from those of the hands-on variety; they merely required a greater focus. And so she gave the task additional impetus, mentally directing the unseen energies toward Kay. Off they sped, heedless of distance or impediment. The fact that Kay turned his back on Morgen only made her laugh. He could not hide from destiny no matter how hard he tried.

Kay started, keenly aware that waves of intense heat were penetrating his frame. Up and down his deadened spine they ran, a prickling pain coloring his senses. "What the blazes are you doing? What makes you think that a scrawny, pampered bitch can succeed where Arthur's physicians had failed?

No matter how insulting, how callous Kay's remarks became, Morgen continued her sacred work, a sweet smile painted upon her unblemished countenance. Kay snorted. Some people have all the luck, or perhaps it was simply that Morgen, like her brother, was born under a blessed star. In any case Kay had to do something that would shock her, something that would make her flee his presence. Nothing, however, came to mind, short of treasonous acts. What would it take to make her stop? What insult had he not already utilized that would send her packing? Oh, yes, he knew that he should not be so cruel to Arthur's sister, especially when she wished to help him, but why did she not heed reason?

Kay paused in mid-thought, his harsh eyes softening quite noticeably. The pain throbbed, then ceased its expression just as quickly as it began. What was happening? All along his spine little tongues of heat ran to and fro. Indeed, his back, an area that had been nearly dead to sensation for months, felt exquisitely warm and tingling. What if it were possible? What if Morgen did possess the ability to restore his body?

Turning toward her so that he could voice that very question, he was startled to find that Morgen was inching closer. That intelligence made Kay's blood curdle. Why did she have to press her luck? Some rules should never be tested. This was one of them. Distance was a necessity of Kay's own invention—one never to be compromised.

"It would help, Kay, if you allowed me to touch your spine," Morgen suggested, oblivious to his inner turmoil.

"No!" he cried, thoroughly humiliated. It thrilled him with a kind of unspoken terror to imagine the touch of her hand upon his person. Morgen was a princess, a goddess in human form, never destined to intermingle with an ogre. Why did she not see that? A wall of Kay's own making rose up between them, severing the mystical connection at its core. Without further ado, he slipped behind a large wine barrel and prayed she would not follow.

"It will not hurt," Morgen reassured, gently pursuing his retreat.

Kay repaid this kindness by removing himself even farther from her reach.

"Why do you deny my assistance? Is it because I am a woman?" No answer came so she continued unearthing Kay's hidden fears. "I know I can help, but you must allow me the chance. Why should you be denied what every man desires?"

Kay whirled on her in a frenzy of embarrassment. "What did you say?"

No sooner had the words left her mouth than Morgen regretted them. She tried to ease the already delicate situation by speaking very softly and with great compassion. "I only meant that you have the same right as every man to find a wife, if you so wish."

"Do not mock me!" Kay cried in a strangled voice. His face grew bright red and the scarred countenance trembled with suppressed rage. "Do not taunt my masculinity! Be you princess or no, I will not bear it!" With that Kay lumbered off into the cellar's lightless depths and was gone.

Feeling hopelessly incompetent Morgen set off for her chambers fairly reeling with regret. Slowly, carefully, she made her way back through the mead hall, ignoring the startled looks of Companions who witnessed her emerge from the cellars alone, even as they marveled at the muddied hem of her gown. What did it matter if they thought foul things about her? Kay consumed her thoughts. King and mage had warned her about the probability of a negative reception. Why then had she tried to force the healing touch upon him when it was so apparent that he accepted her assistance from afar?

Morgen paused in mid-thought. She had just reached her chamber door—which stood invitingly ajar. Perhaps Merlin had finally escaped Arthur's clutches!

CHAPTER 18

The Confession

heedless of her own muddied appearance, Morgen rushed across the threshold fully expecting a lover's welcome. Instead she discovered Arthur, High King of Britannia, dozing in her unmade bed. It appeared that the youthful monarch had cast himself down upon the magnificently trussed raised box and fallen asleep while awaiting her return. Morgen crept closer, gazing at him intently. Soft candlelight played upon Arthur's face, highlighting his rugged cheekbones, the thick golden lashes that liberally framed his eyelids, the determined mouth, and the strong forearm just visible from beneath a gap in her deerskin coverlets. Without question Arthur was an incredibly handsome man. Morgen paused, aware that her heart was beating at an alarming rate. Apparently Arthur had that effect on her. The sisters had hinted that they were already husband and wife, but that was Avalon, another plane, another time—such vows did not register in the mortal realm. If she wanted to reclaim that union, that power over the High King, she would have to begin anew—a not altogether unpleasant task. Why, Arthur's looks alone made her dizzy. Was he handsome enough to capture the heart of a maiden already in love with his best friend, handsome enough to tempt a woman thought to be his own sister? A timely blush painted Morgen's cheeks. She would leave that question unanswered—for the present. In any case an ancient romantic connection did exist between them, one that bound them to each other and Britannia. It was vital that she use this bond to foster peace throughout the war-torn land. *Yes, that was the task set forth by the Sisterhood. Do I have the courage to see it done?*

Aware that she was trembling, Morgen drew near a stark, gray-stoned water bowl situated on a small oak stand opposite her bed and began ridding the muck from her azure gown. Try as she might, no amount of blotting relieved the stain; in fact it worsened, leaving a dark band that transformed the heavenly blue material into a garb few commoners would wear. Finally, when her physical labors fell short, she hailed magic to great success. Positioning her hands directly over the muddied hem, she watched the dark residue soften until it was no longer visible. Life force energy never ceased to amaze her with its scope and abilities. Arthur's amused laughter indicated that he too had witnessed the miracle.

"Where have you been?" he questioned, blue eyes asparkle with intrigue. "I know you were not with Merlin as he has spent all day and much of the night in my presence."

Arthur's graceful stretch reminded Morgen of a large cat, indeed a lion, waking from a long, deep sleep. Quietly he glided to her, placing both hands protectively around her waist.

"Perhaps you will tell me later. I am sorry we were not available to dine with you this evening. I had food brought here if you care to sup with me now."

Morgen cast a glance over her shoulder at the series of pitted dishes, silvery goblets, and elegant foodstuffs that adorned a tiny oaken table propped unceremoniously in the center of her chamber. This was a surprise, indeed. Apparently she had been too preoccupied with Arthur's immense presence filling her bed to acknowledge the fine reception he had arranged. Aged, yellowing tapers sputtered and crackled their approval as something of a half smile played across her lips. What kind of game was this? Did the king have any inkling that she too possessed an agenda?

"Forgive me, Arthur, but I have already supped—quite well I might add. I could not force down another morsel no matter how hard I tried."

"You cannot mean to cast me forth after arranging this elaborate meal."

"I will happily share your company, but you must dine alone."

Arthur raised one fair eyebrow but accepted this edict with little else in the way of outward expression. After seating Morgen on a dragon-backed chair she remembered from childhood, Arthur claimed a companion piece of his own. They stared at each other intently, analyzing every nuance, every expression before Morgen broke the silence.

"How are you feeling, Arthur?"

"My back is fully restored if that is what you mean. It is a miracle, a true miracle indeed," he said, clasping a silvery goblet in his hand. He paused and took a draught of wine, or whatever it was the cooking staff had provided him. "Where did you ever learn such a thing? I know you said it was a gift from the fairies, but..."

"Arthur, do you still have difficulty believing that I am fairy born?"

"No," he replied, gazing directly into her blue-green eyes. "That would explain many things." Many things that kept him awake at night. Many things that routinely assaulted his senses each time she drew near.

"Such as?" Morgen carefully prompted.

"Such as why my men are utterly spellbound by you. Fairies always have this effect on men, do they not?"

Morgen paused, considering this question. She had lived many years in Uther's court without drawing any attention. "No doubt your men are overly desperate for feminine companionship," proved her response.

A crimson flush dotted Arthur's brow, which he sought to camouflage by taking another draught from his goblet. By the gods, she was not making this easy. Yes, it was probably true that the Companions needed more feminine contact in their lives. That still did not explain why *he* was so enamored of Morgen. Everything about her dazzled his senses, fine-tuning them to a keen point he had never experienced before. The rich hue of her waving locks, her luminous eyes, the marble sheen of her skin, her delicate constitution all sang to his heart—indeed, filled it with warmth and promise. She was so intelligent, so sensitive and compassionate; he knew she was precisely the woman for him. Yes, he wanted to possess Morgen, to claim her as his own, just as every other petty king who petitioned for her hand. He loved her as deeply and passionately as his steely adviser did, who had never looked upon a woman before except to exchange a simple greeting. He was utterly, hopelessly lost in her presence. Somehow, some way, he must pull himself together and focus on the task before him.

Although his eyes were downcast, Morgen knew that Arthur was admiring her person. Every nerve, every fiber of his being was focused intently upon her to the exclusion of all other things—or at least it appeared this way. Although she was extremely flattered by this attention, it made her cautious. Arthur had forbidden her to read his thoughts, so she could not begin to guess what revolved within his mind. Whenever their eyes met, however, she saw certain indications of what lay hidden within his heart. This was the proper moment to begin her work. Would he listen or fluff off her counsel as before? It was vital that she not be too delicate, that she give him some impetus to move forward. And so the words spilled from Morgen's lips before she had time to properly soften them.

"What of the treaty, Arthur? Have you finally secured peace throughout Britannia? Will history pronounce you the greatest king of all time or will you linger as some forgotten war lord who did his best but never quite managed to secure the one thing we all desire—peace?"

Arthur rose to his feet, a look of displeasure darkening his brow. The candles gasped and sputtered at his agitation, casting the chamber into riddled darkness. This was the High King who glared down upon Morgen, fixing her with his piercing gaze. She had pushed him too far. He was not to be bullied by a princess, no matter how stunningly beautiful she appeared. "I am not the one whose conduct is at issue here, Morgen. Peace *is* my focus—now and forever—but that may only be achieved when this land is free of senseless raiding, murder, and destruction brought on by the Saxons, Jutes, Angles, and Picts. Solve that crisis, Morgen, and I will say no more about last night."

Silence bled across the chamber. Morgen counted the rapid beating of her heart as she stared into Arthur's eyes, which suddenly possessed a ferocity that she had never witnessed before. Arthur was not ready for ethereal notions of peace. Indeed, he needed hard, concrete measures that he could see, touch, smell, and feel. He wanted a full explanation as to why she had ignored his request to make good her return before darkfall, wanted to understand why Merlin had carried her back limp and unresponsive? That is why the arch mage was so noticeably absent. No doubt he had already questioned his counselor, and now he would weigh her answers against those Merlin had previously supplied.

The chamber, the honey-colored walls appeared to be shrinking in upon them, forcing them closer and closer, two combatants unable to escape the other's magnetism.

"I will resolve it," she demurred, breathless, hopeful, "if only you give me time. That is why I have taken human form. I am here to restore peace, love, and healing to Britannia. But first you wish to question me about last night."

Arthur raised his eyebrows, weighing which move should follow. He had not expected her to be so direct. Since no food had been touched by either of them, he sought to right the situation. "Bread?" he questioned, offering her a thick slice from his own wooden plate.

"No thank you," she said, indicating that he should proceed.

Arthur fell back into his chair and began toying with his uneaten supper. Here it was, the moment of truth. Suddenly the roasted duck and the potato, pea, and carrot concoction that Kay's kitchen staff had so aptly provided appeared altogether unappealing. His stomach was churning, twisting into an inconvenient knot. He must analyze Morgen's responses, just as he had done with Merlin. "There is no easy way to ask this," he began half-heartedly. Throwing the bread back down so that it rocked back and forth amid his stewed vegetables, he took her hand. "Forgive me if I seem indelicate, but I must know. What have Merlin's intentions been toward you?"

Morgen swallowed her pride, aware that he was watching her intently. How should she respond? The look with which he fixed her already indicated that she had been tried and found guilty of thwarting the High King's rule. She was a princess bride stationed precariously upon the auction block for the highest bidder, namely Urien. Suddenly she was spending her evenings with Merlin, his very own advisor. Surely that did not please him. Was it possible to shift his focus, draw him toward ideas of peace instead of this insipid questioning?

"No need to be embarrassed," he continued, scooping up her cool hand so that it fit neatly within the palm of his own, rendering escape or deception impossible. "I know he is in love with you."

Oh, yes, Arthur possessed keen eyes and a startlingly sharp intuition that served him well. Why then did he even bother to go through this inquisition? It was obvious that he had already made his decision. Again she felt drawn toward him, past all boundaries of judgment or decorum; his magnetism was that strong.

"I have known Merlin since I was a child," he continued, unblinking. "The change in him is thoroughly evident to me, if no one else."

Now, after so much speculation, Arthur would know the truth. Merlin's answers had been inconclusive. Indeed, Arthur felt certain his counselor was withholding some vital information. Morgen's glorious sea-green eyes would tell all.

"Has he claimed your treasure?"

Morgen stood then and tried to pull away, but Arthur held her fast, claiming the other hand as he too rose to his feet. Slowly, deliberately, he drew her closer so that they met half way across the table. Escape was not possible. Arthur's eyes bore into her with such intensity that she found it hard to breathe. Trembling animated her limbs, revealing a weakness she had never shown to any man. There was no help for it now. He would find her guilty.

This is what it means to be completely at Arthur's mercy, his puppet. Why then am I so affected by him? How can he so easily wrap my spirit around his finger? Bid me divulge my innermost longings? No man has ever claimed such power over me. Aware that Arthur was awaiting her answer, she turned to those who knew her best.

Sisters, help me. I know not what to do.
Speak the truth. That is the only option.

"I love him," proved the best response that Morgen could utter under so fierce an analysis.

Arthur swallowed involuntarily and closed his eyes for the briefest instant. *Why do I put myself through this? There is no hope. She loves Merlin, not me. Come now, be a king. You can and will conquer this. Look her square in the eye and continue.*

"Yes, I gathered as much. Please answer my question."

A little more than a hair's breadth separated king and princess. Indeed, if circumstances had proved different, they might have kissed. Arthur seemed overly conscious of the fact so he increased the pressure on her hands.

"Answer the question, Morgen. Did Merlin make love to you last night?"

The color drained from Morgen's face. Here lay the heart of the matter, the truth behind the High King's fears. *He wants me pure, unspoiled, and free. Well, last night's encounter was totally blameless.* "We kissed. That is all. I swear it."

Arthur relaxed his grip slightly as a bead of sweat trickled down his brow. "Then he has respected your honor."

"Of course he has!" Morgen cried, finally pulling free. Would Merlin have been punished, perhaps tortured, if they *had* made love? "This is Merlin we are speaking of—your counselor, your friend!"

Arthur drew back as if he had been slapped full across the face. Well, Morgen certainly knew how to twist the blade deep into the wound. "What I am supposed to think, Morgen? When he carried you into this fortress after dark, you lay as one dead. Did he enchant you, cast some kind of spell on you?"

By the Ancient Ones, was this the real Arthur? After all the carefree letters they had exchanged where he appeared to understand Morgen so well, Arthur's true character flooded her senses, left her dizzy, reeling. He cared nothing for Merlin or herself, only his own honor. Morgen's voice grew terse. "No, I had experienced a vision, Arthur. Surely Merlin told you that."

"Merlin told me many things—things that jumble in my mind. I no longer feel I know him. And, if truth be told, I know you even less." The words were cutting, cruel; but if truth be told, they lessened his grief, lent him impetus to continue. "You will deny Merlin's advances until he has made a marriage proposal."

Morgen involuntarily took several steps back. Everything was going horribly wrong. The plans she fostered for freedom were suddenly all but a forgotten memory. This was Arthur Pendragon, High King of Britannia, who questioned her, not some careless boy with whom she once exchanged missives. At last Morgen understood why Merlin, why the people of Britannia and even her own Sisterhood revered Arthur more than any other king who had ever ruled battle-torn Britannia. Arthur possessed the true essence of command. Power ran effortlessly through his veins. He did not have to anguish over problems or solutions, for the answers were already a part of his being. People easily surrendered secrets simply by looking into his eyes. How else had Arthur managed to shift the focus of their meeting? Morgen wanted only to speak of peace, he of her virtue. The question remained—why? What was it he chose not to tell her? There was one way to find out. *He desires me. That much is certain. His eyes are always caressing me. This I will use to my advantage. I will play upon him with the same intensity as Accolon strums his lap harp.*

"I will have your word on this, Morgen."

This is your chance, Morgen, the sisters chanted. ***Do not give in just yet. Arthur trembles at the edge of a precipice. Do you not see how much he loves you? You have only to reach out and grasp his hand. Come, Sister, step forward and claim him as your own.***

Morgen took a deep breath and ignored the sisters chanting and crying her name.

Countless tapers danced higher as she made her approach. Slowly, deliberately, she moved forward, gliding as it were on shadow. A scent of roses perfumed the air. Morgen caught Arthur's hand and brought it to her lips. "What is it that disturbs you most about the prospect of my union with Merlin?" she whispered, drawing her thumb back and forth across his battle-scarred palm. Spellbound, Arthur stared as if waking from a dream. "The fact that I will no longer be a child that you can order around or the possibility that he may achieve the love you so desire?"

A crimson flush assaulted Arthur's countenance. For a moment it appeared he would strike Morgen, yet somehow his fist exploded against the table instead, sending goblets, food, and plates flying in various directions. How could she do this? How could she so callously unearth his hidden affections? "I told you never to read my mind again!"

Suddenly he was in motion, treading wildly around the chamber. Tapers leapt at his approach, and then, just as abruptly, went out, casting the room in bitter darkness, a mood shift that perfectly reflected Arthur's thoughts.

It was all over—all the pretense of sibling adoration, all the facade of brotherly protection. Morgen understood him too well. She was mocking him, casting his heart to the wolves so that she need not entertain it. Why should she when Merlin so dominated her affections? Instead of a golden prince, a High King, she chose a dark, mysterious adviser, one who could easily be her father. Why? What magic did he lack that made him so unappealing? Was it the fact that nearly everyone believed them to be brother and sister; or did her dislike, her revulsion stem from a much deeper source? Arthur did not wish to unearth the answer. Women always pursued a king because of his crown, but not Morgen. At this moment she wanted nothing more than to exit his presence and rush into Merlin's arms! If he could somehow move her, acquaint her with his own feelings, perhaps she would soften. Understanding was the key here. Did he possess the ability to help her adopt this alteration?

"How am I to respond, Morgen?" he said at last, far removed from her vision, using the dark shadows as a canvas to camouflage his emotions despite the fact that two strategically placed tapers sprang back to life full flame. "Nothing I can say will refute such an accusation. Nothing at all. Yes, it is true. I have admired you beyond any other woman since the night of our first meeting. I speak of the night I discovered you at father's deathbed. You are my life's breath, the very blood that flows through my veins. Do you not see?"

A sob involuntarily escaped Morgen's lips. She tried to speak but collapsed back against her chair, defeat welling through her being. This did not bode well. Arthur's honesty moved her as nothing else. Should she follow the sister's promptings and claim him as her own? Did she possess the strength, the courage to take that decisive step?

Sensing the shift in Morgen's perceptions, Arthur drew near once more. Perhaps this was the moment when she would truly see him. If nothing else, he would make her feel his heart. "I nearly became ill when I learned that you were my sister. You must believe me, Morgen. I had no idea that we were bound by such ties; otherwise I would never have allowed myself to feel…" his voice tapered off into the deepening silence. "Now that I know our familial relationship is in name only, my thoughts return to what might have been."

Suddenly he was on his knees before her. Why not make this a proposal? It appeared highly probable that they would never broach the subject again. Why then should he not tell her the truth? The words spilled through his lips with no further prompting. "If the world did not believe you to be my sister, I would have made you my queen." This said, he brought her hands to his lips and kissed them over and over. "I love you, Morgen. Surely you understand that. It is jealousy that makes me accuse Merlin of these crimes—jealousy and nothing more."

There, it was said. No matter what followed, the truth was laid before Morgen and in such a manner that she had no choice but to acknowledge its existence. He did not expect her to leap into his arms and cover him in kisses. If she did he would certainly welcome it, but reality proved a powerful tonic. Indeed, Morgen merely stared at him, tears spilling down her marble-smooth cheeks, uncertain, reeling. When at last she spoke, the words took him completely by surprise.

"Arthur, what are we to do?"

Something of a sad smile graced Arthur's lips. She was asking his advice on how to resolve the situation. If he spoke his heart, then she would probably flee his presence. It was simply a no-win situation. Resolute, he rose, then kissed Morgen's pale forehead. "Nothing as far as I can see. You love Merlin. That is clear enough."

Morgen pulled him close, so close that her lips brushed his cheek. "Forgive me," she whispered, "I never meant to wound you so."

Unable to bear Arthur's broken expression any longer, Morgen sought refuge near her unmade bed. Casting herself down upon its jumbled deer-skin coverlets, she collapsed, sobbing noiselessly. She was vaguely aware of Arthur's steady approach but started when he laid his long, majestic body down beside her. The bed creaked and moaned, echoing their sorrow.

"Take away this pain, dearest," he whispered, placing her hand against his heart, "then we will both breathe easier again. You heal many kinds of illness, Morgen. Perhaps this will be your greatest challenge of all. Heal me of this one-sided love. Heal me now, dearest, and we will never speak of this again."

Morgen, think what it is you must do! the sisters cried. *If you sever this tie forever, then all our hopes will be destroyed.*

The sisters spoke true. She had nearly ruined everything in that moment of confession. Why had she chosen Merlin over Arthur? Was Merlin truly her Otherself? If so, why then did the Sisterhood insist that Arthur was her past, present, and future? Why did everything about him appear so familiar? Surely she should simply throw her arms around his neck and kiss him over and over.

"Arthur," she whispered, drawing her fingertips against the dull stubble that lined his sun-bronzed face. The close proximity of his person, his scent, his warmth, coupled with the fact that they lay opposite each other in bed made her insides tremble. "I cannot honor your request. Indeed, it is vital to Britannia that these feelings remain intact. One day the truth will be revealed to us. One day we will understand why."

"Understand this," he whispered, gathering her face between his hands, "I will never love another." This said, he kissed her soundly, rose up, and without a backward glance, beat a determined exit through the door.

CHAPTER 19:

The Fox and the Hare

"Merlin, why do you refuse to listen? I saw your death! I saw the woman who will fulfill the curse!"

It was another hot summer day, a thick, muggy heat that dampened the very senses, threatened faintness and wreaked havoc with the most even-tempered individual. It made little difference that mage and fay stood knee deep within the grassy, weed-soaked field nor that the blessed forest waited a few paces away with its shady embrace. No, Morgen's passion pierced the heated excess, forcing Merlin to take note of her distress. It was no use. The mage possessed his own opinions regarding her vision, and he was not about to give them credence of any kind.

"A man cannot alter his destiny, Morgen," he said simply, allowing the palm of his hand to play against the tall, stiff grass, an act that shook seeds loose so that they peppered the air.

Morgen sneezed despite herself, but this did not alter her determination. "You have no desire to learn the truth of my vision?"

"No, I do not. It is apparent, however, that you possess a great desire to tell me everything you know or *think you know*."

Morgen kicked the earth with the tip of her deerskin boot and watched as several tufts of midsummer grass flew into the heady air. Why was Merlin so changed? Yes, he had told her that their assumed intimacy—that first encounter under Avalon's standing stones—had merely been a result of the vision. She understood that, and a part of her was thankful for it, considering Arthur's counsel; yet it did not explain Merlin's apparent indifference. Although Merlin's coal-black eyes were trained upon her, they revealed none of their former affection. Indeed, they shone with a degree of perplexity and not a little displeasure. Gone was the lover divine, the man for whom she would have given half her soul. Perhaps that was the point. Merlin, for all his declarations, could never exclusively be hers. Perhaps she had been over-hasty in allowing Arthur to slip away so unsatisfied.

"Are you listening, Morgen? Shapeshifting is not for the fainthearted. Look into my eyes. Focus on the lesson at hand."

Merlin displayed impatience, an ever pressing need to begin. Morgen mustered a brief nod, aware that delay would only heighten his irritation.

"Have you chosen the animal you wish to emulate?"

The air felt increasingly heavy, perfumed with an abundance of pine, perhaps because they stood so very near the ancient forest. This in itself pleased Morgen. What better place could there be to learn shapeshifting? Everything around her waxed hypnotic; she need only heed the lesson. A dragonfly hovered overhead, caressing the air with its iridescent wings, even as a youthful rabbit sought shelter beneath a twisted clump of reed. All this she saw—all this and more.

"I have," she replied, watching the delicate creature's progress.

Merlin nodded. "You need not tell me which creature you have chosen. I will alter according to your decision." He stared at her a moment, black eyes narrowing. "This lesson will prove more complex than mere shapeshifting. That would be far too simple for one of your gifts. You must become the animal to understand its essence. In other words you must experience both the best and worst its life offers."

"You will be the predator and I the prey, is that it?" This information, while not unexpected, proved more than a little unnerving. Merlin was an expert in this art. At present he was demonstrating no hint of his former affections. What if he caught her and...

The tiniest smile curled the edge of Merlin's lips. "I will not lie to you; this exercise carries with it a risk, but its rewards are beyond your wildest imaginings. When faced with a life threatening situation, you may call on the knowledge learned this day and wield it to your advantage." Clasping her hand, he continued, "Yes, Morgen, I *am* quite skilled in this art. If I capture you, I will shift before any harm follows. Remember, you also have the ability to regain mortal form any time you wish."

Morgen kissed Merlin's cheek but was struck by how quickly he pulled away, further dividing their affections. Was it possible she had lost him? No doubt Arthur's edict still haunted his sensibilities. Their relationship must not extend beyond that of teacher and pupil—unless Merlin proposed marriage. If Merlin attempted to woo her without the promise, consequences would follow. Perhaps that was why he chose not to embark beyond a scholarly relationship that day.

Morgen could only smile at this altered aspect of Merlin's personality. His teachings, however esoteric, left her spellbound. Indeed, Merlin's passion for shapeshifting knew no limits. Oh, how she adored the way he spoke of magic, eyes bright as coal fire. Light glittered around him, obeyed the very lilt of his baritone incantations, which were deep, rich, wiser than time itself. The effect was hypnotic, leading her down unknown paths she had never explored before. On and on his chanting echoed until she found it impossible to capture the gist of their meaning. Surely it was midnight, which explained why everything had grown so dark. It took every last bit of determination to keep her eyes open. When at last that seemed impossible, Merlin's hands settled upon her crown.

"Let go, Morgen," he whispered. "Release all connection to your body. You are light, you are energy, not this simple shell." Merlin's forefinger blazed a trail along her spine, setting her essence free.

Warmth flooded Morgen's body, animating her slender limbs with a series of leaps and bounds. She was free—free to explore new hopes and dreams! How wondrous it was to feel so lighthearted! Light blazed around her, within her. No longer simply fay or princess, her womanly form shrank, then compressed into that of a rabbit's delicate mold.

"Good," Merlin whispered, "blend your spirit with that of the chosen creature. Analyze her from every angle. Come, Morgen. Do not be shy," he mused, witnessing her tentative steps with a wry lift of his brow. "You have done this before. In fact, I believe that your life as a mortal is an example of continuous shapeshifting. In other words you need only remember that which you have forgotten."

The transformation was already complete; else Morgen would have immediately debunked such a wild proposition. Slowly, carefully, she wove a path through the tawny grass, hind legs outdistancing the front. Every sense she possessed was heightened, fine-tuned as it were, to brilliancy. Dew drops sparkled as the many facets of a crystal lodged within a bubbling stream. Crickets chirruped their merry greetings with such magnified enthusiasm that Morgen shook her head to clear the sound. Foreign scents filtered through her quivering nostrils, several of which she could not quite identify. She was, after all, newly reborn.

On and on Morgen trod, gaining confidence and with it additional speed. The bladed grass cut at her sweet little nose, and careless brambles scratched her innocent back, but what did it matter? The world was alive with possibility! Suddenly she was hopping. Joy streamed through her body! Up—she leapt over a shallow puddle that barred

her path. Never before had she felt so animated.
Another agile hop carried her across the forest's
threshold. Morgen stopped, fascinated. Dark
cloaking greenery surrounded her on all sides,
offering heightened security. Just ahead lay a thick
patch of blackberry bushes. Something, perhaps
an inner voice wiser than time, urged her forward.
It was folly to remain exposed in the open too long.
Close inspection revealed a blessed parting among
the thicket greenery large enough for admittance.
Morgen took advantage of this at once. Crouching
flat against the earth, she slid through the hole
and landed head over heels within the thicket's
hollowed center. There she lay looking up, wondering what would follow. It did not take long for her
to find out.

High overhead several ebony-feathered ravens
clicked their beaks impatiently. Someone—no,
something—had entered the forest. Morgen trembled. All was not well. What was it they were trying
to tell her?

Just beyond the thicket's sharpened greens,
a movement, subtle in its shiftiness, arrested her
senses. A rust-coated fox prowled back and forth,
its dark muzzle lowered to the ground. Musk
flooded Morgen's nostrils. The fox fixed its amber
eyes upon her and smiled.

Not a sound was heard beyond that of the
fox's heightened breathing. Even the dark cloaked
guardians overhead ceased their warning cries.
Time was of the essence. The fox would only pause
so long before making its move. Instinct counseled
Morgen to stay, but then the fox began pawing

away at the thicket with such fierce determination that she took courage and slid through the opening unseen. Off she sped, wide feet propelling her forward, rear legs powerful. Gracefully she cleared a decaying log, then leapt off toward the promise of a crystal stream. After dipping all four appendages in the water, she doubled back and dove within the log's hollow recesses. A stirring of leaves soon signaled the other's approach.

The fox resolutely plunged through the crystalline stream, bent on unearthing his prey's whereabouts. Water droplets settled along his white haunches and belly, but he did not waver. Upon reaching the other bank, however, something told him to sniff the earth. The rabbit had not passed this way. Trotting back across the stream, he immediately picked up her scent. She had reached this point but no farther. That meant she still hid nearby.

Back he trod toward the thicket, keenly aware of his surroundings. A hush once more animated the air. Pausing just shy of the log, the fox lifted his dark muzzle and sniffed the air. He smelled many things of interest, like the thick mat of decaying leaves at his feet and the family of mice that had recently trod this path. Why then was he unable to pinpoint the exact location of his prey? Perhaps *she had* regained the thicket!

Bounding over the heavy log, he retraced his steps, paying close attention to the leaves, which still lay facing the direction of their original chase. The pretty rabbit had not returned this way. Where, then, did she hide? Vision flooded his senses, pinpointing her exact location. The fox crouched low as he approached the log from a different angle.

Slowly, cautiously, Morgen crept to the tender opening and peered around in all directions. The fox no longer stood guard. This was her chance for freedom! Off she leapt, weaving in and out of the brush at breakneck speed. One goal alone beat within her tiny breast: she must be free to choose her own destiny. Yet the fox, which lay in wait, had another agenda. So quick, so agile was he that Morgen did not even have time to scream. Glancing back she saw him narrowing the distance between them. He was so close, so very close that she could feel the kiss of his breath upon her neck. Morgen's stride lengthened as her legs grew long and slender. Was she hare or was she woman? She could no longer hear the fox's pounding footfalls or see the path that lay ahead. She knew only darkness and the sensation of falling against the leaf-strewn earth. Head over heels she tumbled until she came to rest underneath a patch of wild roses. Morgen gasped for breath as she gazed up at her favorite flower—perhaps for the last time. The fox was upon her at once, its gloating amber eyes ablaze. A snarl escaped its lips as she struggled to slip free. Rusty paws pinned her against escape, yet it hardly mattered, for movement was no longer possible. The lesson was over. Merlin had won. Why then did he not release her?

A shudder laced Morgen's spine as another growl escaped its ruddy lips. Sharp, canine incisors pricked against her delicate throat. Escape was not possible—not this time. Morgen closed her eyes and waited.

Well done, little sprite.

Morgen, the rabbit fair, looked once more upon her captor. This time his eyes sparkled with adoration. She could just decipher Merlin's outline hovering beyond that of her red-coated captor.

Your praise is ill founded. I lost. You won.

The amused fox cocked his rusty head. *Of course I won. I have been shapeshifting into a fox for well nigh twenty years. You actually had me befuddled for quite some time. That is high praise, indeed.*

Fangs softened into lips as the red fox fell away, his body lengthening, pressing Morgen down against the earth. She could not move or even breathe, so fierce was her confusion. What was happening? Why could she not reason? It was Merlin, the enchanter, not the fox who held her— Merlin who kissed her throat and whispered words of passion. They were alone together in the woods, man and woman, elegantly entwined as mistletoe around the steady oak. No separation was possible this time—not unless one released the other.

Merlin smiled a strange smile full of mischief. He brushed his lips against Morgen's cheek, then reached overhead and secured a wild, blushing rose in the palm of his hand. Slowly, deliberately, he offered it to Morgen, then pulled down another and another, hardly aware that the thorns tore his fingers and left bright spots of blood in their wake.

Morgen drank deeply of the fragrant blossom as Merlin sprinkled the excess petals against her body. He was whispering something she could not quite hear. Another rose was pressed against her heart, mingled with soft kisses and blood from her beloved's hands. A spell was at work. Morgen was certain of that. Indeed, her entire body seemed to be unfolding like the many-petaled rose she clutched so tightly against her breast.

"Why do you doubt me, Morgen?" he whispered, gazing deep into her eyes. "You are my heart of hearts. My love, my life."

The fragrant petals rained down upon mage and fay until it was no longer possible to identify enchanted from enchanter. Finally the pupil and the teacher, the fox and the hare were one.

CHAPTER 20:

Choices of the Heart

"An entire month has passed since your first shapeshifting lesson." Merlin paused, offering up an irritatingly superior smile that almost labeled him condescending. "One thing still puzzles me, Morgen. Why did you not shift into a bird and fly away when the fox pounced?"

"Not this again," Morgen groaned, dragging her heels along the crunchy, leaf-ridden ground.

Hand in hand they strolled amid the ever-changing forest landscape, a daily ritual that dwarfed all other obligations. Summer bled into fall, but still they remained constant, unwavering in their mutual affection. Merlin's criticism, which he voiced more for amusement than anything else, would not be muted by anything as simple as love. Morgen knew this, and so she played the part he had grown to expect—that of a willful child who took little note of her tutor's edicts.

"The purpose of the lesson was for you to learn shapeshifting so you may wield it in a life-or-death situation. Forgive me, Morgen, but if that had been a Saxon, chances were you would either be his captive or dead."

"You have no confidence in my abilities," she taunted, sliding free of his embrace.

Merlin's long, slim form wavered hypnotically, a progressive transformation that altered limbs, torso, and head into that of a wizened barn owl. He hooted twice, then gracefully stretched his pale wings so that they caught an air current that carried him several feet to a lowered pine bough where he took up residence, conscious that Morgen must meet his round-eyed gaze.

That is not what I meant.

A brief snort served as Morgen's reply. "I should hope not, Merlin. It almost sounds as if you were not pleased to capture me that day. I know better." Off she marched, leaving the pale owl to his solitary musings. This game was growing old, and she had no patience for further questioning.

Morgen had only managed two paces when the clustered leaves at her feet took flight, a swirling mass that signaled Merlin's approach. There he stood amid the dancing whirlwind, ebony eyes fixed upon her.

"That moment was long in the making. We both know it. It was inevitability. No amount of maneuvering or manipulation could avert it. Surely you know that."

Merlin stared at Morgen, awaiting a response. When it did not come, he continued in altered tones, "I have tried to tell myself over and over that we made the right choice, that Arthur would understand…"

Faltering, unable to voice his thoughts, he began forming a makeshift bow out of some broken reeds. Perhaps it would be fitted with an arrow to serve one of the Companions. Perhaps it was merely a focal point he needed to quell his thoughts. In any case this distraction served Merlin well, for he was soon able to gather sufficient courage to continue.

"If only I could convey to Arthur but a part of what I feel for you." Once again, he fell silent, lost in regret, the reedy bow slipping from his grasp.

Morgen picked up the castoff weapon and began tracing its reedy outlines with careful fingers. "Arthur knows. There is no need to explain."

"We do not speak, Morgen," he said, suddenly pulling her deep into the forest's womb, far from eyes that see too keenly and ears that hear that which remains unspoken—in a word, from Arthur's nearly omnipotent attention. "No, not unless it be over some treaty concern that cannot wait."

Aware that they were cloaked within blankets of pine, she did not hesitate to embrace Merlin, force him to meet her gaze. "You were in the council chambers last night."

"Yes, we were discussing Urien's imminent arrival. He will reach Caerleon within the week, Morgen."

A low groan escaped Morgen's lips. "Do not remind me," she spat, slipping from his arms, legs propelling her forward through brush, weed, and vine, bent on some illusive point where reality dared not follow. "You and your ridiculous treaty.

How in the name of Avalon am I going to escape Urien's clutches? Marriage to that ogre is not part of the plan, Merlin. It is not what I came here to do."

Merlin was fast upon her heals. His long legs easily narrowed the distance between them yet still gave him time enough to train his expression before he voiced the next question. "What is your purpose here, Morgen? You have never told me."

"Perhaps one day I will," served as her reply.

He captured her hand, his stride perfectly matching her own so that they fairly trotted together, navigating the lush, emerald under-growth with a precision few could match. A magnificent array of gold, rust, and crimson-hued trees provided a colorful canopy above them. For a time they said nothing more—so mesmerizing was nature's autumnal canvas. The cool, crisp air had transformed the leaves early that year, offering up a fresh display of sylvan glory. Each step brought them closer to their favorite haunt: a sacred lake that lay half a league from Caerleon.

Morgen burst upon the scene as if viewing it for the first time. Earth, water, stone, and sky inter-twined much as they did in Avalon, a catechism of muted blues, delicious textures that fairly begged to be touched, and glittering cloud formations that always took her breath away. The curiously crescent-shaped lake boasted soft, hypnotic waters that twinkled with an almost iridescent splendor. Silvery mist kissed the smooth pebbled shore as it rose up a dramatic incline well punctuated with standing stones all along its jutting path. Morgen drank of the fragrant air anew and trembled, not with fear but celebration. This was, indeed, a place of eternal truth for all with the will to see.

Merlin glanced down at his love, keenly aware that she was undergoing a transformation of her own. Everything about her person shimmered. She was exquisite beyond expression. They would speak no more of sorrow or regret—no, not just yet. Autumn was the time that suited Morgen best. Indeed, it was the time when she appeared most alive.

"How is it that you grow more beautiful every day?"

"I fear you are bewitched, my lord," she said, playfully pressing him back against a rounded, stone sentinel worn smooth with time.

"If that be true," he whispered, "swear you will never release me from this spell."

Clasping Morgen against his heart, he ravished her with kisses. Lovemaking proved nothing short of bliss, especially when they mingled within nature's embrace. They were the mottled hawk that circled above, the fish that leapt in the crystalline waters, the silvery wolf that trod nearby. They were all this and more. How wondrous such moments were—to be one with the whole of existence mirrored in a lover's eyes.

Morgen acquiesced, allowing Merlin to guide her down among the aging stones until they lay entwined upon crisp leaves of auburn and gold.

The look with which Merlin fixed her spoke volumes. He adored her, he lived and breathed by the very light in her eyes; and at that particular

moment, he wanted her. That much was clear.
Indeed, Morgen saw no reason to deny him. They
were already so akin, so deep in each other's affections that it felt wrong to ignore these feelings. It
made no difference if Arthur disapproved. This
did not affect him in any manner. Well, perhaps
that was not quite true. Arthur very much wished
to usurp Merlin's place, even if it meant that
numerous petty kings took up arms against him
again. Therein lie the rub. Arthur possessed a
double standard when it came to Merlin and his
own royal personage. Why not? He was, after all,
High King. He had every right to tailor his edicts.
Perhaps what terrified Morgen most was the fact
that a disgruntled Arthur, a jealous Arthur might
very well sell her to Urien. If the High King could
not claim his heart's choice, then why should his
adviser? Why not pack her off to the highest bidder? That way he need never see her again.

Merlin's lips called Morgen back to present
moment. This was her true reality. Arthur, no matter how much past history they shared together,
did not converse with her in Merlin's language,
the language that fired the innermost cords of her
heart. Perhaps she was overly hasty in this evalu-
ation, perhaps not. In any case it was her duty to
explore the hidden possibilities this moment held.
And so she did.

Everything spoke at once. Element, tree, mam-
mal, amphibian, each whispered of the sacred mysteries shared by all, yet heard by only the blessed
few. Theirs was a perfect union of physical with met-
aphysical. They were the turtle that crept nearby,

the hawk that cried overhead. When mage and fay finally parted, a faint humming colored the wind. Morgen looked up, startled. Had the stones actually begun to sing? She had never heard any standing stones beyond those found in Avalon offer up a melody. Was this some sort of message sent from the Sisterhood?

"Do you hear it, beloved?" Merlin whispered, ignorant of her concerns. "The song of the universe."

"It is all spice and promise, wind and fire," she said, dashing the leaf-strewn tendrils from her eyes.

Merlin chuckled at the sight. Her flaming locks were virtually littered with an army of clinging leaflets.

"We are going to have quite a time setting your hair aright."

"One look and Arthur will know what we have been doing," she said, laughing a full, rich laugh that painted the air with its music.

Merlin gazed upon her, utterly smitten. Oh, how he loved her; how he wished that this very moment would span beyond eternity's vast embrace. What a dream he wove just in that simple musing. Morgen could never be his though—never in this lifetime. She belonged to another, although neither acknowledged this truth, for it rendered their relationship insignificant.

Catching the thought Morgen felt her stomach twist painfully. It was the topic of marriage that saddened her time and again. Merlin did not wish to claim her as his bride. Yes, he desired her love, her passion, but nothing further. The simple truth was that she had always loved Merlin more. Naturally Merlin would deem this entirely unfounded; but was it? Why would he not do this one simple thing for her? She would do anything for him! No doubt the difficulty stemmed from the fact that she gave Merlin her love, her body, before extracting the promise. Now the promise would never be made.

Merlin started as her inner anguish assaulted his sensibilities. Before he could refute any such notions, Morgen gained her footing. Instantly she was in motion, racing down the narrow rock-lined path at breakneck speed. She did not want to see Merlin, or speak with him again—not until he altered his opinion. But Merlin easily overtook her.

"After all this time, you still do not understand me. I think not of myself but of you." He attempted to stroke her cheek, but she struck his hand away— so hard that Merlin knew he was lucky it had not been his face. "I would give my life for you. Surely you know that. What bliss it would be to know that you belong to me and no other."

"Then why?" she sobbed, falling back into his arms.

"Marriage will destroy us and thereby destroy Arthur. Come, let me show you. The lake will reveal all. I will use the mirror surface to unveil everything I have seen thus far."

A look of skepticism darkened Morgen's brow as she allowed her small hand to be encompassed within the broad expanse of his own. Neither of them dared speak a word until they gained the lakeshore. That is when the true magic began.

They had a sense of being pulled forward by a subtle yet irresistible force far wiser than they. Even the tranquil waters leapt forth in greeting.

Morgen sat down upon a craggy, circular rock that overlooked an exceptionally glittering mass of lake, then indicated that Merlin do the same.

"I thought we wished the same thing," he whispered, "to love one another."

"And so we do." Morgen placed her silken head against his shoulder, furiously blinking back tears.

"But it is not enough. You wish to bind us throughout this lifetime."

Morgen met Merlin's gaze. He looked quite old at that moment, ancient and careworn by the events that were about to overtake them.

"No," came her pointed reply, "I wish to bind us through all time."

Merlin tried to respond, but the knowing waters slapped hard against the rock, commanding his attention. "What would you tell us, gentle lake?"

Mage and fay shimmied out upon the pitted rock until they reached the lake edge, legs dangling toward its tranquil surface. Together they peered into the clear waters, expectant, wondering what missive would unfold. Morgen feared a recital of Merlin's vision, severing them for this lifetime. Merlin merely wished a slight reprieve. Both were startled when a dark presence rose from the brilliant lake's depths. Down it lured them through suffocating blackness until the colors of Lothian and North Wales unfurled before their eyes.

Merlin cursed his own folly. Lot and Urien had just been brought before the king!

CHAPTER 21:

The Wolves at Bay

Flop, flick, flop, flop. Morgen listened to the sound of her deerskin boots as they slapped against the harsh stone floor. Each step brought her closer and closer toward that doom which animated her thoughts, altered the color of her dreams. Onward she trod through Caerleon's sweltering labyrinth, the spiraled halls preternaturally gothic from lack of illumination and deserted, for petitioning enemies demanded all attention. The emerald gown she wore suddenly felt oppressively heavy as if its rich fabric were weighting her down. What was she thinking when she chose to don that exceedingly low-cut garment? Now she would have to endure Urien's lurid taunts. Perhaps that is why she dared not meet her lover's eyes. Why had they remained absent so long? They had been wrong in straying so far from court, especially at a time when Arthur required Merlin's guidance.

"Your fears are unwarranted," Merlin offered in a soothing voice. "Arthur will not give you to Urien." He paused just outside the majestic, glittering Great Hall's stylishly engraved entranceway.

This was the epitome of Roman craftsmanship, a fine veneer that offered no hint that the chambers within proved less than dazzling. Carefully he took her hand, "You are far too dear to him."

"The treaty?" she questioned, with little attempt to hide her cynicism.

"Let us handle that," came Merlin's stalwart reply. "Tonight you need merely appear beautiful and charming, those things that you cannot help but be."

"Yes, nothing more than a piece of meat set out as a prize for the highest bidder."

Merlin's heart twisted despite itself. She was right, and nothing he did could spare her this agony.

The massive, deeply engraved bronze doors, pinnacle of the Great Hall itself, opened at that moment sans pomp or ceremony. On the contrary Bedivere issued forth with such resolute purpose that he did not truly notice Morgen's arrival until he had taken two steps beyond where she actually stood. Something clicked within his brain, however, and he whirled around, delighted. "Thank the gods you are here! Arthur just sent me in search of you!"

The mage spoke first. "Then lead us in and set his heart at rest."

Morgen's third eye throbbed painfully. The old Roman eagle, which stood forever frozen, head held high, imperious in its ability to access every entrant's intents, graced the doors with haughty indulgence, offering an indifferent welcome. For a moment Morgen was reminded of her beautiful falcon, Cerifus. If only he were by her side. If only she had never left Avalon's tranquil shores.

Remember your life's purpose.

It was the Sisterhood, now and forever linked with her being.

How will marriage to Urien help me fulfill Avalon's will?

It is peace we seek, nothing more, nothing less. If marriage to North Wales will help us achieve this, then your purpose **will be** *fulfilled.*

Morgen swallowed hard. Was the Sisterhood actually telling her to marry Urien of North Wales?

Bedivere watched her intently, only partly aware of the private war she waged within. Offering a brief nod, he clasped Morgen's arm, then proudly led her through the threshold of doom. Merlin followed several paces behind, distancing himself from Morgen's anxious thoughts.

The huge chamber, large enough to admit several Roman squadrons, if not a legion, opened its gaping maw, offering up a picture at once dazzling as it was unkempt. Whitewashed timbers, brilliant with false purity, drew the eye at first glance, casting the room's darker secrets into relief. The walls were cracked marble, or some such substance, rose colored and flecked with veins of ebony and gold. Long ago it must have been breathtaking, but a thick coat of dust further camouflaged its worth. Morgen paused, embarrassed by the crumbling pink stones strewn with indelicate haste against the chamber's far corners. No doubt they once been part of a massive fireplace, but age and neglect had brought them to this state of disrepair.

As the only woman in Caerleon, it should have been her responsibility to set this matter aright. Arthur, however, never allowed Morgen to offer such assistance. A network of crimson carpets, laid pell-mell across the humble thrush-strewn flooring, furthered distracted the eye, lending a hint at royalty that all but escaped their ordinary lives. This red subterfuge graced the entourage that comprised the forces of North Wales and Lothian. The Pendragon contingency stood opposite.

Gathering courage Morgen cast her eyes upon the High King, who held her fate between his able hands. The sight of Arthur seated high upon an iron-gray dragon-backed throne drew her focus. She faltered in step, wide eyed, staring. Never before had Arthur looked so regal, so handsome: golden hair falling carelessly against his smooth brow, blue eyes large, luminous, yet glittering their warning that he was thoroughly in command, his long, lean, deeply muscled form barely concealed within a crimson tunic edged in gold, the fiery dragon woven upon his breast. He sported no crown and needed none. What woman could look on Arthur and not be affected? Blood rushed to her cheeks, lending validity to this appraisal. How was it she routinely forgot Arthur's magnetic appeal until it assaulted all sensibility, leaving her defenseless and reeling? He appeared every inch a king, thoroughly prepared for the beasts snapping at his heels. Around him stood the Companions, ever vigilant, determined to thwart any trouble that should arise. The combined parties of Lothian and North Wales peppered the remaining hall.

Keep focus, beloved. Do not allow them to divert you.

Morgen felt Merlin's eyes upon her but dared not look his way. Instead she watched Kay drag himself across the thick layers of bearskins that beat a path from dais to entrance. Pausing before her, his mutilated countenance further distorted as he offered up his best glare.

"You do yourself little favor in keeping him waiting, you thoughtless..."

Here he allowed Morgen's imagination to supply the missing descriptive.

Crimson painted her pale cheeks a richer hue as she looked up at the coarse, if not well-meaning, seneschal. He hated her, as did they all. No doubt Arthur would be thrilled to send her packing.

A triumphant smile twisted Kay's misshapen lips as his weathered baritone announced her arrival.

All the foreign petitioners jockeyed for position as they turned en masse to see Arthur's sister—that reputed beauty who had brought them hither. Morgen drew herself to full height, which was minimal, and glared at them.

Arthur could not help but chuckle. Instantly his feet were in motion, advancing across the bearskins with a determination that left little question who was in command. *Where have you been?* cried his thoughts as he enveloped her in a protective embrace. "It really is not necessary to stare daggers at them," he whispered charmingly near her ear. "They can do no harm."

Morgen looked up at Arthur, uncertain. *What is it you expect of me?*

Arthur shook his head slightly before responding nonverbally.

The success of this treaty depends on your ability to charm Urien. Do you understand me, Morgen?

Was it possible that Arthur also possessed the gift? Morgen stared at him wide eyed, tongue frozen against the roof of her mouth. Speech was impossible so they would have to continue in the realm of thought. **Divert him, dearest, and all will be well.**

I will do my best, Brother.

Sunshine poured from Arthur's expression as he escorted her to the dais, a simple, unadorned wooden platform cut in a graceful oval the Romans had used to receive supplicants. At that moment he knew the night was won.

Merlin silently took his place at Arthur's left, then gestured that Morgen should occupy the right. A pitted, narrow bench was her appointed perch, unassuming in its simplicity, safeguarded by the exuberant Bedivere. Morgen draped her body against this uncomfortable seat so that every contour, every curve of her frame was displayed to its highest advantage. Thankfully *she had* worn the low-cut emerald gown. This would aid her cause as no other. Yes, she was bold, seductive, utterly alluring, perhaps because Bedivere stood just behind her, fingertips caressing the hilt of his sword. Urien sneered despite these precautions. From the corners of her eyes, Morgen glimpsed his leering face, for she would not look at him directly; not until she felt more centered. Urien, however, kept his eyes bent on her instead of the treaty discussions, which recommenced precisely where they had left off. The whole affair proved excessively irritating until Morgen forced herself to meet Urien's insistent stare. This was the man who had nearly claimed her chastity at St. Alban's. What would he do if he knew that Merlin had won the prize instead? Morgen struggled to cast such thoughts from her mind. Urien's surly appearance still reminded her of a predator: trim, hard muscled, masculine to the core. His golden brown hair and narrow green eyes, which displayed a rare gilded hue, were reminiscent of a wolf's. And then there was his insatiable hunger for power.

Oh, yes, smile at me, beauty. You have blossomed— and then some.

Morgen could not help but flush under his intense scrutiny.

"North Wales will have Britannia's protection if you adhere to these few principles."

It was Arthur's voice that temporarily wrest Urien's attention away from his prize. A look of utter consternation darkened his brow. He no longer had any idea what point was being discussed. Indeed, he no longer cared. His eyes kept drifting back to Morgen. Hence, he muttered an affirmative reply.

"What say you, Urien? Is that agreeable?"

"Aye, naturally so," the western king mumbled, never shifting his gaze from Morgen.

"And on the final point?"

A look of utter consternation clouded Urien's expression. Just how much of the treaty had slipped by while he was lost in Morgen's numerous charms?

"If you would allow us a moment to confer," Lot interjected in a silky smooth voice that belied his anger.

A brief nod served as Arthur's reply. He looked to Morgen with a bright, wide-eyed expression, thoroughly pleased with the way she taunted Urien, fed his hunger with careless smiles and alluring ease. Indeed, she draped her form with such sensuous appeal against the cross chair that one might believe it was made out of the softest bedding instead of resolute hardwood.

Well done, beloved, Merlin suggested with just the hint of a smile. ***Now if you can distract Lot as well, we should be free and clear by midnight.***

Morgen turned her attention back on Lot, who was upbraiding Urien in hushed tones. Deliciously tall, the silver-haired patriarch possessed an air of magnetism that issued from every pore of his sun-bronzed skin. Lothian's ruler proved quite the elegant rogue, an aging warlord whose magnetism could not be denied. It was clear why Morgause had lost her heart to him. Indeed, they complemented each other so very well: she beautiful and seductive and he perfectly mesmerizing in appeal. No doubt their sons were glorious creatures to behold.

"Keep your mind on the treaty unless you wish to lose her altogether," Lot counseled in a stern yet faintly amused voice. "Now listen to me. Arthur has just proposed that you may marry his sister if and only if you win her heart. That goes against the original proposition as I see it. What say you?"

A snarl escaped Urien's tightly clenched lips as he faced Arthur. Undaunted he approached within a foot of the dais and spat out his reply, "What game is this you are playing, Arthur? I came here in good faith, and now you deny that which is most precious to me. If Morgen is not a part of this agreement, then the treaty falls."

Arthur smiled, his confidence undiminished. "Do you have any siblings, Urien?"

The king of North Wales quickly relaxed his guard, thinking he understood the question. Arthur was concerned about Morgen's welfare—whether or not she would be of equal station at his court. Surely his answer would settle that query.

"No, I am an only son, sole heir to the lands of North Wales. I would make an excellent match for your sister. She will be treated as an…"

"The point I wish to make is this," Arthur quickly interjected, cutting him off in mid-breath, "Morgen is my only sister." Here he took hold of Morgen's hand and held it fast within his own as if to reaffirm the accuracy of this statement.

Lot leapt at this with a passion. "That is not true! My wife…"

A low growl escaped Arthur's lips. "Say what you will, Lot. Your wife no longer holds any such claims." His right hand involuntarily clasped Excalibur's hilt. "I embrace the well-being and pro-tection of Lothian and Orkney for your people's sake, not hers."

"But your disapproval was with me, not her," Lot said, his hand also drawing far too near his sword. "Now that we have agreed upon an alliance, I see no reason why she may not be forgiven as well."

All across the Great Hall, Companions and followers alike shifted uncomfortably, tapping their swords in case they should be called into play. It was an elaborate dance—one that each warrior knew intimately well. Every eye, every breath was concentrated on the scene before them, a scene which pitted the High King against his most vehement foes, not on the battlefield but within a controlled environment, much like a child's game of fealty.

The haggard and death-ridden image of Uther flashed before Arthur's eyes. It was then he knew with absolute certainty that Morgause had been his father's executioner. How many years might he have shared with his father if not for this murderous fool and his wife? Loss and confusion unsettled Arthur, left him vulnerable. Lot droned on and on, heightening his fury. A moment more and he would most certainly strike him down. Arthur saw it in his mind's eye: Lot lying sprawled across the humble dais, blood pouring from his severed neck.

Remember, anger renders you unbalanced, clouds your thinking. Do not offer Lot this victory. Let him know that you are king.

The effect of Merlin's unspoken counsel was immediate, and Arthur's hand fell back to his side.

"Perhaps in time, Lot, but that is hardly a matter of the agreement. Your wife has greatly displeased me, and I will hear no more of her at present."

Lot was silenced by this, but Morgen saw he stood far from beaten. Indeed, his thoughts were whirling at breakneck speed. Lot possessed an intelligence that mimicked wisdom. Yet this gift, for all its promise, was colored by darkness, a subtle insanity that preyed upon his mind. It was Lot, not Urien, who offered the greatest threat.

"I ask the question," Arthur continued, temporarily thrusting Lot into the background, "because Morgen is very precious to me."

Morgen swallowed hard, terrified of what would follow. The light of Arthur's eyes shone as blue sapphires, brilliant, fiery, and unreadable. Was it possible that he had truly mastered his jealousy, or was this a dazzling mask he wore as High King?

He motioned to Morgen, who quickly rose and took his outstretched hand. "Understand this: I treasure her above all things. While we were laying down the terms of this treaty, I had little idea that my sister's heart had already been given to another."

No!

Morgen tried to wrench her hand free, but Arthur held her fast. Dissension swirled around them, driving the foaming wolf beyond his limited restraint. Lot, selfish in his desire for success, was trying to calm Urien, who had already splintered the chair on which he had been seated. Indeed, the elder man was physically holding the younger back from an apparent attempt to mount the dais.

Arthur's glorious eyes bore into Morgen. How much do you trust me?

What game was Arthur playing? His dazzling eyes bore through her, willing—no, demanding—cooperation. Was he blind to the fact that this pronouncement had just put Merlin at risk? Did he honestly believe that any of them would escape unscathed?

Once again his commanding voice rang through her brain. *Believe me. I know what I am doing. All I ask is that you play along.*

Drawing her head against his heart, Arthur whispered gently so everyone could hear, "Urien should know everything, dearest."

The touch itself proved illuminating, revealing concealed truths that effortlessly spilled through Morgen's veins. It was as if an angel had lighted upon Arthur's shoulder, cleansed him of the darkness that fettered his soul. He looked on her now with nothing but love and respect. Gone was the angst and jealousy Morgen had observed clouding his eyes since that night of confession. Indeed, he appeared fired with possibility. This was his chance to secure peace with two of the most influential petty kings in Britannia. He was not about to allow them an easy victory. No, they would have to fight tooth and nail to achieve an alliance with him. Perhaps that is why the love he felt for Morgen centered him. No middle ground was feasible here; either he would succeed or lose her altogether, the latter of which was not an option.

Morgen marveled at his confidence. She tried to speak, but Arthur brushed his fingertips against her lips. The warmth of this interaction set her heart racing. He was calm, centered, and utterly seductive.

Let me do this. You need not address them. In fact I would rather you did not.

Once more Arthur's strong, protective arms drew her firmly against his chest. He did not wish them to see her—not now, not ever. This was some small comfort, although Morgen lacked the courage to acknowledge why.

"Would you have me permanently sever the cords that bind Morgen to another because of this treaty, Urien? As I recall we left it that I would broach the matter with her first."

"Fie upon your gentle dealings! Give Morgen to me or…"

Arthur raised his hand, claiming further precedence. Mercifully Urien fell silent, his face a darkened grimace of fury; his hair bristled, his eyes glinted fury, but somehow he stilled his tongue.

"I understand your frustration," Arthur continued in a calm voice, "for she is a treasure unparalleled. I therefore offer you this proposition. If you win her heart…"

"But you say it is already given!" Urien snarled, breaking free of Lot's iron grip. He took a step forward, which was readily countered by several of the Companions.

Arthur also advanced, defying Urien to trespass any further. "It is your task to change her mind."

A cry of frustration escaped Urien's lips as he commenced pacing back and forth across the thickly furred rugs, kicking them free of their careful placement. He appeared every inch a caged animal, seeking some, indeed, any means of escape.

Lot merely stood silent, watching, waiting, his age showing more keenly than before.

After a time Arthur spoke again, choosing his words carefully. "I would not betray your trust," he said in a respectful voice. "You have my permission to woo her."

"No!" Urien cried. "I will not compete with some nameless individual for that which is already mine!"

By the gods! How dare you! Morgen's thoughts screamed within her brain. This man, this ape had such gall! How did he imagine that she would consider him a potential husband? Indeed, the thought of his hands upon her each night nearly made her retch.

Stung by the look of revulsion that crossed Morgen's face, Urien's anger flooded anew. "You are mine, Morgen! Do you hear me? I care not who holds your heart, for that is mine as well!"

He rushed the steps at that moment, but the hulking physiques of Bors and Grifflet swelled forward, easily beating him back with synchronized strokes of their well-seasoned broadswords. Offering Morgen a protective nod, they melded in with that impressive unit that comprised the Companions.

Arthur drew Excalibur and placed it firmly before him. He released Morgen's wrist in the process, and she quickly withdrew to the left side of the dais, leaving Bedivere far behind.

"Those are the terms of this treaty," Arthur continued, keeping focus on Urien's grizzled countenance. "You may use your 'charm' to win Morgen. If you should not succeed, I will find you another wife of noble birth. Are we agreed?"

Urien barely heard the words escape Arthur's lips; instead his keen eyes saw what escaped the High King's discernment. She was open, far removed from Bedivere or any other guard, and therefore easy prey. This truth lent him courage, foolhardy as it was, to move forward: he would have Morgen or die. Without warning he sprang up past the Companions stationed at ground level and past Arthur's astute defense, at full gallop, a manic assault bent on claiming the ultimate prize. Thankfully Urien still possessed enough presence of mind not to draw his sword. He had nearly clasped Morgen's arm when a whirl of crimson interceded, juxtaposing itself between predator and prey. Bedivere's broadsword sliced open Urien's good arm, offering an irrefutable warning that halted his ill-advised advance.

"This is ludicrous!" Urien cried, thoroughly bewildered by Bedivere's adept defense, his arm bloodied but not incapacitated. "Tell me who he is! He might be a peasant for all I know!"

"I assure you he is of noble birth," Morgen supplied, "perhaps more noble than any of us who claim to be of royal blood."

A tremor animated Merlin's spine, lending additional warmth and validity to his affections. He knew Morgen had meant that statement more for himself than anyone else and deeply appreciated its intent.

Aware that he was fighting a losing battle, Urien slunk back to Lot's side, tail tucked between his legs.

"There, it has been spoken—and rather eloquently I might add," rang Arthur's affirmation. He had little fear for Morgen's safety. Merlin was well capable of offering protection that even the Companions could not provide. The question was, how much damage had been done to the proposed treaty? Would Urien still offer his consent?

He paused, making sure all eyes were upon him, and then asked the fateful question that beat within his brain. "Once again, Urien, do you accept the terms of this treaty?"

"A word, Urien," Lot cautioned, drawing his friend back into private conference. "I would advise you to accept."

"That is easy for you to say. You have everything you came for!"

"Not quite everything, but that too will come in time, my friend. Calm yourself. I say you will win her within a fortnight. If not, you may take her by force."

Urien sneered, fingering the hilt of his sword, "I like this not."

"It grows late," came Arthur's response, perhaps a little louder than he intended. "What say you?"

"Agreed," Urien conceded through gritted teeth.

CHAPTER 22

Alliances

And so the days sped forward with little regard to Morgen's distemper. Try as she might to avoid the lord of North Wales, Morgen found him tenacious as a guard dog, carefully oozing his presence into her waking hours—morning, noon, and night. In truth he was obsessed with Morgen, obsessed with unearthing the identity of her unnamed lover, no matter what the cost.

Late one afternoon Urien drew up a cross chair in the overly populated mead hall and began calculating his next move. Morgen was an integral part of the plot he had conceived to save his dying kingdom. Yes, his mountaintop fortress was in rapid decline—not so much as a result of Urien's mismanagement but due to irrational choices made by his father years ago. A union with the Pendragon lineage would gain him additional funds and resources necessary for rebuilding and attracting native Welshmen back home. Urien's mind darkened with bitter memories and the waning hope that Morgen would be his salvation. It came as something of a surprise that he was falling

prey to her charms. Oh yes, he had known Morgen
would be a beauty. Even as a child she had proven
most desirable to the eye. Yet, it was her innate
intelligence, her fierce, independent spirit that
drove him beyond despair. Every fiber of his being
cried out for the recognition which she habitually
denied him. Drink after drink passed his lips, but
nothing could quench that insatiable hunger. He
must possess Morgen or die.

As twilight's dulcet shadows slowly lengthened,
casting the mead hall into darkened relief, Urien
fell deep into an intoxicated stupor, banging his
hands against the rough wooden table until they
grew raw and bloodied. This did little to endear
him to Caerleon's increasingly disgusted inhabitants. Finally, once all of the kitchen help had
refused him solace, Urien was left to face the
court's disgruntled seneschal, a task that would
make anyone save the drunken petty king think
twice. And so they set horn against claws, Kay and
Urien: two beasts fierce in their determination
not to let the other gain ground. On and on they
sparred, heated voices amplified to a fever pitch,
driving every last Companion away. They were
trading insults more lethal than blows.

Discord echoed through Caerleon's labyrinth,
spilling around corners, filtering through all but
the most secured chambers. Morgen looked up
from her work—a mottled potion bent on assuring
Urien's impotency—and frowned. It appeared the
lord of North Wales was slathering his attention
elsewhere. Faltering, the clear glass bottle filled
with a virulent green concoction slipped from

her hands and splattered its careful rendering upon the thrush-strewn ground. She would have to begin again, but not before she unearthed the source of Urien's distemper.

Drawn by a sound that reminded her of wolves squaring off over highly desired territory, Morgen crossed the boundary that separated the mead hall from the rest of Caerleon's temperate climate. Several hairs on the back of her neck stood up, heightening her unease; yet she did not pause, not even amid the vicious snarling, which decreased into vocal distemper, a fact easily verified as she stumbled upon Urien verbally abusing Kay.

"What do you mean you won't haul that festering carcass of yours back to the barrel? You're a sorry servant to the king and an even sorrier man. No doubt the ladies flee your approach."

Kay's hulking form slumped forward, arms crossed protectively against his massive chest. The coppery hair that graced his large head and scarred countenance gave him the appearance of a troll threatened by dawn's first light. Although known for his own brand of cutting remarks, nothing prepared Arthur's seneschal for locking horns with the king of North Wales. Wounded but far from beaten, he clamped his twisted mouth shut and wrest the goblet from Urien's grasp.

"Your silence answers me well. When was the last time you were with a woman?"

Kay still did not answer, but kept his steely eyes fixed on Urien, barely containing the anger that raged inside. It would be so easy to snap this imbecile's puny neck and take the consequences later.

Surely Arthur would thank him for such a service. God knows, the whole of Caerleon wished the
petty king dead.

"That long?" continued Urien's sly banter. "No
doubt she saw at a glance that you had been gelded
in battle."

Pain seared Kay's expression, distorting it further into a grim mask that few could gaze upon
without revulsion. Morgen's heart wept blood
tears for him. Sometime that night she would see
him cured of his maladies—all of them—but not
before she first made Urien pay for his injustices.

Walking boldly between the two men, she
watched them turn and leer at her, an almost
comedic reaction that would have forced laughter
to her lips had not the situation appeared so dire.

"I have often heard, Kay, that only a man who
doubts his own masculinity stoops to question that
of another."

The grimace that habitually shone from Kay's
sour face almost twisted into a smile. Morgen
returned the gesture but found her efforts negated
as Urien rose on uncooperative legs to greet her.
The grace that so typically characterized his sober
movements was camouflaged with drink. Indeed,
the lumbering swagger with which he made his
approach reminded her of the walking dead. Urien
perhaps overhead her thoughts, for he stumbled
forward, landing squarely against her small person, an accomplishment that left him well pleased.
Indeed, Morgen was forced to prop Urien up with
the weight of her tiny frame, an act that filled her
with loathing. The stench of his breath, intensified

by the drunken leer that distorted his features, nearly made Morgen gag. Slowly, savoring each touch, he clawed his way up her body, pausing at chest level to mold her sweet bosom between thick, weighted fingers.

"Well, at last, mistress, I see your blood stir. How long has it been for you, sweeting, a day, an hour?"

Disgust flooded Morgen's countenance. How could anyone be so vile? No matter how much he protested otherwise, love never entered the lord of North Wales's mind. He wished only to seduce her, claim her as his mate so he might populate the world with tyrants as single-minded as himself. Unable to stay her temper, Morgen rewarded Urien with a firm slap across his reddened face.

The wolf snarled anew, digging into Morgen's tender shoulders with his fierce grasp. "Enough of that, witch! Try that again and you will regret it. Remember, I am to be your husband!"

"Only if you win my heart, and you are far from accomplishing that feat."

Something snapped inside Urien's brain, and he struck Morgen's delicate cheeks with the palm of his hand, sending her back against a trestle table with such force that she bruised her head, legs and arms splayed wide, lending further indignity. As she lay there in this most deplorable position, a thought crossed her mind. She would win Kay's sympathy by allowing him to rescue her. Afterward she would be only too happy to return the favor— the perfect excuse to enact his healing!

Well pleased with her plan, Morgen watched Kay seize Urien around the waist and cast him into a narrow cross chair, which reared precariously before it fell back into place with a broad thud. Silver flashed as Kay pulled his twisted ring guard free and held the sword against Urien's tawny throat.

"Are you hurt, princess?" Kay cried, never taking his eyes from their mutual tormentor.

Morgen regained her footing, not to mention some small dignity, smoothing her amethyst gown with steady fingers. "No, only a little dizzy. Thank you, Kay, for bringing the drunken fool under control."

"You sly witch," Urien spat, nonplussed by the blade that held him temporary captive. "You treat the cripple with more respect than you do me! If I did not know better, I might think that he is your nameless lover, but it is rather hard to mate with a eunuch."

Kay was about to slam the butt of his hilt into Urien's cheek when Morgen stayed the effort with a touch of her hand. "He is drunk, Kay, and knows not what he says or does."

"Drunk or not, he struck you. We both know how furious Arthur will be when he finds out."

"Why should he be angry with me?" Urien cried, nearly foaming at the mouth. "I was promised a virtuous maiden! That's a laugh! Even you, Kay, must see that the wench has been plucked. The question is, who won the prize?"

The mead hall's vast emptiness magnified the question tenfold as it echoed back and forth among the deserted tables, producing a haunted quality, a mystical amplification that defied discernment. Everything became preternaturally still, lending credence to what followed.

One whom you do not see. One who walks between wind and light.

Urien shook his head as the bodiless chant repeated itself time and again within his brain. He looked at Morgen, then at Kay his jailor, and realized that they did not hear it. Far away a true friend was offering guidance, and so he focused his clouded thoughts, unraveling the clues, coded as they were. *Someone I do not see. Someone whom I never would suspect. Someone who walks on the wind? On the wind? Who would be daft enough to walk on the wind? The falcon, Cerifus, or whatever his bloody name happens to be? Does Morgen have a penchant for mating with animals? That question is just insane enough that it might prove true. Falcon, falcons—how many falcons claim her affection? Has one ever heard of a human falcon? No, certainly not. It is the drink that brings that thought to mind. Perhaps it is a bird of another feather. By the gods, no. It can't be. Merlin, the king's enchanter—that tall, spindly scarecrow that mirrors the walking dead?*

"No," his incredulous cry burst forth, "it is too ridiculous!"

Urien began to laugh uncontrollably at the folly of it, his words spilling out with wild abandon, fists carelessly pummeling Kay's blade without any true intention of attack. "Unless it is that infernal teacher of yours, the one that keeps you so late in the woods. What is it he teaches you, my sweet?"

Morgen said not a word but offered Urien her traditional icy stare that demanded silence. Unfortunately this time she was not accommodated.

"What say you, Kay?" he continued, carefully watching Morgen's face for any telltale signs of betrayal. "The thought is almost too laughable for words. Morgen would have little more success mating with Merlin than with you."

"Enough!"

Without further ado Kay slammed his elbow against Urien's head, an action which thankfully rendered the petty king unconscious.

Morgen rushed forward and clasped Kay's arm. "Thank you, good Kay," she said, beaming approval. "You have just saved me from a rather unpleasant evening."

Slipping back into his typical discomfort, Kay mumbled an incoherent reply and then began the long, slow process of dragging himself across the room.

"Would it not be best to restrict his movements until the wine has worn off?"

A smile flickered across Kay's ruddy face and he ceased his flight. "Are you suggesting I chain him?"

"Perhaps chaining might be too severe. If you could tie him against the chair so the knots must hold, we can conveniently forget he is here."

Kay fell to laughing once more. "You really despise him. You no more wish to marry Urien than Cedric, the Saxon king."

"How true," she said with a mischievous lift of her brows.

Securing a length of rope, Kay's eyes sparkled as he set to work, firmly tying Urien's limbs against the cross section of his oaken chair. For a time neither he nor Morgen appeared conscious of the animosity that once framed their relationship. Instead each worked toward achieving their goal with ingenuity and not a little amusement.

When at last the deed was done, Morgen kissed Kay's cheek and set about bringing her plan to fruition. "Thank you, Kay. You have done so very much for me this night. May I not offer you a gift as well?"

CHAPTER 23

New Beginnings

Kay beat a hasty retreat, dragging his wounded frame deep into the moldering, cobweb infested bowels of Caerleon, where he prayed the delicate Morgen would not follow. The air was foul, thick with fumes from the heated stoves above and fermenting mead barrels peppered here and there. A soft, sucking sound met each footstep, indicating that which he could not see: the mud-covered flooring, an additional deterrent that he hoped would check her advance. No matter how fast he fled, however, the sound of her voice grew increasingly near.

"Please, Kay, allow me to help you!"

Again her infernal offer of healing! Why could she not simply leave him alone?

"Are you blind?" he bellowed, turning to meet her gaze. "I am past all help!"

The steps took an abrupt plunge into darkness just ahead. Kay muffled his torch and disappeared down the lightless descent, hoping Morgen's fears would get the better of her.

Morgen never faltered, however, her feet certain of that which she could not see. "I can make
you whole!" she cried, maneuvering sightlessly
toward his shadowy form.

A shudder raced up Kay's spine. The still, small
voice inside reassured him that this was true.
Perhaps that is why his heart increased its frantic
bid to outrun time. Morgen was behind him—the
sound of her approaching footfalls told him as
much. Still he would not turn and look at her.

"Yes, you felt it," she said, running her hands
along the length of his wounded spine. "I am a
healer, Kay. Allow me to rid you of this agony."

Kay's distorted face twisted miserably as he tore
free of her grasp. Up came the torch—or what
was left of it—so he could better see her expression. "You never thought me such a prize when I
was whole! I remember your looks of disgust at St.
Alban's. Now be done with it. Allow me to live my
life such as it is."

A frown graced Morgen's brow. "St. Alban's?
When did I ever see you at St. Alban's?"

"I was there the night of the insurrection, helping Arthur fight off Lot when you swept past all of
us. I know you saw me, Morgen. Our eyes met and
you quickly looked away."

Something clicked within Morgen's brain as
images of an oafish, copper-haired youth flooded
her senses. Kay's look was far from handsome even
then, overshadowed by his golden foster brother
whose face and form mimicked the god of light.
Overzealous, his blows were wild, erratic, mirror-

ing his temper. Few women, if any, would think on him as a prize, let alone a worthy husband.

Horrified by the accuracy of Kay's remark, Morgen spoke before thinking.

"Forgive me, Kay," she whispered, "I had eyes only for Merlin." A crimson flush colored her cheeks, even as her gaze sought the dirt-laden steps. Perhaps she had said too much.

There was a brief pause. "Urien spoke true, then?"

Morgen met Kay's eyes, which were softer, more inviting. She gave a nod, wondering if it had been wise to bare so much of her soul.

"I only ask," he continued, awkwardly, "because Merlin always thinks of others, not himself. It would really be…" Kay swallowed, searching for words, "…really good if you loved him. He is more worthy of love than all the rest of us lumped together."

At that moment Morgen knew she had won. They had finally reached a common ground. Kay understood her love, even approved of it. This knowledge gave her the confidence to continue, "I do not believe you were meant to suffer this torment, not while I can heal you."

A sigh escaped Kay's tightly clenched lips and his shoulders drooped a little lower. "It is a beautiful dream, princess, but it cannot be."

This said, he resumed a retreat through Caerleon's desolate underworld, his torch sputtering its faint illumination until the oppressive darkness swallowed it whole and Kay's form could no longer be distinguished amid the preternaturally creepy landscape.

Morgen followed at a distance. She found Caerleon's cellars far from appealing, something altogether stifling about their inherent darkness, reminiscent of death. Still she pressed on, maneuvering against a forest of billowy cobwebs that frosted her gown and hair.

"Princess, will you not take nay for an answer?" Kay bellowed in exasperation, still unseen, though he stood but a few paces away. His wayward torch had flared and died, and so he wore the darkness as a cloak of distinction, yet deep inside he could not help but wonder if Morgen was right. What if she could heal him? There was only one way to find out. Much as he was loath to entertain such folly, he grabbed her wrist and pulled her into a chamber that lay directly beneath the bustling kitchens. Kay often sought this retreat when people's comments cut excessively deep.

Morgen was immediately struck by the room's desolate condition. Indeed, four stone walls made up its claustrophobic, infinitely dismal composition. It lacked anything reminiscent of a window, and it stifled all avenues of light. A half dozen people could be housed on cots here—more if stood end to end. Morgen wondered why this knowledge animated her imagination. Indeed, the chamber was so abysmally dark, so oppressively dank that few would seek its shelter. No wonder Kay found it impossible to heal. The place reminded her of a tomb.

"It is an abandoned fruit cellar," he mumbled in a kind of apology.

Morgen nodded. The darkness brought forth a feeling of suffocation that almost made her pause, but then a flick of her fingertips set things aright, and Kay's torch flared anew. Altogether unacquainted with Morgen's abilities, Arthur's foster brother stared at the fiery beacon nonplused, then secured the wooden base inside a dull cast iron holder and watched the room slowly fill with light. Although the air was oppressively heavy, it was possible to breathe once more.

Casting her eyes over a filthy mass of rag-strewn straw that blanketed the chamber in various states of decomposition, Morgen shuddered despite herself. This was where Kay slept. How could Arthur allow his foster brother to exist in such wretched debasement? Did Arthur even know that this was where Kay spent most of his free time now that he could no longer drill with the men?

Kay offered a grunt and indicated that she should sit on a narrow bench directly opposite his makeshift bed. "I want it understood that there will be no touching. I will not have it said that I attacked Arthur's sister in this pit."

Morgen blinked. Suddenly Kay's hesitancy made sense. "I would never conjure such an accusation. If you wish I will remain here on the bench until the healing is complete, but I must warn you that it will take much longer that way."

Kay answered with only a grimace, broader than usual. He then belligerently placed his back against the filthy wall and slid down into what might be thought of as a seated position. This accomplished, he grumbled that she should begin.

It never occurred to Morgen that the very act of sitting would cause him immense pain. "If I am to work on your back, you must face the wall."

The bitter giant gave a snort, then turned away.

A cry of joy nearly escaped Morgen's lips. At last—at last she could begin! *Bridget and Diancecht, mother and father of the healing arts*, her thoughts cried as she placed palm against palm, *Sir Kay is in great need of your compassion. Thank you for allowing me to be the instrument through which this miracle will occur. We ask that this be a total healing of heart, mind, body, and spirit.*

Seven symbols danced within Morgen's nimble mind, each associated with a different form of healing. She chose the first, an empowerment symbol, and then inwardly chanted its sacred name. Although Kay would soon partake of its blessings, he must never know the symbol's true name. This was knowledge for the initiated alone. Soon Morgen's palms grew hot and tingling. She drew the invisible spiral down her own frame to protect against any empathetic reactions and began.

Raising both hands, palms forward, Morgen felt the divine energy blaze within her own being, then directed it into Kay's wounded spine. She saw at once that Kay willingly received the gift, for his twisted back involuntarily flexed and shuddered.

Concern flooded his expression. "What is it, princess? What is happening to me? It feels as if a hundred spears were just thrust through my body."

"Easy, Kay," Morgen replied, a hint of amusement coloring her voice. "Does it really hurt that much, or is it simply odd to feel sensation in your back?"

An oath escaped Kay's lips, as he squeezed both arms tightly against his chest. "If you know so much, you tell me!"

Laughter spilled from Morgen's lips. "I only know that the life force does not usually injure those it heals. Sit up straight, please."

"What?"

"You heard me. Straighten your back."

"You know I cannot!"

"Then forgive me," she said, rising, "I must break my promise."

Without further hesitation, Morgen spanned the distance between herself and Kay until she bent knee and knelt beside him. Softly she pressed one hand against his spine while the other came to rest upon his chest. Energy blazed between the two points, spiraling deep into his core.

Kay bit down on his lip hard until it ran wet with blood.

He was about to make further protest when she said, "Do not shrink, Kay. It is the power of the divine healers you feel now. You are being blessed by Bridgit and Diancecht themselves."

"By the gods, Morgen, how can you bear it?" he gasped, clawing his hands against the wall for support. "You are so tiny. I am surprised this power does not knock you flat."

Morgen chuckled. "Perhaps I am stronger than I appear."

Spasms shook Kay's body as he accepted more and more of the healing energy. This was utterly unacceptable to the embittered seneschal. Embarrassment soon took hold, clouding all perception. Indeed, Kay's torso trembled so violently that he feared it would explode. How was this possible? It felt as if Morgen's dainty hands were working in the depths of his being, stirring the wounded spinal column back to life. Just when it seemed he must scream, an audible snap eclipsed all other sensation. A flood of pain followed, accompanied by an invisible pressure that nearly made Kay stand. Bellow he must, regardless of who might hear.

"Release me! I cannot bear it!"

"No, you are almost whole. Think of what it will mean to be healed! Urien will never dare offer you insult of any kind. Women will seek your embrace."

Through no inclination of his, Kay grasped Morgen's delicate shoulder and watched as violet energy encompassed them both, summoning up visions of a forgotten doorway that lead to those things typically unseen by mortal eyes. Suddenly Kay became aware of countless spirits hovering around the room, lending their energies as the healing reached its zenith. They were smiling at him, offering compassion—the knowledge of which split his heart wide open. Never before had he experienced such a feeling of love, not the type that accompanies passion but the kind that speaks to the eternal in everyone. Tears softened Kay's expression as Morgen touched his gnarled lip. A sharp, buzzing sensation followed. Down upon the moldering straw he collapsed. The healing was complete.

Morgen rose and walked slowly around the room, thanking each of the spirit guides, unprepared for what would follow. A new revelation, a new wonder was about to usurp all previous conceptions. The divine Bridgit, colored by flame, reached forward and touched Morgen's abdomen in blessing. Realization dawned anew. Was it possible? She, a Fairy Queen reborn, would give birth to another? The wonder of it all nearly choked Morgen with its brilliance. Gracefully she bowed before Bridget and the other deities, filled with humility, eyes sparkling, salt bright. At that moment she remembered her charge who trembled pressed against the wall.

"You have just experienced a complete healing of heart, mind, body, and spirit. Be good and cherish it, Kay. Life is a beautiful, wondrous experience. Do not shudder even as it pierces your soul."

Kay fell forward, awestruck, barely conscious of Morgen's departing footsteps until the door creaked its warning. Without thinking he sprang up and rushed after her.

"Would you leave, Morgen, without allowing me to give thanks?"

"Your body offers little resistance now," Morgen replied, turning her radiant smile upon him.

Glancing down at his formerly twisted frame, Kay saw that it was indeed whole. One hand involuntarily caressed the spot where the unsightly scar had marred his face. It was smooth and clear. Words were not immediately forthcoming, so he knelt before her. "I am eternally in your debt."

Morgen felt a certain thrill rush through her veins. This was power indeed. Deep down inside she knew it was wrong to take credit for the healing. She was merely a channel for the Ancient Ones' will, but the power it gave her over mankind was gratifying beyond expression.

"It was my pleasure, Kay," she said, protectively draping one hand against her stomach. "Should Urien or any other man offer me insult, I will claim my reward."

She drew the sacred spiral against his brow in blessing and then set out once more through the murky cellar, unmindful of the dust and cobwebs that clung to her frame. At long last she had discovered her life's purpose!

Upon reaching her chambers, Morgen was vaguely aware that Urien's scent lingered nearby. He had obviously freed himself during Kay's healing. No doubt he spied on her even now. Unwilling to stomach his presence at such a time of joy, she quickly entered the darkened room and set the bolt in place. There was so much to do—so much to tell! Out she strolled onto the balcony, reveling in the spicy, autumn air. Where was her beloved? She must tell him all no matter what the cost. How many days had passed since they were able to exchange anything more than a casual remark? Her soul ached for Merlin, crying his name in a voice that no mortal ear could hear. A moment later, she saw him.

A beautiful hawk swooped low against the starlit sky. Morgen heard its cry even before she caught the first glimpse of his outstretched wings.

The coal-bright eyes so uncharacteristic of his breed, the unmistakably regal bearing—all hinted at his true identity. Still, she would not speak his name—no, not until they were far removed from Caerleon. Gracefully the raptor lit upon Morgen's outstretched arm. She smiled down upon him and placed a swift kiss against his hooked beak.

Urien watched the entire exchange unnoticed from the shadows below. It did not take long before the familiar pangs of jealousy consumed his rapidly beating heart. Even this bird, no doubt another favorite pet, commanded Morgen's affections!

Suddenly, much to Urien's surprise, Morgen evaporated into thin air, or so it seemed in the heavy darkness. A silent raven now occupied the space were once her dainty form had stood. The two unlikely birds began to converse in a language he could not understand. Urien observed this interaction for a time, then marveled as they flew off together into the deepening night. A degree of understanding slowly registered in his steadily sobering brain. The bird Morgen had kissed was not a simple hawk, but a Merlin, a subtle master of disguise. *Merlin was his rival*—not a man, but some magical fiend, well capable of defending himself against a sword.

Chewing on this new tidbit, Urien reentered his chambers and bolted the door against intrusion. It would not do for Arthur, or even Lot to witness what would follow. Lost inside the many folds of fragrant red velvet in a wooden box he kept hidden underneath the balcony window rested an amber amulet. It belonged to a woman whom he counted as the most willing and apt of lovers. She had told him time and again that he need only rub the amulet three times and whisper her name, and she would enact his every desire.

Pulling the trifle forth, a scent of musk filled his nostrils. He had barely offered the piece a single caress when she appeared, locked within his arms.

"Morgause," he whispered, placing his lips against her pearly breasts, "I have a boon to ask of you. One that I believe you will find most rewarding."

CHAPTER 26

Moonlight

"Oh, how delightful," Morgause sighed. "You wish me to torment Merlin."

"No, I want you to kill him."

Morgause paused before making answer, her emerald eyes taking in every inch of Urien's ill-attended chambers. Dark, stagnant, and seething due to an abundance of distemper, the room boasted little to recommend it beyond the regulation raised bed, trussed as Morgen's counterpart in tattered remnants of amber and green. Perhaps that is why Urien kept the windows fettered past discernment and the candles dimmed beyond easy recognition. Perhaps it was his need for subterfuge that fuelled this fancy. No doubt the king's enchanter kept close watch on the lord of North Wales. It was vital they not be understood.

"That will not be easy," she carefully replied, ascertaining their relative safety.

Unmindful of such precautionary efforts, Urien kissed Morgause, moving up the base of her creamy throat. "It should be simple enough for one of your talents."

"Why should I do this? Have I not already gone against all womanly principle by helping you win Morgen?"

A sneer darkened Urien's expression. "Forgive me, but your assistance has hardly paid off. I am still far from claiming her love."

"I never said she would love you," rang Morgause's studied reply.

Urien's eyes flashed fire. She had lied to him again. Once this request was fulfilled he would take pleasure in severing all ties between himself and the red witch.

Aware of his darkening thoughts, Morgause deliberately sat upon the disordered bedding, caressing the deerskin coverlets back into a more ordered composition. "Do not despair. Morgen will be your wife. I have seen it. She will give you a fine son."

"When?" he cried, taking firm hold of her shoulders as if to shake the very truth from her lips.

The blood slowly drained from Morgause's face. "Why should I answer that? When Morgen becomes your wife, I lose my favorite paramour."

Suddenly Urien understood. Morgause had no intention of releasing him. She planned on keeping her claws in him even after Morgen became his wife. Well, two could play that game—a game he intended to win! A subtle shift of movement and she was beneath him, flat upon her back.

"You lose nothing."

"Let me be blunt. I cannot kill Merlin. It lies not within my power."

Morgause slid free of his embrace, then fairly vaulted off the bed. Tossing her fiery black mane, she sauntered toward the ancient window. "Morgen—why must your thoughts begin and end with Morgen?"

"You promised her to me for the death of Uther Pendragon!"

Urien spoke true. He had done Morgause a great service in helping her bring about Uther's demise. Did he not deserve a just reward? Chuckle she must at the thought. Morgen would be no blessing to Urien—no blessing at all. Slowly her gilt green eyes pooled, betraying emotion of another kind. Urien was her own true love. Unfortunately it had been Lot, not Urien, who got her with child all those years ago. Marriage soon followed. Lot wanted a son, and she gave him one. Thus began the bitter cycle. Child after child came, all of them boys, perhaps half belonging to Lot. Morgause smiled at this, remembering the little secret she kept so well. Through it all Urien remained her steadfast lover. She never once doubted his passion—never until Morgen became his obsession.

"I have never asked you for anything," Urien whispered, slowly drawing near so he might wrap his hands about her waist. "Won't you do this for me?"

"I may weaken Merlin by degrees," she sighed, as Urien's lips caressed her throbbing temple, "until he becomes a mere shell of his former self. Once he reaches such a state, you will have little trouble killing him yourself."

Urien lifted her in his arms. "You are magnificent!"

Lost in thought, he momentarily held her aloft; then just as abruptly set her down. "Where are they now? Can you see them?"

Morgause watched her love gain the window and toss the gauzy curtains aside so he might better search the night sky. She was forgotten even then. The gilt green eyes narrowed in anger.

"Do you really wish to know? Such knowledge could make you wretched."

"I am wretched!" he cried, pounding his fist against the blistered casing until powered rock filled the air. "Help me!"

"To win Morgen you must make her lover look the fool."

"Then show me! Show me how!"

"Patience," rang Morgause's triumphant reply. "This night I will see it done."

Doffing their bird habits for those of the human variety, Morgen and Merlin walked hand in hand through cascades of golden mistletoe that bowed tantalizingly low from their oaken perches and tickled the crown of the mage's coal-black head. Moss softened each footfall even as a crunch of an ill-fated leaf revealed steady progress. They were invisible to all but the most discernible eye. Indeed, the barn owl saw them, and so did the bear cub, but no human of note checked their progress beyond she who watched from Caerleon's haunted labyrinth. This was, after all, the woodlands: the sacred haven that magnified their dreams. No one dared fully penetrate the dusky veil that held them so tightly within its protective embrace. They were light and air, thoroughly in tune with bee, brook, rock, and sapling. Wordlessly, they pressed forward, avoiding the obvious topic that continuously assaulted their thoughts. A thick cluster of fledgling yew trees finally gave way, opening up a grand vista: the crescent-shaped lake that had been their stopping grounds for so many romantic liaisons.

Night loomed soft around them, watching, waiting. So much remained to be revealed, so much that demanded inspection. Mage and fay said nothing, however, spellbound as it were, lost in the depths of each other's eyes. Both were silent, wanting so much for the other to speak, but forbidden topics clouded their perception. This was not to be an easy meeting. Finally Merlin clasped Morgen against his heart and willed the interview to commence. They did not kiss or even offer so much as a caress but simply held each other, allowing love full sway.

This night I must do it. I cannot tell her the truth. Morgen will never accept the fact that our marriage will see her dead before she reaches the tender age of nineteen. Nor can she comprehend the bitter rift that will develop between the peoples of Britannia and ultimately lead to Arthur's destruction. She must believe, instead, that I think only of myself.

Merlin swallowed hard, steadying himself against the task ahead. His heart bled at the thought that this might be the last time he ever held Morgen close—the last time he claimed her love. Slowly, deliberately, he broke their embrace and motioned for her to sit.

Drawing a thick, green woolen cloak around her, Morgen complied. She read the seriousness behind Merlin's actions and waited with breathless anticipation. So much depended upon this nocturnal interview—so much she had not fully contemplated. How was she to broach such a subject? Should she tell the arch mage that he would soon be a father? Would he welcome this knowledge or desert her—leave her without another word? Surely Merlin's gentle heart did not allow for such a possibility! One look in his deep, black eyes, however, gave her further pause. Something was wrong, very wrong.

Waves of pearly mist swirled around Merlin, shrouding him in an unearthly glow. Somewhere across the lake, a mournful howl echoed soft and hauntingly sweet. A lone wolf had just drawn near the water's edge. Her amber eyes fell upon the mournful lovers, offering comfort.

Merlin took a deep, steadying breath. It was time to spill his soul but only those parts that would aid his cause. "I never dreamed I would find love, Morgen. I never sought it, not even when it was offered by a beautiful woodland fairy." He gently placed his lips against her silken tresses. "Come let us share our innermost thoughts."

Thrilled by the assumed honesty of such a proposal, the words flowed from Morgen's lips with little prompting. Now they would broach the forbidden subject—the subject that might very well lead to a confession.

"What does your soul say about us—about marriage?"

Aware that his answer must prove utterly convincing, Merlin looked her dead in the eye and replied, "It is impossible, Morgen. Surely you see that. You are a princess, destined to bring about the healing of our people. Your marriage to the right man will facilitate that miracle. I am a counselor, meant to oversee the process—to help arrange the proper match."

Reproach bristled Morgen's luminous expression. "You are my proper match! Surely the people will see that!" Unable to further meet his gaze, she took flight. It was over now and forever. Merlin had effectively renounced her in favor of a unified Britannia. She was indisputably insignificant, unworthy of mention, especially when it came to matter of politics—those things that fuelled Merlin's imagination. Everything else must come first, everything except her heart. Merlin, the arch mage, did not care a fig for her. No, not really. How could he when marriage proved an option, a poison he chose not to imbibe. Off she raced into the heart of the stone circle oblivious to the fact that Merlin was fast upon her heals. Although he was speaking, she only half heard his words. That was enough, however, to make her skid to a stop.

"They will believe that the king's counselor seeks power through a royal marriage."

"No!" she whirled around, gazing full upon him. Suddenly the truth danced unbidden before Morgen's eyes. Merlin was right. The people of Britannia would never accept them as man and

wife or even a couple. They would be outcast, considered vermin, the very scum of the earth, unable
to further assist Arthur or Britannia. The utter bit-
terness of this truth turned her thoughts to bile.
Why did Merlin always have to be right?

Right or wrong, Morgen somehow found herself stationed before the central standing stone,
the tallest and most pockmarked of its brethren,
which she diligently embraced for support. How
had she come to be there? No doubt her mind was
so numbed by the people's assumed rejection—*the
people for whom I gave up everything*—that the act
of moving escaped her attention. In any case she
must offer some kind of coherent answer. And so
she spoke in a dull, colorless voice.

"If this were a perfect world, I would say that
it mattered not. I do not require marriage vows.
How can marriage further knit two hearts as one?
We are already bound by the Ancient Ones themselves. Let the people rest at ease. They need not
know of our affection."

This admission heartened Merlin as no other.
Thus he gathered courage and drew near Morgen.
Slowly, gently, he turned her so she must face him
and seized her hands, covering them with kiss after
kiss as if the answer to his prayers had manifested
without prompting or use of his prodigious talents.

Morgen grimaced, despite her best efforts to
remain calm. The truth proved a bitter tonic. She
saw through Merlin's excess display of emotion
and reacted accordingly. "But, as you so readily
pronounce, I am Arthur's sister. I have no option
but to marry whoever makes the king the most

acceptable offer. If that not be you, then someone else will claim me. Is your soul so unwilling to compromise on this point that it would readily cast me away forever?"

A tremor wrenched Merlin's spine. *She is not finished. Oh, no, not yet. Thus I must play out this theatrical and suffer the full brunt of her displeasure. Why then should I not make it easier for us both? Why should she not know the truth, even if it be partial confession?*

Choosing his words carefully, Merlin convincingly mouthed his reply. "We are eternally bound, Morgen. Nothing can change that. I will always be with you, even if you marry another." He saw her lovely face blanch white, then added, "No matter what happens, you cannot lose me, just as I cannot be separated from you. I will linger always within the tenderest chambers of your heart. You need but peer inside to find me."

"And when my future husband takes me to his marriage bed—what then?"

The mage never flinched. Little did Morgen dream that he had been strengthening himself on this point for quite some time. "I will be there."

Morgen nearly choked at this, caught between laughter and tears. Yes, this was the legendary Merlin—tight, cold, and dispassionate. What would he do if she shared her secret? Would it make any earthly difference? Embracing the ancient stone, cool, gray, omnipresent once more, she turned her back on him. Why did he not speak the truth? He wished to be rid of her—so he might focus all his attention on matters of government.

The mage wove his arms around Morgen, aware that he was but a syllable away from losing her. "We each have our life tasks," he began in a calm, tranquil voice. "Healing will consume your existence. I will help Arthur unite Britannia. Anything else is—*must be*—of a secondary nature. I cannot be controlled by those passions that normally dominate men, not until this miracle, as it were, has been accomplished. Nevertheless, I love you, Morgen. You are everything a woman can be to me, but you are not the totality of my existence."

Morgen opened her eyes—one centered on the moon-drenched lake, while the other rested against cool moss-covered stone. A silvery salmon leapt high, drawing her focus. It would be the greatest folly of all to reveal her secret. The salmon's appearance lent her a wisdom that indicated as much. The truth must, therefore, remain unspoken. "Now I understand," she said, nearly choking. "You wish to be with me only when it is convenient. How selfish—how utterly thoughtless."

Finally the moment was upon Merlin. His mind reeling, his heart bloodied, he communicated with the deepest intimacy of his mind. ***That is why I now set you free. You must decide our fate. I place it in your hands.***

A furrow darkened Morgen's smooth brow. This was so typical, so characteristically like Merlin. "Why must I decide?"

"Beloved, the Saxons are moving once again, plundering the countryside. A return to war is imminent."

"Oh, yes, you must go off to war and I to the Underworld, for I will not live in this realm of mortals if we must keep apart."

Merlin tried to free her from the stone, but she remained immoveable. "And what of all your talk about advising Arthur? What of the good work you will accomplish with your healing abilities? Look at Kay! You have given that lad a new life. What greater gift is there in the world than that?"

Several lifetimes of watching and waiting had taught Morgen the proper response. Indeed, she knew this answer better than she knew her own self. She stood poised, waiting for the precise moment in which her words would wield the most weight. This found, she turned and faced him. "The greatest gift in this world is *love*, Merlin—or have you forgotten that?"

A slight, almost imperceptible tremor animated Merlin's frame. He was failing, failing miserably. Morgen was right, of course. Still, he had to speak the words for her sake. "What good is earthly love in a world that is endlessly fraught by war?"

The fire dwindled in Morgen's eyes. "I have no answer for that."

Back into the center of the standing stones she trod, silently planning her future. She would leave court within the fortnight, return to Avalon, if possible. There the child would be raised a fairy, and the absence of a father would not cut so deeply. Slowly, methodically, Morgen drew the cloak around her, thankful for the additional warmth it provided and sat upon the sodden ground. She heard Merlin's approach but was surprised when he did not take up residence beside her.

The play had all but reached its zenith. Merlin had merely to react to whatever Morgen threw at him, albeit with a docile expression. Perhaps that is why he sat behind her. It would be the highest folly to reveal even the slightest emotion at this time. Slowly, luxuriantly, he relaxed his long legs so they encompassed Morgen on both sides. This done he drew her silken head back so that it rested against his chest. It was vital she not see his eyes.

"Forgive me, beloved. I brought you here this night to demonstrate the depth of my love. Please tell me the innermost whisperings of your soul. Please, my love, say anything. Do not shrink even if you think it will wound me."

Morgen gave a laugh that sounded almost cruel, then replied in a calculated voice, "I have already shared with you my innermost longings. Perhaps you did not hear. I wish to be your wife—to bear your children."

A silent cry escaped Merlin's lips. She wished to give him children? Even now, after all he had said and done, Morgen's thoughts centered on what she could *give him.* Merlin's face contorted in anguish. This was a dream he had never allowed himself to entertain.

"Yes, of course, I should have known," Morgen snapped, interpreting his silence for indifference. "You wish to avoid that topic as well."

The mage felt his heart sink even further. Thankful that Morgen could not see his face, he whispered to better camouflage emotion, "I have honestly never considered such a possibility."

Morgen never missed a beat. "Children are extremely precious to those of us in the fairy realm."

Kissing her softly on the cheek, Merlin said, "Go on."

"We could have one of each," she continued, hoping against hope that she might sway him, "a boy and a girl—to raise in the ways of the art."

"It is a beautiful dream, beloved," came Merlin's careful response. Pictures danced before his eyes of a lovely daughter with ebony hair and alabaster skin: the child waiting to be born should he make Morgen his bride.

Allowing his finger to drift back and forth across her arm, Merlin waited for a reply. When Morgen said nothing more, he deliberately switched topics, thankful that the images no longer played within his mind. "Tell me of your dreams for power. I know they are ever present in your mind. This night, during Kay's healing, you felt a certain rush of it. Tell me, what you would do with this gift?"

All hope evaporated in that instant. Merlin had shown his true face. Morgen could do little but let the discussion run full course, which meant she must offer some coherent answer. "I would accompany Arthur to war and heal all within my reach."

"You are only one person and would find the task of healing all those wounded in battle impossible at best. Look how long it took you to heal Kay—an hour, nearly two. Think of how many others would die waiting for you to finish healing the one lucky enough to claim your attention first. What would that do to you? I can tell you what it did to me."

"But as you have so clearly expressed, we are not the same."

Merlin broke the embrace. "You are not going into battle, Morgen. Arthur will not allow it. There is little use speaking any further on the subject."

Morgen was on her feet at once. "You tear down my dreams before they even so much as leave my lips!"

"Such beautiful lips they are too," he said, following her example. Merlin thereby offered up a passionate kiss that lasted no more than an instant, due to his love's firm rebuff.

"You accuse *me* of leading *you* to distraction!"

"I do the best I can."

"You truly are the spawn of an incubus."

"And you are a reckless, little sprite. What a charming pair we make."

"I never used magic to make you love me. "

"Ah, but you are magic itself."

A slight pause ensued as Morgen took in the compliment. Merlin was staring at her with an almost condescending smile painted across his dusky lips. He was arrogant and conceited, altogether certain that he could not lose her. Did it not follow that she should test this failing, stretch it to the very limits? Certain topics Merlin never entertained. This was how she would decide their fate.

"Merlin, I know of your dreams of peace through Arthur. What else do you desire? What of those dreams that pertain to yourself?"

The first streaks of dawn drew Merlin's gaze. He could just detect the fading outline of the moon. He tried to speak but found it impossible. A haunted wolf cry filled the air with its silvery beauty, followed by a deep, lingering response.

His own dreams? What made Morgen believe that Merlin, the enchanter, was allowed such a luxury?

A light wind played with Morgen's locks, driving them against her pallid cheeks as if they were livid tongues of flame. For a moment the mage thought he saw a tear pool in her eye, but then the walls of defense appeared, and her expression grew terse.

"You have made your decision. Now I must make mine."

Transitions

Why must life be so blasted complicated?
Merlin shook his head, adapting to his new surroundings. He had landed on the far side of a gray-stoned, unevenly sloped hillside that overlooked the heavily thicketed quadrant of Caerleon. Violet light flashed above as the portal he had previously conjured crackled with a fire's ferocity before disappearing from view. Thus, through clever magic, he arrived ahead of Morgen.

This process of severing all ties with Morgen is far more difficult than I surmised.

Scanning the pink-hued horizon, he saw at last a fair swan winging her way homeward, albeit with quiet desperation. Indeed, the pace was too harried, the gait hauntingly uneven for her to escape detection.

My poor beloved.

Softly, he offered wordless apology, but to no avail. The pale beauty swooped low across the landscape, then dipped out of sight.

Mastering the hill's mossy summit with wearied gait, Merlin began his trek home. Down he plunged, sliding several feet on some loose stones before he grabbed a fledgling hawthorn for support. The fragile sapling groaned but held firm, offering Merlin a moment's rest that fortified his resolve. Time and again he found his descent similarly hampered until one particularly stony pass offered such navigational difficulty that he landed flat on his backside. Merlin paused, grimacing. If Morgen witnessed that bit of awkwardness, she would no doubt enjoy a good laugh.

Regaining his footing Merlin dusted off his robes, aware of the comic picture he painted. A lesson resided in this somewhere, although he did not yet see it. Perhaps that was the beauty of his situation. He had done everything within his power to make himself look a fool, and he had succeeded. The ease with which he had accomplished this gave him some pause. In any case if his actions saved Morgen, then no further condemnation would ever enter his thoughts. She was the one at risk. She was the one who would die if he...

It was then he saw her stationed several yards below. Morgen, having doffed her swan form for that of Britannia's princess, stood frozen, gazing around the clustered trees at the courtyard, a look of horror distorting her normally graceful appearance. Indeed, her arms were flung at such odd, impossibly severe angles that they almost appeared broken. A solitary *O* punctuated her ruby lips, yet somehow her very silence magnified the horror, an unspoken anguish that dwelt just beneath the surface waiting tremulously for its chance to break forth as a soul-wrenching scream.

This unparalleled reaction far surpassed that of a woman jilted by her thoughtless lover. It was that of a soul staring straight into the eyes of death, eyes that would never open again. What was it Morgen saw? The answer broke forth from her lips.

Igrainne...

Realization soon shattered the spell, issuing up a magnificent wail that erupted from the depths of Morgen's being, torment and sound blending as one. The shock somehow spurred her forward, racing as it were to overtake time. She must gain the courtyard before it was too late—before the inert figure that lay so fixed and unmoving left the mortal plane forever. The poor child was stumbling, tripping over the elaborate hem of her violet gown even as the huge angel sleeves whipped against her delicate frame. Frustration increased Morgen's frantic pace to such an extent that she nearly fell face down against the dew-moistened grass. Suddenly surefooted, Merlin stayed her descent as he clasped her about the waist and began propelling her forward by sheer will alone.

Pausing near the courtyard gate, enchanter and princess saw at once the tragedy laid before them. An abundance of well-traveled horses, some still lathered with sweat, stood outside the already packed stables. Unfortunately neither handlers nor servants offered them attention. Indeed, the beautiful courtyard they loved so well was literally overflowing with multitudes of dark-robed mourners, both servant and noble. The object of their devotion appeared to be resting on top of a hollowed log, garlands of ivy draped around her docile frame.

Unable to stay the sobs that wracked her body, Morgen tore free of Merlin's grasp. What did she need with him—this man who no longer loved her? A far greater loss consumed her being. Death had claimed her mother: the woman responsible for her life, not in the traditional means of birthing, but one who had offered her a place in this wretched yet hopelessly wondrous mortal world. The finality of this transition affected Morgen's sensibilities as nothing else, for the single-mindedness of its intensity left her raw, bleeding. She would never see this simple, gloriously beautiful woman again, never feel her sheltering embrace or hear her warm laughter. They had been robbed, robbed of what little time they might have experienced together: first by Uther, the jealous, insanely domineering husband, and then by the war itself as it spirited them off in different directions for the proposed maintenance of the family name. What good had it done? She was never a Pendragon, not truly. Merlin knew this, as did Uther. Why had it been necessary to divide them? A subtle voice reminded Morgen that she had spent the last year in Avalon, training, preparing for the peace work she would manifest in the mortal plane. Igrainne could not have accompanied her down this path. A low groan escaped Morgen's lips. She was so far removed from anything that remotely resembled peace work that the whole crux of her existence appeared utterly and hopelessly useless. *It is I who should be lying there, not Igrainne. My life is over, over...*

If anyone beyond Merlin heard Morgen, they gave no outward indication, for, indeed, she agonized within the tortured pathways of her mind.

Each harried footstep brought her closer and closer to that oppressive doom. She had not been present to ease Igrainne through the transition, as was her right. She had failed in this as in so many other tasks. Had Uther's queen tread the darkened labyrinths of the Underworld alone? Morgen slammed her fists against her thighs as she raced forward. *You besotted imbecile! You spent all your thoughts, all your time with Merlin instead of helping your mother through the dark gates! How could you be so careless?* A still, small voice within, gently reminded her that it was also Igrainne's fortitude that had kept them apart. She had, after all, taken vows.

Vows? What on earth do you mean by that?

What had the former high queen been doing throughout those four years of separation?

Narrowing the gap between herself and Igrainne, Morgen felt a far more virulent terror usurp the rest. Her vision blurred then warped, hampered by a veil of unbidden tears. Igrainne was melting, melting down into the very earth, wrapped as she was in an abundance of pale robes—nun's robes! Was it possible that Igrainne had become a nun? No, surely this was a mistake! Igrainne would never adopt the habit of those heartless creatures that had tortured her, nearly destroying every bit of magic that beat within her veins!

Locked within a private tumult of emotion, Morgen only half realized that Arthur knelt at the foot of the coffin, his fair head bowed against distraction. She never saw him look up at her appearance or felt his cool fingers light upon her arm. How could she know that he too felt the same loss, the same unfair twist of fate that denied him a mother?

Yet Arthur innately understood it was the war that dealt him this cruel blow, not Uther. He wanted only to reclaim those lost years but knew at once the utter futility of such a wish, and so he reached for Morgen, his heart of hearts, hoping she might ease the pain. Oh, how easily she slipped through his fingers, bent on attaining some impossible goal. Arthur did not fully gather what Morgen meant to do until it was too late and even then hardly knew how to stop her.

Stumbling past Arthur's kneeling form, Morgen flung both arms around Igrainne and willed her to rise. Surely there was some mistake! Surely Igrainne was merely sleeping! The death chill told another story, one that Morgen could not quite accept. Igrainne was no longer present on the mortal plane. Indeed, she had already assumed another form, one that currently evaded Morgen's perception. Was it possible that the Ancient Ones acted with such brutal complacency? Did they knowingly deny a mother and daughter the chance, the final opportunity to say goodbye? Again the solitary question usurped all others as it preyed upon her increasingly manic thoughts: how could she have allowed herself to become so distracted by earthly love that she had missed her mother's passing? And then it came; the knowledge, the certainty of what Morgen intended filtered through her sensibilities with such strength, such unerring purpose that there could be no denial. She would raise the dead, bring Igrainne's soul back into its mortal shell, force it to breathe the air suddenly so foreign to its composition.

Ancient Ones, it is I, Morgen of Avalon! Hear my cry! I am a divine healer. This you have known from the beginnings of time. Now I beg that which is my right! Allow me to restore Igrainne for an hour—or a day. Please, I beg you! So much time has passed, so many hours wasted. Let me tell her how much I love her!

A golden halo of energy descended upon Morgen, enveloping her in a soft yet unyielding embrace. Mourners far and wide gasped at this seeming miracle. They did not understand Morgen's prowess or that she even possessed magical abilities of any kind. They saw only a grieving princess place both hands against the high queen's chest, eyes bent upon some distant star.

Morgen summoned the life force from its divine origins, oblivious to the increasingly awed cries of the masses. Indeed, her face, her entire countenance was so fixed, so focused on the terrible task before her that she did not fully understand the force with which the requested energy began spiraling inside her frame. Each heightened revolution bereft her of thought, of reason, stripping her already pale countenance of color and stirring tremors throughout her frail body to such an extent that it appeared Morgen herself must expire. And then the horror, the sheer power of the energy rebounded, striking Morgen squarely upon the chest so that she fell as one thunder-struck, landing soundly upon both knees.

The High King was on his feet almost as quickly as she was, but he could not contain her or cease her frantic aspirations. An almost brutal force possessed Morgen as she set both hands yet again against Igrainne's chest, completely oblivi-ous to the fact that her gown was torn and that both knees bled. She screamed in words no mortal could understand, but still the final prize evaded her. The energy originated with such hope, such promise, only to retreat just as rapidly from whence it came. Again and again Morgen tried, each time with increasing desperation. Surely some healing symbol was capable of manifesting her one wish into reality.

"Will no one help me?" she cried to the heav-ens, unaware that it would be a far more earthly guide that answered the call. "Why this silence after all the work I have done for you? Why have you abandoned me?"

Morgen was raving, shaking uncontrollably. Countless subjects who had never seen her before shifted uncomfortably, wondering what sort of mad woman Arthur claimed as a sister. Others bowed their heads and wept at such devotion. Kay, Accolon, and Bedivere struggled through the masses to offer some comfort, but it was Arthur who finally succeeded in clasping Morgen in his arms, Arthur who whispered words of solace in her ear.

"Even a divine healer must accept the inevita-ble. Some souls you cannot save, Morgen."

Suddenly it was as if Arthur's words cut through the fragile bands of time. Morgen blinked, aware that her vision was shifting, propelling her forward to another place, another future. There upon Avalon Tor she knelt, her hands poised over the dying form of Arthur Pendragon. Blood matted his golden hair and dripped into his unseeing eyes. One horror quickly usurped the rest. No hint of energy leaked through her ready fingers. Had the life force itself dried up completely, or did her inability to heal Arthur stem from a darker source? Was it possible that she could no longer wield its power.

"Let me go, dearest. I beg you—let me go."

Arthur's dying words filtered through Morgen's blood, her veins, with such finality that it lent an almost omniscient quality to the entire exchange. Suddenly Morgen split in two: the youthful maiden and her mature counterpart who had conjured the dreamspell. Each watched, increasingly distraught by Arthur's willingness to expire. This was the answer the older Morgen had awaited throughout the course of her conjuring, but the truth did not satisfy. Indeed, she stared wildly at her dying charge as if to infuse him with that very life that slowly dissipated from his wounded body. The vision trembled and then released its hold upon the youthful Morgen's waking consciousness, and she was propelled back into her present state and time. Indeed, a very much alive Arthur held her firmly against his chest, oblivious to her fresh agony. How could she tell him that one day her healing abilities would fail him as well?

"I cannot! I will not accept that!" she cried, flailing against her magnificent restrainer, but Arthur's strength and compassion stilled her frantic movements until they resembled that of a new born babe: weak, feeble, inconsequential.

"Dearest, hear me," he soothed, placing his lips against her damp forehead. "Igrainne is past all pain, all suffering. It is we who suffer now."

Morgen drew back and looked at Arthur, truly met his deep, blue eyes. How was it that a mortal possessed such wisdom? More importantly, how did a mortal acquire the wherewithal to instruct a fairy?

Slowly, deftly, darkness eclipsed all sensibility, and Avalon's misplaced Fairy Queen knew no more.

Time bent its mortal pace as multiple twilights whispered their starry spell. Shadows danced in and out of Morgen's consciousness, lending a further dreamlike quality to the voices and images that played upon her mind. Deeply she lingered within the haunted vale, unmindful of anything, even the soft touch of Merlin's lips. She could feel him probing, prodding her mind but did nothing. Indeed, nothing felt real anymore, not even the arch mage's so-called "love." Eventually he departed and another installed itself in his place. Perhaps it was Arthur, perhaps someone with a far more feminine touch. In any case it made no difference. She would soon leave Caerleon far behind and never look back. What did it matter if this decision went against Avalon's carefully laid plans?

They would soon be in possession of her child. That in itself was payment enough.

The warmth of what undoubtedly was Arthur's hand poised against her cheek put a pause to all such musings. Yes, she would miss Arthur—his strength, his compassion. Even his blind affection which left her so unsettled had stamped an indelible imprint upon her heart. It was a cruel trick of fate that had marked them as brother and sister. Otherwise they might have married. *Might have married? What was she thinking? Marry Arthur, who loved her beyond length and breadth of expression? Was such a thing possible?* Morgen felt the blood run cold in Arthur's fingers, as if he heard her.

"Come back, dearest. Come back to me and we will set all things aright."

If only Arthur knew the truth. He would hardly thank her for breeding with his counselor. Indeed, he might very well execute the pair of them.

"Do not be foolish!" she heard him snap at someone other than herself. "Why does she not wake?"

No, it was not herself but Merlin who stood in the greatest peril if Arthur found out the truth of her pregnancy. Suddenly the fierce anger behind Arthur's words hit home. To whom was he speaking? Who currently garnered his displeasure— surely not Merlin, the enchanter?

Gazing through half-focused eyes, Morgen witnessed her chamber door slam shut with a loud thud signaling Arthur's departure. In his wake stood a familiar presence, one that paused to soothe her fevered brow. A brightness that made her wince enveloped the person, indeed a brightness rivaled only by the solitary candle flame that sputtered fitfully before finally giving out altogether. This was the person who had endured Arthur's harsh tongue.

"Guenevere?" she whispered upon viewing the gleaming locks that nearly blinded her with their brilliance.

The golden goddess offered just the hint of a triumphant smile. Morgen nearly choked at the expression. She had never seen anything quite so lovely. Here truly was a maiden fit for a king. Did Arthur see this? Perhaps that is why his words bit so sharply.

"Morgen!"

Guenevere flung both arms around the invalid princess, well pleased with her timely awakening. "We have been so worried," she said in a pleasantly soothing tone. "Three whole days have come and gone since you fainted at your mother's coffin."

A dull, burning sensation signaled that tears had somehow found their way back into Morgen's eyes. She did not wish to cry, but it felt necessary, vital. Why should she not give into this mortal foolishness when her entire life appeared to be falling apart? Guenevere had no idea what it meant to be a pregnant maid of seventeen. She had no conception of how it felt to be dismissed by an unwilling, disinterested lover, or sanctioned by a brother who just happened to be Britannia's High King.

"No, no," Guenevere said, drawing the fragile princess against her breast, "do not grieve. Once the cold, the illness consumed her breathing, she did not suffer. Indeed, Igrainne's last words were of you. Naturally she left a long message for Arthur; but it was you she spoke of before..."

Try as she might, Morgen could not utter a response. She simply stared like one struck dumb by so much beauty. *Here stands the most beautiful woman in all Britannia—no question!* A rising nausea in the pit of her stomach also gave warning that she was far from well. Here was an additional "blessing" she had no desire to entertain. Why must she be pregnant when the world was falling to pieces? If only she had listened to Arthur, heeded his warnings!

"You were very precious to Igrainne," the peerless maiden continued. "It was her final wish that you be free of those she called 'reprehensible men' who seek to make you their wife."

Morgen choked back the laughter that nearly escaped her lips. It was not necessary for Guenevere to voice the names. Indeed, she had known all too well that Igrainne would disapprove of Merlin. Now it hardly mattered. Marriage with the arch mage was an all but forgotten dream. He had made that clear enough.

Viewing her patient's distress, Guenevere quickly interjected, "Forgive me. I should have avoided that topic."

"Why?" came the dull response. "I will have to face it soon enough."

Understanding something of the delicate position Morgen claimed as Arthur's sister, Guenevere turned away. She knew only too well the sacrifices a princess must make for her people, especially when it came to love. Perhaps that was why the bedchamber seemed oppressively dark, stifling all avenues of hope. Indeed, her own life offered little better. Thus she withstood Arthur's cutting words when it seemed she must scream forth at the injustice of it all or simply implode.

"Well, go on," Morgen sighed, falling back against a mound of pillowed deerskins. "You might as well say it. Mother spoke against Urien and…"

"Lord Merlin," Guenevere deftly supplied, carefully deciphering Morgen's reaction. She had, after all, heard the rumors and even witnessed the enchanter's attentions first hand during Morgen's illness. Still, she was unprepared for what followed.

Anger lanced into the very depths of Morgen's womb, leaving her faint, reeling. Merlin did not love her—or the child she carried inside. Why should she continue? Why not snuff out her life altogether? That was what Arthur feared: that she would never wake up. Why not take that route and be done with it? Arthur would no longer love her now that he had the golden goddess to gaze upon. *Ah, but I came here to guide him toward peace, not garner his affections. That should be reason enough to remain. When all is said and done, I am merely a pawn set forth to claim the ultimate prize. Love was never a part of that picture. I have merely forgotten my reason for being. It is time I reclaim that which is so essential to it.* Placing both hands against her belly, Morgen willed the nausea away.

Unaware of the true source of Morgen's discomfort, Guenevere altered the topic of their discussion.

"How did you fare at Amesbury, Morgen? Did you enjoy being housed with the brides of Christ?"

A hint of amusement colored the question, forcing a groan from Morgen's lips.

"I see," Guenevere replied with a knowing smile as she sat down upon the oversized bed. "You put it very well. In fact, I thoroughly agree."

Morgen raised her brows, surprised that Guenevere had not embraced the faith along with Igrainne. Old questions suddenly resurfaced regarding the maiden who had wielded a sword at St. Alban's monastery. Who was Guenevere? What was the truth of her past?

Such musings were cut short as the radiant maiden continued, "I believe that our creator or creators, whoever they may be, would wish us to be happy in this life, not chastised or beaten because we have done something wrong."

It was then Morgen understood that Guenevere had experienced a fate similar to her own at the hands of the Christian sisters. Before she could question her for particulars, however, Arthur strode through the door. The High King cut an altered figure that Morgen had never witnessed before, one of hardened authority that offered no hint of the compassionate heart that beat within his breast. He looked hauntingly like his father, consumed with a darkness that eclipsed all avenues of light. Was it her illness that had so unhinged him? The gaze he fixed upon her left no further question on that point. Arthur threw back the coverlets and seized Morgen in his arms, oblivious to the fact that Guenevere stood watching his efforts.

"Dearest, you're awake," he whispered to camouflage an all too real concern that his voice might fail. "You've come back." Gently he buried his lips against her temple, her cheeks and crown. Over and over he kissed her, relief flooding his features, softening them back to normalcy. "By the gods, I was so worried. I feared you might have given up this life in exchange for another."

Sound words, indeed, Arthur. How easily you read my soul.

Arthur gazed at her intently, as if he half caught the thought but cautioned silence when she would speak.

I could not bear it, Morgen. I simply could not bear it. I have become a tyrant in your absence, hurling orders here and there, stepping on people's toes when they would help me.

Then I suggest you beg their forgiveness, for that was foolhardy, indeed.

They were conversing easily within the avenues of the mind. Morgen marveled at Arthur's innate ability, then remembered how aptly he had displayed this talent the night Urien and Lot descended upon Caerleon. Did he possess other magical abilities that she had not yet discovered?

Arthur laughed despite himself. "I am so pleased that you are well." He gazed at Morgen intently, as if to fix every nuance, every subtlety of her countenance firmly in his mind. When at last he felt satisfied, he smiled: a dazzling smile that filled the hauntingly oppressive room with light. "Let us have no words of sorrow. Let us speak only of miracles at work here in this court. The miracle that you created with these two hands," he beamed, deftly entwining her slight fingers within the broad depths of his own.

"I am certain she is too modest to tell you, Guenevere," he continued, finally turning his gaze on the lovely, pale-haired maiden who stood nearly forgotten but a few paces away.

"Three nights ago, against all odds, Morgen healed my foster brother of grievous wounds the likes of which you have never seen!"

Pulling the still woozy Morgen out of bed, Arthur clasped her around the waist. "Sister, it is really too wonderful for words. I never would have dreamed it possible. My only complaint is that you did not tell me straight away!"

Morgen, the healer, Guenevere's thoughts turned upon themselves. Suddenly her simple care-giving skills appeared altogether trite. Perhaps it had been foolish to come here when she was so obviously not needed. Once Igrainne's burial had taken place, she would beg leave to return home to Carmalide.

Setting Morgen back upon the bed, Arthur recommenced dispensing his praise. "Kay told me how you healed him. That is why we could not find you when mother's train arrived. Merlin confided that you accomplished the deed all by yourself. No wonder you were so ill! I have never seen him so worried. He could not wrest you from the world of dreams no matter how hard he tried."

A deep, heartfelt sigh escaped Morgen's lips. This was all the answer she could muster. If only Arthur knew why she had blocked Merlin's investigations into her mind...

Such sorrow, such untold anguish clouded Morgen's features that Arthur drew his hand across the length of her cheek once more. *What is it, Morgen?* Something had happened between Morgen and his counselor—something that stifled all avenues of joy. He would not ask for an explanation, not until she fully recovered. Nor would he allow himself to hope that she was free—at least not until he knew the truth. "Tell me you are well."

"As well as one in my condition may be."

The High King cocked his head, puzzled. *They have broken all ties. That is the only explanation. I cannot fault Merlin for this. Indeed, it is what I would have told him to do.* Perhaps if he distracted Morgen with news of celebration, she might momentarily dismiss her sorrows. "Kay has asked the cooks to prepare a feast in your honor. At this moment it is being assembled in the courtyard. Merlin suggested that you would awaken this morning. Will you not take part? Everyone wishes to see you—to congratulate you on this incredible achievement. Come now, Morgen. All the Companions will be there, along with mother's ladies-in-waiting. And it goes without saying," he whispered, drawing very near, "I will be most disappointed if you do not attend. Come, say that you will dine with me."

Again his eyes met hers with an almost intense admiration, one that could no longer be camouflaged within the shallow confines of her chamber.

Does he not understand? Does he not see that Guenevere stands but a few paces away watching us? Surely he cannot be blind to all reason?

Morgen feigned a cough to better hide her discomfort. "Thank you, Brother, but your time would be better occupied pleasing Guenevere, a task that requires you remain in her company."

Arthur met Morgen's gaze as if to make a nonverbal protest. *My heart is already pledged elsewhere. Surely you have not forgotten.*

No, I have not. It was you who said that we could not marry in this lifetime. Unless you find a way around that insurmountable obstacle, then we are condemned to remain apart. A king must have a queen, Arthur. Here stands the most beautiful maiden in Britannia, a maiden who obviously admires you. Why should you not dine with her?

For the simple reason that my heart belongs to you.

By the goddess, Arthur, have mercy. We cannot marry. Turn your thoughts toward Guenevere.

A lovely blush colored Guenevere's countenance as Arthur fixed his eyes upon her. The effect little pleased him. Guenevere lacked Morgen's vibrancy, the impossible war of red and white that comprised her coloring, echoing the deepest flame and palest marble hues, the face and figure that could only belong to one of fairy birth, not to mention the unfathomable depth of her sea-green eyes. Guenevere's beauty, while undeniable, did not speak to him. They did not converse in the same language of the soul, yet somehow he must make amends. If not, the whole court would soon spout his folly.

"Morgen does make a valid point. Would you care to dine with me, Guenevere?"

No words were spoken on Guenevere's part. Indeed, none were needed, for she beamed brighter than the stars that pocked the ever-deepening sky. This new development would please her father, and that alone made her previous inter-action with Arthur tolerable.

Morgen, following Arthur's musings, supplied her own.

Well done, Arthur. That wasn't so difficult after all.

I would be much happier if it were you that clung to my arm.

I fear fate has other plans for us.

After fairly chasing the would-be lovers from her room, Morgen drew near a shallow bowl of water and splashed its rejuvenating liquid all over her aching body. It felt almost relaxing to blot away the stray droplets with one of the many deerskins that had graced her bed. Looking everywhere save her bedside mirror, Morgen drew a comb through her unruly locks until they softened into waves. In time she would grow well again. Until then she must offer up a vibrant outward appearance. A mild glamour, easy to conjure even in her weak-ened state, would do the trick. Setting the spell into motion, she saw it done. Everyone would think her beautiful if they did not look too closely—everyone but Merlin. She would have to deal with him in a different manner.

Setting foot outside her chambers for the first time in three days, Morgen unexpectedly encoun-tered the mage. He seemed surprised by her sudden appearance, quietly leaning against the ancient wall, hands braced upon its crumbling residue. A stiffness in his attitude gave the impression he had been waiting a very long time—like a terribly neglected guard dog longing for his mistress's presence.

Merlin, somewhat awkwardly, resumed a standing position. He wanted so much to embrace Morgen but held back, uncertain. How would she receive him? Not once throughout the entire illness had she called his name.

Are you well, beloved? I have been so worried. I thought for a time you might have given up this mortal existence.

Morgen bit back the laughter that welled against her lips. She wanted to wound him—to make him feel the tiniest portion of the agony that beat within her breast; yet the voice within urged caution.

Softening her response, she voicelessly replied, *What? Leave you behind to fall in love with any number of enchantresses who might cross your path?*

Merlin's frame relaxed as he took in the cleverly crafted words. He smiled and then kissed her brow.

The glamour is most becoming, but I can see that you still suffer. Is there anything I can do?

She paused before allowing his gentle embrace. How much had she successfully kept hidden from him?

What is your opinion of the vision that brought about this fit?

Concern once more darkened Merlin's brow.

Did you see none of it? Morgen's thoughts whispered, inwardly triumphant. He still knew nothing of the child!

Merlin protectively drew her hands against his chest. ***I am afraid not. I tried, but you would not let me in.***

The fragile torch light obligingly sputtered around them, lengthening shadows throughout the narrow hallway.

Morgen watched their eerie dance, then continued: ***That does not surprise me. I was very angry. My mother was dead, my healing abilities failed, and you no longer seemed to care.***

The sound of measured footsteps announced Kay's approach. He paused upon seeing them together, smiled. "Forgive me, I didn't mean to intrude."

Morgen laughed. "You are not interrupting anything of importance," she said a little too harshly.

A frown momentarily darkened Kay's brow. "It's just that the feast is about to begin."

She rushed forward and enveloped Kay in a warm embrace. "You look wonderful."

The poor seneschal blushed crimson, aware that Merlin stood watching this exchange.

"Arthur tells me that mother's ladies-in-waiting are here. No doubt you will find yourself the object of some admiration."

This pronouncement made Kay snort. "Not likely." He caught Morgen's knowing look, then continued, "Well, then," he said, gesturing toward the courtyard, "are you ready?"

Morgen gratefully clasped Kay's arm. "You take the lead."

"But Merlin," Kay fairly bleated his alarm.

"Merlin will find his own way. He always does."

Morgen offered a comely smile, then strolled off toward the courtyard with Kay, leaving a weary and bewildered Merlin far behind.

CHAPTER 28:

Saxons

A bitter chill descended upon Caerleon, turning autumn's brilliant splendor toward decay. The skies shone grayer, the nights waxed longer, but this little hampered the men's daily training sessions. It did, however, send Igrainne's ladies scurrying inside to seek refuge near one of the ill-attended fireplaces that coughed and sputtered noxious smoke, whose origins were disavowed peat. Morgen initially joined them; but after too many sessions during which her companions shirked all activity in favor of misdirected tongue-wagging, she remained ensconced within the confines of her own dismal chamber. What did it matter if they muttered about her being unsociable? What did it matter at all?

As an indifferent dawn blossomed on the sixteenth year of her life, Morgen felt far removed from achieving any real purpose. The healings she would lavish upon the needy, not to mention the peace work she hoped to manifest, were but distant memories lost in the shadow of her ever-expanding belly. Thankfully the glamour kept her secret safe from all. Deep within her core, Morgen knew this was a temporary solution. One day Merlin would pierce through the cleverly conjured haze and unearth the secret she guarded with such tenacity.

You must tell him, Daughter. Waste no more time about it. Tell Merlin this very night.

Time shimmered and split into fragmented acceleration that converted inert matter, bent it, until sentience returned and limbs moved anew. Morgen leapt to her feet, reeling. This was no ordinary sending but an actual visitation—one she had desired with all her being. Long, lean, and willowy, Igrainne's star-bright figure swirled in and out of visual range, draped in cool, translucent mist. This was the former high queen's spirit come forth to converse with Morgen, to offer guidance when all other sources had run dry. A glorious shade Igrainne was, irrefutably beautiful as she had been in life, yet with an ethereal elegance that pronounced her wise beyond ken. Morgen trembled at the contrast it made with her own commonplace, swollen figure. No doubt Igrainne saw through the glamour's clever disguise.

Be not afraid. This child is a natural result of your love for Merlin.

Trembling, Morgen knelt before the awesome presence. She did not wish to speak of Merlin. No, not when they had dissolved all ties. In any case there was nothing to be done. The arch mage had given her up for Britannia, or Arthur, or whatever topic currently dominated his thoughts. She might just as well throw herself into Arthur's arms. At least he loved her, longed for her with a passion that left her heady, breathless. Merlin no longer allowed himself to feel such base emotions.

Forgive me, Mother. We no longer tread the same path. In any case I know you disapprove of him.

Igrainne smiled. *That was in life, child. I now see the beauty of his soul.*

Tears spilled from Morgen's eyes. She tried to speak, but no words proved forthcoming. What did Igrainne mean by this? Surely she was not guiding Morgen toward a union with the king's counselor. That was tantamount to suicide. Indeed, she might as well slit her throat as realign herself with the arch mage. He did not want her or the child.

Be happy, Daughter. You have my blessing. Forgive him and all will be well. Believe me, he thought only of you.

Forgive him? No, Mother, I cannot. I cannot condemn myself to such torment again.

Igrainne blinked twice, a sweet, sad smile painting her lips. Her image wavered fitfully, a clear indication that the energy dwindled behind its manifestation. *I merely wish you to be happy, Morgen. Whatever man can bring you that fulfillment is the one you should marry. If it be Merlin, then marry him. If it be another, he will accept the child as his own. Yes, he will, if he truly loves you.*

Reaching forward with needy hands, Morgen tried to embrace Igrainne, but her airy form flickered twice then slowly faded from view. A subtle creaking of the door interceded, demanding focus. Merlin stood witnessing her efforts, buffeting Caerleon's multifarious noises as the door closed firmly behind him. Everything spoke to Morgen at once: her disordered room, the distended curtains billowing inward due to the careless wind, even the long dead rosebuds still firmly lodged within a bone-dry basin—all paled in comparison with the true source of her amazement. Merlin stood witnessing her endeavors with something of a bemused smile coloring his slim lips.

All thought of camouflage was forgotten as Morgen found her footing. It was Merlin come to see her—Merlin, with whom she had not exchanged a single word for an entire month! Was it possible that Igrainne's appearance had been a portent of his unexpected arrival? Did forgiveness truly reside within her breast? There was only one way to find out. Expertly navigating through downed pillows and discarded gowns, Morgen threw herself into Merlin's arms. She did not look up at him or even attempt to meet his eyes. The pain was still too fresh. Slowly, exquisitely, the mage's tapered fingers caressed her arm, uncertain as to her reaction. One of them must break the spell. And so it was that Merlin chose voiceless communication.

Will you spend this Samhain with me, Morgen? I know I have been distant, preoccupied with governmental affairs. Tonight I wish to put all that aside. Let us welcome those spirits that slip through the gates. Please say you will. My very soul cries out for you. Let us celebrate your birthday together.

Morgen paused, shocked that Merlin mentioned that which she had taken great pains to forget. "You actually remember that today is my birthday?"

"Of course," he whispered, gently nipping her ear, "how could I ever forget that my Morgen turns sixteen this day."

This said, Merlin draped his arms around Morgen's waist and began to propel her across the floor. Round and around they spun as two mario-nettes governed by a master puppeteer's hand. This was to be the last time, the last night they shared together. He could no more usurp what destiny decreed to be Arthur's place. Morgen belonged to the High King. The fairy once cloaked in moss and roses had served her purpose. He would always cherish her for that. The mage stooped to kiss his love once more, then froze, a perplexed look painted across his brow. It was evident that Morgen zealously withheld vital knowledge from him. He took in the disorderly trappings, the dis-carded gowns, which nearly tripped his fair con-sort. Something was wrong—something that went far beyond the clutter that met his eyes.

"Let there be no secrets between us. What is it you are trying to keep from me? I need not read your thoughts, for it is clearly stamped across your countenance."

Words failed Morgen miserably; thus she broke free and began straightening her chambers with a deft, albeit trembling hand. Back and forth she fluttered moth-like, continuously in motion. Here a chalice, there a coverlet, each item was carefully placed back into its appropriate corner. She did not look at Merlin or even glance his way for fear of detection. This, however, offered him only greater impetus to unearth her secret.

"I see you have the glamour about you. Why is that? Are you ill? Come, Morgen, drop the concealment. Show me what you are hiding," he whispered, clutching hold of her fair arms. This magical prompting forced the glamour open, split its core, revealing Morgen's rounded abdomen, so foreign to her normally lithe frame. Merlin's dark eyes widened with comprehension, and his dusky countenance took on a paler hue. His seed had taken root in Morgen's womb.

"Why did you keep this from me?"

"Think back on our last meeting," she snapped, her nerves bristling against rejection.

Remembering that ill-fated evening, Merlin realized with a thrill of self-loathing that Morgen had intended to make the confession at their favorite haunt, but his one-sided obsession with saving her life left him blind to all other propositions.

"You should have told me," came his soft reprimand.

Sinking to his knees Merlin placed his lips against Morgen's belly and covered it with one kiss after another, acknowledging the priceless treasure she harbored inside. Morgen carried a child in her womb—his child—no, *their* child. Surely this was reason enough for them to forget all prophecy, all futuristic, mind-numbing probability, and claim each other as man and wife.

"I tried to tell you, but you seemed so against the idea of children," came her affected reply. She knew not what to do or think. Was it advisable to admit Merlin back into her heart?

"Oh, my love," the mage sighed, burying his face against her stomach, that soft, round addition that fostered life anew.

"Remember, I never said a word. I fought so hard that night to free you of the tragedies our marriage would inspire."

Once again Morgen questioned her sanity. What impediments had Merlin conjured to free himself from her clutches? "I do not understand. What tragedies?"

Merlin sensed her displeasure but continued, confident in his ability to make her understand his actions. "Your death—Arthur's destruction—the fact that you are bound to him by ties which supersede any hold I claim on you; it is all very muddled at present. Please, believe me, I thought only of you. When you spoke of children I nearly cried out with longing. I was behind you, remember? You could not see my face."

Confusion colored Morgen's expression. How was she to reconcile this seeming inconsistency within Merlin's character? "Is it true? You honestly love me—and our child? You are pleased to be a father?"

Merlin kissed Morgen's lips over and over until no further doubt could remain. *Marry me, beloved. Our child will need both mother and father. Surely some spell may be conjured to avert your death.*

A low, dull chill shook Morgen's spine. "Death? I don't understand."

Merlin froze, tongue-tied, unable to express further thought. *By the gods what have I done? This was to be our last night together and now I speak of marriage? I cannot be hers. The fairy that sought the fledgling enchanter so many years ago, who dreamed of teaching him the art of love, has served her purpose. I have experienced the one thing lacking in my existence: love of a feminine being. Our union, sweet and fruitful as it is, does not extend beyond this point. The child of our union belongs to Avalon. Indeed, the Sisterhood will demand the child as payment. What need has the babe for an earthly father when she will have elementals at her beck and call. Oh, my poor Morgen. This will be so hard for her to accept. Yes, I will always love her, worship her, but our time together ends this night. There is no other way. Destiny decrees that she belongs to Arthur. I have seen this time and again. Suddenly I can no longer deny the deep bond king and fay share. They are founders of Britannia, the mother and father of my race.*

This deep-seated knowledge communicated itself to Merlin and he swayed unsteadily with its import; yet this was not the full breadth of the vision's communication. Indeed, a sea of ruby fog bled across his vision, shrouding everything in its wake. This was not the red of blood—not at first— but the deep red of Morgen's mane. It appeared alive and heartily zealous, lashing Merlin's face, spilling into his eyes, nose, and mouth. A sweetness was present that reminded him of the precious tide that swelled within each human being, but still he would not believe. Down came the stars, shattering icy shards all around him. Hearts were ripped free of their bodies. A vast darkness enveloped Caerleon as the crimson life force increased its flow. Every last soul—Companions, maidens, king, even Morgen herself—was drowning, trapped within the fortress walls. A miracle was needed and soon.

Saxons...

It was essential that Merlin find Arthur before the vision deprived him of reason. Releasing Morgen, the mage gained his footing and raced through her chamber door. Down the narrow hallway he plunged, casting Companion and maiden aside. Indeed, Merlin did not pause until he burst full into the deserted courtyard, heaving. The sky grew black overhead, aiding his purpose. A low rumble shook the earth underfoot. He was grounded, ready. A fierce cry issued from the core of his being.

"The City of Legion is under attack by night! Red Dragon, arise and come forth!"

Morgen rushed to his side, gasping for breath. Never before had she witnessed the depth of her beloved's powers first hand. Utterly spellbound, she stared transfixed and unblinking. This was more than mere magic. It was an elemental shift equivalent to the abilities wielded by the Ancient Ones themselves. Who was Merlin? How did he come by such power?

Cries of alarm spilled throughout the deepening air, the sound of anxious footsteps racing toward them. Merlin's voice increased its volume, "The white seeks to cripple the red on his own ground. Britannia's Red Dragon must take action, or we will all perish by the sword!"

Footfall after footfall pounded the earth, thundering the approach not of the Saxons but of one hailed by the arch mage himself. Arthur appeared running full tilt, his hand locked in that of the lovely Guenevere, who struggled to match his frantic pace. Countless others, Companions and maidens alike, stood equally perplexed, draped in the cloak of darkness—darkness at noontide.

"Saxons spilling across the land, hacking their way through the City of Legion!"

"Legion?" Arthur's dismay rang clear. "That is Caerleon!"

Merlin's eyes blazed white as he turned his gaze on the speaker. "Britannia calls the Red Dragon back into service. You must triumph here this night—or your children will perish under Saxon rule."

The King swallowed involuntarily. "They intend to attack Caerleon on Samhain?"

A silvery lightning bolt colored the air, followed by a low, menacing rumble. Several women screamed as Merlin spewed his warning, "Cedric thinks to descend upon us during Samhain festivities, but we will give him a celebration of our own making!"

Arthur nodded, his mind awhirl with activity. "We have until nightfall?" Thankfully the sky had already reclaimed much of its bright hue.

"We do."

"Bedivere, get the foot warriors ready. Companions, see to those on horseback. I will be with you shortly."

No further words were spoken. Indeed, none were needed for every last man, sans Merlin, the king, and a silent Urien of North Wales, were already in motion. Lot had returned to Lothian some weeks earlier with a score of Arthur's men so they might still an insurgent Angle uprising. It was quite a stroke of luck that Urien had remained behind. Arthur knew he must ask the next question very carefully.

"Urien, will you honor the treaty and fight by my side?"

Something of a wicked smile graced Urien's lips as his eyes shifted between Arthur and his intended bride. "You may count on me for this fight. Next time Morgen will determine my allegiance."

This said, Urien kissed Morgen passionately, then strolled off to rally his men.

Morgen's eyes were drawn back to Arthur, who approached with rapid gait.

He knew what she was thinking. Oh yes, Morgen clearly intended to join the fight, not wielding a sword but healing the wounded. Arthur felt his stomach churn. He could not lose her. Not now. Not ever. That meant he must come up with some plan that kept her safely inside. In a trice he saw it clearly unfold within his reeling mind.

"Dearest, I have no time or manpower to transport you and mother's ladies to a safe haven. I therefore place you in charge of their protection."

Here it was again: Arthur always standing between her personal safety and her life purpose. Surely he was wise enough to see the truth. "But Arthur, I must heal the wounded!"

Thoroughly prepared for her protestations, Arthur grabbed her fair arm with such conviction that his fingers left marks upon her fair flesh. "Heed me and obey," he said through gritted teeth. "Use whatever magic you deem best to safe-guard yourself and the women. Remember, I am counting on you." He punctuated the command by kissing her full on the lips. Guenevere trembled at the sight. The king was in love with his own sister. She had witnessed their odd, almost romantic relationship time and again. No wonder she often found such heartbreak reflected in the depths of Arthur's eyes. This was a forbidden love—one that could never be consummated—something she understood all too clearly. Perhaps she was a better match for Britannia's king then anyone had yet realized. What other man of noble blood would comprehend the dagger so firmly lodged within her own soul? The firm press of Arthur's fingers against Guenevere's arm forced her back to the present.

"Guenevere, my sister must place all her focus on spell work. I therefore ask you to take charge of the ladies. Will you do this for me?"

Arthur's expression was so genuine that Guenevere felt her defenses melt. Gone was the cruel monarch who had met her care-giving with bitter indifference. Here in his stead stood a man who proved strong, yet compassionate and hopelessly beguiling. This was a man willing to risk his very soul if it might save his people—a man she could love if only given time.

"I would be honored."

Without further ado she offered a quick bow and started off toward the women, many of whom were sobbing in fear and confusion.

Arthur stayed the motion by clasping hold of her petal-smooth arm. "When this madness is over, I would speak with you."

The golden beauty nodded, a faint smile coloring her lips. Arthur brushed his lips against her hand. So consumed was he with purpose that he turned, ignorant that Morgen stood waiting to catch his eye, then bent his steps toward the stables.

Morgen's thoughts churned inward. *Ancient Ones, what have I done? He is going to marry her! This is my doing—just as surely as I draw breath. I have lost him forever—ruined everything. I have cast aside Arthur's love when it is the one thing I should have treasured most.*

Then tell him—tell him how much you love him! It is the one thing he needs to hear above all others!

Morgen recognized the Sisterhood guiding, instructing her as they had so many times before. If only she had listened to them sooner! Suddenly her feet were in motion, rushing forward as if to overtake time. Through the cluttered courtyard she wove, avoiding Companions, commoners, and even Merlin. The air felt oppressively heavy in her lungs. It was now or never. The truth must reveal itself or lay dormant, unexpressed for this lifetime. Somehow she cleared the distance that separated her from Arthur, whose broad step carried him ever near his waiting mount. He turned at her approach, a startled look coloring his brow. Morgen chose this moment to reach high and grace his forehead with the protective spiral.

"May the blessings of the Ancient Ones be upon you now and forevermore, Arthur Pendragon.

I love you—I love you with all my heart. Be safe, dearest," she whispered, kissing his cheek, "and come back to me."

The affect of this exchange clearly played across Arthur's countenance, reflecting an emotion so pure that he could not speak. Pulling Morgen tightly against his chest he allowed his lips to brush against her glorious locks. His eyes were filled with wild tenderness that defied description. They had so little time together before the madness consumed them. Indeed, perhaps they had this moment and nothing more. One, if not both of them could die in the coming fray. It was his task to ensure that did not happen—that they both lived to see a unified Britannia. And so he extricated Morgen's fair form from his person and held her at arm's length so she must meet his eyes.

"Thank you, dearest. You have given me strength to move forward. I battle for you and the people of Britannia. There can be no further delay. The Saxons make good their approach. Heed your own advice, Morgen. Be safe. Now go to the women and do not fail me."

Without another word Arthur mounted his pale steed, Lughan, who pawed the ground with anxious hooves. The act was seamless; indeed, man and horse practically merged as one entity so suited were they to each other and their common purpose. One touch of Arthur's heals sent Lughan into a gallop, and the two disappeared into the gathering forces.

Morgen felt hot tears spill against her cheek. Would she ever see Arthur again? Would they ever fully realize the love that until this moment lay dormant within them? She had no time to fully absorb these questions, however, for a dark form usurped all thought, all sensibility, looming before her, claiming precedence even as it grasped hold of her arm. "Come with me," Merlin said, pulling her far from the warriors that swarmed the stables with the same tenacity as wasps overwhelm an active nest. "Something I would give you."

Startled by his appearance, Morgen wondered if Merlin had actually witnessed her blessing of Arthur Pendragon. Did he comprehend how her heart suddenly feared for him above all others? Arthur was, after all, High King. That meant the Saxons would target him first! Yes, she knew that Arthur was the finest warrior ever birthed upon Britannia's shores. She need not fear his skill; yet battles were not always won by the best fighters. The decision often favored those that displayed the best tactics, the greatest feat of the mind. Thankfully Arthur was equally gifted in this area, and he also utilized Merlin, Bedivere his captain, and countless others who knew Britannia better than any Saxon.

Back through the courtyard they rushed, down the darkened hallway and into Merlin's well-tended chambers. Morgen could not help but mark the difference in tidiness with her own. Everything, from the flawlessly turned bedding to the countless phials filled with rare herbs and magical properties, was perfectly ordered. Indeed, even the well-trained tapers sprang alive at their approach.

Reaching for the pouch that hung perpetually at his side, Merlin said, "Close your eyes."

Morgen readily complied and soon found herself rewarded as Merlin draped something cold and metallic upon her chest.

"Now look down and tell me what you see."

A golden medallion drew her gaze, glittering and roughly hewn in aspect. Through its middle ran a deep cut, punctuated with an engraved letter "M." Morgen touched the precious metal and inwardly thrilled at its lyrical response. Deep magic centered in this medallion, magic that would assist them through the coming siege. Glancing up, Morgen saw that Merlin was in the process of hanging a similar token, the missing half, around his own neck.

"Thank you, Merlin. Now I will always feel you are with me, even in the coming battle. I need only look at the medallion to know you are there."

"A gift to my sweet Morgen on this her sixteenth year," he whispered, placing both tokens together so they became one. "The medallions demonstrate that each of us are but a single part of the unified whole."

Merlin felt odd voicing this belief now that he knew she was Arthur's true love, but if it helped save her then they would both be served. "Never forget that, Morgen," he continued, increasingly justified in his actions. "Together we are strongest."

Anger lanced Morgen's heart. *Is Merlin always this changeable? Was it not he who wished us to remain separate?* she cried inwardly.

Instead she somehow managed a coherent response. "How can I forget when it rests against my heart?"

Merlin's lips flashed a smile, but he was not finished, no, not yet. Fumbling through his corded belt, he wrested a bright dagger free and held it aloft. "In return I wish a lock of your hair to guide me through the coming darkness."

A half smile graced Morgen's lips as she helped Merlin choose the glossy strands that he would carry throughout the night. *I will not read into this or hope for more than this moment offers. Merlin is not mine. He no more belongs to me than the wind or the moon. We are but two entities that temporarily walk the same path.*

Merlin stared at her with glistening eyes, only half hearing the thought. Somehow they must accept destiny's edict, make a new beginning, and place all the romance, the passion behind them. Somehow they must survive this night and start afresh. "Live, beloved. Live for our child. Do nothing foolish. Wait until the battle is over before healing the wounded." He kissed her once more, willing her cooperation with the intensity of his coal-black eyes, then wordlessly took leave.

After counting to three, Morgen shadowed Merlin's wake, careful to remain hidden from his discerning gaze. Down the deserted hallways they trod, silent, stealthy. Long shadows distended beyond recognition, conjured by the fiery torches that blossomed within their iron hangings. Morgen had all but determined to follow Merlin through the courtyard gate when Kay's hulking form arrested the effort.

"I have been looking for you everywhere," he said, gently taking her arm. "Follow me. The ladies are currently lodged below."

Morgen came to an abrupt halt. "Is that wise? If the Saxons set Caerleon ablaze, we will be trapped."

He nodded and commenced escorting her into the bowels of the fortress. Forward they pressed through cobweb-infested walkways that seldom saw such marked attention. Morgen wondered how she could shake free of Kay without offering him insult or landing him in trouble. She did not, after so much former discord between them, wish to injure their newly conceived friendship. Suddenly he was speaking and she took pains to hear him.

"On the far side of the chamber where you healed me is a door. Go through it, bear right. Follow this tunnel to its end. You will find yourself well beyond the gates that border the forest. Should fire engulf Caerleon, you must use that tunnel to escape."

He stopped just short of the steps that plunged into the underground labyrinth and commenced buckling on a coat of leathern armor. Morgen marveled how well it molded against his recently healed frame. Kay looked every inch a warrior. Indeed, his size alone demanded respect.

"You are going into battle?"

"Thanks to you," came Kay's warm response. A rare smile colored his lips as Morgen reached up on her tip toes to trace the protective spiral against his brow. Once done, he bowed and then set off in search of the Companions. Morgen's thoughts spoke far more clearly than words.

Perhaps I will see you there.

CHAPTER 29:

The War Within

A dull pain throbbed against Morgen's temple as she entered the familiar chamber where Kay's healing had transpired. Several torches illuminated the oppressive gloom, revealing a cramped, tight mead cellar, far smaller than Morgen remembered. Gone were the rags and filthy straw, replaced by an abundance of women, some overly concerned about the condition of their newly soiled gowns, others sobbing quietly into the flickering light. The night would be a long one—should Morgen choose to stay among this lot. Arthur's image wavered before her eyes.

Remember your promise.

Yes, she would safeguard the women—a task easily accomplished by drawing life force around the chamber and then sealing it tight with the appropriate symbol. This done, Morgen stole out the side door as Kay directed, then made a sharp right—a foolish move to say the least, for she was plunged into bone-chilling darkness. Morgen paused, heart pounding. Why had she not secured a torch from the women? The answer proved simple enough. She was unwilling to endure their questioning, unwilling to adopt any tagalongs who wanted to partake in her private adventure. An unseen companion with scores of tiny legs swept over Morgen's hand as it braced the stone wall for support. She was not alone. Indeed, the darkest, most loathsome insects walked by her side. That was small comfort, indeed.

We are all one.

Honoring this truth, Morgen offered silent thanks for their assistance and pressed forward, hands scouring the slimy walls—her single compass amid all absence of light. Every now and then she heard a crunch underfoot, some unfortunate invertebrate that crossed her path at an inopportune time. Morgen saw nothing but willed her other senses into heightened display.

Slowly, carefully, she maneuvered through the haunted abyss. Decay painted the air with reek; something larger than an insect had met its end just ahead. It grew so extreme, so revolting that Morgen attempted to eradicate the scent with a bit of sleeve pressed against her delicate nose. This proved a most unfortunate choice, for she lost contact with the wall and tripped over what felt like a dead body. The scent's origin was revealed in that instant, though she could not see its source. A scream lodged within Morgen's throat. Was this a Saxon who had already penetrated the fortress? Morgen pulled herself up and rushed blindly forward, listening for any sound of enemy approach. The only thing she heard was her own heightened breathing and the careless pounding of her booted feet as she raced forward. The body was long dead; her sense of smell indicated as much. Upon her return she would make certain the poor soul found its way home. Home…

Morgen longed for Avalon with all her being.

Footfall after footfall carried Morgen forward, her hands scanning the crumbling walls searching for clues her eyes could not detect. A hidden door leading to the forest must reside somewhere in this forgotten labyrinth, as Kay had intimated. Yet how was she to find it, cloaked as it were in ebony supreme?

Just when it appeared that things could get no worse, Morgen's feet sent a spray of chilly water up against the tunnel wall. Thinking it a puddle, Morgen plunged her booted toe into the untold depths but found it to be part of something far more substantial—that of an underground stream. Morgen's hands fumbled the walls once more for any hint of a doorway. This time she found it! A broad chain dangled from the ceiling. Dancing on tiptoe Morgen reached up and pulled with all her might, producing a creak and a groan as the hinges gave way. She also heard an unexpected whinny. A horse? What was a horse doing so near her exit? The trap door was flung open in that instant. Morgen trembled, wondering what horrors were about to befall her.

"Princess, is that you?"

The throbbing in Morgen's temple increased its pressure. That voice—she recognized that voice!

"It's Accolon. Can you hear me?"

Morgen's relief spilled forth with one heartfelt exclamation. "Accolon?"

"Here, let me help you. Grab hold of my hand."

Standing on tiptoe Morgen reached forth and caught hold of the extended appendage. She was surprised at Accolon's steely grasp, considering his hands were gloved for battle, but he lifted her free of the darkened tunnel with relative ease. Down she collapsed against the ground, aware that her cloak and gown were muddied beyond repair. Accolon lifted his leathern helm and smiled his greeting.

"How did you—?"

"How did I know to meet you here?"

Morgen nodded, her eyes still adjusting to the twilight surroundings. They were in the woods but a stone's throw away from the hollowed log where she had hidden from the fox. That meant the trap door's entrance was close to the stream, just as she had imagined. Accolon's beaming countenance drew her attention.

"It was Kay. He somehow knew you would use this tunnel to mount an escape."

"How clever of him. I am here to heal the wounded."

"Yes, I know. I am here to help you."

Morgen blinked. "You are?"

Accolon's smile increased in warmth—if that were possible. "This may be hard for you to believe, but I received a sending—a message from the Sisterhood of Avalon. You know of whom I speak. They asked me to escort you through the battle and safeguard you from wounding or even worse. Come, take my hand."

Morgen did just that, momentarily surrendering her control to Accolon, who skillfully led her through the forest. Why had the Sisterhood approached Accolon with this task? Surely he was devoted to her and trustworthy beyond reproach, but what of the fealty he owed Arthur, not to mention Britannia?

"I serve Arthur, Britannia, and indeed Avalon by safeguarding you," he replied to her unspoken prompt. Pausing at the familiar blackberry thicket, he drew forth a dark tunic, breeches, cap, and cloak, offering them with steady hand.

"They belonged to my little brother. Use them well this night, and he will be avenged."

Morgen drew breath to question Accolon for particulars, but he motioned her to silence.

"Not now. The pain cuts far too deep. I need all my wits about me." This said, he turned his back and waited for Morgen to adopt her new guise.

The material felt course and well worn, but it was warm and would allow her to move with little restriction. Morgen easily slid into the breeches and tunic, which proved a loose fit for her, then belted them with a length of reed. Once or twice she caught Accolon peering round but said nothing, aware of the great debt she already owed him. Twisting her thick curls into a knot, she further concealed her femininity with the aforementioned cap. Her courtly gown and cloak were next stowed in the thicket. This done, she motioned Accolon to take the lead, which he did for a brief time.

Crickets chirped around them, blissfully unaware of impending doom.

Once warrior bard and princess reached the forest's edge, they paused to ascertain the relative safety of their position. Morgen quickly shut her eyes against intrusion so she might call Merlin's form into view. There he stood, high upon the hillside, conversing with a strangely garbed figure that sported horns on its shaggy head and cloven hooves: *Cernunnos, Lord of the Underworld*! No wonder Merlin boasted such elemental power! Think of what he could accomplish united with an Ancient One. God and mage had just finished a tremendously complicated spell that shrouded Arthur and his men in a thick blanket of fog, which stretched well beyond visual range. This bit of magic left them virtually impenetrable to attack. Morgen pitied the Saxons. They would never know what hit them.

Night blossomed full and deep, while the air swelled with anticipation, calling all participants into play. Accolon drew Morgen behind him and waited, sword drawn. A low, incessant, thunderous sound that was not of elemental origin rattled and grew, signaling the Saxon's approach. Ravens cried overhead, while the tiniest of mice sought shelter, rushing past warrior and princess without pause. Morgen tried to secure a better viewing position, but Accolon threw her behind him with such force that she knew any further attempts would be equally futile.

As time shifted and warped its onward pace, the Saxon warriors penetrated Merlin's elemental ring and found, to their great surprise, nothing but an empty meadow flooded with billowing mist. The City of Legion had seemingly vanished into thin air! Every last warrior came to a halt. Not one of them understood what had happened. Perplexed, they wandered aimlessly, tracing back and forth across the area they knew once housed Arthur's fortress. Round and around they turned, searching, seeking that which evaded their eyes. Spirits sank, and with them bodies relaxed, spears were lowered, while formations condensed into a single whole.

Morgen trembled. This proud race was about to be slaughtered as beasts sent to a butcher. Did they not see what had happened? Did they not comprehend how easy it would be for Arthur to catch them, walled up as they were in the circle's interior?

True to plan Arthur's forces set upon them at that moment, breaking Saxon command from every angle. The clash of metal upon metal sent Morgen's heart racing. Every torch, every flame commanded her attention, magnifying the screams of the wounded tenfold. Men were dying in untold numbers. Was she able to do anything about it? No! Try as she might, Accolon would not let her move forward—not until the battle had eased, or so he told her time and again.

A change of tactics was in order. Morgen possessed neither torch nor flame but still fashioned a bright beacon from Merlin's golden medallion that hung about her chest. Light flashed against the keepsake just as a bloodied warrior sought

shelter within the woods. Saxon he was; Morgen
felt sure of it, yet he bore a pinched, weasellike
look that branded him a deserter. Why else would
he abandon the fight? Calling upon the magical
properties of the golden relic, she watched it flash
fiery brilliance. If only she had thought of this
sooner—when she faltered in the cavern's bitter
darkness! Suddenly the talisman became the perfect tool to easily lure the weasel toward her hiding place. The weasel paused, catching Morgen's
eye, a smile further distorting his overly thin face.
Pointed yellow teeth only heightened his repulsive
nature. Believing himself well positioned to claim
a necklace of some value, he drew within striking distance, but Accolon's sharp defense stalled
the effort. The fight would be short lived. Morgen
saw that at once, for the weasel could not match
Accolon's prowess.

Slipping away unnoticed, Morgen sought the
fallen, like some dark angel, fluttering earthbound. In and out of the frenzied blades she wove,
pausing to assist downed Briton and Saxon alike.
Merlin's words soon came back to haunt her, for
she either reached the wounded too late or came
across individuals whose souls had already taken
flight. Was it possible that her first journey into battle had all been for naught?

*Sisters, guide me. I am here to help the wounded.
Show me someone that I can heal!*

"My lady, please, please help me."

The voice was soft, merely a rush of wind, but
Morgen soon found its source: a boy, a mere lad of
ten or eleven lay partially hidden among his fallen

comrades, gasping for breath and reeling from the arrow he had taken in the chest.

Using all her strength, Morgen dragged him into a grassy hollow situated between two holly bushes that shielded a narrow, albeit winding brook. Yes, it was damp, but that hardly mattered. The boy's impending death superseded all such concerns. Darkness eclipsed Morgen's senses so completely that she paused, uncertain how to proceed.

How can I heal him when night shades my eyes? I cannot claim a torch or light a fire, for that would signal our position. What is it? What can I use to aid my mortal vision? It was then her agitated fingers happened upon Merlin's gift. *The medallion! Yes, the medallion's golden rays will serve me well. If only it would heed my summons and shine again.*

Without further prompting the golden relic answered her prayers, blazing afresh amid the starless night. Morgen set to work immediately, molding the healing energy so that it flowed beyond her earthly fingers: a clear ivory field that she fine-tuned into gentle digits. Delicate and agile as her fingers, the white light easily penetrated the boy's chest and reached inside it, coaxing the lethal arrow tip out so gently that it missed all of the major organs and arteries. This was a miracle that Morgen could not have accomplished with her own two hands. The wound closed of its own accord once the foreign object had been extracted, but Morgen did not stop there. How could she? The lad was still bleeding inside.

Once again the medallion blazed forth, illuminating a spot near the lad's heart that still demanded attention. Morgen placed both hands against his bony chest, oblivious to the fact that a one-eyed warrior, drawn by the light of her broach, bore down upon them. A shriek escaped the boy's lips as he became aware of their impending doom, but with a rush of wind and flash of blade, Accolon, faithful to his word, deflected the spear, sending its wielder sprawling among the hapless reeds.

Morgen pressed the young lad against her heart to better seal the healing, while Accolon struck the head from their downed adversary. Blood splattered her fair countenance, but the boy reached forth with his own sleeve and blotted it away.

"Thanks much, my lady," he said, lifting the cap from her head to confirm her femininity. "It feels like I was never struck down. What do they call you?"

A single tear slid down Morgen's cheek. "I am Morgen—Morgen of Avalon."

The boy's eyes grew wide. "A healer lady from Avalon." Instantly his feet were in motion. "I'll tell everyone your name!" Off he sped into the deepening night, the hat still tightly clutched in his hand.

"I fear I have lost your brother's cap," she mused, grasping Accolon's hand as he lifted her free of the reeds. "How can I ever thank you? Avalon has chosen her champion well."

"Avalon has chosen their healer well," he replied, mussing her knotted hair so that it spilled free. "Let there be no more illusions as to your true identity. This night you are Bridgit incarnate, goddess of healing."

Morgen smiled, offering silent thanks for the boy's recovery. She then set out once more about her work, fluttering moth-like between downed Briton and Saxon alike. Miracle after miracle transpired, all without any further attempt on Morgen's life. Accolon stood by ever watchful, witnessing her great gift, assisting when possible. Within the course of an hour, the wounded and dying were calling her name, reaching out desperately for the healing powers she possessed. The numbers were so massive, however, that Morgen found it impossible to reach them all. At one point she drew near Merlin but did not acknowledge his presence, her eyes haunted by images of death and dying—those she did not reach in time. One healer could only do so much, even if she were gifted by the gods. This was a lesson Morgen found nearly impossible to accept.

And so the night wore on. Victory for Arthur and his men was nearly complete—with a few unfortunate exceptions. Cedric, the Saxon king, had escaped with a band of followers who somehow stumbled beyond the circle's magical boundaries. Arthur gave pursuit but without any real intent of engagement, his own forces not fully gathered. Caerleon, the former City of Legion, was safe—for a time.

It was then Arthur turned his thoughts on Morgen. Oh, yes, he knew she had defied him, the knowledge of which wounded him to the core. How could she have spoken words of affection that filled him with the promise of a life they would share together and then cast it all to the wind? She did not love him. No, not really, else she never would have stolen out to heal the wounded while the battle still thundered its fury. It had all been a ploy—a ploy conjured to distract him! Indeed, over half the Companions told him of the fallen calling Morgen's name. Drawing near her side, he remained cloaked and unrecognizable. He witnessed Accolon offering assistance and knew at once the breadth of his duplicity.

"Traitor, draw your sword," he whispered through gritted teeth.

Accolon looked up, horror-stricken. "Forgive me, Arthur," echoed his gentle apology. Instantly his sword was cast down, his head bowed, the perfect embodiment of submission and respect.

"You chose beauty over Britannia. Draw your sword, traitor, or I will run you through without further provocation."

Arthur was already off his pale steed, Lughan, sword ready to execute a final judgment.

"No!" Morgen cried, throwing her arms around Accolon's bowed head. "Arthur, your anger lies with me, not Accolon!"

"How could you, Morgen?" he questioned, pulling her up by the shoulders, as if he would rattle the truth from her lips. "Do I mean nothing to you? Are my commands to be ignored?" His eyes blazed fire, still consumed with battle frenzy. When she did not answer, his anger burst forth ungoverned.

"I will deal with you momentarily, Morgen. Now I must execute a traitor."

Everything happened so quickly, Morgen knew not what to do. She saw Arthur move forward, sword raised, but could not fully understand what was happening. Surely this was some nightmare. Arthur would never execute one of his own Companions.

A desperate prayer formed within her reeling brain. ***Ancient Ones, by all that is sacred, protect your champion!***

Light blazed through the darkened gloom, flashing and swirling around them even as it stalled Arthur's advance. Here was the answer Morgen awaited, the very assistance she had so aptly summoned. Indeed, Britannia's Warrior King appeared frozen, Excalibur raised high, teetering precariously near final judgment. How long this enchantment would remain intact, she dared not entertain. It was critical that she transport Accolon to safety. Merlin's appearance, however, changed all that. With bold step he crossed the portal's threshold and deliberately placed himself between Arthur and his prey.

"The battle has ended," Merlin soothed his calm benediction. "You have no need to use Excalibur against a friend. If I am not mistaken, Accolon defended Morgen throughout the fray. He is to be praised, not executed. Morgen would have found her own way into battle even without his assistance. Am I not correct in this assumption, Morgen?"

"Yes, oh yes!" she cried, regaining her footing. "Forgive me, Arthur. Healing is my life's work.

Avalon sent me for this very purpose just as Avalon bid Accolon protect me this night."

Arthur shook his head, reeling. "Avalon? You hail from Avalon?" She had lied to him or at the very least withheld this vital information. Did she take him for a fool? Surely she knew that he would never ignore a messenger from Avalon. Why then had she kept silent on this topic?

Aware that Arthur's fury had reached its zenith, Morgen softened her response. It was vital she heal the relationship she shared with the High King, or they would never accomplish the great work set forth for them, never bring peace upon the land. The sooner Arthur understood this, the better. "I tried to tell you many times, but so much has always remained unspoken between us."

"Enough!" Arthur cried, cutting her short, his eyes wild, ungoverned. "Accolon, return to the Companions. This is not finished between us."

Accolon bowed low, quickly glanced at Morgen, and took shelter within the thick cloak of night.

"You must forgive us," Morgen began, approaching Arthur with measured tread, careful not to anger him further. Danger issued from the very pores of his blood-spattered skin. The killing frenzy was still upon him. What did that mean for her fragile life? Had the love he professed evaporated because she had challenged his authority? Were men not to be trusted at all?

Arthur glanced at her, eyes seething before quickly looking away. "I am sending you back to Amesbury in three days' time."

"No!" Princess and mage spoke at once.

Morgen grasped hold of Arthur's bloodied sleeve, but he easily shook free. All the anger, the horror of betrayal, spilled forth in one great cry. "Look at you, Morgen!—your hair, your cloak— your very hands caked with blood!"

"As are yours! I see no difference between us— unless it be that I heal people, while you slaughter them!"

"Morgen!" Merlin tried to intercede, but he was too late.

Arthur grabbed Morgen by the wrists and held her fast. "Were you really out there healing Saxons—the very people who would have murdered all of us without a second thought?"

Understanding broke through Morgen's defenses, softening her heart. Arthur thought only of safeguarding the people by whatever means possible. War, at the present moment, was the only means *he understood*. Softly she reached up on tip-toe and draped her arms around his neck. "Is it not possible that we each use different means to achieve the same goal? It is peace we seek now and forever. Surely we need not punish each other for that?"

A certain trembling animated Arthur's frame. This alone made sense in the great vast muddle of their discontent. She had not betrayed him, not in a conventional sense, for her healing worked toward a unified Britannia, one that honored Briton, and—he could barely think it—Saxon alike. What if Avalon's counsel pointed in this direction? Could he take that foreign, ultimately unpopular path? Unable to meet Morgen's gaze any longer, he buried his lips in her hair. "Forgive my harsh words, but you must understand that I cannot lose you. Is that clear? The hope of a unified Britannia that we might share is the only thing that keeps me sane. That is why I am sending you to Amesbury."

Merlin cleared his throat, waiting as Arthur broke free of the embrace.

"If you wish to say something, Merlin, I suggest you do so now."

"Send Morgen to Glastonbury instead. House her with the holy sisters near Avalon. She will be happier there. Moreover, Kay will be lodged nearby, overseeing the construction of your new fortress. He can keep watch over her. Otherwise she might follow us on the campaign."

"That is well bethought," Arthur conceded, brushing the bloodied hair from Morgen's eyes. She was still hauntingly beautiful, even after suffering the grossest, basest warfare. Indeed, she appeared elfin, dressed in the tattered tunic and breeches, hair askew, painted an even deeper crimson, hardly the fairy that had so captured his heart. Yet that otherworldly aspect of Morgen's being troubled him, for it could not be contained or understood. Truthfully the validity of her so-called love proved impossible to decipher. It was foolhardy to contemplate anything more stable than a passing friendship with this changeling if he wished to keep his sanity. Gone was the dream, the passion. She could not be his now or ever. And so it was with a heavy heart that Arthur set out once more for Lughan, who grazed but a few paces away.

Guenevere would make a fine bride, a noble high queen. Why wish for better than that? Up into the saddle he sprang with the clear intent of making good his departure, but Morgen stayed the effort by placing a firm yet gentle hand upon his wrist.

"You cannot cast me back into the keep of nuns. I am Avalon's Fairy Queen! I will not be subjected to nuns' cruelty or their doctrine."

Arthur fixed his eyes on Morgen, his mind reeling, his heart broken. *Queen of the fairies?* Why had she never told him this before? They were equal in every sense of the word and so blatantly unrelated that marriage should have been the most logical of options. Yet all that had changed this night with her thoughtless dismissal of his love. She did not care for him—no, not in the slightest. He could no more bind himself to Morgen than the wildest star! All those poor dreams he had cherished when they first met—that they were bound together through several lifetimes—suddenly appeared nothing more than a product of his imagination.

It appears I have made the right decision. I have lost her forever.

He gave a sharp bob of his head before pulling free. "Do as you please, Morgen. I wash my hands of you."

CHAPTER 30:

The Veil Torn

The finality of Arthur's dismissal cleft Morgen's heart, leaving it numb: a raw, gaping wound that no salve could heal. That fateful moment did more than tear the scales from her dull eyes. It unlocked her spirit so that previously repressed feelings and knowledge broke forth in a cascade of emotion. The Sisterhood had spoken true. They were bound together through past lives, a bond so unerring in its purity that it dwarfed all other relationships. No one knew her, understood her soul, her dreams as well as Arthur, not even Merlin. This oneness could never be replicated or understood. They were mother and father of Britannia and this union heightened their love as no other. She had not realized the depth of love she bore Arthur, no, not until he was irrevocably torn from her grasp. The agonizing silence that followed bereft Morgen of all sensation save that found in the conjecture of how she might win him back. Conjecture it was, for Morgen never saw Britannia's High King after that tortuous exchange. No, many months would pass before the one needed the other so desperately that each forgot their past dissolutions. Morgen, however, suspected nothing of this. Indeed, her own thoughts were so dark that even the Sisterhood's guidance went unnoticed. Merlin, too, offered council, and he renewed his offer of marriage, but Morgen was so certain of his indifference that she little entertained its value. Even his proposal, romantic as it appeared, felt false, conjured for appearance's sake. Every dream, every goal she had ever imagined shriveled by the weight of an unyielding Excalibur and the monarch that wielded its influence. How was she to win reconciliation when Arthur so adamantly refused her company?

Caerleon was abustle, men and women absorbed, stockpiling rations, re-plating leather armor, fortifying swords, aware only that they must prepare the Warrior King and his Companions for departure. Yes, Arthur would rid Britannia of Saxons this campaign; annihilate all who threatened his people. Perhaps that is why every curtain remained drawn, and no hint of light or fresh air penetrated Caerleon's defenses. Peace was apparently obliterated from Arthur's thoughts, as was Morgen. And so, the displaced Fairy Queen agreed to Arthur's terms, quietly allowing Kay full supremacy over her movements as they made painstaking progress through the emerald rolling hills that comprised Glastonbury and its surrounding territories.

Kay felt certain that this marked symbol of obedience would win Arthur's respect before midwinter. Indeed, Arthur often employed this enforced silence when things went contrary to his liking. It was the only way he knew to ensure obedience. Morgen was not so certain. And so, as she watched Kay ride off toward the new fortress that he and countless promising yet bedraggled artisans hoped to create, she prepared herself for more than a fresh dose of heartache. Arthur was dead to her. It was vital for her own state of health to eradicate him from her thoughts. Perhaps then she could make a life for herself among the holy sisters. Grief consumed her being, labeling her alone, friend-less—that was before she truly assimilated her surroundings; that was before she actually recognized the wise woman who bid her welcome.

"The abbey? This is the abbey?" Morgen cried, certain only that it was Tyronoe who stood before her smiling. "Have you yet again adopted the habit of a nun, or is this some kind of bizarre dream?"

"Glance around you, Morgen. Tell me what it is that you really see."

Following Tyronoe's council, Morgen saw a plain, whitewashed, and roomy church made from timber, with few adornments and only the necessary benches, tables, and an odd cross chair here and there. Tall, unfettered windows ushered in large gusts of chilled air from the broad, green hills above. New thrushes lined the dirt floor, sweet and inviting. Seated at a long, narrow wooden table, a number of white-robed women were enjoying a meal of pitted bread and cheese.

Morgen peered closer, certain that her heart could not be mistaken. This was the Sisterhood welcoming her home. Each rose to her feet, beaming, then in turn walked forward and embraced Morgen. The exchange was magical, unexpected, though why Morgen should be surprised at their appearance remained a mystery. Cliton and Gliton placed their hands against her belly, honoring the priceless treasure she harbored inside, their flowery faces lit with unmatched joy.

"The first of our kind conceived by a mortal father," chimed Glitonea with shining eyes. "Our first true daughter of Avalon. Such a gift is precious beyond imagining."

Slowly Morgen allowed herself to be drawn to the table and seated at its head. The bench proved uncomfortable, or so she noted in her compromised position. Pregnancy did not agree with Morgen, especially once her abdomen grew so large it blotted out all other sensation.

Glitonea's words further distempered her humor. A low voice inside bid her remember that Merlin was not a mortal but the son of Cernunnos himself. The validity of this statement filtered through her being without further assurances. Certainly she remembered their initial meeting. Merlin had adopted the guise of Cernunnos just as he had near the fountain the day they embarked on their forest excursion. And then she recalled Cernunnos's most recent appearance at Caerleon— father and son they were beyond question. The true mystery was why it had taken Morgen so long to absorb this revelation.

"All the better," Glitonea smiled, reading her thought. "The child will wield power."

"Do not jump to conclusions," interceded Tyronoe. "Merlin's mother was a mortal woman. I fear Merlin possesses many of the failings found within his mother's race. The child may likewise be tainted."

"I do not understand," Morgen said, rising to her feet, an act which eased her scrunched belly to an elongated state. She was so blasted uncomfortable! Perhaps that was the point of it all. Mortal life was filled with warts and imperfections that fairies and elementals could only begin to comprehend. Suddenly the church, the tall windows, the thrush floor, even the white robes that cloaked her sisters all melted away. Morgen found herself standing at the base of Avalon Tor, windswept and dazzlingly free. The birds had departed, no doubt bent on some distant climate that boasted warm winds and bright sunlight. Britannia's winters boasted little if any such endearments. The sky, a cold, clear gray, shrouded the beckoning mountains, far beyond water and tumultuous sea foam. Gone was the color, the floral abundance that scented the air, dazzled the mind. This was not to suggest that Avalon lacked beauty or appeal. No, that could never be the case. Why, the magic alone that swirled through its arteries colored the air a translucent hue, painted everything from reed to hillside a mystical silver that lulled the senses and rejuvenated the mind.

"The waddle church was an illusion conjured for Arthur's foster brother and the men who brought you hither. Whenever Kay seeks you, he will find you housed within that church. It is a simple matter of thought manifesting into reality," explained a smiling Cliton.

Morgen brushed her hand against the stark, pruned rose bushes that had once boasted lush blossoms, pausing only when a stray thorn drew a prick of blood. "You have changed the subject. What is it you fear about Merlin and our child?"

The sisters glanced at each other, uncertain. Tyronoe once more clasped Morgen's hand. "Forces are at work, Morgen, that seek to destroy Merlin and your unborn child. That is why we made certain Arthur sent you here. Remain within Avalon's gates and all will be well."

Merlin is in danger. The knowledge of this crept as quicksilver through Morgen's veins. It had been a seeming eternity since their lives had intertwined as one. Merlin had loved her and had left her, a connecting thread found over and over again in the best romantic tales. Suddenly all the love she had shared with this mysterious, magical being burst forth ungoverned. Surely the Sisterhood understood that if Merlin was in danger, she would do everything within her power to save him. He was, after all, the father of her unborn child!

Glitonea drew near before speaking. "Merlin is dying, Morgen. I cannot put it more simply than that. The war is killing him."

Killing him? Yes, war slowly eats away at all who promote its gross delights. Horror eclipsed Morgen's sensibilities leaving her shattered, shaking. No conceivable means existed by which she could convince Merlin to leave Arthur's side. If the war extinguished his light, he would deem it a necessary price extracted to solidify Arthur's place upon the throne. For a brief moment, Morgen considered informing Arthur of Merlin's precarious condition, but then she remembered that they were no longer on speaking terms. Tears spilled from her eyes at the utter futility of her situation. How could she help Merlin—help anyone—locked away within Avalon's impenetrable gates?

Sisters flooded around Morgen, offering comfort, compassion, and warm arms entwined around her neck.

Britannia's breath and being originate within our blessed realm. We are the beginning and end of all thought, all action. No one is ever forgotten here. Once your child is born, you may seek Merlin. We will watch over her as if she were our own.

This enticing revelation did not surprise Morgen one bit. Indeed, she had thoroughly anticipated that the Sisterhood would offer to raise her daughter. Demand was probably a more accurate word. In any case she had no objections. Something deep within her being whispered that the outside world needed her. And so she allowed the sisters to govern her actions, quietly watching the various characters play their parts.

The vast sum of a day bled into a fortnight, and the fortnight into a darkling month. Precious little delight was in evidence anywhere, for battle, bloodshed, and an endless display of severed limbs became Britannia's regular fare. Morgen was not suffered to offer hands on healing as she had at Caerleon. Instead she blended her energies with

the sisters, ever striving toward the peace that currently evaded the land and her people. The precious babe lodged within Morgen's womb grew
large, so large that it became apparent her birthing would occur well before a mortal nine-month
period. Indeed, fairy births, rare as they were,
often occurred within the span of a few months.
Daily she conversed with Merlin through the well's
mirror reflection, conscious of his decline. Deep
down inside she knew that salvation lay within her
reach. "Time will tell," the sisters avowed. And, so,
the days and the months crept by.

One morning as dawn's pink fingers laced the
burgeoning sky, pain lanced Morgen's belly, signaling the onset of childbirth. It was vital that she contact Merlin and tell him of their child's impending
arrival. And so she stepped before the Chalice Well
ignoring the agony that threatened reason. The
crimson waters swirled once, revealing the mage
as he watched the horizon, his face brightened
with the same wonder she had expressed but a few
moments earlier. Arthur's men appeared equally
transfixed. A large quantity of water swirled at their
feet—a river or lake, no doubt, bent on reflecting
the miracle of color and light. Reeds swayed sensuously back and forth, and a lone heron teetered on
its left foot, scouting for easy prey, a renegade fish
that drew too near his haunt.

Merlin, hear me. See me. It is time.

Merlin shook his head as she called him from
his silent reverie and into the cold realization that
she needed him. Even then it took him several
moments to recognize the loathsome creature that

wreathed within the river's callous bosom. Indeed, the red witch's curse altered Morgen's fairy shape and form into a horrific banshee: ghoulish, utterly devoid of that beauty Merlin so associated with her person. Anger enveloped his soul. Had the foul being murdered his poor love?

Who is it? What game are you playing? Step forward and show your hand.

Morgen froze, terrified at the response. Something was wrong, something that lay just beneath the surface, something she could not quite see. A great burst of water struck hard against the well's stone casing, revealing darkness, upheaval, and madness. It was indeed madness that facilitated Merlin's undoing, madness born of deceit.

It is I, Merlin. Come see me for what I truly am.

The mage looked upon her again, staring as if hopelessly perplexed. A fine layer of sweat misted his brow, soaking his dark locks, which appeared increasingly silver. Suddenly a new possibility arrested his thoughts: this was not a ghoul, but his love sickened unto the point of death.

Morgen, what has happened to you? Why did you not tell me you had grown so ill?

Puzzled by his reaction, Morgen conveyed the obvious. *I am not ill, but our child is coming.*

Merlin stared at his beloved's reflection, reeling and thoroughly unconvinced. *Not ill—surely she is dying!* Madness grossly distorted Morgen's reflection, altering her form into little more than skin stretched over bones, quickly belying the huge belly that thoughtlessly drained her of life. That is what Merlin saw reflected in the River Tribuit's rising waters, though Morgen did not comprehend it at first.

Do not move! I will come to you!

The promise proved enticing, quickening Morgen's heart, warming her very soul; but it was not to be. A northern tribe of blue-dyed Picts crept forward, awaiting the proper moment to strike. Overhead three ravens mindlessly circled, signaling the assault. Indeed, sound, sight, and anger blended in one transparent scream as the river exploded its fury. A thousand agile feet plunged through those watery depths with a single goal: annihilation of the Britons. Arthur and his men had traveled just short of the borders, hardly anticipating what would one day be called a highland charge. The immense array of colorful Picts that bore down upon them, spears raised high, however, set every Companion in motion. Torn between love and duty, Merlin bowed once more to Britannia.

"May Bridgit protect you, beloved," he fairly sobbed. "I must take action or all is lost!"

Down into the river's watery embrace he plunged and was seen no more. The pain in Morgen's abdomen increased its expression, bent her double; but she somehow willed herself to shift form, meld with the very air, until she reappeared high upon the Tor. The sisters were waiting, well pleased with her arrival. Morgen rendered the circle complete, and they could not, would not offer assistance without their Fairy Queen. Purposefully she cast the golden medallion down so that it demanded attention. Each sister responded accordingly, channeling healing into this orifice, a metal surrogate fashioned to represent Arthur, Merlin, and Britannia's forces. Light shimmered and split off the relic, dividing into nine points that enveloped the Sisterhood in rainbow splendor before spiraling off in one great sending toward the River Tribuit. The golden talisman rose several feet, revolving round and round, creating a gilded mirror that illuminated Arthur and his forces as they met the Picts within the river's watery embrace.

The Sisterhood watched the enchanted exchange with heavy hearts. Yes, Arthur and his men were protected, but at what cost? The Pict warriors were also children of Britannia. What right had the Sisterhood as guardians of the land to safeguard one people over the other? Several of the sisters wept, unable to stomach the part they had played in the Picts' destruction. Magic had been their undoing. Sensing their sorrow, the medallion gave a shudder and plopped down hard against the earth.

Sweat beaded Morgen's fair brow, soaking her hair, discoloring her emerald gown. Aware that the pain would soon bereft her of reason she clasped the medallion between her numbed fingers and gazed into its center. There she saw Merlin, trembling at the water's edge, eyes clouded with madness.

"Morgen, is it possible that I am too late?"

"I am here, Merlin. I am here." She offered subtle reassurance, conscious that he could not see or hear her so deep was his grief.

"Oh, beloved, can you ever find it in your heart to forgive me? I am sorry I turned my back on you. It is this war, over and over again, which destroys me."

Indeed, Merlin had never been at ease with battle tactics. The idea of one man killing another had always made him ill. This day, however, the screams of the dying magnified his despair tenfold. They were human beings, after all, not merely Picts, but brothers battling over a territory they wished to call their own. One by one the painted warriors died horrible, bloody deaths—all because of his thoughtless intervention.

Merlin fell to his knees sobbing. All life was sacred. After an entire lifetime of mouthing this belief, the mage suddenly understood its meaning. He was no longer the king's councilor but a member of the brethren that beat against Annwyn's dark gates. Never again would he be involved in so brutal an act.

"Sisters, help him," Morgen cried, conscious that the feminine waters streamed between her legs. The time had come. Her child's birthing could no longer be abated.

"First," Glitonea replied, "we will attend you and the babe."

Tor, medallion, earth, sky: all faded from view, so great was the fresh onslaught of pain. Morgen found herself crouching in a dark, shallow chamber that boasted no bed but a series of ropes that dangled from the timbered ceiling. They were lodged in the basement of what would one day be known as the maiden's chapel of Glastonbury

Abbey; in her day, however, it was the timber and wattle church. Glancing up, Morgen was preternaturally aware that she could see through the chapel's skeleton, glancing beyond timber, rock, and wattle to see a solitary grave perched upon a rising slope that haunted her sensibilities. *Arthur lies at rest there, or so the locals say...*What trick was this of her wreathing mind? She had just seen Arthur proclaimed supreme victor over the bluish Picts. Why must she witness this perplexity now? Casting her eyes back upon the humble birthing chamber, she noted that straw lined the floor in huge mounds that tickled her calves and toes.

"Clutch tight, sweet sister, and let nature do the rest."

"But Merlin—where is he? Will no one help him?"

Soft arms surrounded Morgen from every side. She wanted so much to see, to call the mage's form into view, and so she closed her eyes and did just that. The pain of the babe increasing her bid for freedom made it difficult to connect at first, but slowly Merlin's tall, dark form loomed into view. Round and round a circle of downed standing stones, dark, misshapen, foreboding, he trod oblivious to everything but the fever that thrilled his brain. Funeral pyres danced wickedly amid the deepening twilight, filling the air with the scent of roasting flesh. Try as he might, Merlin could not help but retch. His knees met the ground in humble delirium.

Ancient Ones. Take me from this earth. If you will not honor me in this request, then I will claim the right with my own two hands.

Morgen screamed anew. "Please help Merlin!"

Intuition guided Merlin's hand to the pouch that hung about his waist. A lock of Morgen's hair remained lodged within. Slowly, carefully, Merlin drew it forth and drank of its rosy perfume. Again and again he pressed the delicate strands to his blistered lips.

"Come to me, beloved, do. I know that the dead still walk the earth long after their bodies have decayed. Come to me now, Morgen."

"Merlin... Merlin..."

Merlin paused, listening. Was this not Morgen's voice calling his name? Suddenly she appeared before him, untouched by childbirth, slender and beautiful. They had barely kissed in greeting when she pushed him back against a fallen ring stone. Not a word passed between them. Indeed, none was needed, for Morgen lay her sweet body upon his, coaxing love. Merlin was feverish and delirious, unable to clearly see through the thick, red haze that coated his eyes. How could it be otherwise? Morgen's lips were everywhere at once, fueling the fire that burned within his brain. He could neither speak nor think, but watched spellbound as their bodies joined as one.

It is Morgause that holds you, Merlin—not I! It is the curse come to claim your life!

Morgen's thoughts were screaming, straining against the pain that threatened to tear her apart. The child was struggling so hard to be born but finding it difficult to break free from her tiny body. Merlin felt her agony as if it were his own. His body was heaving, splitting in two as their child increased its desperate bid for freedom.

Merlin!

The mage opened his eyes and saw her smiling down at him with a sweetness that belied any such trauma. Surely there could not be two Morgens. The lock of hair flamed once more, burning him with its unspoken missive.

Merlin, Merlin! Heed my warning!

Echoes of Morgen's agony shrieked inside his soul. It was nothing short of the death cry. This made him sit up, but the gentle Morgen merely slowed her lovemaking until he could do nothing but lie back down and allow desire full sway. She had nearly drawn him to release when an image of horror clouded his senses. Morgen was wreathing in a timbered church, hands clutching a series of birthing ropes, the child unable to break free from her tiny body.

"Merlin, I know you can hear me!" she screamed mentally and aloud, the medallion clutched tightly against her breast.

Merlin, heed me while you still can. It is Morgause that holds you in her arms, not I. It is her desire to fulfill the curse. She has awaited this moment throughout time. You still have the power to break free. Claim it now!

A wave of crimson mist flooded Merlin's vision, severing the cords that bound him to the real Morgen. It was then he saw the red witch's face— clear, unmasked. Morgause was gloating, laughing at his folly, claiming the seed that spilled within her womb.

"You see, Merlin," she taunted in a low voice that dripped honey, "at long last you *have* fallen prey to my charms. Now my curse has destroyed you thoroughly. You have lost both Morgen and the child just as you are about to lose your own soul!"

Destiny's Playfellow

Light—fierce, mind-numbing excess—streamed through Merlin's fingertips, a full-bodied explosion that hit the red witch's gloating face and cast her aside as if she were no more substantial than a rag doll. Surprise colored her countenance, indeed, forced an uncommon *O* shape to those ruby lips, birthing a horrific wail that shattered the night air and called all from their slumber. In a flurry of motion, Arthur, the foot soldiers, and Companions grappled for their swords. Somehow the blade that Merlin never deigned touch found its way into his trembling hand. Following instinct alone, he began to stab at his tormentor.

"Surely you can do better than that!" Morgause laughed, effortlessly evading his blows. "Strike true, great mage, or one day my son will wear the crown!" Round and round she danced, hands raised high, while a series of unintelligible gibberish escaped her lips. Clouds shrouded the haunted sky, deepening ebony to passionate excess. It was difficult to discern shape or movement, only the heavy breathing that escaped her lips.

Merlin alone saw beyond this conjured haze, saw straight into the heart of prophecy, his eyes blazing that familiar telltale white that foretold use of the Sight. The ground heaved underfoot, the skies trembled their warning. Blood blotted out all other perception and consumed thought in a thick crimson tide that clouded vision, twisting it beyond the humble workings of the mind. Another prolific scream colored the night. Companions were racing everywhere. Did they not see that the very river ran red? A crimson wave burst up over the sodden riverbanks, a wicked progression that painted the grassy plains a macabre hue. Surely Arthur and the men would drown if he did not stop its progress.

Laughter pierced the night air, drawing men of all rank and distinction ever closer, chilling them with broad malice. Merlin shut his eyes and ears against their puzzled visages and demanding cries. These were men who respected him, who relied upon him to light the path. Surely they must not see him so disarranged—no, not disarranged but distraught. The untimely death of Morgen followed by Morgause's appearance fairly ripped the veil from his clouded eyes. He must annihilate the red witch once and for all. No middle path was possible; either he won this battle or simply surrendered his life altogether. So sweet was the second prospect that Merlin momentarily faltered, but then his inner voice pulled him back to the present with such severity that he had no choice but to redouble his efforts. Light flashed from his fingers, his eyes, faster than thought, soaring through the night, bent on Morgause's cackling form. She danced, she dodged, she spun, avoiding most bursts; but now and then her hair would singe or her skin burn, evidence that the mage had grazed her. Sweat streamed down her fair brow, but she had no time to wipe it free, no, not when Merlin leveled volley after volley at her. Leaves sputtered and crackled, burgeoning flame where the razor-sharp lights went wide. Brilliant hellfire colored the night, or so it appeared to the bedazzled warriors.

"Over there!" screamed Bedivere, brandishing his sword toward the fantastic light that played between witch and enchanter.

White, green, and deep crimson beams flashed back and forth with such rapid succession that it was impossible to know whether they originated from witch or mage. Indeed, it was difficult to decipher one from the other so bright was the illumination. And then it happened. Morgause unexpectedly caught one of Merlin's volleys, forced her delicate fingers round its glowing mass. Pain seared her sensibilities, forced tears to the eyes that never cried; but still she held on, molding the energy to her desired goal, a white light that obeyed her bidding. The act was ferocious, malevolent, but somehow she cast the brilliant glow back from whence it came. Merlin saw the white light but did not comprehend its new consistency. Indeed, he only understood its altered state when the mass hit him square between the eyes. Blinding pain ensued followed by the sensation of falling; then Merlin, the enchanter, found himself face down upon the dewy grass, impossible to move or think, so shattered was his focus.

The witch's laughter increased its passion. Footfall after footfall brought her closer to Merlin's paralyzed form. Well satisfied, she bowed low and smiled. Words framed themselves skillfully as they spilled from her ruby lips. Indeed, the spell waxed full, encompassing Morgause and her victim in a hauntingly lurid glow; yellow green, it was the color of spring, or deepest bile. Within this sallow reckoning, a black gate swung wide jaws taut, poised to claim its due. The ease with which Morgause drew the weakened Merlin down into this fathomless pit gave her pause. Surely this was just a ploy to put her off guard. Merlin would never surrender his soul so easily unless...

Home...he shuddered, seeing the vast crystalline cave yawn wide before him. *She has led me home.*

Round and round Morgause danced; her eerie silhouette was cast into shadow by hypnotic flames that took root and spread, remnants of the fiery volleys that bled astray. Each spiral, each rotation birthed an enchanted prison, not of rock as Merlin feared, but a stark, wooden cocoon that boasted heartwood, sap, and phloem. Roots sprang from his leaden feet, even as his dull fingers sought the sky. He was one with trunk, leaves, and peeling bark, a shade trapped within a thriving hawthorn tree. Why, the very effort it took to inhale bereft him of reason. His lungs ached with the exertion and threatened to give up the fight altogether. Bark, twig, and trunk encompassed his emaciated body, rendered it inconsequential. He was no longer a solitary individual but a symbiont fully dependent on its host for survival.

"Sleep, great enchanter, sleep now and for all time."

Merlin knew that he was trapped, unable to free himself or aid others, but that did not stop him from witnessing one final vision.

No longer content to rest upon the Tribuit's soggy plains, the red tide reared up, then just as quickly slapped down hard upon the earth with such fortitude that it necessarily streamed forward. Down the length of Britannia it spilled, growing thicker, a sticky cacophony of all that is vile. No one was immune to its grotesque progress. Deep into a vast, pale fortress the tide spilled, casting aside king, court, and all who dwelt within its pristine walls. The bloody waters did not stop there but swelled around a gray dragon throne so that it tottered back and forth before it pitched forward. There it lingered a moment and was seen no more.

The message was clear enough even to Merlin's unsettled mind. Morgause would destroy Arthur just as she destroyed him—if he did not break free—and so he did, divorcing himself from Morgause's mind-numbing trickery that was nothing more than a false vision conjured to weaken him—there was no hawthorn tree, no sylvan prison, only the darkest fears that haunted his mind. Clasping hold of the sword he never deigned use, he drove it to purpose and struck true. Merlin lashed out again with greater surety. This time his blade made contact with flesh. A sharp intake of breath followed, heightened by a low cry.

"What ails you, Merlin! It's me, Bedivere!"

Somewhere through the thick bands of delirium Merlin almost heard the voice, almost deciphered what it was saying, but Morgause's laughter drew him forward until he struck again with renewed vigor. A substantial mass took the brunt of his efforts and fell down hard. Thinking it to be Morgause, the mage made ready to inflict the deathblow but just short of impact, a strong blade struck the sword from his hand. Merlin looked up, trembling. There before him stood the battle-clad Arthur Pendragon wielding Excalibur, disbelief imprinted on his handsome face. Light, sound, senses: all shifted dramatically into focus. The red witch had long since made good her escape.

Bedivere lay on his side, gasping for breath, his right arm twisted in a bloody mass beneath him. "Arthur, it was the witch. She's here. See how she has unsettled Merlin. Guard yourself."

The crimson tide reasserted its pull, drew Merlin back into vision's heady embrace. His eyes rolled upward, his mouth spewed venomous portent. "Britannia split in twain," he raved, tearing his increasingly silvered hair. "Father and son sacrificed as one, their blood spilt to wash the land clean!"

Although far superior in strength and prowess, the High King had a devil of a time subduing Merlin. Indeed, the mage proved so wiry, so bloody slippery, that Arthur finally threw his whole weight against him, catapulting them both down upon the grass in order to secure Merlin's hands behind his back. This accomplished, he turned attention toward his captain, simultaneously pulling Merlin back up onto his feet while maintaining control over his arms. "Bedivere, are you—?"

"It will heal," came Bedivere's forced response. He was trying very hard to belie the seriousness of his injury, but even his ready smile dripped pain. There he lay rocking back and forth, favoring his bloodied right arm that appeared to have been severed and hung sickeningly attached by a few threads of skin. Bedivere did not question why he was not overcome with blood loss or why his artery no longer bled; it was as if Merlin's sword had magically cauterized the wound so that the injured warrior had more than a passing chance at survival.

"You are wrong, Bedivere," Merlin exclaimed, still caught within his visionary bindings, "It will never heal. You will bear this wound until the day you die."

Bedivere paled further, yet this time held his silence. Indeed, it would have made little difference if he had spoken, for Merlin turned his crazed eyes on Arthur.

"Just as you, Red Dragon, will bear Morgause's mark—until the day you die."

This warning hit the mark. The tone, the very rasp of Merlin's voice unsettled the king, and Merlin momentarily slipped free. "This is madness!" Arthur cried asserting his grip at the throat of his dark robes. He then shook the mage with such vigorous intent that the scarlet malady momentarily took flight. "I alone control my destiny! Follow my example and break free of her!"

Merlin did just that, regaining his freedom from Arthur's vicelike grip with a flick of his wrist. His feet were alive, pacing frantically back and forth as if to overtake time, recall all the madness, all the hatred that tainted the air. "Beware her son, Arthur. Make ready—they intend to destroy you."

"Which son?" Bedivere questioned, struggling to regain his footing. Twisting a blanket around his shattered arm, he prayed no one would take notice of his wounding. Indeed, more important matters were at stake. The Companions were gathering around him. He had no idea how to keep them ignorant of the information that passed between counselor and king. "Gawain...Gareth? Tell us which one so we may stop this thing before it happens!"

"You know of which son I speak."

Arthur took two steps backward, his senses reeling. "No, that's impossible. You cannot mean that he lived. Lot would never accept a bastard son unto his brood."

"No less than two of Lot's so called sons are sired by other men."

"What precisely are you saying, Merlin?"

"They are lurking everywhere, Arthur, waiting for you to slip. Do not give into them. Do not allow them to destroy you as they have destroyed me."

"Destroyed you?" Arthur questioned with growing concern. "Surely this will pass. You must rest."

This said, Arthur helped his friend and mentor gain a seated position, but the tormented enchanter would have none of it. On his feet again, he howled to the heavens, an action that rivaled the most mysterious wolf. "I will seek the kingdom of my father—open the sinewy gates of Annwyn! Morgen cannot have traveled far. Perhaps there I will meet our child."

Arthur's face grew crimson at the mention of Morgen's name. A seeming lifetime had passed since he had allowed himself to think of her, to dream of her. Suddenly Merlin's words indicated that she was no longer alive. If that were the case, then he might as well rip out his heart and live for Britannia alone. No matter how much Morgen had wounded him, life without her was inconceivable. And then something else hovered outside his grasp, something he could not quite decipher— something about *a child.*

"What are you telling me, Merlin? That Morgen bore you a child? Are you speaking true or is this just another one of Morgause's tricks?"

"I would ask your forgiveness, but it is too late for that. She is dead by my hand."

A sharp cry filled the air, this time originating from Arthur. His own true love, his precious Morgen was *dead*, stolen from his faltering grasp, the culprit none other than his very own counselor. How was this breach, this betrayal to be answered? Payment must be extracted, payment in full. Arthur's eyes darkened into twin points of obsidian, battle ready, fierce, volatile, a terror that reasserted its grasp on Merlin's robes and forcibly conveyed him several feet across the wind swept plains, pausing only once he came to rest against a standing stone, pinned at the throat and chest against movement of any kind. The stone, which boasted a wicked crack through its middle, a stone that mirrored Arthur's own cleft heart, held fast, restricting all movement. Twist and contort as Merlin might, there could be no escape, not until Arthur willingly set him free.

Weak from the pain that threatened to bereft him of consciousness, Bedivere staggered to Arthur's side. "Pause, Arthur. Think what you are doing. This is Merlin—not some fiend of a witch."

Arthur silenced the well-meaning Bedivere with a single glance. Turning his gaze once more on Merlin, he said in a surprisingly controlled voice, "I know not what Morgause has done, or if you are even conscious of thought, but you must tell me true—is Morgen dead?"

A weak nod of the head served as Merlin's reply. He had seen the child caught within her, undoubtedly so large that it could not break free. Indeed, that final image of her bloated, twisted form, her bloodless face had spoken more clearly than Morgause's taunt. Yes, Morgen was dead. No woman, not even a fairy, could survive so brutal a delivery.

Arthur increased his grip tenfold. Slowly, he brought the tip of his silver dagger against Merlin's tawny throat. Just what it was he meant to do proved uncertain, but the action itself further heightened his manic fury. "Tell me this is a lie."

The mage offered no response.

Bedivere stood helpless—caught between loyalty to both adviser and king. Little could he do but rein in the unsettled warriors that drew increasingly near before they overheard the contents of this heated discourse.

"She died giving birth to your child—is that it?"

The mage collapsed full against the unyielding stone, his limbs riddled with spasms that jerked at horrific angles capable of breaking a mortal bone. "Take me from the world, Arthur. I beg you do it now."

For a moment Arthur felt himself capable of striking home, his anger was that extreme, but soon images of the years they had spent together as student and teacher flooded his brain, and the dagger found its way to the ground.

"Why did you not tell me she was pregnant? I would have done anything to see her safely delivered. Surely you know that! How could you have left Caerleon knowing that she was in danger?"

"I believed that Britannia needed me more."

Arthur released his grip, reeling with the import of this statement. He, too, had placed Britannia before Morgen's concerns. Had she not plead with him to send her somewhere—anywhere but a nunnery? Had he even listened to this request? What did nuns know of childbirth? What of his own harsh indifference to her pleas? They had not exchanged a single word since the battle at Caerleon due to his stupidity. He had sent Morgen, his own true love, to her death.

Ignorant of the king's self-condemnations, Merlin pitched forward and commenced writhing amid the cool, gray megaliths that had long since fallen from their original placement. "I will seek her in the land of my father. I will leave no stone unturned until I find Morgen's spirit and beg her forgiveness!" The words were wild and garbled, practically unintelligible. Arthur might also have joined him in abasement had he not caught hold of a rounded sentinel and allowed it to support his grief. There he remained unmoving until a silvery howl pierced the night air.

Staring in amazement Arthur watched a silent gray wolf approach Merlin's side, tail tucked tightly between its legs. It bowed low before Arthur and the Companions, demonstrating subservience, then cast his golden eyes on Merlin. Slowly, gently, he washed Merlin's tear-stained face with his long, pink tongue. The two commenced communication, although how this was accomplished not one of the Companions could truthfully reply. Somewhere amid the unintelligible gibberish, one phrase alone captured Arthur's attention.

Red Dragon, heed the dictates of your heart. End the war and set us free.

Merlin crouched low next to the silver-furred beauty, utilizing all four limbs. Suddenly agile beyond years, he set them in motion. Round and round he whirled, chasing an invisible tail. This was not the hapless gesture of a madman but an intricate invocation that set the act of shapeshifting into play. Gracefully the wolf followed suit. Together they danced as one entity, one being until the spell completed its work. The night air trembled and split its passion, rendering mage and lupine waif as one. A low, mournful wail spilled from the beast's noble lips. It took one look back at

Arthur then set off at a gallop across the darkened plain, vanishing.

"What have I done?" Arthur whispered, frozen with grief. Sight, sound, passion—all blended as one, setting him in motion. "Merlin! Merlin, come back!" he cried, racing full after the wolf's retreating form. The Companions wanted only to follow him, but somehow, even in his wounded state, Bedivere held them at bay.

The sentient night kept pace with Arthur's progress, urging him forward, increasing his speed past the bounds of mortal endurance until he collapsed, unable to complete the chase. "Merlin, forgive me," he gasped, curling into a fetal position. "I cannot fathom how I will continue without your wisdom, your good council. You have been a part of my life for as long as I can remember. Now I linger alone, forsaken by you and the woman we both loved.

"Love, Arthur? Do you truly love me?"

The soft, familiar scent of roses caressed Arthur's nostrils. Was it possible that Morgen's spirit watched over him even now? She was, after all, a fairy. Hope burned anew in his heaving breast. Instantly he regained his footing.

"Come back to me, dearest. I know that you are near. I can feel you. Do not leave me alone, searching the darkness for some shadow that reminds me of your beauty, your grace. I am waiting for you."

The air shuddered its warning, offering up a dim, shadowy figure that shaped itself into the being Arthur most desired to see.

"You are not alone, Arthur. I, too, await the coming dawn.

Golden hairs bristled on Arthur's head, neck, and arms. "Morgen, is that really you?"

CHAPTER 32:

The Dreamspell

"Where are you?" Arthur cried, spinning wildly around in an effort to visually capture her illusive face. The phantom slid in and out of view, echoing the cloud-draped moon. Surely this was not a dream. "When will you return to us? When will you return to me?"

A shaft of moonlight pierced through the deep clouded excess, spilling down into a glorious cascade that cast a halo around Morgen, unveiling waves of deep, red hair that fairly undulated around her slight frame. Arthur gasped despite himself. The image was so longed for yet so unexpected that it took several moments for his eyes to attune to her translucent appearance. He often forgot how tiny she was—not impossibly small, but fragile, ethereal—a woman, an angel whose head barely reached his chest.

"Time will tell," echoed her soft reply. "I live in Avalon now. One day you will visit me there."

The voice so lyrical, so melodiously sweet, flooded his heart, his mind. Arthur could not gather Morgen against his heart fast enough. She

felt misty soft at first, cottony, as she slowly gained
definition, but Arthur held fast and was soon
rewarded when her lips sought his. The sensation
proved so lush, so real that he knew that it was
Morgen who filled his arms. Time and strain had
not aged her. She was more beautiful, more sensuous than any memory that haunted his dreams.
What was it about her that had changed, altered as
it were into starlit bliss? Did it stem from the fact
that she lived in Avalon and claimed her fairy title?
"Show me the way, dearest," he whispered, burying his face in her luxuriant hair. "Guide my path.
Lead me to your magical isle."

"When the time is right, you will find your way."

Again she kissed him, but even this did not
allay the nagging concern that assaulted Arthur's
thoughts. Not everything was as it appeared. The
rolling hills that sprung up around them, the stars
whose altered configurations pockmarked the sky,
even the water that incessantly lapped the rock-
lined shores all pointed to the fact he could no
longer ignore. Their surroundings were shifting,
altering beyond recognition.

"And so you will leave me too?" he questioned,
unable to bear the answers that weighted his soul.

Pearly light flashed around them, encompassed them in its soft, warm glow, eradicating
every last hint of the blackened landscape that
comprised Tribuit's battlefield. Together Arthur
and Morgen stood, looking down upon a golden
bed, bloodstained and empty, awaiting the return
of its wounded charge, a bed that rested high upon
Avalon Tor. Time warped and bled its expression.

This was their true reality. Arthur was dying, sustained only by Morgen's dreamspell, a spell that forced him to revisit his life in the hope that some pearl of knowledge would be revealed to secure his healing.

"I am with you now and always, Arthur," Morgen said, smiling. "When you gaze into the blackest night and watch shadows fall across the land—I am there. Together we witness visions of the past and await the promise of a new day."

Morgen softly placed a kiss on Arthur's cheek as he lay down once more upon the golden bedding, his head still swollen, his bandages bloodied. The spell of remembrance claimed this moment to catch a well-deserved breath before completing its first night's work.

"And when that day comes?" he asked, breathless.

"Then we too will awaken in the land of dreams."

Arthur shifted his lips as if he wanted to say more, but his eyes closed on the vision and he fell back into a deep sleep.

CHAPTER 33:

The Dreamer Awakens

A solitary cricket chirped the final note of its twilight symphony as dawn's first light pierced the sky. Morgen had fallen asleep against the reed woven bedding that encased Arthur Pendragon's wounded frame. The spell had offered up more information than she cared to assimilate. Arthur stirred fitfully beside her but showed no real indication of waking. She had called him back from the dream realm, excited by the revelations that burst forth within the spell. Arthur had realized their love, their eternal connection, understood that they were bound to Britannia, parents divine long ago. Yes, this great country was their offspring, their child, and as it declined so did they. In other words she must save Arthur to resurrect Britannia. Daylight streamed over the eight curvaceous standing stones that wordlessly observed Morgen's progress. The Sisterhood was never far away. Indeed, their melodious song spurred her up onto bent knees. It was early morning: the best time to begin anew.

Morgen placed her delicate hands just above Arthur's bloodied skull and breathed a prayer for assistance. Surely this day his healing would be rendered complete! Energy surged through her outstretched fingers into the exposed brain matter. All breath and focus was centered on this naked mass.

Heal, Arthur. If you accept this gift then the spell may end here and now. Neither of us will have need to relive the past.

Light crackled around Morgen, intensifying the healing flow to its zenith. Sound, scent, color all mingled as one. Slowly, painfully, Morgen felt her empathetic powers intercede. Why did this always occur when the life she aided was most dear to her? As if healing was not fraught with enough peril. Few people realize that healers die a thousand deaths every time they use their gifts. Not that healing demands such sacrifice, but those who are truly committed always offer up a bit of their soul every time they heal another. Morgen's fair skin turned an unpleasant pink, stinging painfully as if it were being stabbed by a thousand fiery knives; yet she could not falter. Blinking back the sweat that seeped into her eyes, she tried not to succumb to the black stupor that threatened consciousness. Although Morgen was not in the habit of fainting, she lingered very close to collapse—the pain was so intense. If this was a true reflection of Arthur's suffering, she marveled how he still lived.

Arthur, you must fight—fight for your life! Do not give in, dearest. I am here beside you. Take the light from me and continue on.

Morgen, are you mad? Arthur's voice flared inside her brain. *I will not steal your life away in an attempt to reclaim my own.*

A tremor rattled Morgen's stiffened spine. Arthur's spirit was speaking to her, offering direction, commanding her to stop.

"I cannot! I will not cease—not while there is still breath in my body!" she cried with such passion that several ravens formerly intent upon her progress took flight from their rocky perch, the twisted standing stone.

Arthur's eyes flew open. They were still blue as the summer sky. He stared at her intently, then sighed. "Some things never change."

A sob escaped Morgen's lips. "Arthur?" Her hands wavered as if she would relinquish the healing effort, but resumed their task with even greater fervor. She was making progress. If Arthur could speak to her, then some aspects of his wounded brain had been restored.

"Morgen, dearest, I truly appreciate the effort, but I must ask you why? Why heal me when I have done all that I came into this world to do?"

Morgen took a deep breath to ease her rapidly beating heart and replied, "Britannia is once again at war, Arthur. You—I—we both came into this world to bring peace upon the land."

Moving his cramped, blood-stained fingers so that they brushed Morgen's fair arm, Arthur replied, "And so we did—for a time."

Another tremor wracked Morgen's frame. "Are you telling me that it has all been for naught, Arthur?"

His voice came as no more than a whisper. "Britannia has always sought conflict, Morgen. Remember Agned, remember Badon. I suppose you intend to wrack my brain with those memories as well."

"It is all a part of the spell," she sighed, gazing out over Avalon's veiled horizon. Beauty waxed hypnotic as the familiar vista sparkled a steely blue, melding tree, hill, and lake into a misty delight. "Together we will relive the past. Only then may we understand why Britannia—why *we* are failing."

"What would you have me do? Race back onto the battlefield so that I may rally the tribes around me again? They hunger for conflict. I merely distracted them for a time with promises of peace."

"Distract them again."

"I am dying, Morgen—in case you haven't noticed."

A single tear spilled from Morgen's downcast eyelashes. "Not if I have anything to do with it."

Arthur's frame shuddered as he made a tremendous effort to clasp her hand, an act that fell short of its purpose but finally drew Morgen from her healing work. "What is it, dearest? What is it you want of me?"

"Hold me," he sputtered, straining with all his might to keep his thick voice from failing.

Morgen did just that, wrapping her slim arms around his chest. Softly, her head came to rest against his heart, an act that brought tears to the eyes of both healer and wounded king. "Is that better?"

A sharp nod of the head served as his reply.

"Come, then, the spell must continue its work. Let us remember the great wars and how they ultimately brought us together…"

CHAPTER 34:

The Adversary

This time Arthur and Morgen had neither well nor cloud to reflect their past experiences, only the simple hooding of their eyes. They relaxed to purpose and were rewarded as image after image swirled as quicksilver through their minds. Avalon faded even as the Companions took precedence. Arthur stood among them tall, golden, handsome—attributes that the immense sorrow that consumed his features could not mask. They were searching for Merlin, an unending task that left young and old increasingly frustrated. Was it possible? Had the enchanter in his madness actually disappeared into thin air?

Do you see it, Arthur? Do you see how much you missed him even then?

It was not just Merlin I mourned. Remember, I thought you were dead.

The search for Merlin extended the length of six nights—six nights during which every last member of Arthur's forces forsook sleep in a desperate attempt to unearth the famed enchanter. Spirits ran low until Lot's youngest son, Gareth, a fourteen-year-old maverick with the breadth and musculature unmatched by many adult warriors, appeared on horseback, galloping frantically down a steep embankment, an act further hampered with loose rock and feeble vegetation. The fact that he bore a desperate summons from the people of Lothian immediately commanded their attention.

"Great king," he cried, struggling to calm his jagged breathing as he cast himself down on both knees before Arthur. "Forgive this rude intrusion, but I know not where else to turn. My father has been captured by a renegade band of Saxons who have penetrated far into our northern territories and now terrorize the countryside. Gawain, my eldest brother, has taken command of your men that still lodge within our keeping. How much longer they can hold out is impossible to say. I only pray I may have reached you soon enough to save them."

Arthur stared at Gareth's golden brown hair and clear gilded green eyes, aware that this might very well be a trap. The lad's look was innocence itself—bordering on worshipful in respect to his own person—but Arthur did not put it past Lot to use his own son for evil, even if it be without Gareth's knowledge. In any case the need for action was paramount. The men were ripe for new conflict. Thus, Arthur led his forces north through harsh wind, snow, and the sucking mud—so thick that at times it nearly pulled the boots from their feet—stopping only once they reached a steep volcanic plug known as Agned, situated at Lothian's rear door. A series of jagged cliffs jutted out around them, some soaring to impressive heights, while others remained squat and fertile. Arthur noted that these crags fairly surrounded his forces, hemmed them in or buffeted them against attack, depending on how one viewed the situation. In any case Arthur hoped that this lofty vantage point would help him weed out all miscreant activity— a sound plan until the snows came down in an unrelenting veil. It was the winter solstice and daylight was scarce when Arthur and a few of Gawain's locals went scouting for shelter.

Back at camp the men were speaking of their lost loves.

"Come on, ladies, we are waiting," the ginger-haired Gawain began, hoisting his notable personage up on both legs so he might better scan the low valley in which they lodged. He was a handsome young man who lacked the dazzling perfection of the High King but still cut a striking figure. It was evident he had inherited Lot's good looks as well as a healthy dose of his charm. Gawain and some four score of the king's men had joined up with Arthur's forces shortly after their arrival.

A faint chuckling rippled among the men. Perhaps they knew Lot's eldest son a little too well. Even at sixteen years of age, Gawain was something of a ladies' man, a fact clearly evident by his frequent attempts to woo every farmer's daughter that crossed his path. He was not quite as tall as Gareth nor so well physically defined, but he possessed a strong, wiry build capable of great speed, a fact that heightened his already remarkable combat skills.

Gawain offered a mischievous smile as he pushed a handful of rusty, snow-dampened hair from his brow. "What ladies, you ask? Why, those Saxon beauties who haunt the crag."

"They would as like slit your throat as give you a kiss," interjected the ever-steady Grifflet, sharpening his blade against a jagged rock that already boasted a wicked cleft due to his amorous attentions.

Gawain approached Grifflet grinning broadly, a smile that stretched deceptively from ear to ear. With one swift move he fearlessly captured the red-hot blade, thankful that his hands were gloved—otherwise he would have been rewarded with a well-sliced palm. He winked at his fellow warriors then brought the sword tentatively to his lips. "Never fear, friend, even a Saxon lass can be made to swoon." Grifflet cuffed him, reclaimed his lost weapon, and recommenced sharpening, a bemused expression coloring his pinched face.

Bedivere laughed heartily. "What say you men? Shall we conquer the Saxons by wooing their women?"

"All of us except baby Gareth," quipped Gawain, jabbing his younger brother's shoulders and chest.

Gareth rolled his eyes, used to the treatment. Yes, he was the youngest man present, but that did not signify for he had already witnessed a lifetime of hardship. A person did not grow up in Lothian without having experienced marauding Picts, insurgent Angles, or renegade Jutes. Everyone was laughing—even Grifflet. Gareth's large golden-green eyes sought his one, true friend, his silent comrade with respect. "What of you, Lancelot? Would you take part in this folly?"

Gray-eyed Lancelot looked up, haunted by some shadow that consumed his thoughts. Conscious of his surroundings, he knew what had transpired—even if he was not altogether present. He was fond of young Gareth. Indeed, the lad's innocence both on and off the battlefield had garnered his attention. Lessons in sword combat naturally followed. Obviously Lot had never schooled Gareth with such necessities.

"My heart is already bespoken," he answered at last. "I wait for her alone."

"Why speak of love when the princess has been taken from us?" Bedivere wistfully sighed, his eyes fixed upon the heaving sky. Pristine snowflakes landed on his face and tongue, and he trembled accordingly, the wound being still fresh.

Accolon tensed despite the aching cold in his joints. Bedivere was speaking of Morgen, and he could not allow the mention of her person to pass upraised, so deep was his devotion.

"The kindest, most beautiful woman ever to have graced this earth," he said in a voice that did not conceal its emotion. "She was indeed a treasure among women."

Bedivere seemed not to hear, his good arm tucked behind his back. "I can still see her now, red hair blazing, brighter than the deepest sunset."

"I believe you are right," Accolon quickly added. "She is with us even now."

Everyone stopped what they were doing and turned sharp eyes on Accolon. Was it possible the warrior bard knew something they did not?

"Well, go on," Bedivere urged, sitting up, his right sleeve flapping ever so slightly where the amputated limb had once been. "Explain yourself."

Accolon's head drooped ever so slightly. How could he ever lay bare his thoughts before so many unfeeling eyes? Kay had been unsuccessful in recovering her body. Did it not then follow that Morgen might still live?

"We all have such dreams about women, especially one as beautiful as the princess," the quiet Lucan unexpectedly volunteered. "They are nothing new for warriors of our plight." His eyes lingered on Accolon then swiftly darted away. No one spoke a word. Instead they listened to the wind's haunted symphony as it played upon the cliffs. The snow increased its downward spiral, blanketing Lucan's thoughts, coloring the air a fine, virgin hue that made rock, tree, and crag appear newborn.

Arthur, climbing a footpath that narrowed dramatically into sheeted rock which accepted his bulk and little else, caught a glimpse of his beleaguered followers, sheltering within the chilled levels below. He was slowly working his way up the steepest crag in search of a massive cavern that several locals had suggested might house his men. Glancing down upon the carefully huddled troops, he could almost hear echoes of defeat. The men needed inspiration that he alone could offer. Drawing a deep breath, he planted both feet against the rocky ground and thrilled as earth energy took note, surging beneath him, a heady flow that spilled up through his veins, enlivened his heart and mind. Next he looked to the pale, flake-hued sky.

As above, so below.

Everything happened at once, a lush cacophony of celestial events that dazzled the eye: Clouds parted on cue, even as the snow ceased its amorous attentions, a prelude that several ravens celebrated, throatily welcoming the long-awaited sunshine that flooded the snow-capped levels below. So brilliant, so beatific was the sphere that it cast a halo around Arthur's body, highlighting his fair locks in an unearthly glow. Many fell to their knees as they caught sight of the king, who seemingly commanded the sun's movements, indeed, mirrored its radiance with the mere wave of his hand.

Arthur breathed a sigh of relief. Merlin had taught him well. This was the Pendragon returned unto its power. He was about to hail his men when a certain play of light fell upon the rust-hued cliffs above. There amid the snow and bramble lay a gaping chasm—no doubt the cavern mentioned by several well-meaning locals. Arthur followed the golden expanse of morning light toward the promised haven, far from the watchful eyes of his followers. Perhaps there he would find some peace. Perhaps there answers would appear forthcoming.

Up, up he climbed, hand over foot. Pausing briefly at the smooth-lipped crest, he hauled himself onto a leveled plateau that appeared deliberately made for viewing pleasure. Gazing down he marveled at how quickly the powdery snow had covered much of the red hued countryside, dusting it a sugary, fairytale white. What a thing of beauty Lothian was—vast, craggy hills that jutted their massive necks blissfully into the clouds, before spilling down into windswept plains that touched the azure sea. And then there was the plug itself, a high conical mount, so lyrical, so breathtaking in its composition, that the locals swore it once spit fire. "Arthur's Seat" Gawain was already calling it, although the High King never dreamed his current resting place had adopted his name. There on that lonely plateau Arthur saw no hint of conflict or strife. One day Britannia would be truly peaceful as this glorious climb. Merlin had prophesied as much, a fact that inherently made it so.

No sooner had the thought crossed his mind than it was followed by a sharp tinge of regret. The unthinkable had happened. Morgen was dead, the knowledge invoking an emotion that Arthur could neither voice nor allow himself the luxury to express fully. He had attacked Merlin as a result and nearly killed him. The student who had so worshipped the master that he hardly dare walk in his footprints now faced the future alone due to a moment of indiscretion—no, not indiscretion, insanity. If anyone had been insane that night it had been Arthur. All his immediate hopes and dreams dwelt upon a single wish: that Merlin would reclaim his rightful place, thereby rendering all past dissension and heartache forgotten. Each might move forward in time—after appropriately mourning mother and child.

The wind shifted subtly. Arthur's eyes flew to the cavern that lay no more than a few feet away. Senses alert, he saw a shadow swell full then give birth to a figure that leapt with wildcat precision and wrestled him to the ground. Suddenly, a dagger pulsed against Arthur's jugular vein, the justice of which nearly brought laughter to his lips. The figure that held him at bay was surprisingly light and small of bone. Clad in a vast array of animal hides to ward off the chill, the attacker brushed back its hood, revealing an unexpected hint of femininity with its long eyelashes and streaming hair.

"You, warrior of Britannia, tell me where to find the Pendragon!"

Before she could finish the declaration, Arthur promptly wrest the dagger from her hand. Sliding across the flat plain, the weapon paused in its dramatic escape just short of flight, dangling precariously against the ledge's outermost lip, finally disappearing into the deep gap below. Arthur had just regained his footing when a stream of Saxons issued from the cavern's gaping maw and surrounded him on all sides. Placing hand to the golden hilt he knew so well, Arthur pulled the bejeweled Excalibur free. The reaction was just what he anticipated.

A general exclamation broke forth as the sacred sword glistened majestically, light flashing off the well-placed rubies encrusted here and there along the hilt's cross section, shimmering along the Celtic runes that embossed the length of the blade's clean lines, offering warning for those foolish enough to trespass against its master. Excalibur was born of magic. No one knew that better than Arthur Pendragon.

Arthur's initial attacker was the first to speak. "So you are war lord of the Britons," she began, placing one booted foot against a low rising rock. Fair-skinned and green-eyed with an abundance of blonde hair, barely restrained by an unraveling braid, she reminded Arthur of how Guenevere might have appeared had she accompanied him on the campaign.

"Strange," she continued, smiling at him in a sly manner, "I expected to find you better attended. What made you come here alone?"

Arthur raised his fair brows in a bemused manner and offered her a careless smile. Well versed in the currency of how to handle and, if need be, force information from a foreign prisoner, he was not going to make this easy for her.

The woman trembled ever so slightly, certain he had just dealt her an insult. Taking up her prized spear from a cleft stone that appeared expressly made for that very purpose, she was upon him.

"Answer me!" she cried, whirling into attack stance. Her eyes swept over his unarmored body but found no hint of weakness or gap in clothing— nothing that would help her vanquish this giant of a man. Indeed, her head barely reached the Pendragon's chin, and she was considered tall for a Saxon woman.

The lithe wildcat sprang forward, spear fixed upon Arthur's chest. She made a quick thrust downward, but Arthur blocked with such force that the spear nearly flew out of her hand. Regrouping with lightning precision, she gained the crest of a low-lying rock that lent her several inches of additional height and lashed out again and again. She was darting around so quickly it would have unsettled even the steeliest warrior, for it was impossible to know from which angle she would attack next. Arthur said nothing, however, and whirled around just as fast as she, meeting each thrust, each attack with tempered defense—without any real intent of inflicting harm. He had little desire to wound a woman, even if she be a Saxon. The duel stood at an impasse for several minutes until the adversary's limbs began to show that telltale tremble. She was weakening, indeed, on the verge of collapse. Arthur heard the whispers of his inner voice suggest that it was vital he understand the enemy. Only then would the war see an end. In other words he must allow himself to be captured. And so Arthur struck the spear from her shaking hand and watched as a wave of Saxons swept over him, knocking him off his feet with the sheer weight of their numbers. His fingers flexed momentarily to ease the fall and Excalibur slipped free. It came as some source of amusement that the Saxon warriors kicked the blade several feet from his reach, yet none dared take hold of its hilt. He was then forced into a kneeling position, both hands tied behind his back with a length of rope.

"Now Pendragon," the adversary said, barely disguising triumph that colored her voice, "Why did you come here alone?"

"May not a High King travel anywhere he wishes in his land?" came his light reply. His eyes sparkled as blue sapphires, charming yet fiery deceptive.

Fairly grinding her teeth, she spat out a reply. "He *may* when it is his own land!"

Arthur echoed her passionate outburst. "Which it is! You are the invaders! You are the ones who are not welcome on our shores!"

The adversary leapt forward and hit him in the stomach with the dull end of her spear. Arthur doubled over with the impact. Thankfully he had not eaten anything for some time, for he would have had a devil of a time keeping it down; he drew a deep steadying breath. Pain washed over his senses, but it did not unhinge him. Evidently he had touched upon a nerve. It was essential he register this information for future use, providing he lived that long.

"We were welcomed by Vortigern! It was your family that forced us away!" she cried, fairly dancing around his bent form. She took some delight in having bested him and shared this with her amused warriors who demonstrated their approval by slapping hands upon their thighs.

Arthur held firm to his purpose. "We would have no need to *force* you away if you did not rape, pillage and murder at every turn."

With that one brief statement, the Saxon good humor kindled into a firestorm. Up rose spear, axe, and sword, ready to execute their mistress's fury, but it was not to be.

"Stand down," the woman said through gritted teeth, "Pendragon is mine."

Offering Arthur a swift kick that further bent his form, she began arranging her warriors into distinct ranks. She ordered the first group to find her father, a task, if Arthur understood their reactions, would take them far from Agned's rocky crags. The second wave was told to shadow Britannia's troops. This left the High King increasingly unsettled. What had he been thinking, allowing himself to be captured? This could be the end of his dream—the end of Britannia as he knew it—unless his gut, his heart proved right. *Hold fast to your purpose, Arthur,* his inner voice cried. The Saxon warriors clapped hands over their hearts then rushed off in mass, obviously nonplused by the fact that they were leaving this woman alone with an enemy leader. What did this tell Arthur about her true identity? She was quite skilled with the spear. He had already seen that, but what about a battle of wits?

Once they were alone, the woman addressed him in a manner that sounded almost respectful; her stance grew less feline, and her eyes no longer spit flame.

"Now, my captive Pendragon, tell me something. What will your people give for your freedom?"

Arthur's words came easily. "Nothing. They will not barter for me."

This set her on edge, a fact that she camouflaged by placing one booted foot upon his knee. The act was sensuous, appealing, especially since Arthur could discern the outline of her leg straining to reveal itself through layers of animal skin. She was long limbed and very alluring.

"Are you suggesting they do not honor and respect their king?"

Amused by the gesture, he claimed another glance at the lovely hide-clad appendage and replied, "I have warned them never to bargain for me."

Catching the look she quickly stepped back and said with a careless laugh, "Then it seems you are of no use to us."

"It would seem not," rang his amused reply.

Arthur watched the adversary size him up, returning the favor, allowing her almond-shaped eyes to register every aspect of his appearance. He was used to women admiring him—because he was king. Why, even Guenevere… He paused, aware that his captor drew near with spear in hand. A half smile played upon her lips as she sidled forward, the tip of her spear dipping down to touch his torso. Slowly, suggestively she pulled the weapon upward, leaving a thin trail of blood in its wake until the spear paused to bite his tender throat. How cool the flint felt against his fevered skin. This is what Merlin must have experienced the night of their confrontation. He paused at the thought. What would Merlin have done at this moment? The answer lay locked inside the woman before him. To understand her he must become her.

"How cool you are, Pendragon," she whispered, placing her chin against the spear's well-worn handle. "Do you not fear death?"

"I fear it as much as any other man," he answered truthfully, analyzing her every movement down to the smallest rise and fall of the breast.

"And what if I kill you? Would it not shame you to die at the hands of a woman?"

Straightening, she situated the spear's tip so that it pulsed against his jugular vein. One false move and death would claim him.

Arthur did not bat an eye. "No, my lady, it would not."

Something in his response made her laugh and brought instant release upon the spear. "My lady? Is that not fine!"

Drawing up to her full height, which Arthur calculated would probably meet him at chin level, she said, "As you can see, I am no lady. I am Roweena, daughter of King Cedric."

"I would bow, if I were able, but as it is..." He gestured to his humbled state.

The feline smile returned. "You would bow before me? That I would like to see."

"Then help me to my feet and we will see it done."

Roweena grabbed Arthur by the shoulders and accommodated with a harsh push. Hands tightly bound behind his back, Arthur bowed from the waist in a most dignified manner. Perhaps the key to securing his freedom lay in treating her as an equal. Thus the words, "My princess," sprang to his lips.

Rage flooded her expression and she struck the handle of her spear against Arthur's shoulders so that he fell to his knees. This time Arthur met with solid rock and the lower portion of his body flooded with pain. He had miscalculated and suffered as a result.

"How dare you mock me? I am not your princess!" Up to a craggy ledge she sprang, twisting her lip between her teeth. This king, for all his apparent ineptitude, knew how to belittle her as no other.

Arthur regrouped and tried sincerity. "It was not my intention to anger you. I merely wish to understand you better."

At that moment his eyes locked on hers with the kind of intensity that would make even the fiercest warrior flinch. He was struggling to read her soul. What made the Saxon princess want to fight for this land they both shared?

More puzzled than uncomfortable by the gaze, she asked quite abruptly, "Why do you stare?"

"I am striving to become you in heart, mind, and soul."

This set her pacing, back and forth on the crusty ledge to better calm her wildly beating heart. "Why, so you may escape?"

"Would that be inappropriate?" he responded with a sly smile. "Actually I am struggling to understand your people. If we are ever to find a common peace, then the raping and plundering must end."

Quite unexpectedly, Roweena sprang down and taking three determined strides, smacked him across the face. "I do not rape or plunder!"

A moment of silence passed before Arthur responded. "Many Saxons do."

"I do not speak for others. My people merely seek a place to call our own—here in the land of our forefathers. Yes, for scores of years my family has lived and ruled in Britannia."

Arthur chewed this over in his mind. The Saxons thought of this land as their own, every bit as much as those who called themselves Britons. Did he really possess the right to force them from these shores that were so precious in their estimation?

"Then you really are a princess."

Roweena took this as a challenge upon her honor and immediately drew back into warrior stance. "Do you doubt it?"

"At first I may have," he sighed, "for I would never have allowed my sister to lead warriors in battle, but she is..." he paused, remembering Morgen's fate, then continued on with renewed vigor, lest Roweena question him, "...an enchantress, and such things would not interest her."

The fair eyebrows drew together, calculating how such information might further her cause. All at once she saw an option for peace no one else had thought of to date.

"Is your sister married?"

He took a deep breath and gave voice to the deception, "No, not yet."

The next question followed without missing a beat. "Are *you* married?"

Arthur's sapphire eyes grew wide. All at once he understood her line of questioning, a fact that did not make him altogether happy, so he began working the knots that bound his hands with fingertips and determination. "I am promised."

She pondered this over for a time, chewing her inner lip in a most attractive fashion, and then made the pronouncement in one breath. "These are the terms of your release. You will break the marriage contract."

"Indeed," Arthur muttered, pulling, twisting, attempting any means to break free; but the knots held fast.

"You will break it and marry me. Such are the terms of our agreement. You wish our people to live together in peace. The only way that such peace may be obtained is if Briton and Saxon royalty join."

With one deft motion, Roweena pulled Arthur's head back and kissed him full on the lips. It was a fierce, aggressive action, meant to instill admiration and respect. Instead she found herself slipping under the Pendragon's spell. Her father could not help but be impressed with such a man—the leader of Britannia's countless tribes. She would initiate peace between Briton and Saxon by marrying their king.

Carelessly releasing him so that his chin bounced upon his chest, Roweena stood back and placed one hand against her hip, quite certain he could not fail to be impressed by her charms.

Arthur's thoughts were whirling at breakneck speed. "It is a sound plan, princess," he managed, affirming its validity, "one that speaks of a true desire for peace; but I cannot comply."

The full import of Arthur's words now hit Roweena squarely between the eyes. This was not just a rejection of herself but of her people.

He would join with a perfect Britannia lass who knew nothing of battle or peace treaties. No doubt he found her person bestial and utterly unworthy of marriage. Fury fired her veins, engulfing her otherwise calculated sensibilities. Fingering her spear grip, she made ready to see the insult paid in full. Indeed, one thrust through the heart and Britannia's High King would be no more.

"Pendragon, prepare to meet your God..."

CHAPTER 35:

Agned

Arthur took heed, steeling himself against the deathblow, his muscles tight, cramped, and desperate for escape—for another chance at life. It was vital that he concentrate as never before and claim the Ancient Ones' assistance, or Britannia would be lost. Sight, sound, breath—all condensed into one vibrant sensation that pled his cause as no other.

Ancient Ones, if you still have work you wish me to accomplish, aid me now!

Roweena's spear split the air with such purpose that Arthur felt his skin tingle where the point would strike home. Still, he was unprepared for the deathblow, unprepared for the swirling, violet flame that interceded between his body and the flint head. Roweena doubled over as if she had been punched in the stomach, then was flung backward by an irresistible force, a look of astonishment painted across her lovely face. Cast against a craggy ledge, her figure crumpled then moved no more. Arthur stared in disbelief. What was happening? A sharp ringing filled his ears. The violet flames danced higher, encircling him within a warm embrace, caressing his tired, wounded frame. He watched spellbound as the restrictive bindings fell from his hands.

"Let no man, no woman, nor spirit divine enter the sanctity of this sacred circle."

Recognition flooded Arthur's reeling mind. Surely that was Morgen's voice! Was it possible that she—his own precious angel—still lived? A gentle stirring of flame revealed the face, the being he loved above all others: the willowy form, slender, yet decidedly feminine; the pale complexion that rivaled fairest marble; the luminous sea-green eyes so wide, so doelike that they mirrored his reflection as if it were part of their own composition; and the deep red hair, so long, so deliciously silken that it floated in luxuriant waves down her narrow back. Never before had Morgen appeared so ethereal, so thoroughly untouched by time.

"Morgen, is it really you?"

The shade smiled but made no answer. Unable to stay the action, Arthur cast his arms around her, an act that confirmed her validity. This was definitely not a dream. Gathering Morgen against his pounding heart, he drank in her rosy scent, kissed the soft, lush tresses that spilled across his hands, the warm, supple body that affirmed life as it pressed against him. Yes, Morgen had returned to him, his own precious love, his savior.

"I thought you were dead," he whispered, trembling with joy that could no longer be abated.

"It should be quite obvious that I am not. You, on the other hand, might have beat me to the gates had not the goddess Cerridwen heard your call. She is the reason that I am here."

Arthur kissed her softly upon the forehead and cheeks, framing his next words carefully. "I am so sorry, dearest, so sorry that I drove a wedge between us. Somehow, someway I will make it up to you. I swear it. I am, after all, forever in your debt. How may I repay you? Tell me, dearest, and your every wish will be granted."

Morgen met Arthur's startling blue eyes then swallowed hard. His offer was genuine. She saw that at once. *Goddess help me. If he asked me now, I would bind myself to him forever.* How could she make such a confession when the Saxon guard drew near? How could she even hint that the love Arthur once so desired welled within her heart? *The only gift I would ask of Arthur is himself.*

Keenly aware that such an admission would render them both unstable, Morgen instead focused on Arthur's healing. Training her hands, which were trembling badly, she placed them against his torso, intimately conscious of the hard, smooth muscle beneath the multi-layered garments that shielded him from the cold. ***Ancient Ones, help me focus; help me be cognizant enough to offer the healing Arthur so desperately needs.*** The requested energy spilled through Morgen's palms without further prompting, flooding his aching frame with warmth and renewed vitality.

The exchange lasted less than a minute. Indeed, there was no time for further attention. The Saxons were stirring, moving forward, bent on total and complete annihilation of the Britons. A low moan escaped Arthur's lips as he straightened into battle stance.

"How do you feel now?" Morgen asked, aware that he was indeed free from physical trauma.

"Much better," rang his heartfelt reply. "Thank you, dearest. I have so many questions I wish…"

"Let us speak later," she quickly supplied, holding him off when he would kiss her again. "First we must spirit you back to the Companions."

"Is she dead?" Arthur asked, indicating Roweena's stiffened body that lay death-like but a few feet away.

"She will recover soon enough to lead her warriors against you in battle. Now take my hand."

Arthur readily complied. No words were spoken. In truth none were needed, so volatile was the situation. A thick cascade of snow resumed its downward migration, decreasing visibility. How were they ever to escape this lonely crag? Inwardly cursing himself for having climbed so far from his men, Arthur wondered they would ever meet the coming siege in time.

Thankfully neither snow nor wind possessed the power to overwhelm Morgen's spells. Clasping a handful of icy dirt and loose stones between her fingers, Morgen threw the earthen mixture up into the frosting air and was rewarded when a low, dull explosion followed, purple—like a burgeoning wall of flame. This portal would be their medium, their means of escape.

"Morrigan, goddess of the battlefield, heed my cry! Guide the dragon back unto his brood so they may feast upon this carrion!"

The flames commenced a spiral rotation, devouring king and fay in their wake. Arthur found himself catapulted through a long, winding tunnel that spun round and round without any apparent beginning or end. Indeed, the violet flames at his feet kept him in constant motion. On and on he raced, feeling increasingly dizzy. Surely his men could not be that far away!

Following this nonverbal prompting with preternatural precision, the tunnel opened its gaping mouth: a virtual window that maintained shape amid the roaring flame and revealed both warriors and Companions huddled below. The men looked frozen, ill humored, scattered here and there around camp, hardly anticipating the battle that loomed before them.

It was difficult for Arthur to grasp what was happening, difficult for him to understand the principle behind portals and why he did not fall through or suffer burns from what appeared to be substantial flames, but somehow he found voice and cried, "Companions, rouse yourselves! The enemy is upon us!"

A sharp ripple of disbelief brought man and boy to their feet. They had been awaiting just such a message! Surely this was the call to arms, yet from where did it originate? As if in answer to their question, the High King appeared out of thin air—no, not air but a burst of flame, running at full clip, his clothes and fair hair not even smoldering. A feminine figure, hampered by a rather long, uncooperative gown, emerged behind him in the same unsettling manner, surrounded by dancing amethyst fire that heralded her arrival then disappeared just as fast from whence it came. The men did not recognize her at first. Indeed, few guessed that it might be Princess Morgen until the hood flew back from her emerald green cloak, and her deep, red hair swung free.

"Princess…"Accolon felt the breath catch within his throat. He reached out to her, uncertain. She responded by clasping his hand. Their eyes met in welcome, then she quickly moved on.

Friends rallied their neighbors, pouring themselves into battle attire with a rapidity that belied chilled fingers and half-frozen limbs. Perhaps they were not so ill humored after all. Arthur was already struggling with his own protective garb when Morgen entered his makeshift tent, the only such shelter that had withstood the increasing winds. His eyes met hers in brief recognition, then fell back to task, with no time for further discussion. Indeed, his frosty reception indicated that she should leave. Instead Morgen claimed her first wish when she began lacing the well-worn leathern armor against Arthur's chest and arms. This afforded the High King an opportunity to hurl orders.

"I know of at least two squadrons, if not triple that already on the crag. I think it safe to say they are right behind us. Take formations! Bedivere…"

"Here," he cried, rushing to Arthur's side, but not before he gave Morgen a pleased smile.

"Get the foot soldiers ready! Have Lucan see the horsemen prepared! Lead them into the valley, but tell them not to mount!"

Bedivere rushed about, whipping the ranks into shape, while Morgen fastened the last of Arthur's armor upon his body. Her fingers worked feverishly as they brushed his skin, shielding it from harm. The touch, the sensation of this assumed intimacy worked upon her soul. What if she never saw Arthur again? What if this battle ultimately claimed his life? He was mortal after all. This could very well be the last moment they ever spent together. Should she not tell him the truth? The folly of such a notion instantly applied itself to her feverish brain. Arthur needed all his wits about him. Why would she risk that which she held most dear?

"You must leave now," Arthur whispered, carefully kissing her brow. "Find a place to hide and remain well out of sight." Two strides brought him to the mouth of the tent. "Come back, if you can, when the battle is over."

Morgen was fast upon his heals. "Arthur, I…"

"We will not negotiatiate this point. I will not lose you twice."

"I think it far more likely that I will lose you."

Arthur reached down and kissed her softly upon the lips then brought his forehead to rest against her own. "Have faith, dearest. The fighting may end this very day. Come now, give me your blessing."

Placing her fingertips upon Arthur's third eye, Morgen drew the sacred spiral. She watched Arthur straighten as he accepted the gift.

"So many things I wish to know, so much I need to convey…Meet me here after the fighting ceases."

This said, Arthur strode off toward the formations awaiting his command.

Terror eclipsed Morgen's being. Indeed, her nerves were wrung so tight that she felt capable of retching. This was war: the very thing she despised above all others, the thing she was born to eradicate. What was she to do? A shrill incessant wail filled the air, demanding her wholehearted attention. There in the deepest shadows stood Urien, a tiny bundle clutched against his chest. Was this real or a sending? Surely Urien would never bring a baby into a war zone. Morgen could hardly draw breath as the precious babe turned his green eyes upon her.

Will you deny me a chance at life?

Life? The child had yet to be born. That meant this shadowy intrusion was a vision, a warning. The lord of North Wales was near, no doubt plotting against Arthur. His mysterious disappearance after the battle of Caerleon was still hotly debated. Had he sided with the Saxons? No doubt he was angry that Arthur had denied his proposal, angry that Morgen would never be his bride. Suddenly this vision indicated another possibility. One day this child would be brought forth from her union with that self same man. The child was offering her an ultimatum—save the father or he, the babe, would never see the light of day. She must act quickly. Arthur had already led his horse, the snow white Lughan, to the head of the columns and stood stroking the bridge of his tremulous equine nose.

"Urien of North Wales," she whispered into the frosting air, "I offer you this warning. Side against Arthur, and vision or no vision, I will see you dead."

The image trembled; then child and shade faded into the air. Morgen quickly thrust it from her thoughts; she had no time to take in this information, for every last man was in place. The foot soldiers had hidden themselves among ragged stones that littered the hillside, an easy task since the snow instantly camouflaged their garb with a soft, white dusting that mirrored the surrounding landscape. Tents, pots, wood: all were stowed safely behind tree, brush, and shrubbery. This left Arthur and the Companions, *the men on horseback,* to complete the picture and solidify the ranks, a task that appeared to miss its mark as they feigned unease, struggling with frozen, uncooperative fingers to secure the rigging on their charges. Morgen felt certain that this was a ploy to make them appear vulnerable. Had she not already seen the horses readied firsthand? Roweena's warriors would think them ill prepared when in reality one and all were eager to draw blood. Arthur and the Companions would meet their Saxon opponents in the valley, while the foot soldiers took aim at them from the hillsides above, clever tactics indeed, but would they be enough to stall the Saxon advance?

Sound, fury, and determination proved the only answer. Indeed, a thousand agile footsteps came thundering around a huge outcrop of rock that divided the opposing forces from the volcanic plug that loomed high above. Deep into the valley the Saxons streamed, spears raised high. Roweena proudly led this squadron, eyes brightened with vivid hate. She would not be defeated this time. The Saxons swarmed as bees to a hive, ready to consume Britannia's ill-prepared forces. But just as they saw the prize within their reach, Arthur's horsemen swung into their saddles as one entity and drove their chargers forward into a solid wall of flesh. Roweena's warriors faltered, startled by the feint, many falling under driving hooves before they could ever use their spears.

The first advance thus stalled, Saxon fury rekindled and blazed anew. A second squadron spilled down the southern hill that led into the valley, thoroughly intent on sealing Arthur and the Britons within a frozen tomb. Morgen stood powerless, witnessing an increasingly hopeless scenario unfold. Arthur's men were clearly outnumbered. How would they ever prevail unless she wielded Avalon's power in their favor? The thought spurred her forward with little attention to safety.

Racing at breakneck speed, Morgen wove in and out of Arthur's men stationed along the eastern cliffs, bent on achieving a knoll situated due north of the mayhem. Down this northern gap she climbed, conscious that Saxons had already once used its narrow entrance. They could at any moment do so again. Time was of the essence. Morgen slid to a stop just short of the knoll, gasping, her breath staining the air. This momentary pause cost her dearly, and so she began the upward trek, inwardly cursing the fact that she had not worn better boots, for each new step up its slippery climb forced additional snow and ice through their ill-made stitches. Numb from fatigue and the knowledge of what she was about to do, Morgen drunk deep of the frosted air. This was a sacred place, one that would serve her purpose quite well. What better place could she have found to call the Morrigan undisturbed?

"Morrigan, goddess of the battlefield, hear my cry! Arthur and the Britons need your strength, your support, to turn the tide of this battle. I call on you to aid them now!"

The air trembled purposefully, birthing the battlefield deity in triplicate form. Virgin, matron, and crone stood analyzing Morgen's soul with the very weight of their slow, black eyes.

We understand that which you seek of us. Truly it is within our power to give it you, but only if a bargain may be agreed upon.

Morgen stood her ground, awaiting the full statement of terms.

Fear not, Morgen of the fay, we will extract payment only upon you.

Now came the rub—the very fly in the ointment that could render the agreement mute.

The crone offered up a toothy smile. *A price will be determined upon the reckoning. We will determine both price and reckoning.*

Morgen swallowed nervously at the thought of this so-called bargain. Instinctively she knew that Merlin would never agree to such terms, but she was not Merlin, a fact that repeated itself over and over again. She would win this battle for the fay. This time she would be acknowledged as the enchantress at Arthur's side!

Fatal sounds of the wounded and dying called Morgen from her musings. This time she faced the trio with a renewed passion. She would garner their power and worry about the consequences later. As her eyes fell upon Morrigan, it became apparent that the three distinct shapes had melded into one being: the tall, battle-clad Morrigan with fierce dark eyes and legendary spear.

I am waiting, Morgen of the fay. What will it be? You cannot expect me to linger when so many demand my attention!

The time for hesitation was over. "I accept your terms, providing that you will not ask me to bring about the deaths of Arthur or Merlin."

The goddess laughed loud and full, her wild, black hair lashing the sky.

My request will be of a different nature, far different than you may ever dream.

The earth began trembling as Morrigan struck her spear through a sheath of jagged rock as if it were of no more consequence than well-churned butter.

Your request has been grounded in stone. This will stand as a reminder of your words until the end of time.

The fierce goddess pointed one tapered finger at Morgen's heart. *Think carefully, Morgen, before you act. Arthur has planned this confrontation to perfection. He knows exactly what he wishes to accomplish. This may prove far different than you ever imagined. I counsel you, as an Ancient One, not to interfere with his strategy. No matter what happens, do not wield this power for which you have bartered your soul. Protect him, yes, heal him if necessary, but allow him this victory on his own terms. Merlin would tell you no less than the same.*

Flashing her wicked smile of frosty white so blinding in its brilliance that it thoroughly eclipsed her being, Morrigan wavered, then was seen no more.

Tears streamed down Morgen's cheeks. What had she done? Was it really necessary to barter her soul? Certainly Arthur did not think so. By all accounts he had the situation—indeed, the entire battle—well planned. Why, then, did she feel that he was about to be overthrown?

The question haunted her thoughts, her sensibilities, driving her higher up the knoll's jagged climb. Several tiny hairs on the back of Morgen's neck bristled their warning. Indeed, the moment flashed upon her with such unexpected clarity, she knew not how to intercede. Arthur, one of the most brilliant equestrians Britannia ever birthed, was cast off Lughan when Lancelot's dark charger, who had been mortally wounded with a spear through the chest, reared high, then came crashing down upon king and steed. It took but a moment for Arthur to right himself, but Lughan did not move, pinned by the dying charger. Arthur tried to free the pale steed, his own true friend; he pulled, he struggled to untangle equine limbs, but with little consequence. Indeed, Roweena, witnessing the High King's vulnerability, instantly rallied a charge against him. Everything happened so fast it was impossible to intercede. Saxons swirled around Arthur, tearing him from Lughan, who raised his pale face, whinnying furtively at his master's departure, life having almost departed him. Arthur felt Lughan's despair, watched his glorious head fall back against the snowy ground, but could do nothing more. The sheer weight of the Saxons pressed him, forced him up the southern bank, effectively cutting him off from all support.

Moving with a grace that belied the seriousness of the situation, Arthur drew opposite Roweena and waited. One of his gloved hands caressed the hilt of Excalibur while the other tore the helm from his own fair head. It was a sign to the many foot soldiers stationed above. Morgen saw that at once. Why, then, did they not fire their well-placed arrows? Had Arthur actually signaled them to stand down?

This action further sparked Roweena's fury, for the Pendragon appeared to think himself invulnerable. She began to circle Arthur, utilizing the same tactics as before, springing forward with well-aimed spear thrusts from every side, moving so blindingly fast that few could see which angle she would choose next. Revenge colored each motion, each thrush of her spear; but Arthur met her attacks with equally swift rebuttal. The ease with which he accomplished this led Morgen to believe that he was withholding his full skill. What was it he had in mind? Every fiber of Morgen's being grew strained, raw and feverish. *Let the battle unfold as Arthur planned it,* Morrigan's warning repeated itself steadily through her brain.

And so Roweena continued her lightning swift assaults until the pace, the sheer instability of her mood lent an increasingly erratic quality to the exchange. Arthur sensed the shift and acted accordingly. He was so strong, so well versed in his craft that one well-aimed blow split Roweena's spear, sheared it in half, the force of which wrenched her wrist out of joint and forced her to her knees. There she knelt trembling before the great Pendragon, so tall, so impossibly grand that his shadow thoroughly enveloped her bent form. Not a word escaped Roweena's tightly clenched lips, but the hatred burning in her eyes spoke most eloquently.

So it is with all Britons. They must thoroughly dominate and destroy whatever they cannot understand.

"Go ahead—finish it, Pendragon!" she cried at last, tears streaming down her flushed cheeks. "Kill me and watch your sweet dreams of peace fade into dust!"

The echo of this fierce challenge called young and old to attention. Indeed, every last warrior stationed throughout the valley and the surrounding crags froze, preternaturally aware that the slightest movement might bring about the death of the Saxon princess. All eyes turned upon Arthur, who appeared every inch a monarch, ready to extract punishment upon a mortal enemy. No one moved; few even dared breathe so tense was the situation. Another scream colored the air. This time it was Roweena's frustration spilling forth at the humiliation of being mocked by so many eyes. Feeling nothing but compassion, Arthur offered his hand.

"We may end this now with a single word."

Roweena stared at Arthur through half-dazed eyes. The Pendragon was offering her salvation, a way to save her people, the sheer magnitude of which left her breathless with possibility. She had

not the power to end the conflict between her people and the Pendragon. That honor belonged to her
father alone, and he was several leagues away. No,
the best—*the only*—thing she could do was surrender her forces and await her father's return. Rising
to her feet, she clasped Arthur's outstretched hand
so that no doubt could arise as to her motivation. It
would be all too easy for one of Arthur's followers
to assassinate her due to uncertainty.

Arthur raised his hand high; triumph coloring
his eyes an even more startling blue as he motioned
the Companions to cease all fighting. Briton and
Saxon forces began standing down, each side settling into a cautious optimism. Arthur had just
moved to examine Roweena's dislocated wrist
when a ghastly form emerged from deep within the
Saxon ranks. Few among the Companions could
fail to recognize the silver hair, the falcon crest of
Lothian's illusive king; yet all remained stationary,
powerless to intervene. Had not Arthur told them
to stand down?

Lot said but a few words when he broke through
the Saxon ranks and boldly rushed Arthur from
behind. "He lies, princess."

With a swirl of cloak and a flash of metal,
Lot's blade bit into the gap where the armor had
recently come unlaced at Arthur's side. Blood blossomed, filled the huge gash, splattering Roweena,
as Arthur yanked the offending weapon free. One
look into Roweena's distraught face told the High
King that she was just as surprised as he was. This
was Lot's doing alone. Arthur struck, keenly aware
that the wound he had just received might prove

fatal. Each new thrust of the blade brought on a burning sensation that nearly bereft him of reason. Blood streamed down his right torso, coloring the snow beneath his feet a crimson hue. Still, he fought on, driving Lot back against the wall of Saxon warriors that encircled them. This did not bode well with the Saxons, several of whom pushed Lot forward so that he almost skewered himself on Excalibur. Arthur twisted, turned, gracefully insinuated the sacred blade, evoking a lethal string of blows that belied the seriousness of his wound. Betrayal proved an ugly word. Lothian's king had done just that when he cast their treaty to the wind. Roweena's presence further clouded his thoughts. Perhaps she would think Britannia untrustworthy. Somewhere amid this upheaval of emotion, Arthur heard Morgen's voice whisper that all would be well, even as the invisible touch of her hand came to rest upon his side. The bleeding slowed, thickened, then ceased its flow altogether. Delicious heat sutured the raw flesh, rendering it whole. Suddenly the pain was gone! Arthur struck with a ferocity that nearly bereft Lot of his sword. Yes, all would be well. Morgen, his bright angel, had offered healing from afar!

Lot's eyes widened in disbelief. Was it possible that Arthur no longer ailed?

Blow for blow they met, white hair spilling free from its leathern helm against a sea of silvery blonde. And so it was that Lot, king of the Angles, challenged the "bastard" Pendragon, utilizing every last trick he possessed to gain the upper hand. Arthur's defense, however, was so impressive that Lot could neither trip nor snag the good king's cloak, nor even cast snow dust in his eyes. Indeed, Excalibur was everywhere at once, stalling such tactics. Lot found it increasingly difficult to keep pace or manage even the simplest defense. The Saxons watched, spellbound, hardly daring to support Lot in favor of Britannia's king, who could heal a mortal wound so readily.

Although the tide had shifted, although Arthur had all but beaten Lot into the ground, Bedivere refused to remain inactive during such peril; disregarding Arthur's orders he rallied the Companions forward, smashing through the stationary Saxon circle. Bodies flew this way and that, a tragic dance cast in shadow by the sun's descent. It was almost twilight.

"NO!" Arthur screamed, his cry rendered impotent by the sound of hooves crashing forward and the Saxon's bitter anguish as they fell. They had been so close, so close to realizing a lasting peace. Arthur could all but taste sweet success on his feverish lips. It was Lot's selfish desire to wear the crown that had defeated Britannia's hope, Britannia's prayer. Again he cried forth, "Stand down!" but no one heard him—no one but Morgen, who trembled at his anguish. Arthur did not want the Companions to save him. He wanted to end the war now on his own terms. That is what Morrigan had been trying to tell her!

Truth proved a bitter tonic. Lot's duplicity had overshadowed anything Arthur might have done to achieve peace at Mt. Agned. He had nearly cried out as much, but Lot's zealous attack magnified tenfold. It was as if Lot knew he had but one chance left before his great plan dissolved. The moment passed, then was gone, for Arthur's apt defense allowed no further wounding. Blades crashed and bloody snow flew in all directions. Lot staggered, near collapse. This left him no alternative but to hail his own sons.

"Gawain, Gareth, your fight is here! Help me secure your rightful throne!"

The young men turned as one entity, flushed with glory, to find their father fighting the High King. Joy was instantly replaced by horror, disbelief. It was evident that neither Gareth nor Gawain knew of Lot's plans. In a strange way this pleased Arthur.

"What are you thinking?!" cried Gawain as he rushed toward Lot, an expression of unspeakable rage painted across his countenance.

Registering Gawain's level of disgust, Lot did not properly block Arthur's next blow, which penetrated his torso at the unprotected gap in his breastplate. *A wound for a wounding,* he mused, coughing, choking back the bile that sprang to his foaming lips.

"Come, join me, Gawain!" he cried, clutching the fresh wound that wept sweet refuse. "This is your fight!"

Bright spots of blood tinged the snow beneath Lot, staining it a color not all that dissimilar from Morgause's favorite gown. Confident that she would not desert him, he fought on.

"Come, Morgause, I need you now! Send me your dark blessing!"

A ripple of shadow pooled wide, its charcoal mirror reflecting the red witch both in face and form. Slowly, sensuously, she wavered before him, a tantalizing display that distracted rather than aided Lot.

I thank you, husband, from the bottom of my heart.

Morgause's untimely appearance, unseen by everyone but Lot, cost his blade, a steep price indeed. Another butt from Excalibur's hilt sent Lothian's petty king sprawling flat upon his back, with no time to move or even breathe, for Arthur placed his foot squarely upon Lot's chest and pressed down hard.

"Morgause, do something! End this now!"

Laughter spilled from Morgause's ruby lips. *Your blood will pave the way for Mordred's ascension to the throne.*

"Mordred?" Lot's breath faltered and threatened to cease expression altogether. How could it do otherwise when Arthur commanded this—the most basic of necessities?

Indeed, who better to wear the crown than Arthur's own son?

Lot barely saw the Companions crowding around him, barely heard the words of condemnation echo far and wide. Surely this was all a dream. Mordred was *his* child, a son born of his seed!

Morgause placed a phantom kiss upon his lips, a tantalizing, unforgettable morsel that spoke their dissolution stronger than words. *Goodbye, my love. You have served me well.* Red velvet blazed through Lot' senses, unsettled his already volatile mind, then the face, the form he worshipped above all others, was gone.

Aware that his heart was near bursting, Lot made one last attempt to rise, which was instantly refuted by Arthur's seemingly immoveable weight. A low groan escaped his lips. The damned witch had never loved him. It was not Arthur that had laid him low. No, it was Morgause who had effectively killed him with a thrust of her well-aimed blade. She had used him to achieve her own purpose, realize her own goals. Bile swirled up from the deep recesses of his soul, shielding truth from reality. Where were his sons? A subtle stirring of snow directed his attention toward Gareth, who stood watching him with tear-stained eyes.

"Gareth, my only son, help me!"

The young lad trembled, then moved forward, an almost involuntary action that made his legs appear weak or ill matched. His father needed aid, something that should not be questioned, yet this was combat against the High King. No, that could not be right. Certainly his father had disagreements with King Arthur, but he would never attempt to usurp the throne!

A wall of snow flew up between Gareth and his father, an icy barricade, Gawain's apt intercession, blocking the intended path. "Take another step, Brother, and we will cross swords!"

"But he is our father…" the protest all but died on Gareth's lips. The good king was staring at him, sorrow coloring his eyes.

"He made his decision. We must stand by the king."

Gareth directed his gaze upon Arthur. "Please," was the only word he could muster before angst interrupted, overwhelmed all further expression. The warrior lad fell to his knees, weeping, unable to stay the emotion, unable to forgive the unthinkable.

Arthur acted without hesitation, rendering Lot unconscious with a swift blow of Excalibur's hilt to his head. Gareth rose, and with three determined strides, brushed past Gawain, never pausing to see if he would be challenged, never ceasing his approach until he gained Lot's side. Once more he knelt, this time to better clasp his father's icy hand against his tear-stained face. He would not weep again—no, not until darkness fell; then no one else need experience his shame.

Shadows lengthened, consuming the dry ditch, the snow-clad valley that housed Arthur's men. After so much warfare, the virtual silence proved deafening. Above, the sky spewed more white effluvia, an unwelcome return that chilled hands and stiffened limbs. Arthur found his way back to Lughan and saw at a glance what he refused to believe. Casting his gloves free, he placed fingertips against the charger's ivory nose bridge and stroked ever so gently. A soft snort served as his reply. Lughan opened his great wide eyes one last time, a kind of smile playing upon his muzzle. He nudged Arthur as he had done so many times before, shuddered briefly then drifted back into the vast unknown. Arthur swallowed the tears that threatened his stability. So much he needed to address, so much that demanded his attention. He was, after all, High King.

The Saxon's departure solidified that point as no other. It was not altogether clear how it had happened; but somehow after Lot's fall, the remaining Saxons secured their retreat. Perhaps they possessed a subtle magic of their own. Only the wounded stragglers remained behind, anxiously awaiting judgment. This unexpected departure raised many a questioning eyebrow, and Morgen chuckled at the shortsightedness of their dismay. Yes, she had followed Morrigan's counsel and allowed Arthur to win the night, intervening only when he needed healing and ultimately sending the Saxons packing once Lot's vile interference rendered Arthur's peaceful dreams mute. Arthur would claim peace for Britannia one day when all Britons sought the same goal. That day was not long in coming. Until then she must somehow appease his sorrow. A smile graced her lips. She could think of more than one way to make the High King forget his regrets.

CHAPTER 36:

Britannia's Savior

L ot grudgingly passed through the Otherworld veil late that night, unattended by anyone save the gentle Gareth. Morgen watched from a safe distance, biding time before she approached Arthur. The blood, the murder, the mayhem sickened her, made her regret what little aid she had offered. War: that all consuming passion to dominate, control another people's destiny, proved the culprit. *Why must mortals kill each other?* she inwardly cried. The utter futility of Morgen's life purpose turned to bile, eating away at her soul. No wonder Merlin had gone mad. War offered but three resolutions: death, victory, or insanity. Perhaps that is why she could not move beyond the Fairy Knoll or the shadow of Morrigan's spear. One day the battle goddess would claim her due, and nothing Morgen did could free her of that iron pact. Thus Avalon's displaced Fairy Queen sat frozen, unable to move beyond the bitter darkness.

The Saxon captives fared little better. Repulsed and terrified by the huge funeral pyres that consumed their fallen brethren, they did the thinkable and cast themselves into the vivid flames rather than await execution. Arthur trembled despite himself. How was such an atrocity to be answered? Was not he responsible for their horrific deaths? It had been his belief that the pyres, a Celtic honoring of the dead, might garner respect. Instead he felt the weight of each and every one of their sacrifices darken his soul. How could he have anticipated such irrational behavior? It had been his intention to eventually free the prisoners. Execution had never entered his mind.

Arthur tried to move beyond the horrific screams of the dying, beyond the stench of roasting flesh that filled his aching lungs. A cold chill beaded his brow, rendering him nauseous. Sickness and spasms followed, forcing him down on both knees until he could no longer contain the bile that spewed from his lips, coating the icy ground.

Utterly debased, Arthur straightened, perhaps a little too quickly, hoping that no one had witness his shame. He waited and waited for an answer, but none appeared forthcoming. The Saxon martyrs keenly reminded him of the proud, noble race with which he shared the land. Surely some way existed to end this war and honor each people's customs and thereby maintain their originality.

Follow that thought to its manifestation.

A sigh escaped Arthur's ruddy lips. *Thoughts become reality, yes, but I am too tired, too ill to contemplate such a goal.*

Sit down, dearest, and allow me to heal you; then we will speak of peace.

Morgen?

Arthur fell to his knees, conscious only of the soft arms that wound around his battered frame. He had remained strong, so utterly in command for such an extended length of time that it proved a relief to allow Morgen complete control over his healing. Indeed, he would allow no one else in the entire world such absolute domination over him, no one save his own precious Morgen. Oh, how he loved her! A soft sigh called him back to the vast sloping valley that undershot Mt. Agned and the countless pyres that lit the night. Morgen stood before him wrapped in a halo of billowing mist, or was it merely ghostly smoke that issued from the voracious flames? In any case she was so beautiful, so hauntingly feminine that words escaped him. Morgen softly pressed her lips to Arthur's cheek then gently began unlacing his tunic, her hands finally pausing against the cool flesh of his belly. Delicious heat coursed up and down Arthur's aching torso. If this were a false vision, Morgause or any other fay who wished him dead, he was powerless to intercede. Every thought, every prayer began and ended with Morgen.

"Where have you been hiding?" he whispered, ever conscious that her hands pressed against him in a most provocative manner. Surely she felt it too, or was it possible that healers never confused their gifts with love, with passion, never allowed them to meld and become one.

When she did not answer, Arthur tilted his head back so he could see her expression. He felt so warm, so deliriously happy that his words sounded almost slurred, as if he had consumed too much

492 CDORGEN OF AVALON

drink. "Dearest, how may I repay you for saving my life three times this day?"

Laughter spilled from Morgen's lips. "Oh, I can think of many ways, some of which you will enjoy while others may give you pause.

"I like the sound of that," he said, brushing his lips against her fair arm, "the joy part I mean. Let us leave the other requests for later."

"So like a man," Morgen beamed, refocusing her attention on his troubled stomach. Arthur had not eaten anything for a very long time. That was part of the problem—that combined with the emotion brought forth by betrayal, the severing of his dreams, and the Saxon martyrs' untimely fate, not to mention his own near-death experience. "Britannia before pleasure," she said, holding him off when he would kiss her again. "I ask only that you heed my counsel."

Arthur paused, uncertain as to whether he had heard her aright. It sounded almost as if she would welcome his advances, but she wished to offer him counsel first. Well, if that was the necessary price for a night in her arms, he would willingly pay. Nodding his fair head, he wordlessly indicated that he would listen. How beautiful she was, even then, bright hair mired with falling snow. He wanted nothing more than to hold her until the world fell away. Watching her lips move hauntingly in the shadowed firelight, Arthur knew it was vital he maintain focus. The counsel she offered would be that issued by Avalon itself.

"This next battle must see the Saxons defeated," she breathed, increasing the healing energies tenfold. Arthur gasped at the sensation, but she continued, demanding that he meet her eyes. "Then and only then may you offer them freedom on terms agreeable to both parties. Wait any longer—or worse, forfeit your next fight—and chaos will consume Britannia."

Arthur's stomach twisted painfully, demanding further solace. Thankfully Morgen graciously complied. The exchange took on a heightened quality, a bonding that drew them closer than ever before. Arthur felt his belly slowly relax into its original state. Morgen's love, her great gift, had healed him again. Yes, healed he was, although his soul still cried for answers. Perhaps Morgen could resolve some of the countless questions that buzzed within his brain.

"We think along the same terms," he began, placing her fingers against his lips. "The next battle for Britannia must be its last. Pray the gods I may succeed. No doubt I will with you at my side."

Drawing his tunic closed, he added, "Thank you for healing me, dearest. I feel quite renewed. Perhaps I can find something for us to eat."

Morgen produced a fine apple from the folds of her emerald gown and offered it to him. "Do not dismiss my words so lightly," she gently admonished as he took the proffered fruit from her hand.

"Believe me, they are forever engraved upon my heart," he said, offering the apple a swift bite. "By the goddess, that is glorious. Will you share it with me?"

"No, it is from Avalon and will sustain you. Enjoy it while you can. I fear this evening will prove a long one."

Arthur offered her a sideways glance. That was not what he had hoped to hear. Perhaps his dreams of a romantic union with Morgen were ill founded, yet she still took his hand as they followed a well-defined path that slowly wove its way up toward a bright, gaping cavern seemingly lit by a hundred candles: the aforementioned shelter Arthur had sought earlier that day. Crossing this welcome threshold, Morgen marveled that the cave had not caught fire, for indeed, torches were thrust into every available nook and cranny that yielding rock allowed. Arthur's foot soldiers crowded the huge chamber, having shunned the burnt offerings below. Most had stretched out their bedding, hoping to ward off the night chill. Indeed, some were already asleep, snoring lightly amid their comrades' songs and victorious tales.

Arthur paused outside a makeshift tent of deerskin stretched tightly between two posts thrust into graveled crevices. The sight was decidedly unassuming. Following his bidding Morgen plunged into the dimly lit confines which proved small and cramped, not unlike those often inhabited by the Companions. She saw a thick mass of bearskins used as bedding, partially hidden by one misshapen table upon which rested a silver urn and goblet—the only possessions that revealed any hint of royalty.

"Tell me everything," Arthur whispered, kissing her forehead. Although her hair was damp from the falling snow, it still smelled of roses, which greatly pleased him. Dull torchlight flickered just outside the tent, lending added brightness to their surroundings. His eyes caressed the delicate plains of her face. Morgen smiled back at him, expectant. Something in her look heartened him, something he had never witnessed before. Had it been Caerleon at Midsummer, he might have called it love. Was Morgen, Avalon's Fairy Queen, actually in love with him?

"Where should I begin?" she questioned, deliberately resting her head against his chest.

The act, so warm, so sensuous amid the freezing night, nearly bereft Arthur of reason. "So many questions plague my mind. Right now, however, I cannot express one of them. I think I am in great danger of losing myself in you."

Morgen reached up and took his face between her hands. "Would that be such a terrible thing?"

"You tell me," he sighed, drawing her down upon the bearskins. "I seem to recall that you love another." Slowly, deliberately, he placed his fingertips underneath her chin and waited. This way she could not avoid his gaze.

Lacing her arms about his neck, Morgen deliberately lay back so that Arthur could not help but follow her progress. "Times change, Arthur. People change, as do their loves, their desires. I am not the woman I was last midsummer."

Conscious that Morgen lay beneath him, Arthur felt the sweat trickle against his brow. He wanted to kiss her, to ravish her as he had done so many times in his dreams, but her words sounded strangely hollow. What motivation lay behind this seemingly innocent change of heart? Was Merlin so easily forgotten? Was he, Arthur Pendragon, just another passing fancy? If they were to enter a union this very night, he would want it to be lasting, not just a temporary means of helping each other forget the nightmare that was their existence. How was he to broach these concerns when she appeared so eager to love him? To offend Morgen now would be tantamount to suicide.

"Dearest," he whispered, still holding himself off, still supporting his weight with steady hands. "I am honored beyond all expression that you want me. I simply need to understand why."

"Why?" she cried, drawing him down so that his battle hardened body came to rest against her graceful curves. "I love you. Is that not reason enough, you great, big oaf?"

Laughter spilled from Arthur's lips as he reveled in the warmth of her, the sensuous curvature of her delicate frame. He was conscious of the brush of bearskin, the scent of roses. What little resolve beat within his breast was rapidly dissipating. Pure intoxication it was, pure bliss to lie there entwined, ignorant of Britannia and its incessant demands. And so his lips found hers, eager to begin the dance. The exchange was so satisfying, so welcome, as if he had at last come home, the knowledge of which made him pause. Yes, this was all too familiar. Had not Morgause used Morgen's face and form to deceive him? What if this was another ploy to render him weak as a newborn babe? He knew nothing of Morgen's past six months—where she had gone, how she had escaped death. And what of the child? What of Merlin? It took a great deal of determination to do it, but somehow Arthur extricated himself from Morgen's loving arms.

"Have mercy, Morgen," he whispered, struggling to ease his heightened breathing as he rolled free. "I love you beyond length and breadth of time, but tell me true. What of Merlin, dearest? I thought your heart belonged to him."

Morgen felt a deathly chill tighten about her heart. He spoke of the arch mage, her dark consort, the grand falcon of the night, whose love and passion she had placed before her Otherself—and why? She was unschooled, untried, her fledgling human emotions too volatile. Merlin had needed her as much as she needed him to smooth out these inconsistencies. They both had benefited from the exchange and emerged wiser, more attuned to love's nuances—that is until Morgause's curse preyed on Merlin's weakness. Morgen had tried to follow his spotted path that led deep into the nethermost realms, but she found he had covered his tracks too well for anyone to find him, lest he wished to be found. Surely Arthur saw that. Perhaps if she reminded Arthur of his initial concerns, perhaps if she conveyed even the tiniest bit of anguish she had suffered at Merlin's hands, the issue would fall away, at least for this one, precious evening. "Your warnings were well bethought, Arthur. Listen carefully. I do not wish to slander the man, but the truth must be told no matter how painful. Merlin used me, as all men use women; and when he was done, he cast me aside."

A sad look softened Arthur's countenance. Merlin, his own treasured teacher, a seducer? Surely there was some mistake. Merlin would never wound another soul, never use another strictly for self gain. Undoubtedly Arthur and Morgen weren't seeing some missing piece to the puzzle. And so Arthur spoke the only response that made sense. "I would never have thought it possible, but men are a rascally lot, Morgen. Trust none of us."

"You question how I can so easily forget Merlin?" she continued, barely hearing his words. "I tore Merlin from my heart. It practically killed me to do it, but I tore him free and cast him to the wind. The truth is that you and I are bound together, Arthur, through Otherworldly ties that supersede any feelings we may have experienced for Merlin or Guenevere. They have touched our hearts, but they cannot replace the deep love we have shared through many lifetimes."

Arthur rose to his feet, almost involuntarily, as memories flooded his sensibilities, drawing him back to their initial meeting. Thrusting his fingers through the damp forest of his hair, which still bore remnants of snow, he gleaned the truth of their past, believed in its validity without failing, but he still could not reconcile the fact that the Morgen he knew loved Merlin.

Sensing this hesitation, Morgen thrust the bearskins aside and gained her footing. She knew not what she wished to accomplish until the previously viewed goblet captured her attention. And so she shuffled forward, heedless that her emerald gown fairly hung off one shoulder. "I think we both need some wine," she whispered, clasping the silver treasure between her hands.

Arthur forced his numbed legs into submission so he could gain her side, a genuine look of concern darkening his brow. He had wounded Morgen, denied her loving nature when she had been so eager to give him joy. Surely that made him little better than Merlin in her estimation. If they had shared lifetimes together, then why was this time so different? Perhaps they, perhaps *he* was not ready for such intimacy. The thought was not a pleasant one, but Arthur claimed the other side of the goblet and tilted it back so that its contents strengthened Morgen. He then added what little was left in the urn and took a deep draught for himself. The conversation must move forward if either of them were to know peace.

"And the child, Morgen? What became of your child? Merlin assured me that you were both dead. It drove him mad."

Must all Arthur's thoughts begin and end with Merlin? Could he not simply voice the question without mention of that thought-consuming mage? Perhaps she was being unjust. Perhaps she merely did not wish to speak of her baby, but Arthur's words filled her with a certain dread. She had not been wrong when she suggested that the evening would be a long one. "Make no mistake about it, Arthur. The war drove Merlin mad. As to my child," she said, a careful smile coloring her lips, "my daughter is with the Sisterhood in Avalon. When I left she was doing quite well. We were never in any danger."

Arthur could not envelope her in his arms fast enough. A mother, his precious Morgen was a mother. It never struck Arthur until that moment how much he wanted children, how much he wished that Morgen would be the vessel through which they entered the world. Morgen would be the best, the most gracious, caring mother—one that put all others to shame. A low voice bubbled up inside him. *Perhaps if she were given the choice, but as it stands that is not quite true.* The truth settled squarely upon Arthur's shoulders, forcing a chill up his spine. Morgen was there in his tent, attending him, not the child; she was there helping him win the war. Feeling utterly divided by this knowledge, he nearly choked out his response. "A little girl? Oh, dearest, she would do well to remain in Avalon until this madness is over."

"Perhaps she would do well to remain there permanently. That is what the sisters intend."

Arthur's could not conceal his surprise. This child was a precious commodity; the Sisterhood's actions could not be viewed otherwise. "How do you feel about that? Surely you wish her to be a part of this world."

"Yes, I do—once Britannia is free of fighting and turbulence."

Arthur took hold of Morgen's hand and led her back to the bearskins. "I will see what I can do about that," he said, helping her down into a seated position. Taking residence beside her, he continued, "What does she look like, Morgen? Does she resemble you?"

"I think she is the best of her father and mother. She has my fairness of skin but Merlin's dark hair and eyes."

"Quite a striking combination," rang his honest response. He gazed at her intently, musing over her beauty and the complexity of their conversation. Something here of magnificent import lay just beneath the surface, something that had not yet been revealed.

"Can you tell me what happened to Merlin?"

Why must they speak of Merlin? Naturally the topic would appear some time or other, but why now when there was so much to celebrate. At that moment she thoroughly questioned whether or not Arthur would ever be hers. The Sisterhood's inner council spurred her forward, however, refuting any such uncertainties. And so perhaps she revealed more information than was wise. "He has run wild through this world and the next, seeking his father. Merlin believes that it will be only through Cernunnos and the eternal Cerridwen that he will reclaim his sanity."

Arthur considered her words. "Are you telling me that Cernunnos is Merlin's father?"

A low, dull sound thudded at the back of Morgen's brain. A revelation was coming, one that she did not wish to hear. "Yes, I am."

Arthur's face was transformed. "Then he is a half god!" His mentor, his teacher was aligned with the Ancient Ones. Suddenly Merlin's tremendous powers made sense. He was immortal!

The direction that the conversation sped did not please Morgen. Indeed, it left her breathless, uncertain. What terrors was Arthur conjuring in his mind? "Merlin would never think of it that way."

"And your child," Arthur said, practically beside himself, "that makes her…"

"You must think of her as a fairy, nothing more."

Suddenly, with an alacrity that defied description, all the pieces fell into a unified whole. Britannia's salvation began and ended with this child! "Think of the power she will wield! She will be a queen, a woman capable of charming our worst enemies!"

Morgen's throat constricted painfully. Was her daughter to be offered up as a prize? Was this the reason the Sisterhood guarded the child so dutifully? "I cannot even claim her until she achieves womanhood—by then she may be so much a part of their world that she will little relish this one."

"She will wish to meet her parents," rang Arthur's undeterred response. Indeed, he knew all too well how much an apparent orphan dreams of meeting his or her family. Perhaps that is why the next words escaped his lips with ease.

"We will give it out that you and Merlin were secretly married. Indeed, we will see it done—once Merlin is himself again. That way the child will be accepted without question."

Morgen felt as if he had slapped her across the face. Had Arthur listened to anything she said? Did he not realize how much she loved *him*? Did he not comprehend that Merlin was all but dead to her now? And what of the child, her daughter, condemned to a loveless marriage? "I will not hear this!" Morgen cried, fighting back the tears that betrayed her anguish. "You cannot speak of promising her to the Saxons!"

Arthur deliberately slowed his breathing. This child that sprang from no less than two otherworldly parents was destined to save his country. If he offered the Saxons such a prize, could they deny him? The answer was rendered mute by the very weight of Morgen's pooling eyes. How strange that this gifted peaceweaver, who had devoted her life to the cause, did not share his enthusiasm. Strange, but true...perhaps, in time, she would soften her objections. Perhaps this very night he might find some means to convince her. Visions of love and romance reaffirmed their presence, but they seemed an inappropriate medium to such a task. Indeed, Morgen would believe that he had used her, hardly a good beginning to an eternal relationship.

"Forgive me. I am overhasty. The Ancient Ones will determine the course your daughter's life must take. Come, dearest, tell me that all is forgiven."

When she offered a faint smile, he continued, "I trust you will allow me to watch over you this night."

"If you so desire," came her soft reply.

"I do," he declared, kissing her forehead. "It's time to rest. Lie down and I will ensure that no harm comes your way."

Morgen paused, shivering as she watched Arthur arrange his bedding so she might easily slip inside. It was a struggle to divorce her thoughts from what might have been, but somehow she managed the task. A heartbeat later Arthur rested his tired frame beside her, albeit on top of the bear-skins, his great cloak pulled tightly around him. Morgen rolled onto her side and prayed that he would say nothing further.

Lacing his arms around her, Arthur whispered, "You never told me. What is her name?"

CHAPTER 37:

The Vision

The night proved long, especially since Morgen found little solace in Arthur's arms. How could she when his words, his actions proved so calculated, so cruel? Why did every man she had ever loved place Britannia above all things? Why did they profess ardor and passion and then show themselves to be completely disinterested? Perhaps it was something within her soul that fostered this standoffish behavior. Perhaps it was merely the fact that Britannia had lingered so long at war. In any case she spoke no further words with Arthur that night. None were needed or welcome for that matter. Instead Morgen allowed the High King's steady embrace to both warm and protect her as the cave grew increasingly chill. Before dawn's first rays lit the sky, she knew what tragedy had transpired while they slept. She thought once or twice of informing Arthur of their perilous position but understood that nothing could be done. They were trapped, virtually immobilized by nature's white fury.

Near daybreak, Morgen heard the foot soldiers discover this truth, but she remained stationary, carefully anticipating the moment Arthur would awake. When it came she knew that she had waited too long. Indeed, the High King and his forces hardly knew what hit them, for the snow only increased its downward spiral, offering little reprieve. Suddenly they were trapped, unable to attain the wintry levels below. Rats scurried about the deep cavern, carefully avoiding human contact. The horses sheltered deeper still, growing increasingly nervous. They, too, sensed impending doom. What little reserves the Britons' forces possessed would be gone within a few days time. No one had anticipated such an event. No one ever dreamed they would be cut off so effectively from all other life forms beyond those with whom they shared the cave. Like it or not, the rats might look quite appealing in due time.

Round and round Arthur paced trying to ward off the horror that threatened his very sensibility. This disaster was retribution incarnate. Had he not condemned the Saxon prisoners to the flames? If only he had pursued the retreating forces instead of taking time to honor the dead. Why did he not give the order to move forward instead of spending the night with Morgen? He had wanted so much to love her, to comfort her; but instead the entire exchange had gone terribly wrong. That should have been his first indication that trouble was afoot. The child, Britannia's savior, had driven a wedge between them, and that chilled him to the core. Somehow, some way, he must win her back.

First, however, it was vital that he save Morgen, save them all before nature exacted full payment for his personal crimes. Thus began Arthur's downward spiral. The lack of sunlight and dwindling food reserves, coupled with enforced immobility worked upon his soul.

It took a massive effort, but Morgen ignored the hurt that consumed her being even when it threatened her very sanity. Kindness, compassion, and a soft voice were the things that Arthur needed most. And so she set her feelings aside and gave him everything that he required, everything but the kisses that fired his imagination. She counseled him night and day that destiny proved the chief architect directing their path. Once the first thaws arrived, the curse that held them in its icy grip would lift and be replaced by a myriad of blessings. Any attempt to depart before then would spell their doom.

Days slowly lengthened into a fortnight. Many warriors lost hope of ever seeing another summer. As food grew increasingly scarce, the few trees that dotted Agned's rocky climb became the single means of supporting the forces' dwindling horse population. Bark soup, a traditional staple in times of hardship, ranked as a luxury rarely afforded the men. Agned's animal populace of rabbits, squirrels, and the occasional deer that fed them so admirably at winter solstice also disappeared. Dead horses were then harvested for what little flesh they might provide. That was when the sickness claimed countless good men. While Morgen possessed the ability to heal, she appeared unable to conjure sustenance of any kind amid this complete desolation. It did not enter the High King's mind to question why.

Arthur grew despondent, refusing repast of any kind while his men suffered. Anguish altered his features, chiseling them into a perpetual grimace that bore no resemblance to Uther Pendragon's twenty-year-old son. This was an Arthur that Morgen had never seen before—an Arthur who doubted his own authority. Darkness slowly poisoned his soul, eclipsing everything he once believed true. Each new dawn broke cold and brutal as the day before. And the snow remained an impassable barrier that held them tightly within its frozen embrace.

Unable to watch Arthur's downward spiral, Morgen spent all her waking moments attending the ill. On occasion she was accompanied by Accolon and his lap harp, which proved quite a boon. A certain undeniable healing power resided in Accolon's songs. Everyone paused to listen, transported, if only for a fleeting moment, to some distant memory where beauty lingered true. And so Morgen and Accolon worked side by side, at one point lulling a pneumonic sixteen-year-old to sleep. This tactic proved essential to avert the danger that the healing energy would evoke a coughing fit that forced the air passages to close even further. Morgen hoped that the sleeping Lamorak would stand a better chance of recovery.

Accolon offered a slight bow of his head before turning to the next patient. Returning the gesture Morgen called the healing powers to play. If all went well, this very night she would see Lamorak whole. Placing her hands against the lad's chest, Morgen momentarily forgot the sorrow and depression that plagued her companions. Healing was her true passion. Yes, it was healing that made her feel most alive, regardless of the death crone lurking around every corner. This grim reminder recalled her attention to the High King. Why did he steadily creep into her thoughts even when she focused on another? Surely something could be done to ease his despondency. The thought carried her forward longer than she had anticipated. Indeed, when her eyes cleared and all the internal musings ceased, a miracle had transpired: Lamorak stirred beneath her hands, offering thanks. Taking a deep breath to still the rapid beating of her heart, she looked down upon his thin, tired frame. It was obvious that he needed food—preferably meat—warmth, and rest. But health was glowing within his youthful face. This was a battle won—the first of many that would follow!

As the day wore on, Morgen slowly made her way from one patient to the next, passing hibernating bats along the way. Each new stop brought with it a fresh dose of reality. The men were failing, not merely in body but spirit. It was only a matter of time before they surrendered altogether.

Once the faint light that graced Morgen's wanderings slowly ebbed toward darkness, she drew apart from her patients, tripping past the cave's entrance where the Companions had cleared a narrow path that ran along Agned's icy ledge. The moon shone full above. Twilight swelled around her vast and deep. Surely this was the time to use her almost forgotten power as Avalon's Fairy Queen to summon assistance. And so she drank deeply of the frosty air and mentally pushed free of the snow that threatened their existence.

Where are you, Ancient Ones, defenders of men? Come, you will not deny Avalon's queen—even if she be cloaked as a mortal.

With a flash of antlers and a scrape of hooves, Cernunnos, lord of animals, appeared tall and proud, cloaked in a vast mantle of moonlight. This was the Ancient ancient One one as she had never seen him before—rugged, commanding, yet noticeably softened by the pearly lunar beams. Starlight sparkled in his large, dark eyes, which were fixed upon her in an almost quizzical manner. His imposing figure dwarfed her—indeed, dwarfed any mortal she had ever seen, including Arthur. The humanoid portion of his frame was dark skinned and boasted thick furs that could only have originated from a wolf. The antlered head and shaggy legs, which ended in decidedly pronounced hooves, reminded Morgen of a wise, old buck that had witnessed many such times of deprivation. Indeed, the words that spilled from his lips hinted as much.

Seasons come, seasons go. Each has an individual purpose. Each "seasons" us for rebirth. It is folly to alter destiny's course, or dream of achieving such a goal; for life cannot renew without these times. Bide the hours, Morgen, and ride the winds. One day soon you will walk free of this mountain, and then the future will claim its due.

Morgen shivered despite herself, certain of what Cernunnos inferred: her own promise to Morrigan. But she quickly thrust this aside and asked the question that suddenly plagued her mind.

What of your son? What of Merlin?

A lone voice, shrill in its despair, hauntingly familiar, yet altered beyond common recognition swirled through the deepening twilight.

Morgen's heart thudded painfully within her chest. *It was Merlin.*

"Merlin?"

A gateway rose before her, preternaturally macabre. Black as pitch it was, sporting a jagged display of toothlike bars. Behind it cackled a dark skinned hag, barring entrance. Slowly, methodically, she stirred a bubbling caldron, a full-bellied sow lulling at her side.

Morgen started with recognition. This was the gateway to the Underworld, guarded by none other than Cerridwen herself, in the guise of a crone. *I have seen all this before.* A hint of regret prickled along the base of her spine. Was she not supposed to act as an Underworld guide? Was she not destined to help those who could not easily cross over?

A sharp knock on the toothy barrier shattered Morgen's focus—a petitioner waited at the gate, a tall, gaunt petitioner with long, white hair that spilled down the length of his back. Bent from suffering, this man shuffled between two bootless feet, swollen and bloodied. Morgen's heart beat a little faster. The petitioner's hair was thickly matted, sometimes covering one, if not both, eyes. He drew a gnarled hand to his chest and began toying with a golden chain that hung ceremoniously about his neck.

Merlin.

Was it possible that madness could so consume a person, weaken him beyond recognition, steal his soul?

"Son of Cernunnos, you have traveled far from the Land of the Living. What is it you seek?"

Altering composition Cerridwen cloaked herself in a rich, dark beauty that dripped compassion. She was suddenly the great mother, the matron capable of nurturing her wounded children, guiding them back toward life, if that choice be for the benefit of all.

Merlin fell upon the gate, hands twisting desperately against the toothlike barricade that denied him entrance.

"Dark Goddess, I seek the treasure of my soul. It is I who killed her mortal frame, I who robbed her of life. Please, let me pass! Let me know that she still continues in your care."

The plea cost Merlin much. Time and again he writhed against the sharp barrier, drawing blood on his hands, face and arms.

"Morgen is a fairy. She belongs to the other realm."

"But I cannot find her—anywhere!"

The anguish of this cry nearly bereft Morgen of reason. Why had she forgotten Merlin? Why had she cast all thought of him aside? Yes, Arthur needed her, but what of her child's father? True, the love, the romance they had once shared was gone; but heartfelt warmth remained. She could no more cast Merlin aside than sever a limb from her body, for he was part and particle of her being. Cerridwen's lush voice called her back from such musings.

"It is not Morgen who is lost, but you, Merlin. First find yourself—and Morgen will soon follow."

A rush of wind and a flash of light followed, and Morgen found herself standing once more upon the same snow-clogged cliffs that she and Britannia's troops had inhabited for the past fortnight.

Before Morgen could even realize what she intended to do, Cernunnos blocked her path with his immense frame.

Do nothing, Morgen. You are needed here. Simply follow the path set before you. It will lead to my son.

Gesturing across Agned's wintry summit, he revealed an unexpected surprise: a herd of deer attempting to strip bark from trees already thoroughly flailed by their equestrian counterparts. At the heart of this herd was a white hind, ethereal in her nearly translucent beauty.

"This is my boon to you, Morgen, for loving my son and bearing his child," Lord of the Animals supplied. "I ask only that you honor those lives willingly laid down for you with appropriate respect."

Morgen knelt, placing her frozen lips against the Ancient Ancient One's cloven hooves. Time and again she kissed him, knowing full well she could never repay so great a boon.

"Cernunnos, you have no idea what this will mean to us. How can I ever thank you? We will certainly honor you and the spirits of your children. Is there nothing else you ask in return?"

He smiled and cocked his shaggy head. "Be mindful of the white hind. She offers vision to those who are lost. Do not sacrifice her with the rest of the clan."

The antlered god bent low and kissed Morgen's forehead. "Grieve not over my son, Morgen. Prepare your heart for change. It is coming whether you will it nor not." Cernunnos twisted his lips into a half smile that faded before it achieved full expression. His dark eyes followed, twinkling brightly as they eclipsed hooves, torso, and all. Fever thrilled through Morgen's veins. She had so much to tell Arthur—so much! Raising her arms in a gesture of blessing, Morgen cast a white, protective light around the beautiful hind. This done, she rushed past a myriad of bemused warriors, who wondered at her strange behavior. Into the king's tent she plunged, unprepared for what would follow. Arthur did not look up but sat unmoving, his thoughts dark, oppressive. Never before had Morgen seen him so defeated. The sun had just begun its amber trek across the sky. Apparently the entire night had slipped away while she was in the presence of the Underworld deity.

"Arthur, wake up!" she cried, shaking him soundly. There was no response.

"Arthur, please listen to me! You must take action—now!" Still he did not move.

Kiss him, Morgen.

The words sounded so assured so confident as they rattled her brain.

Morgen's heart thudded painfully against her chest as she knelt before Arthur's great bent frame. Slowly, deliberately, she took his anguished face between her hands and pressed her lips against his.

It came as some surprise that Arthur broke this exchange first, his face registering a mixture of anger and disbelief. "What game is it you're playing, Morgen?"

"Come, dearest, make ready!" she cried, thrusting a quiver and bow into his seemingly frozen grasp. "See what blessings Cernunnos has gifted us!"

Arthur settled upon her a reproachful glance then fell back to his private musings. "Morgen, I have little patience for games."

She kissed him again. "I assure you this is hardly a game."

Confused by her foreign behavior, he rose, frowning. "You have my attention now. What is it you want of me?"

Using an almost super human strength, Morgen pulled Arthur free of his tent, through the staring crowd, never relaxing her grip until they reached the cavern's gaping maw.

"Look—there upon the summit!"

A cry broke forth as men young and old crowded around Arthur, eyeing the glorious herd.

"By the gods, we are spared!" croaked Bedivere, instantly shifting purpose so he might gather his hunting tools.

"Look at the size of them!" rang Gareth's astonished appraisal. "Why, there is enough meat to keep us until spring!"

Blankets and extra coverings flew in all directions. Everyone was talking at once, arming themselves for the coming hunt, limbs stiff, numb, and complaining. Something of Arthur's old spirit stirred within his breast. "Thank you, dearest. I suspect you are behind this miracle."

"It was Cernunnos," she said, struggling on tiptoe to kiss his brow. "Go, honor him, and thereby restore faith in yourself."

Although the snow was high and the men were weak, a hunting party soon set off in pursuit of their prey. It came as some surprise that the deer did not flee their approach but merely allowed the arrows to pierce their hearts without uttering so much as a dying scream. Only the hind tripped away, observing the sacred ritual from afar.

Arthur was near delirium as he drew upon the felled herd, seeing double—at times triple—their numbers draped against the bloody snow. Fever actively consumed his brain, rendering those things substantial that normally escaped his notice. Perhaps this is how his eyes met those of the pale hind. Never before had he seen a creature so lovely, so ethereal. The hind bowed her head then blinked three times, offering guidance. Light, air, sound all ceased expression, rendering the vision complete. Arthur wavered uncertainly and then fell to his knees. The hind's dazzling white purity blurred and reconfigured itself into a blue-robed woman who clasped a silent infant against her breast. Beside her stood the divine Bridgit cloaked in summer green. A raven-haired babe, dressed in feminine swaddling, a little girl, somewhat older than the boy, who boasted ebony eyes and ivory skin, every bit as vibrant as Merlin's, was tucked softly against her heart. Behind them followed a holy man, and perhaps one other. As the blue-robed woman slowly approached Arthur, her precious cargo, a king of kings, cooed its pleasure.

"Will you offer him up as host?"

Arthur stood transfixed. It was the holy man who asked the question. Certainly he did not mean the child.

The blue-robed mother nodded ascension, then gracefully relinquished her treasure. A stone alter became his new manger, the patriarch his confessor supreme. Up rose the sharpened blade. Cold metal flashed its sacrificial smile. Arthur stood frozen, unable to intervene upon the child's behalf.

Not the child! Not the child!

Time—perspective—froze, ceased its forward path, spiraling Arthur around so that he faced the smiling Bridgit, who presented her lovely charge to a fair-haired warrior, garbed not so unlike himself.

"Will you accept her in good faith?"

It was Cedric, the Saxon king, welcoming this darling raven-haired child, the pretty cooing lass, his arms spread wide. Suddenly affirmation dawned through the thick bands of Arthur's delirium. This was truly the answer to his prayers—the very request he had breathed so many times. It was a blending of the many peoples he sought—in this case through the combining of their religions! Joy flooded his senses. This was his life's purpose—the reason he came into being!

Arthur cried Morgen's name but felt uncertain as to whether or not she actually heard him. He was far, far away, lodged in another place, another time. It was not winter there but early spring! Green, not white proved the predominate color.

Time shifted its ever-changing face once more, revealing the first innocent child as it was sacrificed, drained of blood, bereft of flesh, the gentle mother, passive, unmoving.

Sickened beyond expression, Arthur's blazing hand fixed upon Excalibur's hilt and up rose the sacred blade. Three steps brought him level with the murderous patriarch. It would be a clean, easy strike—one that severed the head and neck. The execution was in motion when the patriarch's hood flew back, and horror of horrors, Arthur saw Merlin's face staring back at him. *Merlin!* Arthur tried to stall Excalibur's advance, but it was too late. The blade was too fast, too eager; yet somehow, just before settling upon its mark, a swirling mass of blue silks intervened—the Madonna! One touch of her soft hand stopped the bright blade, forced it back into the sheath without further prompting.

Round Arthur spun once more and watched as Bridgit transferred her raven-haired babe into Cedric's waiting arms. Everything looked so familiar. Where had he seen this before? Glancing across the countryside, he could just distinguish a score of shadowy figures making good their approach. One, in particular, drew his focus: a tall, golden female with hair the color of ripe wheat. So bright was the illumination that rose from this being, there could be little doubt she was anything other than divine. Arthur swallowed hard. This was a goddess to whom the Saxons paid homage.

Cedric lifted the lovely infant high overhead, which set the crowd cheering. People far and wide celebrated this day, this hour.

"Fulfill our destiny," the babe whispered, her black eyes bent on Arthur.

"Be at peace, Pendragon," the blue-robed matron said dreamily. "All will be well."

Arthur found himself drawn forward. The gentle mother was offering him a chalice filled with her child's blood.

"Come, partake in the body and the blood of the Christ. He has made the ultimate sacrifice so understanding may fall upon the children who wander lost and alone."

She then placed the simple chalice in Arthur's hands and willed him to drink. Somehow a bread-like substance also found its way into his mouth. At that precise moment, a faint, gurgling sounded nearby. It was none other than the sacrificed child, smiling at Arthur, apparently unharmed.

"Will you follow his good example and bring peace upon this land?"

Arthur nearly laughed at such a prospect—since peace, let alone freedom of movement, seemed impossible at this time of elemental repression. The smile wavered tentatively then froze upon his lips as the blue-robed matron gifted him with a crystal cross.

"Wear it in remembrance of my son's sacrifice," she said, scooping up the giggling babe.

Bridgit drew opposite mother and child, stopping just short of Arthur's reeling frame. There within her palms burned the fire of illumination, drawing each toward their destiny as moths to a flame. The blonde Germanic goddess approached Bridgit's right, while the blue-robed Madonna appeared at her left. Together, with almost unparalleled precision, the three turned their eyes on Arthur and smiled. It was the Eternal Goddess in triplicate form. This incredible sight lasted only a heartbeat, for one by one they melded into a single entity, each chanting a sacred name.

Friya
Mary
Bridgit
Do we not all occupy the same space and time?

Bridgit crinkled her starry eyes and smiled, reflecting all the sacred manifestations joined as one.

Come, good Pendragon. The future of Britannia lies within your reach. Gaze into the flames of destiny. Allow them to illuminate your path.

Arthur collapsed upon the icy snow, unaware that it was Morgen's soft arms that encompassed him.

"Dearest, can you hear me? It's Morgen."

Opening both eyes Arthur saw the face he cherished above all others staring back at him. "Morgen," he whispered, "did you see? We will become one."

CHAPTER 38:

Badon

Late the next morning, winter finally retracted its icy claws. Many believed that Arthur's miraculous vision had something to do with this happy alteration. Spirits ran high among those who had survived the storm. In all, over forty men, some of them little more than beardless children, lost their lives due to illness and exposure. Everyone knew that divine intervention alone had spared them. Few questioned which god was behind their salvation. Arthur remained their leader. Whatever gods he honored would receive their respect as well.

Although Arthur's thoughts centered on his men and the terrible hardships they had endured, one goal inspired his imagination: a unified Britannia that encouraged religious tolerance, something he welcomed. Why else had the divine Bridgit appeared next to the God of Christ, not to mention the Saxon fertility goddess? A unified land—one that welcomed peoples of all faiths— was his goal, but first the war must reach its conclusion. Thus, Arthur resumed training exercises—a task greatly simplified when his venue changed.

Long before Lot's capture, Morgause and her younger children had made good their departure for the more "hospitable" shores of Orkney. This allowed Gawain to offer his inheritance, the Lothian fortress, as training grounds. The fortress was a large, winged, timber and thatch holding that boasted a courtyard and several outbuildings well situated on a rising crag that flattened into a plateau, good for farming and equally well suited to training. It proved a much needed change. Plied with warmth and food, everyone reclaimed their former strength—everyone but Morgen.

Prophecy slowly animated Morgen's waking vision, leaving her increasingly unsettled. How could it be otherwise when her sleepless dreams involved malevolent fire sprites, wildly unprincipled, oblivious to elemental laws—sprites that ultimately birthed monstrous funeral pyres that slowly consumed Britannia? Time and again she saw Arthur and the Companions struggle to forestall the advance, but somehow they always succumbed to the flames. Morgen often awoke screaming Arthur's name—the empty fortress magnifying her terror tenfold—but with no one there could she share such concerns, no Merlin to help her unravel the increasingly cryptic theme. Arthur spent all his waking moments training the men, training that extended far beyond midnight. Rarely did he inhabit the private chambers allotted him. Oh, how she missed him, missed his arms warming her and lulling her off to sleep. Morgen forestalled this inevitable meeting until the internal whisperings became so incessant she could do nothing but seek her confessor.

And so one night, after a an especially unnerving dream, Morgen threw the emerald cloak over her shift, taking pains not to make a sound as she opened her chamber door and slid out into the empty, dimly lit hall. No one was stirring, no other souls so tormented by dreams that they could not sleep. Heart wildly pounding within her chest, she crept forward, a low, dull fear gnawing her innards. What if Arthur did not believe her? What if the love he once felt for her had melted with the crusty snow?

This is ridiculous! her spirit cried. *Do not allow fear to eclipse your mission. You are here to help Arthur instill peace throughout the land."*

Gathering courage Morgen pressed her hand against the chamber door that guarded Arthur's possessions and found that it was already open. In she walked, unprepared for the immaculate setting—the perfectly tended fire, the untouched bed, the armor readied for lightning-quick adornment. Arthur stood at the window lost in thought, free of all kingly adornments save a simple blue tunic and pants. Did he too sense the impending storm? Arthur turned at the sound of her entrance. Firelight bathed his features, rendering them a dazzling amber and gold hue. He was at once devastatingly handsome, sensuous, the very man for whom untold numbers of women would lay down their chastity without thinking twice about it. Arthur was that magnificent.

"Dearest," he began, easily traversing the distance between them. "What is wrong? Has something happened? You cannot know how I have missed you." This said he cast his warm arms around her tiny frame and squeezed tight. His lips found her lustrous hair, her marble-smooth forehead, but fell short of touching her mouth. "We finish training so late each night that I hesitate to visit you. I have no wish to disturb your dreams."

Morgen took a deep breath and met his gaze. "That is why I had to see you, Arthur. My dreams, my visions, grow increasingly dark. I fear we must take action or Britannia will be lost."

His eyes flashed brilliantly, mirroring the firelight that warmed their skin. "What is it? What have you seen?"

A sob broke forth from her trembling lips. "Fire—flames—a living funeral pyre surrounding, consuming our forces."

Instantly he conveyed her to a thick, oaken bench positioned so near the fireplace that Morgen found it necessary to avert her eyes. Arthur claimed focus instead, as he knelt before her, resting his hands upon her knees. "Tell me everything."

The close proximity of his person, his scent, his warmth, sent Morgen spiraling back into the abyss. Prophecy commanded her voice, her expression. "The Red Dragon's lair is aflame! See how the Saxons burn your new fortress and her inhabitants alive! They target Kay, the artisans, and all who labor on Camelot. None will be spared, Arthur. None. Do you hear me?"

"By the gods!" he cried, never altering position. "It is as I feared. They are coming for us now, Morgen? Is that what you are telling me?"

Morgen reached forward and clasped her arms around his neck. "They attack in two days' time."

"Two days?" Arthur's mind raced toward its conclusion. "How will we ever reach Camelot in time?"

"There is a way," she said, steadying her gaze. "You must trust me without question. If you can do this, if you join with me, there is a chance. Your men already stationed at Camelot will fight and defend their keep. That will win us some time. Listen carefully, Arthur. We must never allow it to reach that point. We must thwart the Saxons well before they gain Camelot. We must stop them at Badon. That is where they have wintered: Badon hill fort near the old Roman baths. At Badon we will realize our destinies. A pair united in their common love for Britannia and for each other, the Warrior King and his Fairy Queen must work as one or Britannia falls. Magic must inspire the sword; sword must solidify magic. The joining begins now."

Morgen pitched forward into Arthur's ready arms. "Dearest, stay with me," he said, warming her face between his hands. "There can be no delay. We have only this moment before the action consumes us. Do you see how it is done? How can we save Britannia?"

"I become you; you become me. We are one and the same."

Words gave birth to transformation, altering the room, conveying its charges deep within a swell of pale moonlight so bright, so blinding that it eclipsed Morgen, Arthur, bench and all. High upon the windswept Tor the High King and Fairy Queen found themselves transported, shrouded by the shadow of eight megalithic stones and one decidedly ancient tree.

"What magic is this?" Arthur whispered, not quite trusting his eyes.

"We are in Avalon—my home," Morgen supplied. "Hold fast to me, dearest. The joining will soon begin. My sisters will aid our efforts."

"Sisters?" he questioned with raised eyebrows. "You never told me you had siblings. Where are they?"

A shimmer of light and a ripple of stone passed before them. Glitonea slid free of her rocky haven, the tallest and most curvaceous megalith, a steely blue beauty that rivaled the fairest star. A smile graced her lips, a decadent expression not altogether reassuring. It was a curious sight to see this transformation—one rarely gifted a mortal even if he be a king. Arthur, however, was different. They all knew it. This Warrior King was no less than one of their own. "We are not so foreign as that, Arthur. You have met us before."

One by one the Sisterhood stepped free of their stone haunts, arms raised high. The air, the very mist appeared to bend in upon itself, giving birth to these winged messengers who held time momentarily at bay. Light dazzled the senses, altered the very course of fate. They had but one purpose in mind, the salvation of Britannia. Indeed, it was to that end that they had indentured their souls.

Arthur nodded his greeting to each sister, cognizant of their beauty, yet never let his gaze stray too far from Morgen. *She is my goddess, my other self, the one with whom I have shared many lifetimes.* Tracing his fingers along the delicate planes of her face, he said, "I do not understand. What is it I am supposed to do?"

"Do you trust me, Arthur?" she whispered, throwing her head back so that moonlight played upon her features, vibrant, otherworldly, and utterly fay.

"With my life."

Arthur's words reverberated through the mist, lending a kind of affirmation that drew the very stars earthward. Lower and lower they sank until three glittering spheres centered over Avalon. The High King watched spellbound as a bright, pearly light encompassed Morgen, eclipsing her frame, altering it beyond recognition. No longer the petite, flamed-haired maiden that he loved so well, she rose up a silver-hued fairy, her flowing locks and moon-drenched eyes colored that same otherworldly hue. Shimmering, translucent wings aided her purpose, propelling her so high that she met Arthur's gaze. Arthur gasped at the transformation, thoroughly enthralled. Pressing her forehead against his, Morgen placed one hand upon his heart. Arthur mimicked the action, resting his hand against the warm swell of her breast.

"I have always thought you the most beautiful of women, Morgen. Now words fail me. This is your true form?"

"Yes. Now it will be your form as well."

Relaxing every part and particle of her being, the Fairy Queen altered, compressed, and condensed her composition until it liquefied as shimmering quicksilver, pure essence itself. Down into the very pores of Arthur's skin she spilled, weaving her magic, blending her blood, senses, and soul with his. It was an intimate task—one that demanded complete dependency of each individual upon the other.

"Arthur Pendragon, High King of Britannia, my thoughts are your thoughts. My heart beats in time with yours. Our actions are one and the same. Together we wield magic and the sword with equal measure. We are one entity."

Arthur struggled against the lulling magic that altered his thoughts and clouded his senses.

"Yes, but not in battle. You cannot mean that we will be one in battle."

"No other choice is before us, Arthur. I was born for this purpose—as were you. This is how we will save Britannia."

Arthur broke through the stone circle, reeling, sickened by the realization of what was to come and the knowledge that he could do nothing to alter it. He staggered to the ancient yew tree, tall and red, its spicy scent perfuming the deepening night. Aware that it was her haunt, he hoped and prayed with every fiber of his being that she would take shelter within its leafy embrace. "By the gods, Morgen, I love you with all my heart. Believe me, I want nothing more than to join with you, but I cannot risk your life this way. I have no assurance that we will survive this firestorm. While I would gladly sacrifice myself, I cannot sacrifice you."

The Sisterhood spoke as one, drawing his attention to the magnificent picture they painted—fair Valkyries, deadly, capable of aiding or striking down all who crossed their path. Shrouded by moonlight they stood frozen before their stone edifices, otherworldly sentinels unaffected by mortal emotion. "You have no choice. This is Morgen's destiny whether you will it or not."

Swallowing back his anger, Arthur spoke again. "Then tell me how we will transport Britannia's forces here when they currently reside in the north."

Tor, moonlight, standing stones were eclipsed by the light that issued from their eyes, a blinding response with the power to transform. Arthur found himself standing near the same rustic fireplace, within the same well-tended chamber that he had originally inhabited. Morgen's human self resumed its seat upon the bench, her form an unsettling, translucent blue.

"Several portals in Avalon can be used to transport the men. Call each and every one of them into readiness. I will ensure that they manifest through a cleft yew tree which boasts a central, circular portal mid-trunk. Once there, we will race to Badon. If all goes well, we will arrive before dawn lights the sky."

Casting the heavy, oak door open, Arthur rushed into the darkened hall. "Companions!" he cried with such force, such amplification that no one could miss the summons. "War is upon us! Gather your belongings! We depart immediately!"

A single look over his shoulder told him that Morgen no longer inhabited the chambers. Had she returned to Avalon? If so, how would he ever find her?

"We are one," she breathed through his consciousness. "No need to search for me. I am here."

Bedivere arrived first, sliding into place, his feet still bootless, clothing half covering his frame. Slipping his good left arm through the leather sleeve, he laced the jerkin in record time. It was amazing the speed with which the Companions followed, many stirring up the foot soldiers and those who slept farther off. The assembly met in record time, fully geared, prepped for battle.

Arthur drew a deep breath and told them of Morgen's vision. Many, especially those who did not know her well, shifted uncomfortably, but this made little difference. The Companions knew Arthur believed her, and that was good enough for them. Thus, single file, he led them into his private quarters, trembling at the uncertainty that plagued his mind. The numbers were so vast that they could not all inhabit the chamber at the same time. How would they understand what he was about to do? How were they ever going to pull this off?

Do you see the moon, Arthur? Morgen's voice soothed his frantic thoughts.

Arthur cleared the distance between door and window, cast back the thick russet curtains that graced its frame, and watched moonlight flood the chamber.

This is our portal. Tell the men to race through it one by one, allowing the count of five between each departure. This will ensure that each warrior has cleared the tree before the next arrives. Everyone must run at full clip and not stop until they reach the Chalice Well. I will see to the horses. Tell them. Do it now.

And so he did. Arthur spoke with such authority that no one dared criticize the plan. It was agreed that Gawain would remain behind until the last warrior found his way through the portal.

Taking a deep breath to center himself, Arthur glanced back at his men, who looked as disconcerted as he felt; but this was not the time for wariness, however, so he raced for the patch of moonlight, uncertain of precisely what would follow. He experienced a sensation of falling, flailing through the vast unknown. Thankfully he caught himself and ran on. Iridescent light blinded him, leaving him uncertain as to which way was up or down. Still his legs moved forward, determined. Reddish wood, branches, and leaves offered encouragement, filling his nostrils with that spicy, glorious scent possessed only by yew trees. He was almost there. Suddenly he sprang through a wooden hole, moonlight still guiding his path. He heard the sound of water guiding him—the sacred well at last! He was in Avalon! He heard the sound of rapidly advancing footsteps. Bedivere appeared, followed by Gareth, Accolon, and the Companions. One by one Britannia's elite forces joined him. Morgen proved better than her word! If anyone doubted this fact, they need only observe the horses that grazed nearby.

Gathering the mane of an ebony charger, Arthur swung up into the saddle. They had but seven hours before daylight filled the sky. All element of surprise would be lost at that moment. It was essential that his men reach the ancient fortress situated just east of the great Roman baths while it was still dark. Off they set at an accelerated pace, the Sisterhood of Avalon conjuring a magical bridge that appeared to be comprised of glass yet easily sustained the Britons as they crossed the vast lake that separated them from the mainland. Stars beamed forth encouragement, surpassed only by the vibrant moon. The journey itself proved invigorating after so much stagnancy. Spring was clearly evident in the roaring streams, fed by freshly melted snows. Thick mud routinely challenged their pace, but this only increased focus. The safety of Britannia was their one thought, their goal.

They came upon Badon almost too quickly. Arthur knew it was Morgen and her sisters who had assured their early arrival. His heart swelled with gratitude, but they still had a battle to win— time enough to offer thanks later, or so he prayed.

Are you still with me, dearest? he asked, half hoping for no response.

Yes, her voice played inside his brain. *You know what to do. Battle strategy is your forte, not mine.*

Casting a glance heavenward, Arthur drank full and deep of the dewy air. It was time: the hour just short of sunrise when the world yawns before falling back asleep, ready for that final, blissful rest that stalls daily tasks and dreams anew. Oh, how he wished to wake from this living nightmare that was his existence! A leader of men, he was daily forced to live with the realization that he was often their executioner. Each time he lead men into battle, it was the same. How many of those souls who surrounded him, the souls that survived Agned's horrific winter, the souls that only wished to return home to their families—wives birthing babies while their husbands, their support, slaughtered Saxons—how many would actually still remain standing by nightfall? The morning lark trilled its welcoming song, calling him back to the present. There was no help for it. They must move forward. If not, Britannia as they knew it would cease to be. Few words were spoken. Indeed, none were needed. The men grew wild with anticipation, brandishing sword, axe, and spear.

"Our salvation is the sun," he said, glancing heavenward. "We attack with the first morning light."

Thus began the ascent of Badon Hill—it really was a hill, though many often called it a mountain—horsemen first, foot soldiers directly behind, silence and stealth incarnate. It was hard to imagine that bloodshed lay ahead, so beautiful was that early morning climb. Birdsong warmed their hearts, banishing the mists with dawn's smiling countenance. Somewhere in the distance a wolf howled. The sun took this as its cue and burst upon the scene with unparalleled vivacity, its fierce golden rays showering the hill, drawing all who slumbered within its ancient fortress into contented wakefulness. They didn't understand the sun's promise or the part they were about to play in the blood bath ahead.

The events that followed almost defy description. Arthur and his warriors did clear the eastern summit at dawn's first light. A smattering of Saxon lookouts that tended the early morning fires started at the sight of them, blinded by the rising sun, unable to mount a proper defense against the Pendragon's stampeding fury. A cry of disbelief penetrated the air. Where were their brethren? Many were just rising, still clad in breeches alone, as the foot soldiers penetrated Badon's decaying fortress. These half-naked warriors plunged onto the summit, seeking shelter behind outbuildings that lingered dangerously near collapse. Cedric, the Saxon king, was chief among this group, his fierce presence stirring them into action. Huge pieces of wood and refuse were torn free of their crumbling frames and then piled high upon the long, snakelike burial bounds that littered Badon's countenance.

Cedric ordered his men to create a barricade as Arthur's assault intensified. Men were falling faster than the stars. Everywhere he looked enemy warriors were raining down upon them. That is when Cedric remembered his original plan. He would burn the Britons, even if it cost Saxon lives. Torches soon fulfilled his purpose, fueling the ancient fortress, barricade, and outbuildings. Orange tongues of flame danced higher and higher, lashing out with a widening grin. Vengeance fed their voracious appetite. It was only a matter of time before they consumed Briton and Saxon alike. None of them could last much longer. Explosions shattered all thought, all objectivity.

Morgen, do you see this? Arthur was desperate. *This is your prophecy incarnate. Can you do nothing to stop the flames before we are all burned alive?*

Keep your thoughts focused on the battle, Arthur. I will see to the fire. Peace now and forever. Peace blanket Britannia. Peace be upon all beings and peoples of the earth. Feel it. See it manifest before you. Claim peace now!

Thunder rumbled its approach high overhead, even as the sky grew foreboding. The warriors looked up, heated blades blistering their hands. Soft rain spilled upon their anxious faces, cooling passion, tempers, and smoke-darkened skin. Lightning flashed its welcome smile, followed by watery torrents that slowly eclipsed the flames. This temporary lull fostered new determination. The battle resumed its cataclysmic pace, racing toward its resolution. All was blood and tears. Arthur appeared godlike, impervious to blade, axe, or spear. No one could touch him, so blessed he was that day.

Desperate to forestall annihilation, Cedric struck his renowned spear into the kindling and watched the fire take root. Well pleased with his efforts, he raised it high, the red-hot tip centered and ready.

Weaving his way through a thick blanket of smoke that hid foes and addled the mind, Arthur made good his approach, oblivious to the spear that marked his heart. A relatively small Saxon leapt in front of his driving horse, a risky move, one that would only pay off if the spear wielder actually hit its mark. Arthur never gave him the chance. Indeed, one stroke of Excalibur shattered the upraised spear with such force that the small-boned Saxon fell backward, leveled in its wake. Arthur's dark mount danced around this coura-geous yet foolhardy Saxon, taking great care not to trample his form. Several hairs stood up on the back of the High King's neck, commanding attention.

Raise Excalibur to your chest without delay!

Following this inner prompting, Arthur did just that, a timely response that saved his life. The fiery missile struck Excalibur's enchanted blade with such force that it exploded into untold frag-ments, showering splintered wood and molten iron everywhere. Arthur's horse reared, unseating him. Down onto the smoky ground he fell, finding him-self remarkably near the small Saxon. Something about the moan that escaped the warrior's lips stirred memory, but he had not time to unravel this, however, for he was keenly aware that who-ever had wielded the spear would follow. Rocking up onto his haunches, Arthur quickly regained his footing, Excalibur ready to extract judgment.

A low cry, bestial in its dismay, escaped Cedric's lips. Pulling his sword free, he raced toward Arthur, heedless that this action forced him to push through the Companions, press beyond the comfort—what little there was—of his own war-riors. Cedric place himself within striking range of Britannia's elite fighters as they enveloped him, effectively cutting him off from his men.

"Father—no!" cried a feminine voice, desperate but inconsequential in its feeble display. It was Roweena, the slight Saxon who lay vanquished at Arthur's feet.

Cedric was upon Arthur before anyone could thwart the attack, his sword, smaller and more agile than Excalibur, worked blindly to find the opening that would save his people.

Arthur knew that this fight would determine the battle. Destiny whispered success but at what price? If he killed Cedric, the Saxons would never cease their attacks. No, it was essential that he bring Cedric to his knees. That meant shattering the king's sword, the symbol of his power. Calling upon the elemental guardians, the Sisterhood of Avalon, and his most beloved Morgen, Arthur watched the maneuver manifest in his mind. There he held the image, waiting for the perfect opening. When it came Arthur sliced Excalibur across Cedric's weapon. Miraculously the solid metal blade gave way at the hilt just as he had foreseen. It was over! As Cedric fell backward, the Companions swarmed around him, swords raised high. They looked to Arthur, waiting. Arthur, in turn, scanned the battle scene. His foot soldiers currently surrounded what was left of the Saxon forces. The Companions subdued their leaders, Cedric and the dazed Roweena. The battle was won!

Arthur raised Excalibur high, a victory cry escaping his lips. The Britons followed suit, some singing their ecstasy with such passion that it pierced the heavens. All eyes centered on Arthur as a silver light poured from his skin. Many blinked, startled by the beautiful fairy that hovered before him. Oh, what bliss it was to know, to conceive that they had achieved this fragile peace together!

Morgen, is this not beyond all imagining?

The fairy offered up an enigmatic smile, slowly altering her form into that of the flame-haired Morgen.

Cedric and his remaining forces silently watched this transformation, awaiting judgment on bent knees. Who was this Fairy Queen that had aided the Britons? Why had she not lent her powers to the Saxons instead? Questions lingered, unanswered. They had nothing to do but wait. It was beyond their comprehension to beg for mercy so great was their inherent pride. The Pendragon who consorted with elementals would decide their future.

Arthur stood unmoving, his body illuminated against the heavily banked funeral pyres that would consume the dead. Unable to speak, he gazed full and deep into Morgen's blue-green eyes. Elation flooded her fair countenance. That is when the High King took command.

Clasping Morgen around the waist, Arthur crushed his lips against hers, hardly caring that the Companions lingered nearby. This was the final moment of their joining, embodied as it had never been before, flesh pressed against flesh, bodies entwined. Morgen surrendered her will to Arthur, and Arthur conceded his power to Morgen. Both were surprised by the length of this exchange. Slowly, willfully, their passion increased until Bedivere's apologetic voice forced them apart.

"Arthur, Morgen, forgive me...I..." he stammered. "...Cedric is waiting to hear your terms, Arthur."

I love you, Morgen, more than life, death, and all other events in between.

Morgen did not respond, aware that they tottered near a precipice. The cost of this triumph was steep. Once Arthur realized this truth, his feelings would alter. She must be ready, centered.

Slowly Arthur opened his eyes, taking in the full weight of destruction that lay rotting around him. Certainly the gods had not intended such brutality. Bodies of both Briton and Saxon lay strewn across Badon's blood-soaked countenance—lives carelessly cast away at a moment's notice, and for what? A simple dream.

Morgen slid free from his arms, aware of the change. She, too, had participated in this bloodbath. How would she—*would they*—ever heal the scars it wrested upon their souls? Arthur's thoughts echoed her sorrow.

By all that is sacred, I swear—this is the last time I will ever command troops in battle, no matter how noble the cause.

The gods had created him to manifest a peaceful Britannia. Now that he saw the terrible price extracted to ensure such a lofty goal, a sorrow welled inside him that no accolades could staunch. He, Arthur Pendragon, was nothing more than a butcher of men. How was such an atrocity to be answered? .

Drawing the back of his hand against droplets that colored his eyes, Arthur hardly knew what it was he wished to say until the words poured forth of their own volition.

"I once believed that Briton and Saxon could live in a common land as one people, but the many battles we have fought have taught me something different. You are a people seeking to reclaim what is considered a birthright. That makes union with the Britons unacceptable on any terms."

"Pendragon, you misunderstand us!" Princess Roweena cried, tearing the helmet free so that her fair hair flowed unbound.

Cedric said nothing, opting to watch all further proceedings behind seething eyes. This was not over no matter what Arthur thought. One day they would rise from the ashes like the mystical Phoenix of old.

"You seek a place to call home, a place in which to practice your own beliefs, worship your own gods, and honor your own royalty. Your princess helped me see that. As High King of Britannia, I offer you this—on one condition."

The many Saxon voices that had steadily cried approval fell silent, awaiting final judgment.

"I only ask that you put down your swords and live peacefully among my people. Any attack upon a Briton or other people who live in this land will be punishable by death. If you must fight, fight among yourselves. Leave us in peace. This is all I ask of you. I do not ask you to follow me, to pay tribute to me or my gods, but you must honor this land and her people. If you can agree to this in writing and in blood," he suggested, slicing his palm against Excalibur, "you are free to go. If not, you will join your brethren this night. What say you, Cedric?"

Scanning the wounded faces before him, Cedric steadied himself for the inevitable. They were all nodding to him, urging him to accept the treaty before they, too, were thrown upon the funeral pyres like the hapless Agned captives. Cedric drew himself up to full stature, which happened to be an inch or two taller than the Pendragon. Pulling a dagger across his palm, he approached to accept the treaty in "good faith."

Adding further insult to injury, Bedivere disarmed him before he could even reach the king.

"Your terms are acceptable to us, Pendragon," he said, placing his hand against that of his former adversary.

Parchment was then drawn up to place the words in unalterable text. Both Cedric and Arthur signed with their blood, honoring those who had died to make this "enforced" peace a reality. Cedric's eyes found Morgen time and again. It was vital he understand the part she had played in Arthur's victory.

"You are lucky, Arthur, to count the fairies as allies. How did you ever manage such a union? Is she the one to whom you are promised?"

Arthur met Morgen's uneasy gaze. "It is time they know the truth," he breathed, taking hold of her hand. "This is Morgen, Fairy Queen of Avalon, raised as my sister, but no more related to me than you are."

Pursing his lips, Cedric drew breath before he made reply. "Would that my house was so allied."

"There is a way," Arthur replied, his voice warming with purpose. He paid but a simple glance at Morgen before the words tumbled out that effectively severed all ties between them. "I have a gift that I would like to offer you, Cedric. Let me emphasize that it is a gift beyond all imagining."

Morgen listened in numbed silence as Arthur promised her daughter to Cedric's teenage son. He had not even asked her permission or questioned whether or not she approved of the match. Did she mean nothing to him? Was the oneness they had shared so easily cast aside? What of her daughter? The utter heartlessness of Eliana's fate burned within Morgen's breast. Somehow she would keep her precious child from Cedric.

Once the weaponless Saxons began their trek down Badon hill, Arthur threw his arms around Morgen. He was babbling something she had no desire to hear. Still, she allowed him full expression until satiated. The only response she made was to extricate herself from his broad embrace.

Arthur frowned, puzzled by her lack of enthusiasm; then he felt a sharp prick of regret as she marched deep into the night. Suddenly his legs were in motion, overtaking her.

"Morgen, this is what we were born to do. Surely you see that. Your child will unite Briton with Saxon. It is her destiny."

Speechless, Morgen stared at him, tears clouding her eyes. Again she strode off, unprepared for the strong arm that pulled her back against her oppressor's chest.

"Do not leave," a desperate Arthur whispered, reeling. "I need you beside me."

Arthur speaks true, Morgen, the Sisterhood intervened. *Your work is with him. Avalon is but a stone's throw from Camelot. You may visit us anytime you wish.*

I wish to see you now—to ask why you allowed this atrocity to happen!

You agreed to Eliana's betrothal long ago when the world was still young. Forgive Arthur. Forget your anger. Help him be a king for all time.

Book One

"A king for all time…Do you hear me, Arthur?" Morgen gazed down upon her dying charge, remembering the angst, the betrayal, the fury that still haunted her imagination. Was this the reason she could not heal him? Was there still some part of her that blamed Arthur for Eliana's fate?

Opening his eyes the wounded Pendragon shuddered, his lips fluttering softly against the pale moonlight.

"Forgive me, Morgen. Can you ever find it in your heart to forgive me?"

The story continues with
Morgen of Avalon: Child of Destiny